Murder at Half Moon Gate

Center Point
Large Print

Also by Andrea Penrose and available from Center Point Large Print:

Murder on Black Swan Lane

This Large Print Book carries the Seal of Approval of N.A.V.H.

Murder at Half Moon Gate

A Wrexford & Sloane Mystery

Andrea Penrose

CENTER POINT LARGE PRINT
THORNDIKE, MAINE

This Center Point Large Print edition
is published in the year 2018 by arrangement with
Kensington Publishing Corp.

The text of this Large Print edition is unabridged.
In other aspects, this book may vary
from the original edition.
Printed in the United States of America
on permanent paper.
Set in 16-point Times New Roman type.

ISBN: 978-1-68324-881-1

Library of Congress Cataloging-in-Publication Data

Names: Penrose, Andrea, author.
Title: Murder at half moon gate / Andrea Penrose.
Description: Center Point Large Print edition. | Thorndike, Maine :
    Center Point Large Print, 2018.
Identifiers: LCCN 2018019940 | ISBN 9781683248811
    (hardcover : alk. paper)
Subjects: LCSH: Large type books. | GSAFD: Mystery fiction.
Classification: LCC PS3554.A15 M87 2018 | DDC 813/.54—dc23
LC record available at https://lccn.loc.gov/2018019940

Murder at Half Moon Gate

To my perfect partner-in-crime
(You know who you are)

"Blood only serves to wash ambition's hands."

—*Lord Byron*

Acknowledgments

Writing is a very solitary endeavor . . . which makes the support of family and friends even more special.

And so, I shall begin with a big shout-out to all my family, who love books and the nuances of language as much as I do. It's such fun to talk about ideas and the craft of writing with you.

As always, I'm so grateful to my fellow Word Wenches—Joanna Bourne, Nicola Cornick, Anne Gracie, Susanna Kearsley, Susan King, Mary Jo Putney and Pat Rice—for all your help in brainstorming plots and characters . . . not to speak of all the hugs and copious amounts of cyber wine and chocolate you send when I'm sniveling about how badly The Muse is behaving. It's a pleasure—and a privilege—to be part of such a wonderful BFF sisterhood of writing.

Special thanks also go out to John R. Ettinger, whose suggestions for plot and character twists are even more devious than mine! And I'm profoundly grateful for beta readers and dear friends Lauren Willig, Deanna Raybourn, Amanda McCabe and Patrick Pinnell for all your suggestions and support.

And lastly, a heartfelt Regency curtsey to

my wonderful professional partners—my agent, Gail Fortune, my editor, Wendy McCurdy, the Kensington PR team, and the Kensington Art Department, who have created such a fabulous cover!

Prologue

A thick mist had crept in from the river. It skirled around the man's legs as he picked his way through the foul-smelling mud, drifting up to cloud the twisting turns of the narrow alleyways. He paused for a moment to watch the vapor ghosting through the gloom.

A shiver of gooseflesh snaked down his spine.

Shifting, he peered into darkness, trying to spot the wrought iron arches of Half Moon Gate. But only a shroud of black-on-black shadows lay ahead.

He was unfamiliar with London, and must have confused the directions. From Red Lion Square, he had taken three—or was it four?—turns, only to find himself lost in a maze of unlit alleyways. Squat warehouses, all sagging slants and filthy brick, were squeezed along the crooked turns, while the boarded-up rookeries rose up at drunken angles, blocking out all but the smallest slivers of sky. A glance up showed only a weak dribbling of moonlight playing hide and seek within the overhanging roofs.

"Logic," he murmured. "There's no conundrum that can't be solved by logic." Turning in a slow circle, he sought to get his bearings.

Left, he decided. Heading left would quickly

bring him back to the cobbled streets of the Square, where he could start over.

He set off again, sure that he'd soon see a glint of light. And yet, the shadows seemed to darken and creep closer. He tried to draw a calming breath, but the stench made him gag.

"Logic," he reminded himself. Just another turn or two would bring him—

He stopped abruptly.

So, too, did the scuff of steps behind him. But not quite quickly enough. By the laws of physics, it couldn't have been an echo.

"Who's there?" he called sharply. His wife had warned him to ignore the note requesting a meeting. He'd intended to do so, but the second missive had been impossible to ignore. So much depended on making the right decision . . .

There was no response, save for the rasp of rusted metal swinging in the breeze.

He chided himself for being too jumpy. The crooked walls and overhanging roofs distorted sounds, that was all. He resumed walking, turning left, and then right, and then left again—only to have the sinking sensation that he was walking in circles. There was no flicker of light anywhere. The shadows seemed to darken and creep closer.

From out of nowhere came a low, rasping laugh.

He quickened his pace.

Steady, steady, he told himself. The Square had to be just ahead.

And yet, his boots seemed to have a mind of their own. *Faster, faster* . . . Behind him, the echo seemed to be gaining ground. It seemed to be coming from the right—he must head left!

Slipping, sliding, he lost his footing as he turned the corner of a deserted warehouse and hit up hard against the soot-dark brick. Pain lanced through his shoulder.

"Hell's bells." He braced his back against the wall, drawing in a shaky breath. No educated, intelligent man of science should let himself be spooked by nonexistent specters. Logic . . .

And yet, against all logic the pursuing steps were growing louder. And then, out of the shadows rumbled a taunting voice.

"You may be brilliant in the laboratory, but here in the stews there's no fancy formula for escape, Mr. Ashton."

Pushing away from the wall, Ashton took off at a dead run.

What devil-cursed hell had he stumbled into?

Straight ahead, a wall loomed out of the blackness. He hesitated for an instant, and then the sound of pursuit once again drove him to his left. After skidding through yet another turn he tried to summon an extra burst of speed. But a slip sent him sprawling.

He hit the ground with a thud, rolled through the ooze and was halfway up on his feet when a gloved hand—black as Lucifer—shot out and caught hold of his collar. His assailant swung him around and slammed him against an iron grate.

Instinctively, he threw up his arm to parry the blow aimed at his skull. His assailant rocked back, and Ashton heard the whisper of steel kissing leather as a knife slipped free of its sheath.

He was no longer young, but he'd spent most of his life shaping iron with hammer and chisel. His arms were still muscled, his hands still strong. He had no intention of giving up without a fight.

Throwing his weight to one side, he broke free of the other man's hold and lashed out a hard punch, taking grim satisfaction in feeling his broad knuckles crack against the other man's skull.

A grunt of pain, a vicious oath. Shifting the knife from hand to hand, his assailant retreated a step, then pivoted and moved in more warily. The moon had once again broken through the clouds, allowing a dappling of light to reach the slivered alleyway. It slid along the razored steel now cutting slowly back and forth through the night.

Ashton fished out his purse and threw it down. "Here, take my money. I've nothing else of value with me."

His assailant let out a nasty laugh. A mask hid his face, but a malevolent glint showed through the eye slits in the silk.

"I don't want money. I want the drawings."

How did a common footpad know about the drawings? "W-What drawings?" he stammered.

In answer, the blade flashed a series of lightning-swift feints, driving Ashton back up against unyielding iron bars. He was now trapped in the narrow gated recess between two warehouses. In desperation, he lashed out a kick, but Evil Eyes was quick as a snake. Dodging the blow, he smashed a knee to Ashton's groin.

"I'm tired of playing cat and mouse games with you."

"I don't have—" gasped Ashton.

But a vicious elbow to the throat crushed his windpipe before he could go on.

No, no, no, he mouthed in silent agony. Dear God—not now! Not when his momentous discovery was on the cusp of changing the world.

"Please, just let me live," he managed to whisper.

"Let you live?" The knife pierced the flesh between Ashton's ribs. "I'm afraid that's not possible."

There was no pain, just an odd tickling sensation. *How strange,* he thought. Steam was always so pleasantly warm, but the silvery mist caressing his cheeks was cold as the Devil's heart.

"You see, Mr. Ashton, letting you live would ruin everything."

Evil Eyes let the lifeless body drop to the ground. A search of Ashton's pockets turned up nothing but a pencil stub, a coil of twine and a scrap of wire. Uttering a low oath, he wrenched open the dead man's coat and set to slitting open the lining with the still-bloody knife.

Nothing.

Trousers, boots, stockings—the blade sliced through the garments and still not a scrap of god-benighted paper was to be found.

As disbelief gave way to fury, Evil Eyes slashed a series of jagged cuts through the pale flesh of Ashton's exposed belly.

"Damn you to hell! Where *are* they?"

Chapter 1

"Why is it that *I* never win at dice and cards, Wrex?" Christopher Sheffield kicked aside a mound of rotting cabbage before leading the way through a low archway. "While *you* always walk away from the gaming hells with your pockets stuffed with blunt." He expelled a mournful sigh. "It defies logic."

The Earl of Wrexford raised a brow in bemusement. "Hearing *you* invoke the word 'logic' is what defies reason."

"No need to be sarcastic," grumbled Sheffield.

"Fine. If your question was truly meant to be more than rhetorical, the answer is I watch the cards carefully and calculate my chances." He sidestepped a broken barrel. "Try thinking, Kit. And counting."

"Higher mathematics confuses my feeble brain," retorted his friend.

"Then why do you play?"

"I was under the impression that one doesn't have to be smart to gamble," protested Sheffield. "Didn't that fellow Pascal—and his friend Fermat—formulate ideas on risk and probability? I thought the odds should be roughly fifty-fifty for me winning simply by playing blindly." He made a rueful grimace. "Bloody hell, by *that* calculation, I must be due to win a fortune, and soon."

"So you weren't actually sleeping through lectures at Oxford?" said Wrexford dryly.

"I was just dozing." A pause. "Or more likely I was cupshot. Aberdeen was awfully generous with his supply of fine brandy."

"Speaking of brandy," murmured the earl as he watched his friend stumble and nearly fall on his arse. "You've been drinking too much lately."

"Hell's teeth, since when did you become such a stick in the mud?"

"Since you led me into this putrid-smelling swamp of an alleyway," he retorted. His own wits were a little fuzzed with alcohol, and he winced as he slipped, nearly losing his balance. "Pray, why are we taking this route past Half Moon Gate? Tyler will raise holy hell at having to clean this disgusting muck from my boots."

"Heaven forbid we upset your valet." Sheffield made a face. "You know, you're in danger of becoming no fun to carouse with."

Wrexford came to a halt as the alley branched off into three twisting passages. "Which way?"

"The middle one," said Sheffield without hesitation. "As for why we're cutting through here, there are two reasons. It's much shorter than circling around by the main street." A grunt, as he slipped again. "More importantly, there's a chance we'll encounter a footpad, and given my

20

recent losses at the gambling tables, I'm in the mood to thrash someone to a bloody pulp."

The earl tactfully refrained from comment. Like many younger sons of aristocratic families, his friend was caught in a damnably difficult position. The heir and firstborn usually had a generous stipend—and if not, tradesmen were willing to advance generous credit. But those who trailed behind were dependent on parental purse-strings. Sheffield's father, however, was a notorious nipcheese, and kept him on a very puny allowance.

In retaliation, Sheffield made a point of acting badly, a vicious cycle that did no one any good.

It was, mused Wrexford, a pity, for Kit had a very sharp mind when challenged to use it. He had been of great help in solving a complicated crime a handful of months ago—

"Has Mrs. Sloane decided to move to a different neighborhood?" asked his friend, abruptly changing the subject.

"The last time I paid her a visit, she made no mention of it," he replied.

Sheffield shot him an odd look. "You didn't *ask?*"

The *squish-squish* of their steps filled the air. Wrexford deliberately said nothing.

"Never mind," murmured his friend.

Charlotte Sloane. A sudden stumble forced a sharp huff of air from his lungs. That was a subject he didn't care to discuss, especially as the throbbing at the back of his skull was growing worse.

He and Charlotte Sloane had been drawn together—quite literally—by the gruesome murder of a leading religious zealot, a crime for which he had been the leading suspect. *Secrets twisted around secrets*—one of the more surprising ones had been that the notorious A. J. Quill, London's leading satirical artist, was a woman. Circumstances had led him and Charlotte to join forces in order to unravel a diabolically cunning plot and unmask the real miscreant.

Their initial mistrust had turned into wary collaboration, and then to friendship—though that was, mused Wrexford, a far too simple word to describe the bond between them.

Chemistry. As an expert in science, Wrexford could describe in objective detail how the combination of their special talents seemed to stir a powerful reaction. However, they lived in different worlds and moved in vastly different circles here in Town. Rich and poor. Aristocrat and Nobody. Charlotte had made it clear after solving the crime that said circles were unlikely to overlap again.

Despite her assumption, he did pay an occasional visit to her humble home—simply out of friendship—to ensure that she and the two urchin orphans she had taken under her wing were suffering no consequences for helping prove his innocence. But given his own reputation for being a cold-hearted bastard, Sheffield didn't need to know—

"We turn again here."

Sheffield's murmur drew Wrexford from his brooding.

"Mind your head," added his friend as he squeezed through a gap between two derelict buildings. "A beam has broken loose from the roof."

The alleyway widened, allowing them to walk on side by side.

Wrexford grimaced as a particularly noxious odor rose up to assault his nostrils. "The next time you want my company while you try your luck at the gaming tables, let's choose a more civilized spot than The Wolf's Lair. I really don't fancy—" His words cut off sharply as he spotted a flutter of movement in the shadows up ahead.

He heard an oath and the sudden rustling of some unseen person scrambling to his feet and racing away.

"Don't fancy what?" asked Sheffield, who had stopped to light a cheroot.

"Strike another match and hand it over," demanded Wrexford. "Quickly!"

Sheffield dipped a phosphorus-tipped stick into a tiny bottle of nitric acid, igniting a flame.

Wrexford took it and approached the corner of a brick warehouse. Crouching down, he watched the sparking point of fire illuminate what lay in the mud and then expelled a harried sigh.

"I really don't fancy finding yet another dead body."

Setting aside her pen, Charlotte Sloane took up a fine-pointed sable brush and added several bold strokes of blood-red crimson to her drawing.

Man versus Machine. Her latest series of satirical prints was proving very popular. And thank God for it, considering that there had been no sensational murder or flagrant royal scandal of late to titillate the public's prurient interest. As A. J. Quill, London's most celebrated gadfly, she made her living by skewering the high and mighty, as well as highlighting the foibles of society.

Peace and quiet put no pennies in her pocket.

Charlotte expelled a small sigh. Financial need had compelled her to take over her late husband's identity as the infamous Quill, and she was damnably good at it. However, her income would disappear in a heartbeat if it ever became known that a woman was wielding the pen. She, of all people, knew that no secret—however well hidden—was perfectly safe. But among the many hard-won skills she had acquired over the last few years was the art of survival.

Forcing aside such distractions, she turned her attention back to her drawing. The recent unrest at the textile mills in the north had struck a raw nerve in the country. A heated debate was now raging over whether steam power would soon replace manual labor. Many people lauded the new technology.

And many feared it.

Charlotte leaned back in her chair, studying the violent clash of workers and local militia she had created, the human figures balanced precariously on the iron-dark pistons and condensers of a monstrous, steam-belching engine.

We are all creatures of habit, she mused. However awful, the known was preferable to the unknown.

The thought caused a wry smile to tug at the corners of her mouth. She seemed to be one of those rare souls drawn to exploring beyond the boundaries of convention.

"Not that I had much choice," she murmured.

Not to begin with, perhaps. But honesty compelled her to admit that the challenges, no matter how daunting, were what added a spice of excitement to the humdrum blandness of everyday existence.

Raising her gaze, Charlotte looked around at the half-packed boxes scattered around the room and was once again reminded of the current theme of her art.

Change.

"Change is good," she told herself. Only unimaginative minds saw it as terrifying.

But at the sight of all her earthly possessions—a rather unimpressive collection of flotsam and jetsam—lying in disorderly piles, she couldn't help feeling a twinge of trepidation.

For several months she had wrestled with the idea of moving from her cramped but cheap quarters on the fringes of the St. Giles stews to a more respectable neighborhood. The previous week she had finally made up her mind, and, with the help of a trusted friend, had leased a modest house on Buckridge Street, near Bedford Square.

Her art was now bringing in a handsome salary from Fores's print shop. And along with the unexpected windfall she'd received for partnering with Lord Wrexford . . .

Charlotte expelled a long breath. She had not yet come to grips with how she felt about taking the earl's money. Yes, she had earned every last farthing of it. And yet . . .

Beggars can't be choosy. She silenced her misgivings with an old English adage.

All those lovely gold guineas would allow Raven and Hawk, the two homeless urchins she'd taken under her wing, to have a chance at bettering themselves. Basic schooling, decent clothing, entrée to a world outside the sordid alleyways in which they had been abandoned.

Rising, she rolled up her finished drawing within a length of oilcloth and carefully tucked in the flaps, readying it for delivery to the engravers. A glance at the clock on the rough-planked table showed it was past midnight.

The boys had not yet returned from their nightly rambles and Charlotte tried not to worry about why. From the first time she had found them sheltering in the outer entryway of her tiny house, there had been an unspoken understanding that they were free to come and go as they pleased. She tried to make sure they had more than pilfered scraps of food to eat and better than tattered rags to wear. They were very bright and clever, and under her guidance they had learned to read and write . . .

But there were moments when she thought she detected a half-wild gleam in the depths of their eyes. A fierce independence, an elemental wariness that refused to be tamed.

What if they hated the idea of a nicer house, and proper schooling?

What if . . .

Whatifwhatifwhatif—

Steeling her spine, Charlotte cut off such thoughts with a self-mocking huff. Hell's bells, if she had a penny for all the times in the past she fretted over the consequences of a decision, she'd be rich as Croesus.

She had done her best to always be forthright with them and be deserving of their trust. Unlike John Dee, Queen Elizabeth's legendary seer and spymaster, she didn't possess a magical scrying glass in which to see the future. She could only try to deal with the present.

And at this moment, the present was grumbling for a cup of tea.

At least she could now afford the luxury of a spoonful of sugar to sweeten it.

A sharp hiss slipped through Sheffield's clenched teeth as he leaned in over Wrexford's shoulder.

"Is he dead?"

"Yes." Wrexford had felt for a pulse, though the three bloody stab wounds piercing the left ribs indicated the victim couldn't have survived. Sitting back on his haunches, he surveyed the violence of the attack—the ripped clothing, the slashed boots, the mutilated flesh of the dead man's belly.

"Holy hell," muttered his friend, fumbling to light another match. The flare of light showed all the color had leached from his face.

"The Devil's own work," he agreed.

Sheffield swallowed hard. "It's an awfully brutal attack, even for this part of Town." The man's neck had been broken and a knife slash had badly disfigured his face.

Lifting the dead man's hands, the earl examined the broad knuckles, noting the bruising and scrapes. "Looks like he put up a fight."

"That explains the victim's wounds." Sheffield

averted his gaze. "The footpad must have panicked at the resistance."

"Perhaps." Wrexford frowned, sensing there was more to it than met the eye. "But that doesn't explain the cut-up clothing or the slashes made to the body after death—"

"How the devil can you tell that?"

"There was little bleeding from the cuts on his belly. Which means his heart had stopped pumping."

Sheffield was starting to look a little green around the gills.

"Footpads strike for pragmatic reasons," mused the earl, as much to himself as to his friend. "They want money and valuables—which they assume are in pockets or on fingers. They don't waste time searching seams or mutilating their victims. Unless . . ." He took a closer look at the ripped lining of the coat and ran a hand between the wool and satin.

"Unless the fellow's attacker knew the fellow had something special hidden on his person," suggested Sheffield.

"There's that possibility," conceded Wrexford. "But given the signs of blind rage, it's more likely personal. Perhaps a betrayal or a business deal gone bad."

His friend appeared unconvinced. "But by his clothing—or what's left of it, the fellow appears to be a gentleman."

Wrexford arched a brow as he continued to examine the coat. "Meaning a gentlemen is never involved in anything sordid?"

A fresh match caught Sheffield's answering grimace. "Point taken."

He nodded absently, his attention caught by a small tailor's mark sewn in discreetly at the back of the collar. It appeared that the victim was from Leeds. Which added yet another layer of mystery as to why he was lying murdered in one of London's most dangerous stews. A stranger to the city did not simply stumble by chance into these fetid alleyways . . .

As the stinking sludge began to seep through his own boots, Wrexford shrugged off the conundrum. Whatever reason had brought the fellow here was none of his concern. After draping the remains of the coat over the death-distorted face, he rose.

"There's nothing more to do here. Let's find a watchman in Red Lion Square and alert him of the crime." A pause. "Assuming you know your way out of this cursed maze."

"That way," said his friend indicating the passageway to their left.

As they turned, the earl spotted two wraith-like shapes flitting, dark on dark, within the shadows.

"The Weasels," he muttered.

"Where?" demanded Sheffield. "I see nothing."

"You wouldn't." Already they had disappeared

in the gloom. "They're more slippery than quick-silver."

An instant later, two boys darted out from a plume of mist on the other side of the alleyway.

"Oiy," grunted the older of the two. "Another dead body, m'lord?"

"Don't be insolent to your elders," shot back Wrexford.

Sniggers greeted the rebuke. Unlike the beau monde, the Weasels weren't intimidated by his lofty titles.

The younger boy grinned. "I gotta new toof coming in." He raised a hand to his lower lip—or perhaps it was a paw. It was too filthy to be sure. "Here, would ye like te take a peep?"

"Good God—do *not* put that finger in your mouth," he snapped. "You'll likely get the plague."

The older boy—whose name was Raven, though the earl pretended not to know it—made a rude sound. "Our tutor, Mr. Keating, says there ain't been an attack of the plague in London since 1665."

"Yes, well, ingesting a mouthful of that disgusting muck could very well change that."

Hawk—like his brother, he, too, had an avian moniker—obediently dropped his hand.

Raven hesitated, then turned his attention back to the corpse. He crossed the footpath and leaned in for a closer look. "Cor, that's a nasty bit of blade work."

"It's a nasty part of St. Giles," replied Wrexford. There was no need to mince words. The brothers had grown up amid the brutish realities of life in the stews. Hoping to forestall further questions, he added, "Which begs the question as what you Weasels are doing here at this time of night."

Raven ignored the question. "It's odd for a cove te have his togs shredded like that," he mused.

Damnation—the boy was too sharp by half.

"Not if a thief thought he was being diddled by his partner," said the earl. "My guess is it's a quarrel over money that turned ugly."

"I s'pose that makes sense," allowed the boy.

"Are ye gonna find the murderer?" demanded Hawk.

"Absolutely not. I've resolved to leave solving crimes to the proper authorities," replied Wrexford firmly. The boys had played a role—far too great a one—in helping catch the Reverend Holworthy's killer, and he didn't wish to encourage the thought that it might happen again. "As is the duty of any law-abiding citizen, I'm going to alert a night watchman. And then I'm going to seek out my bed and sleep the sleep of the innocent."

Though he knew it was pointless, he moved slightly to block the younger boy's view of the mutilated torso. "I suggest you two scamper home and do the same."

The boys continued to stare at the body.

"It's just a commonplace murder, one of many that likely occurred here in Town tonight," he murmured. As if the taking of any life, however flawed, could ever be thought of as meaningless. "No need to study the gruesome details. There's nothing about this crime that will interest Mrs. Sloane."

Raven nodded and slowly turned away. "Aye. M'lady says her skills ain't needed te tell the public about nasty truths of their everyday life. She thinks that her pen is more useful fer exposing the evils in society that can be changed."

The pen is mightier than the sword. It was true that Charlotte's drawings had a rapier-like sharpness. And the fact that she unerringly cut to the heart of the problems facing the country or the hypocrisy of the ruling class was elemental to their popular appeal.

Feisty courage and lofty principle—a dangerous combination if ever there was one.

Repressing a grim sigh, Wrexford watched the two boys disappear into the fog-swirled darkness. The pounding in his head now felt like a spike was cracking through his skull. "Come, Kit, let's find—"

"Halloo!" A flash of lantern light and a sharp hail cut him off. "Who goes there?"

"Ah, excellent. Here comes a night watchman. We can hand things over to him and wash our hands of this damnable business."

Chapter 2

Wrexford gingerly took a seat at the breakfast table and darted a pained squint at the mullioned windows overlooking the back gardens. Sleep had done little to temper the ill effects of the previous evening. During the night, the throbbing in his skull had turned into a dull ache, whose bilious tentacles now reached down into the pit of his stomach.

The footman standing by the sideboard tiptoed across the carpet and quietly adjusted the draperies to block the blade of sunlight. Like all of the well-trained townhouse staff, the fellow was very good at reading his employer's mercurial moods.

"Tea and toast, milord?" he asked in a low, soothing voice.

The earl gave a tiny nod, though the movement made him wince. "And ask Tyler to prepare—"

"To prepare his special Hair of the Dog concoction," finished his valet, who at that very moment appeared in the doorway bearing a tall crystal glass filled with a ghoulishly green liquid. He circled around to the head of the table, and let out a reproving *tsk-tsk*. "It's an elemental axiom that combining brandy, champagne and Scottish malt is the devil's own recipe for a hellish morning after."

"Thank you for the basic chemistry lecture," said Wrexford sourly.

"You, of all people, ought to know what comes from mixing together volatile substances without careful measurement and timing."

Within London's scientific circles, the earl was acknowledged as one of the leading experts in chemistry. A fact that was often overshadowed by his erratic personal behavior. His scathing sarcasm and blatant disregard for the rules of Society—coupled with his notorious hair-trigger temper—frequently landed him in the headlines of the city's scandal sheets.

"Give me the damnable glass," growled Wrexford. He took a small sip and grimaced. "Did you add an extra measure of horse piss?"

"And two pinches of sheep dung," replied Tyler, who was well used to the earl's irascible comments. He arched a brow in bemusement. "You're out of practice, milord. Which doesn't bode well for the coming weeks if you're going to start carousing with Mr. Sheffield."

"Remind me again why I shouldn't give you the sack and hire a more obsequious servant?"

"Because no one else knows the secret for removing chemical stains from your expensive evening coats."

Wrexford chuffed a laugh, and then drained the drink. "Consider yourself fortunate that I'm a vain popinjay about my appearance."

His valet gave a long look at the earl's uncombed hair and carelessly tied cravat. "Quite fortunate, milord." He picked up the now-empty glass. "Is there anything else you require?"

"Other than a pistol to put me out of my misery?" Wrexford sighed. "Has Avogadro's book on gases arrived yet?"

"The package came in from Hatchards this morning. It's on your desk in the workroom."

"Put out the books by Lavoisier and Priestley as well," said the earl. If anything could chase the devils from his skull it was scientific inquiry. "I wish to review some of their early experiments with oxygen."

"Very good, sir," answered Tyler. Seeing the footman approach with the breakfast tray, he turned and left the room without further comment, knowing the earl's mood was always less testy when his breadbox was full.

A plume of steam rose from the silver pot's swan-like spout. Inhaling the pungent scent of smoky spice, Wrexford let out an appreciative sigh as he poured a cup of the sin-dark brew. He took a long, scalding swallow, feeling the coffee begin to burn away some of his malaise. His toast, cut thick and buttered exactly as he liked it, was—

A sudden knock on the door ruined the moment. "Bloody hell," he muttered.

His butler eased the portal open. "Your pardon,

milord, but there is someone asking to see you on a matter of grave importance."

"I don't care if it's the Grim Reaper, tell him I never receive visitors before noon," he snapped.

"It's well past one, milord." A pause. "And it's not a he, but a she."

Even worse.

"The lady's name is Mrs. Isobel Ashton."

Wrexford frowned. The name sounded vaguely familiar, but he couldn't place it. "And pray tell, what matter of grave importance does Mrs. Ashton wish to discuss with me?"

"The death of her husband, sir." The butler cleared his throat. "Apparently it was you who discovered his body last night."

"Eggs and gammon?" Hawk inhaled deeply and then let out a gusty sigh. "Are we celebrating something?"

"Yes," replied Charlotte, turning away from the bubbling frying pan to cut off several thick slices of soft white bread. "The last of legalities have been signed. The lease for the new house is now official."

Hawk gave an uncertain smile, but looked to his older brother for a reaction.

"When do you move?" asked Raven.

Charlotte felt a clench in her chest but pretended not to notice his use of the word *you*.

"Next week," she replied. "The carter comes

today to count the boxes." A glance around showed that the fellow wouldn't need more than the fingers on his two hands. "There is a great deal more space in the new house . . ."

Would that sound appealing?

"We shall have to acquire more furniture," she went on. "Like proper beds for the two of you and an armoire for your clothing."

Raven's face betrayed no emotion. Neither did his wordless grunt.

"Beds," breathed Hawk. At the moment, both boys slept on the rag rug in front of the stove. "Just like a grand lord?"

"Indeed," she replied lightly. "You shall be Duke of the Downy Pillows."

He giggled, but his brother's expression remained guarded.

"Speaking of lords," said Raven, breaking the sliver of silence, "we met His Lordship last night in St. Giles."

"Oh?" Charlotte busied herself with turning the browning meat. There were only two reasons aristocrats ventured into that section of Town—the gaming hells and bordellos offered the sort of dangerous pleasures that couldn't be found in the staid streets of Mayfair.

Not that the Earl of Wrexford's exploits were any of her concern . . .

"I trust he was looking well," she said.

"Actually he wuz a little green around the

gills," piped up Hawk. "It might have been the drink—he smelled like the inside of a brandy barrel. But more likely it was the dead body he'd just found."

Charlotte jerked her head up, and then swore as hot grease spattered her fingers.

"Language, m'lady," said Raven primly, which drew another chortle from his brother.

"A dead body." She carefully wiped her hands on a rag. "As in someone expiring from natural causes?"

"Being butchered ain't natural," he replied.

"Don't say *ain't*," whispered Hawk.

"You mean it was a murder?" asked Charlotte, though the answer seemed clear enough.

"Aye, and a grisly one at that. The man's clothing was slashed into ribbons and his belly was cut up something awful," answered Raven.

She felt herself stiffen.

"Lord Wrexford said it were likely a falling out among thieves," added Hawk.

Ah, thank God—an ordinary murder. One that had no deeper significance than greed and desperation. The footpads who prowled through St. Giles were known as some of the most violent criminals in all of London.

"I daresay he's right," said Charlotte, feeling an odd rush of relief. For any number of reasons, she was glad that the circumstances would not draw the earl into being a subject for her pen.

Again.

No doubt he was even more pleased than she was.

Thrusting aside thoughts of Wrexford, she focused on a more pressing concern. "And it is a grim reminder that St. Giles is a dangerous neighborhood, especially late at night." She dared not voice more than an oblique warning. Raven was fiercely independent and the ties that bound them were those of trust, not blood.

He shrugged. "Death is everywhere, m'lady."

"That doesn't mean you should cock a snoot at the Reaper."

Her words elicited a grudging smile. "We're careful."

Not nearly careful enough, thought Charlotte with an inward sigh. But she let the subject drop.

"Come help me carry the plates to the table. As an extra treat, I also purchased some strawberry jam."

"Thank you for agreeing to meet with me, Lord Wrexford." Smoothing her skirts, Mrs. Isobel Ashton settled herself on the drawing room sofa. "I know I have no right to ask for your help. But . . ."

She drew a measured breath. "But my husband was a great admirer of your intellect and incisive logic, so I thought perhaps . . ."

Her words trailed off, leaving Wrexford still

wracking his brain to recall his connection to the murdered man.

"My condolences for your loss," he murmured, falling back on the sort of platitudes he hated for lack of anything else to say.

"Elihu was particularly grateful for your advice on the chemical composition of iron," went on the widow. "And how to achieve a metal that withstands heat and pressure.

Ah—the inventor! Wrexford now recalled their correspondence from the previous year. A fellow member of the Royal Institution had suggested that Ashton contact the earl about a problem he was having with the boilers of a new steam engine design.

What a damnable loss for the world of science that the victim was Ashton.

"Your husband possessed a remarkable talent— he had both the imagination and the technical genius to implement his ideas." Wrexford rarely felt compelled to utter compliments, especially about another man of science. "It's a terrible twist of fate that he was the unfortunate victim of a random robbery."

He paused, wanting to choose his next words with care. There was no reason to upset a bereaved woman with any hint that the circumstances of her husband's death had raised some unsettling questions—

"But that's just it, Lord Wrexford," said Isobel

41

before he could speak. "I don't believe for an instant that my husband's murder was a random robbery."

The earl sat back in surprise.

She looked up from her lap. Her face was as pale as Lord Elgin's Parthenon marbles, but despite the grief shading her fine-boned features, her expression was as hard as sculpted stone. "You may think me a hysterical female, but I promise you, I am not falling victim to a fit a vapors. Elihu was on the verge of a momentous discovery, and I believe there were those who were prepared to do anything—*anything*—to steal his idea."

The first question that came to mind was *why?* Wrexford shifted on the cushions, trying to think of a tactful way to phrase it. But after another glance at her face, he decided the widow didn't need to be treated like delicate porcelain.

"For what reason?" he asked.

"For the same basic urges that have caused man to murder his fellow man since time immemorial—greed and envy. You have only to read the Greek tragedies to see the truth of it."

An interesting answer. His first impression on meeting the lady was that she had little substance. In his experience, beauty and brains rarely went hand and hand—and there was no question that Mrs. Ashton possessed striking looks. Her glossy, jet-black hair accentuated the milky perfection of her skin, and the exquisite symmetry of her face brought to mind an ancient sculpture of a classical goddess.

As for her eyes . . .

She met his gaze and didn't flinch.

"The Greeks were wise about a great many things," agreed Wrexford. But they weren't infallible, he added to himself. No one was. Even the great Aristotle had his weaknesses—he was completely bolloxed in his ideas on science.

For an instant, a hint of a smile touched her lips. "I understand that you are skeptical, sir. It's assumed that women are ruled by an excess of emotion rather than rational thought." Isobel expelled a sigh. "Alas, too many of us confirm the judgment."

"As a man of science, I try to base my conclusions on empirical evidence, not preconceived notions," answered the earl. "So far, I have no reason to believe you're acting out of hysteria."

"But nor do you believe that I have any logical reason for suspecting a more sinister reason for my husband's murder than mere bad luck."

Wrexford's opinion of her rose another notch.

"If you will allow me to impose a little longer on your time, I shall endeavor to explain . . ."

A nod signaled her to continue.

"I have every reason to believe my husband was on the verge of creating a revolutionary new steam engine, one whose power would make possible a whole new world of manufacturing." Isobel paused to draw a deep breath. "Such an invention is not only exciting intellectually, but it would make someone rich beyond their wildest dreams."

Wrexford needed to think for a long moment before the realization dawned on him. "I take it you're referring to a patent." Her fears suddenly seemed far more substantial than mere figments of a flighty imagination. Money *was* a powerful motive for murder. And owning the rights to such an important technical innovation would indeed be worth a fortune.

"Precisely, milord."

"What was this new innovation?" asked Wrexford, his scientific curiosity piqued.

A look of sadness darkened her amber-colored eyes. "My husband confided a great deal in me. But on this, he remained very secretive. Perhaps . . ." Her hands fisted together. "Perhaps he feared that speaking of it aloud, even within the privacy of our home, was dangerous."

Wrexford took a moment to consider all that she had told him. "It seems to me that your concerns are reasonable, Mrs. Ashton." He pulled a face as the pounding in his head came back with a vengeance. "But what I don't understand is why are you coming to me. The authorities—"

"The authorities think I've been reading too many horrid novels!" she exclaimed. "I met this

44

morning with a Bow Street Runner—a large, untidy man whose wits seemed as slow as his shuffling steps." The Runners were a group of men under the formal command of the Magistrate at No. 4 Bow Street, and one of the few official forces tasked with solving crimes.

"He made it clear that my husband's murder was—as he put it—an unfortunate result of a man straying into the wrong place at the wrong time," continued Isobel. "And that the chances of capturing the culprit were virtually nil."

However slow-witted the Runner was, Wrexford tended to agree with his assessment. Most murders in the stews remained unsolved.

"Be that as it may," he replied. "I have no expertise in criminal investigations."

"That's not what Humphry Davy of the Royal Institution says," countered Isobel.

Damnation. Davy was so fond of the sound of his own voice that he tended to talk too much.

"Mr. Davy was kind enough to call on me and offer his condolences," explained the widow. "When I expressed my worries about the authorities, he mentioned that you were instrumental in solving a recent murder."

Before he could respond, she added, "And I, like most of the public, saw the series of prints by A. J. Quill. The artist implied that it was through your efforts that justice was done."

Wrexford squeezed his eyes shut, wishing he

had followed his first instinct on waking and gone back to sleep.

"They both have greatly exaggerated the truth," he muttered. "Contrary to what you may think, I am no crusader for justice. Any efforts I made were to save my own neck."

"Please," she said softly, lowering her gaze. "I don't know where else to turn."

Feminine wiles bored him to perdition. But Ashton was a colleague. And a brilliant man of science. Recalling the corpse lying in the muck of a deserted alleyway, he let out a long breath. "I can make some inquiries. But I can't promise that they will do any good."

"Bless you, milord," she said, fixing him with a beatific smile.

"I doubt the Almighty would agree," murmured Wrexford. "It's the Devil who's more frequently invoked when people mention my name."

"Nonetheless, I have great faith in your abilities, sir."

In his experience, faith rarely aligned with probability. But he kept such skepticism to himself.

"If I am to be of any help, I need to know everything I can about the possible reasons for your husband's murder. To begin with, do you have any idea why he was in that part of Town so late at night?"

"He told me he was spending the evening at

46

White's with some fellow members of the Royal Institution. But upon our arrival in London several days ago, he had received a note from someone who seemed to know about his research and wished to discuss some very important implications—"

"Who?" interrupted the earl.

Isobel's lips tightened for an instant before she answered. "The note was signed *A Kindred Spirit in Science*. I counseled him not to respond. But Elihu was trusting—too trusting—of people." She looked down at her hands. "I fear he may have arranged a meeting despite my objections. Other than that, I can think of no earthly reason why he would have strayed to the stews."

Wrexford made a mental note to learn whether Ashton had a taste for gambling or women. Wives, however sharp, didn't always see a man's every weakness.

"Do you still have the note?" he inquired.

"Yes."

"I should like to see it." The earl doubted it would be of any value, but at this point, any scrap of evidence was worth collecting.

"Of course," she replied. "One of Elihu's investors kindly offered us the use of his townhouse for our visit. I shall have one of the footmen bring it to you."

"One last thing—I should like to see a list of all the people who knew about your

47

husband's research, and how close he was to a breakthrough." He steepled his fingers. "And I should like your assessment of who among them might be willing to kill to possess it."

Isobel shifted uncomfortably and averted her gaze. Shadows skittered over her profile and yet he could see that her face had turned deathly pale.

"Mrs. Ashton?"

"I'll compile a list and send it to you, along with the note," she whispered. "It pains me to think that anyone on it would wish my husband ill." The skin tightened over the bones of her face, giving her beauty a fragile edge. "But if you must begin looking at possible motives, I suggest you speak with my husband's personal secretary, Octavia Merton, and his laboratory assistant, Benedict Hillhouse."

Isobel paused, and to his eyes her expression seemed to harden.

"Given how closely they worked with him on his experiments," she said carefully, "they will know the most about any secret animosities."

Chapter 3

Charlotte picked up the woven straw hat and carefully shook the dust from its floppy brim. The motes floated through the still air, sparkling like bits of gold in the sunlight slanting through the narrow window. It was, she told herself, only a figment of her maudlin memories that the musty back room suddenly seemed redolent with the summer-warm fragrance of cypress and thyme.

Italy had been a time of simple pleasures— ethereal light, glorious art, breathtakingly beautiful landscapes, cheap wine. She and her late husband had been poor as church mice. And yet they had been happy there.

With a pinch of her fingers, she fixed a crick in the paint-stained crown, and then set it atop a neatly folded pile of Anthony's clothing. The hat had been a great favorite of his—he'd worn it every day while painting outdoors amid the classical ruins of Rome. They had both loved the sense of old and new that one saw in every vista of the city. It made life seem eternal.

But it was now time to truly put the past behind her. Anthony's death had been . . .

Avenged? Charlotte hesitated, running her hand over the soft folds of a linen shirt. No, that wasn't the right word. Perhaps the emotion defied definition. Knowing the truth had at least allowed her to make peace with her demons— and his.

It had been a senseless death. But life was capricious. All the more reason to look to the future.

Charlotte quickly finished sorting through the box of Anthony's clothing and returned to the main room.

"Raven," she said, after scribbling a short missive and folding the paper. "Would you and Hawk kindly take a note to Mr. Henning?" The surgeon ran a clinic for wounded war veterans. She was sure that a donation of clothing would be most welcome.

The boys looked up from their schoolbooks— too quickly, she thought with an inward sigh. With all the distractions of readying for the move, they had been neglecting their studies.

"Aye, of course, m'lady!" said Raven, shooting up from his stool.

"And we'd be happy te run any other errand for you," added Hawk hopefully.

"Thank you, but the note may wait until *after* you have finished the chapter on the Glorious Revolution."

"History's boring," grumbled Raven, reluctantly sitting down.

"Actually it's not," she countered. "It's all about the fascinating people—the politicians,

50

the philosophers, the artists, the soldiers, the musicians—who shape the world."

Hawk looked thoughtful. "William of Orange does seem a like wery interesting fellow."

"William—now there's a good, strong name." Charlotte seized the opportunity to change the subject. It was a sore point between them, but much as she disliked pressing the boys, it couldn't be put off much longer. A decision had to be made.

Raven muttered a word she pretended not to hear. "I don't want a new name." His chin took on a pugnacious tilt. "Wot's wrong with the one I have?"

They had been over that question countless times during the past week. The new neighborhood was only a scant half mile away. But it was a different world from the stews of St. Giles. To fit in, the boys needed real names.

"Think of it this way," she reasoned. "Life is all about change—a caterpillar turns into a colorful butterfly. You are simply shedding your old skin and taking on a new one. It will be . . ."

A loud knock on the front door saved her from having to utter yet another platitude.

"That must be the carter." Charlotte hurried through the entryway and threw back the bolt.

"You're late," she chided as the portal swung open.

"Am I?"

The Earl of Wrexford was wearing a superbly tailored coat, a rakish low-crown beaver hat—and his usual sardonic smile, noted Charlotte.

"That should be of no surprise," he went on, stepping past her without waiting for an invitation to enter. "You know conventional manners bore me to perdition."

"Indeed I do. So I take it this isn't a social call?" she replied with a harried sigh. It had been a fortnight since his last visit, and the unexpected appearance caused a tiny hitch in her heartbeat—though she was too preoccupied to think about why.

Ignoring her question, Wrexford took off his hat and ran a hand through his wind-ruffled dark hair. It looked like it hadn't been trimmed in weeks.

"Halloo, Weasels," he called to the boys.

"You see, m'lady," challenged Raven. "His Lordship doesn't give a rat's arse about calling us by a heathen moniker."

Charlotte bit her lip in exasperation. Given the earl's penchant for sarcasm, this was not likely to end well.

"I seem to have intruded on some sort of altercation," he murmured. "Pray tell, what's the problem?"

"Never mind," she said through gritted teeth.

He arched a brow.

"She wants us te have proper English names," volunteered Hawk. "So when we move te a new neighborhood no one will know we're nuffink but orphan guttersnipes."

"It's bloody stupid and I won't do it!" cried Raven hotly. "I refuse te be a Charles or a Nathaniel—or any other cursedly idiotic name."

"*Merde*," muttered Charlotte and then tried another tactic. "Come, there must be *some* choice that doesn't make your skin crawl."

Raven's expression turned even more mulish.

"Ye god," murmured the earl. "All this *sturm und drang*, when the answer is laughably simple."

She fixed him with a look of mute appeal. "Please, sir, this isn't a game."

"Allow me to explain," he replied.

She hesitated and then gave a brusque nod. So far, all her arguments had been for naught. There was little to lose.

Wrexford turned to Raven. "Pick a proper Christian name—any choice will suffice."

"But—"

"Just do it, lad." A note of command edged his voice.

The boy drew in a wary breath. "What was yer brother's name—the one who's dead?"

"Thomas," answered the earl softly.

"Then I choose Thomas."

"Excellent." Wrexford performed an elaborate formal flourish.

Drat the man—he was clearly enjoying himself, thought Charlotte. *At my expense.*

His deep, plummy voice drew her back from her momentary brooding. "Allow me to present Thomas Ravenwood Sloane—known to all as Raven."

Charlotte started to speak but he waved her to silence. "In the beau monde, men are very rarely called by their Christian name. It's a time-honored tradition that you acquire a nickname. I am always called Wrex, John Nottingham Allerton is Notty . . ."

The earl shrugged. "So there you have it—two birds with one stone, if you will. The lads need only mention their full names once, and then never have to deal with the question again. And you have what you need for any official purposes."

"Yeah, I s'ppose I can live with that," allowed Raven.

"But I—" she began.

"If you are concerned about the choice of Sloane as a surname, my thought was, you can explain the lads are orphaned relatives from your late husband's side of the family. Again, it seems the simplest solution, but it is entirely up to you if you wish to choose another."

She drew in an uncertain breath. "No, what you suggest makes sense."

"Excellent." Wrexford shifted his gaze to Hawk. "Your turn."

"Wot's *your* Christian name, sir?"

The question seemed to take him by surprise. Charlotte realized that she, too, had no idea of the answer.

"I can't remember," quipped Wrexford.

"Come, sir, what's good for the goose is good for the gander," she murmured.

He frowned in mock concentration for a long moment. "I believe it's Alexander. But I ought to check Debrett's Peerage to confirm it. It may be Agamemnon or Aloysius."

Raven snickered.

"I choose Alexander," said Hawk solemnly.

Another flourish. "And here we have Alexander Hawksley Sloane—known to all as Hawk."

"Alexander Hawksley Sloane," repeated Hawk in an awestruck whisper. A delighted smile spread the width of his narrow face.

"It's an awfully big handle for an awfully small runt," teased his brother.

Although the older boy was very good at hiding his emotions, Charlotte could sense that he was secretly just as pleased.

"Thank you, milord," she murmured.

Hawk took up a pencil and began to write out his new name in large, curling copperplate script letters.

"I see that no more serious study can be expected," observed Charlotte wryly. "So you two might as well take your swift feet—and exalted monikers—and fly off to Mr. Henning with my note. Lord Wrexford and I have some private matters to discuss."

"How do you know that?" inquired Wrexford as he watched the boys gratefully snap their books shut and scamper for the door.

"Because, as you've take pains to point out, you despise social pleasantries. You're a pragmatic man, milord. So since you are here, I assume there's some sordid matter in which my skills or my knowledge can be of use to you."

Am I really that unfeeling to my friends? Sheffield's oblique criticism suddenly cut a little more sharply against Wrexford's conscience. Despite the complexities that shaded their relationship, he *did* think of Charlotte as a friend.

"Perhaps I have come to wish you well in your new residence."

She let out a low laugh. "And perhaps pigs have learned how to fly."

Some men might have been offended. However, he liked to think hypocrisy was not one of his many faults.

"I may always count on you to bring my vanity down to earth," he murmured.

Charlotte turned away and began straightening up the jumble of books and papers on the table. "It was merely an empirical observation, not a criticism. We both know you despise tender sentiments." Her hands stilled on the paper

56

bearing Hawk's carefully written name. "That said, I'm truly grateful to you, sir. Your solution resolved a very thorny problem."

"As we both know, seeing a problem from a different perspective often reveals a simple answer."

More shuffling. Charlotte shifted her stance, and in the flickering of the shadows, he thought he detected a look of uncertainty pinch at her features. However, it was gone in a flash as she looked up and tucked a loose strand of hair behind her ear.

A thin smile twitched on her lips. "Which, I take it, is why you are here."

Wrexford allowed an answering smile. "Close enough to the truth that I won't quibble over semantics."

She sighed and signaled for him to have a seat on one of the stools. "Why is it that I suspect this concerns last night's murder?"

"Because you have very good instincts."

"I thought you told the lads it was merely a falling out among criminals."

"And so I believed at the time," he replied.

She sat down opposite him, her expression unreadable. "Go on."

Tit for tat. He'd debated with himself on whether to draw her into this conundrum. But given her profession and her network of informants throughout the city, there was little chance that the suspicious circumstances wouldn't come to her attention.

That didn't mean negotiations would be easy, he thought wryly. As in chemical experiments, putting two explosive elements together was always a risk. She'd never settle for vague generalities, which would force him to balance on a razor's edge of truth and diversion.

"If I had my druthers, I would prefer that the scandalmongers not stir up a tempest of lurid speculation," he began.

"Cut wind, milord," she interrupted. "Who was it?"

There was no point in prolonging the inevitable. "Elihu Ashton."

A ripple of awareness darkened her gaze. "The inventor?"

He nodded. "And owner of the most productive textile weaving factory in the country."

"Ye god," she murmured. "You must be mad to think this won't stir the press into a frenzy." A pause. "So why come to me with the secret when you know my bread and butter is scandal?"

"Because you'll find out soon enough. The news will very shortly become public," admitted Wrexford. "However, there are facts to which only I am privy. And I'm hoping that if I reveal them to you, I may count on your sense of justice to temper your pen until the authorities have a chance to uncover the truth."

"The truth?" Her tone mingled mockery and regret. "We both know what an elusive concept that is."

Her view of the world was nearly as cynical as his. The difference between them was that her principled idealism had remained uncorrupted by harsh reality.

"Be that as it may, I would rather not drag a man's name through the mud until more facts are known. I think you can help with that."

"You drive a hard bargain, sir," muttered Charlotte.

"We expect no less from each other."

The warring of emotions was writ plain on her face as Charlotte took a moment to consider what he had said. "Look, I can't very well ignore the murder. It's exactly the sort of thing A. J. Quill would comment on, especially given my latest series on *Man versus Machine*."

"I understand that," he replied. "But perhaps the thrust of your next print could simply be the shock of a notable figure meeting an untimely death, rather than your usual insightful commentary that digs deeper into the heart of a crime."

Seeing her scowl, Wrexford quickly added, "We both know you have the power to fan the flames of public opinion. And that, in turn, influences how the authorities handle an investigation. Any hope of a fair assessment can easily go up in smoke if the prints are too incendiary."

"That's a low blow, sir." They had first met because the earl was the main suspect in a heinous murder—and her satirical drawings had whipped up speculation that his neck would soon be in a noose.

This time his smile was more pronounced. "Yes, well, I'm an unscrupulous fellow. I'll stoop to any means to get what I want."

Her eyes narrowed, but not quite enough to hide the flicker of humor. Unlike most people, she understood his sarcasm. "Before I agree to your terms, I need to know how you learned that the victim was Ashton. More importantly, I need to know why you care."

Wrexford blew out his breath. It was for good reason that A. J. Quill was recognized as the sharpest, savviest commentator on human nature in all of London.

"His wife—or rather, his widow—came to visit me earlier this afternoon," he answered. "And knowing your next question will be why, Ashton and I were acquainted through the Royal Institution. We didn't meet in person, but corresponded regarding a question on the chemical composition of iron. I was able to help him solve a technical problem he was having."

After reaching for a pencil and paper, Charlotte started to make some notes.

"Mrs. Ashton was aware of my connection with her husband," he continued. "She had also heard from Humphry Davy that I'd been involved in solving another diabolically difficult murder."

Charlotte looked up. "I take it you're implying she thinks this is not the work of random footpads."

"Correct."

"For what reason?" she pressed.

"Ah." Wrexford stretched out his legs and stared down at the tips of his well-polished boots. "Now we have come to the metaphorical Rubicon, Mrs. Sloane."

She set down her pencil and tapped her fingertips together. "You mean if I cross the river, there is no going back."

"I see your classical education goes beyond a command of Latin," he said dryly. "At some point, I would be curious to know how that came about."

"At some point, I may be willing to satisfy your curiosity. But now is not that moment." She raised her brows in challenge. "What promises do you need from me?"

"That the information I tell you will be held in confidence and not color your drawings."

"What if I learn the same information from other sources?" asked Charlotte quickly.

"Bloody hell—are you training to be a barrister?" he grumbled.

"It's a pity women aren't allowed to practice law," she shot back. "We'd be far better at it than men because we care more about practical results than prosing on like pompous windbags."

Wrexford chuckled. "Point taken." He hesitated, his expression turning grave, and then added, "As for what promises I require, I will trust you to decide what is right, Mrs. Sloane."

A spasm of surprise flitted over her face, along with an emotion he couldn't read.

"But allow me to repeat that I am deadly serious about the dangers of inciting wild speculation merely to sell more newspapers or satirical prints. Innocent lives can be put at risk, reputations can be ruined, and the guilty party may have leeway to manipulate the truth."

"Have you reason to think I don't take such responsibilities to heart, Lord Wrexford?"

Their eyes locked.

"If I did, I wouldn't be here," he replied softly.

Chapter 4

Charlotte rose abruptly and went to put the kettle on the hob. "I feel in need of some tea. Would you care for some as well?"

"I would prefer brandy, but tea is probably a wiser choice."

She had noticed the dark hollows beneath his eyes and the taut lines etched around the corners of his mouth, but refrained from comment. The earl's moods were best described as mercurial. However, his personal life was none of her business.

After adding several heaping spoonfuls of Lapsang Souchong leaves to the pot, Charlotte turned and set a hand on her hip. "Nebulous as they are, I agree to your terms, milord." A sigh. "Though likely we will clash incessantly over their interpretation."

A glint of amusement lit in his eyes. "That goes without saying."

"You speak as if that is . . . entertaining."

"My valet tells me that I am a very difficult fellow to live with when I am bored," he replied. "You never bore me, Mrs. Sloane."

The kettle began to hiss, sending a cloud of steam into the air. "No, I drive you to distraction."

"Let us just say you challenge me. Few people do."

"I'm not sure whether to take that as a compli-ment or a castigation."

"Yes you do," murmured Wrexford.

Impossible man. At times she was sorely tempted to strangle him. And yet, a smile curled at the corners of her mouth as she carried the tea tray to the table.

"Enough of verbal sparring, sir." Charlotte passed him a cup. "You've come here to discuss business."

A plume of steam rose up, blurring the sharply chiseled planes of his face. And yet, even when softened by the silvery vapor his features radiated an elemental strength.

Or perhaps stubbornness was a better word. Charlotte ducked her head to hide another smile. *Birds of a feather.* Honesty compelled her to concede that she saw the same unyielding expression every time she glanced in the looking glass.

The earl took a sip of the scalding brew, then set it aside. "Ashton's widow is convinced her husband was murdered because he was on the verge of a momentous discovery." He pursed his lips. "I'm inclined to give her suspicions credence because of the state of the body."

Charlotte went very still. "How so?"

He raised a brow. "The lads didn't describe it to you in gory detail?"

"No. They merely said you had stumbled upon

a body and were of the opinion that it was a quarrel among thieves."

"Don't look daggers at me," he replied. "That *was* what I thought at the time. Given the information I have now, I see things differently." The earl took up a spoon and turned it slowly between his fingers. "Ashton's clothing was ripped at the seams —clearly his murderer was searching for something. And his belly was slashed, indicating rage at not finding it. Logic says it wasn't a random crime."

"What was the murderer after?"

"Presumably technical drawings or a description of the invention. According to Ashton's widow, a patent on it would be worth a king's ransom."

Patents. While researching her latest print series, she had become aware of how powerfully profitable they were. That ideas were, like estate lands and Old Master paintings, valuable property whose rights could be owned had been an unfamiliar concept. But she could well understand how a new technological innovation— and the riches it would generate—might be a motivation for murder.

"I take it you found no clues at the scene."

"No. I heard someone racing away from the body, but it was too dark to see anything. However, I do know that Ashton was lured to the area by a note from a so-called kindred spirit in science who wished to discuss a special partnership."

"In *St. Giles?*"

65

He made a face. "Both Ashton and his wife are unfamiliar with London. He had no idea that he was heading into the very heart of the city's darkness."

Charlotte felt a welling of anger at such deadly deceit. It seemed horribly wrong than a man's brilliance should cost him his life.

"Does she have any idea who the culprit could be?"

"I asked her to send me a list of those who knew of the invention." He shifted on the stool. "She was very careful not to make any outright accusations, but she did suggest any questioning ought to begin with his secretary and laboratory assistant."

"Did she say why?"

"Not in so many words. But it was obvious that there is no love between the three of them."

Interesting. But first things first. "Getting back to the actual murder—describe the corpse and its surroundings as precisely as you can."

His mouth tightened.

"For God's sake, milord, the lads saw the scene —and I daresay they can tell me every bloody detail even more accurately than you can!"

"I don't doubt it." Wrexford chuffed a grunt. "What I was about to say is, I'm hoping you won't show the slashed clothing or mutilation in your drawing. If the murderer doesn't suspect that the crime is being seen as anything other than a random act of violence in a dangerous part of the city, it will make it easier to investigate and learn the truth."

"I'm aware of that, sir," she said softly. "Just as I'm aware that my livelihood depends on being one step ahead of my competition. I survive by feeding the public's need for speculation." A pause. "Misery loves company."

Wrexford rose and began pacing the perimeter of the room. He was a big man and his long-legged stride made the space seem even smaller than it was.

"I realize that I am asking a great sacrifice on your part," he said. "I would offer recompense for your loss of earnings—if I didn't think you'd hurl it back in my face."

"Taking a bribe to suppress facts would be the first step down the road to perdition." Charlotte expelled a sigh. "Which is not to say I won't act on moral principles, even if it means starving."

"You're the most popular satirical artist in London," he murmured. "I daresay you won't starve."

"An exaggeration. My stock in trade." Charlotte stilled the twitch of her lips. "I asked about the details only to decide how else to frame my drawing. The angle of the building, the lighting, the depth of the muck. I'd at least like to get some of the scene depicted correctly."

Acknowledging her reasoning with a curt nod, he went on to describe the setting without further protest. His eye, as she well knew from their previous encounters, was just as sharp as his sarcasm.

"Thank you." Charlotte added another few notes to her paper, then offered the earl her pencil. "Do me a favor and draw the distinctive Z-shaped slashes that you just described."

"Why?"

"Because visuals help stimulate my thoughts about a crime."

He made a face but circled back to the table and did as she asked.

She stared at the sketch, feeling unaccountably unsettled by the image.

"My apologies for lacking your artistic skill," he said. "It's crudely rendered but relatively accurate."

"It's not that. I simply find it macabre a murderer would take the time to carve up the flesh of his victim."

Charlotte quickly shrugged off the thought and turned her attention to the facts she'd just heard. For now, it was difficult to see any pattern that might help them start piecing the puzzle together.

"You said the authorities are involved. What does Mr. Griffin of Bow Street have to say about all this?"

"Nothing. At least not as of yet," responded the earl. "Another Runner was assigned to the crime, and he told Mrs. Ashton that there is virtually no hope of capturing the culprit. But I intend to have a private talk with Griffin this evening and get his opinion on how best to proceed.

"Assuming he believes there's reason to proceed," pointed out Charlotte. At first blush, Griffin—who had handled the murder investigation involving Wrexford—gave the impression of being a slow, methodical plodder. But they had both come to respect his tenacity and commitment to ensuring that justice be done.

"True," conceded Wrexford. "The widow may be seeing specters where there are none. However, she did not strike me as a woman given to fanciful delusions."

"Just one more question, milord."

He stopped pacing.

"You still haven't explained why you came to me in the first place. What is it you want from me?"

"Your network of observers and informants is by far the best in the city," answered Wrexford. "Can you make inquiries as to whether any of the footpads in St. Giles might have been responsible for the crime? If, in fact, it does turn out to have been a random robbery turned violent, then we need not expend any further thought on it."

"But you don't think that is the case?"

"No. I have a feeling that when we dig a little deeper into the muck of St. Giles, we'll find a serpent's nest of intrigue."

Charlotte felt a chill snake down her spine. "As do I," she said slowly.

The earl's footsteps beat a grim tattoo on the bare wood floor as he made his way around a stack of corded boxes. "Unless you have any other questions, I'll take my leave and start tracking down Griffin."

"I'll make the inquiries among my sources, however they won't be up and about until midnight," she said in reply. "I'll send word as soon as I learn anything."

"Thank you." Wrexford halted at the door to the entryway and turned to face her. The wall lamp was not yet lit, so his features were wreathed in shadows.

"By the by," he said softly, "I *do* wish you well in your new abode, Mrs. Sloane. It would be entirely understandable if you have reservations about the decision. Change is never easy. But for whatever it's worth, I think it a wise idea. I admire your intelligence—and your courage—to make the change. Expanding one's boundaries allows for greater freedom of choices."

Praise from Wrexford? His words were so unexpected that Charlotte found herself momentarily speechless.

The earl set his hat on his head and pulled the brim to a rakish angle. "Good hunting, m'lady."

He was gone before she could muster a reply.

"Choices, choices," she muttered as she rose and moved to her work desk. The sight of her paints and pens helped calm her mind.

Through art, she had the confidence to express her thoughts and observations with a cutting clarity.

While conversing with Wrexford seemed to arouse naught but a tangle of indefinable emotions.

He enjoyed keeping people off kilter, she told herself. Most likely because his own equilibrium veered to all points of the compass.

Taking out a fresh sheet of watercolor paper, Charlotte set to work on a preliminary sketch of Ashton's murder. As she had told the earl, the people she needed to speak with wouldn't be awake until well after dark, so she might as well use the time for something constructive, rather than brooding.

Imagination slowly took precedence over intellect, and as the lines and textures took shape, Charlotte lost herself in the creative process. Though she wouldn't show them in the final drawing, she had copied the distinctive Z-shaped slashes drawn by Wrexford onto her sketch of Ashton's body, just to give herself a sense of the actual scene.

And it was then that the realization suddenly dawned on her.

"Bloody hell," she whispered.

They weren't just random cuts. The lines formed a crudely drawn symbol.

One that Charlotte was fairly certain she had seen very recently.

• • •

Spotting a flicker of red through the beery haze of tobacco smoke, Wrexford turned back to the barman and purchased two tankards of ale. The tavern was crowded, forcing him to take a roundabout path to the far side of the taproom.

Griffin slowly looked up from his kidney pie as the earl set the drinks down on the table. His expression gave nothing away, but Wrexford had learned that the Runner's beefy body and shuffling movements belied the sharpness of his wits.

"Another dead body, milord?" Griffin took a long draught of the earl's gift. "I would have thought that you'd had enough of the Grim Reaper's company."

"A chance encounter," he replied.

The Runner's grunt was noncommittal.

Wrexford took a seat. "I imagine Bow Street is no more happy than I am about the discovery of the corpse. The murder of a well-known gentleman never reflects well on the authorities responsible for keeping the criminal element in check."

Another grunt. Griffin didn't waste words.

"Your compatriot, Mr. Fleming, is of the opinion that it's simply a random robbery," went on the earl. "But I have reason to believe it isn't."

The Runner put down his fork and wiped his fingers on his sleeve. "According to Fleming's account, Mr. Ashton was stabbed and his purse was nowhere to be found. It is, alas, a more

72

common occurrence than we would like when a gentleman makes the mistake of straying into the stews."

"Did his account also mention the state of Ashton's clothing and the fact that his body was mutilated?" asked Wrexford.

Griffin took another swallow of ale. "Those details do raise certain questions."

He made a rude sound. "An understatement, if ever there was one."

The greasy lamplight caught the sharpening of the Runner's heavy-lidded gaze. "And you, milord, have answers?"

"That depends on what you're willing to ask." Wrexford held the other man's eyes for a long moment before continuing. "Fleming seems stubbornly set on ignoring all signs that this was no ordinary attack by footpads. Ashton's widow has offered him both a compelling motive and a list of possible suspects who would profit from her husband's death. And yet he chooses to ignore them."

"Have you any evidence that this was a premeditated murder. Or merely conjectures?"

Wrexford swore under his breath. "At least agree to hear me out."

That brought a rare smile to Griffin's lips. "Very well. But it will cost you another ale."

The earl waved a brusque signal to one of the barmaids, then edged his chair a little closer to the table. "Let's begin with motive. I happen to have been acquainted with Ashton. He was a brilliant inventor, and according to his wife, he was in the final stages of finishing a new technological device that would have been worth a fortune."

"How so?" Griffin's expression remained neutral, but a slight inflection in his voice indicated his interest was piqued.

"Are you familiar with patents?"

"I'm a humble thief-taker, not a fancy aristocrat," responded the Runner. "I've heard the term, but how a simple piece of paper magically begets bags of blunt is a mystery that only you wealthy toffs can comprehend."

Wrexford chuffed a low laugh. "Actually it's a mystery that only the damnable barristers and solicitors can understand. Nonetheless, I shall endeavor to make a brief explanation."

"For that I'll need a wedge of Stilton and an apple tart."

"A small price to pay for justice to be served," he murmured as he counted out a few more coins.

"And another ale while you have your purse open," murmured Griffin.

"Very well," acquiesced the earl. "Now, pay attention. To understand patents and profits we need to go back to 1602 and the Case of Monopolies, which was about a patent for playing cards."

"A case that is no doubt near and dear to your

heart, milord." A pause. "And that of your friend, Mr. Sheffield."

"There is, I admit, a certain irony to the fact that we discovered the body on our way home from a gaming hell. But let us not digress."

The Runner nodded absently, his attention momentarily diverted by the arrival of his cheese and tart.

"The idea of patents was not new," continued Wrexford. "King Henry VI issued the first letter patent in 1449 to a glazier for his special formula for making colored glass. It took another hundred years for the second one, again for a glass-making technique."

"Then, in 1598, Queen Elizabeth issued a patent to Edward Darcy, one of her courtiers, for a monopoly on the import and sale of playing cards. Darcy then sued a merchant who was doing the same thing. The defendant in turn challenged the patent in court by right of common law."

Griffin broke off a morsel of Stilton. "And what happened?"

"Fierce arguments were presented by both sides to the chief justice. The crux of the merchant's defense was that the Crown couldn't grant a patent merely for the personal gain of an individual. Only an idea that created some actual improvement to the making of playing cards could be protected," explained Wrexford. "In other words, a patent was for some new invention or unique innovation, not merely for commerce."

"I wonder how many Runners have the privilege of getting an Oxford education along with their supper," murmured Griffin through a mouthful of custard and apples.

Wrexford found the parsing of intellectual concepts endlessly interesting but was wise enough to recognize that not everyone shared his sentiments. He could see that he was in danger of losing the other man's interest.

"Bear with me—I'm almost done," he said. "Darcy's patent was thrown out by the court and in 1623 an Act was drafted to clarify the rules of patent grants. Known as the Statute on Monopolies, it still serves as the basis of our modern day patent laws."

"I take it you are now going to explain to me why Ashton was about to become a very rich man."

The earl smiled. "Yes."

Griffin leaned back in his chair and unfastened the bottom two buttons of his scarlet waistcoat. A low belch ended with a twitch of his lips, which may—or may not—have been meant as a smile. "Do try to make this quick, milord. Unlike you, I must eventually rouse myself from the table and go back to earning my living."

"Very well, but to fully understand the laws today, there's one other key concept that comes into play," explained Wrexford. "It's based on the ideas of the philosopher John Locke concerning property."

"I'm a pragmatist, not a philosopher."

"Which is why it behooves you to listen just a moment longer," replied the earl. "Locke believed the concept of property rights was derived from man's labor. To whit—a farmer possesses the right to his harvest not because he owns the land but because by the sweat of his brow, he's created the crops."

The Runner's expression of boredom altered.

"Locke's thoughts on property, labor and the accumulation of wealth were very influential around the turn of the last century. In 1710, the Copyright Law was passed, which was in a sense a complement to the Statue of Monopolies. In a nutshell, it said that in addition to hard goods, ideas were property too, and could be protected by law."

Griffin let out a grunt. "It's hard enough for me to protect the silver and jewels possessed by the beau monde. Now I must also worry about what goes on inside the heads of you fancy aristocrats?"

Despite the quip, Wrexford could sense he had the man's full attention.

"The Engravers Act was passed in 1735 protecting the work of artists," added the earl. "And now, we come to the heart of the matter. In the past, inventors, along with a great many other intellectuals, were often very secretive—they were loathe to share their discoveries or innovations for fear of them simply being stolen. But now, with the right to protect their ideas, such valuable information flows more freely to the public. And in the case of practical inventions, they offer ways to stimulate the economy and create wealth for both the creator and the people who will use the innovation."

The lamplight flickered as a draft stirred the smoke-filled air. Wrexford set his elbows on the table and leaned in a little closer. "For example, imagine an invention that makes steam engines more powerful. All manufacturers of engines will want to add it to their products because everyone who owns a steam engine will want the latest model. And they will have to pay for the right to use the inventor's patent."

The Runner was now sitting up straight. "Every steam engine in the country?" he mused. "That would be—"

"A bloody lot of engines," finished Wrexford. "And a bloody lot of money."

Griffin pursed his lips and gave a thoughtful nod. "So," he murmured after several long moments. "I concede you've spelled out a compelling motive, but have you a shred of proof to give me?"

"*I'm* not paid to solve crimes," retorted Wrexford. "You and your compatriots are."

A glint of wry humor lit in the Runner's eye. "Yes, well, as your friend Mr. Locke points out, labor and wealth are connected. Bow Street won't assign a Runner to do more than a rudimentary investigation unless there is some proof it's not a waste of time and effort."

"I'll hire you to follow the clues," said the earl. Runners could be hired privately for those wealthy enough to do so. "Mrs. Ashton is sending me the note that lured her husband to his death, along with a list of people who knew about his work. With a methodical—"

Griffin held up his hand. "I'm presently engaged in a case, Lord Wrexford. And to be frank, even though you've piqued my interest, unless you can bring me more than conjectures, I'll not waste your blunt. Trying to track down the villain with only what you mention would be like looking for a needle in a haystack."

"You've sharp eyes, as I well know," answered the earl.

"As do you, sir." The Runner's chair scraped back over the rough planked floor. "If you find a trail—even a faint one—I'm willing to talk again." He rose and patted his belly. "Preferably over another excellent supper."

Charlotte darted a glance up and down the crooked lane before stepping out from the slivered alleyway. Not that she needed to check for trouble—she was sure that Raven and Hawk were lurking somewhere in the shifting shadows, keeping watch over her.

But this was a particularly rough part of St. Giles, and even though she had taken the precaution of disguising herself as a tattered street urchin, the threat of danger was not something to be taken lightly.

Quickening her steps, Charlotte darted through a narrow opening between the sagging buildings on her right and made her way to the back of the gin house. Set deep within a recessed nook was an iron-banded oak door, black with age. She rapped out a private signal—three sharp taps, three fisted thumps—and waited.

The shadows shuddered as the fitful breeze blew through the cracks in the rotting fence, stirring the fetid smells of decay.

Charlotte felt a shiver slide down her spine. A scent of hopelessness pervaded the area, thick and viscous as the foul mud beneath her boots, and she offered up a prayer of thanks that Fate had offered her a way of escape.

But Fate, as she knew, was fickle. And cruel.

She drew in a steadying breath. Wrexford's description of the murdered inventor must be unsettling her thoughts. That brilliance could be snuffed out in an instant—

The door opened a crack, cutting off such musing.

Charlotte hurriedly slipped inside. A man—short, fat and dressed in a greasy coat that was threatening to split at the seams—relocked it and turned to face her. The spattering of weak light flitted over his bulbous nose and unshaven cheeks, catching for just an instant the alertness of his beady black eyes.

"Wotcha need, Magpie?"

It was Charlotte's street name. A bird had seemed apt, given the boys, and what better species than a sly one who darted to and fro, stealing shiny bits and baubles to take back to its nest.

"Information on the footpads near Red Lion Square, Sam," she uttered in a raspy growl that hid her true voice. "A toff was brutally murdered. Any word on who might have turned violent?"

Sam scratched at his bristled jaw. "Naw, nuffink like that. Bad fer business te poke a stick up Bow Street's arse."

She held up a purse. "You're sure?" He knew that payment would dry up if his information wasn't accurate.

"Aye, Roger the Razor was in here earlier, nabbering about how they's all madder 'n hornets that sumbody fouled their nest."

"They have any idea who? A rival gang from one of the other rookeries, perhaps?"

"Naw," he said again. "They has their way 'o hearing iffen that were true. Ain't no cutpurse what did the dirty deed." A nasty smile spread over Sam's face. "Must be anudder toff what got blood on his lily-white 'ands."

Charlotte was satisfied that her informant was telling her the truth—and indeed, given her knowledge of the mutilation done to the murdered man, she had expected no less. She would confirm it with several other people, but her gut instinct was that Sam was right.

The footpads and cutpurses of London weren't the villains in this particular crime.

"Thank you." She handed over the purse.

With a few quick flicks of his fingers, Sam undid the lock. "Any time, Magpie."

Charlotte slipped back out into the night, the damp air feeling even chillier after the stuffy warmth of her informant's lair. She turned to make her way to the next stop on her list.

But her mind was already at work on how to learn more about the symbol that had been carved into Elihu Ashton's flesh.

Chapter 5

"Damnation," muttered Wrexford as he booted shut the door to his workroom. Ignoring the crucible and neatly aligned bottles of chemicals on the center table, he took a seat at his desk and set down his cup of coffee, trying to tamp down his rising frustration. It was nearly noon and still no package had arrived from Isobel, leaving him naught to do but stew in impatience.

Priestley's scientific magnum opus lay open to the section on "dephlogisticated air," and yet much as the earl was interested in reading the early experiments on oxygen, he couldn't bring himself to concentrate.

Damnation. Something was bothering him about the whole affair, but he couldn't quite put a finger on what it was.

"Milord." His valet's entrance kept his brooding from turning any darker. He brought over a thin parcel. "The information from Mrs. Ashton was just delivered."

"About bloody time," muttered the earl as he ripped off the paper wrapping.

Packed between two pieces of protective pasteboard was the short note to her late husband and a sheet of floral-scented stationery with a list of eight names, each followed by a short explanation of how the individual was connected to Ashton.

Wrexford cleared a spot on his blotter and carefully laid them out.

Tyler came around to stand by his shoulder. "Perhaps we could examine the note under the microscope," he murmured. "The composition of the ink may give us some clue."

The earl frowned. "The odds against that are astronomically high, but I suppose it's worth a look." He leaned in closer. "Hmmph."

"What?" asked his valet.

"Whoever penned the note has a distinctive style," said Wrexford, after making a closer study of the handwriting. "Take a look at the curlicue looping of the letters *f* and *g*."

Tyler took a moment to fetch a magnifying glass from the worktable and make a more thorough study. "You're right."

And yet, the discovery only caused Wrexford's frown to deepen. "It's too good to be true to think that any murderer would be daft enough to leave such a calling card."

"Unless," mused Tyler, "he didn't intend to kill Ashton."

A reasonable explanation, he conceded. It was possible that Ashton and the self-proclaimed Kindred Spirit in Science had quarreled over partnering in the new invention and things had turned violent. However, all the earl knew about Ashton argued against such a scenario. The inventor was well-known to be an altruist. Wrexford couldn't quite imagine him involved in any havey-cavey dealings.

But then, everyone had faults they wished to keep secret. A fancy polished veneer could hide a core of rot.

"I suppose we must consider that," he finally said aloud.

"But you don't believe it, milord?"

"No," replied Wrexford flatly. "I don't. However, as a scientist I must keep an open mind and base my assumptions on facts." He smoothed a finger over a crease in the paper. "Let us set up the microscope and see what the murderer's note can tell us."

As Tyler began to rummage in the storage cabinets, the earl slouched back in his chair, still wrestling with the strange prickling at the back of his mind. Perhaps it was merely the murder of an acquaintance—and a horribly foul one at that—that had him feeling unsettled. And yet, that was too glib an answer. His friends would cheerfully vouch for the fact that he was not the sort of fellow prone to tender sentiments.

Understanding the physical world and how it worked was the sort of intellectual conundrum he enjoyed solving. Chemistry was all about logic. One could puzzle out answers through empirical observation and analysis. Murder was all about emotion. It defied the clockwork laws of the universe. Which, conceded the earl, offended his orderly mind.

So why the devil had he been moved by the lovely widow's appeal for help?

Wrexford shifted uncomfortably. Beneath her grief and uncertainty had been some elemental quality that intrigued him. No milk and water miss, like most of the well-born ladies of the beau monde, Isobel had radiated a steely strength of character, a sense of calm resolve. Indeed, he had never met any woman quite like her.

Save for . . .

He chuffed a sharp exhale, forcing the image of Charlotte Sloane's face from his mind.

Bloody hell, it wasn't like him to allow thoughts of women to bedevil his brain.

Perhaps it was a sign that he needed to choose a replacement for the diabolically lovely Diana Fairfax, with whom he had parted ways a number of months ago. The beautiful—and pragmatic—courtesans of London understood the rules that governed such liaisons. Money had its privileges, he thought sardonically. It helped ensure there were no complications or complexities of feelings to confuse the relationship. As for more personal entanglements . . .

"Milord," called Tyler. "The lenses and lights are all adjusted. Would you care to come have a look?"

Wrexford rose, happy to have a practical problem shove away his brooding. "Anything of interest?" he asked as his valet relinquished his spot at the worktable.

"Not that I could see at first glance." Tyler leaned in and made a slight adjustment to the reflector. "But perhaps you'll have better luck."

The earl squinted through the eyepiece at the note that had lured Ashton to his death. But luck was proving as mercurial as his mood.

"No," he muttered after taking a few moments to confirm his first impression. "There's nothing unusual about the ink or paper."

Tyler shrugged. "We expected as much."

"True. But at the moment, I can't think of anything else to try." Wrexford rubbed at his temples. "You might as well attend to other things. I'm simply going to do a bit of reading on Priestley."

However, after his valet quitted the room, he took the note from beneath the microscope's lens and placed it on his desk, the pale, crinkled paper standing out in stark relief against the dark leather of his blotter. Wrexford shifted his empty cup, and after ringing for a fresh pot of coffee, he sat down and leaned in for yet another searching look.

What am I missing? As of now, the only tell-tale clue was the handwriting. But given that London's present population was over two million souls, the odds of identifying the author were . . .

"Virtually nil," muttered the earl.

"Nil?" repeated Sheffield as he strolled into the room. "Good God, it's far too early in the day to be reading Latin." He looked around and let out a mournful sigh. "Why are you here and not the breakfast room? I'm famished."

"I'm thinking—a concept with which you are unfamiliar."

His friend contrived to look injured. "I do, on occasion exercise my brain." A pause. "But never on an empty stomach."

Ignoring the hint, Wrexford reached for the magnifying glass.

Another sigh. "Pray, what's so interesting that it's caused you to forsake those lovely silver chafing dishes full of shirred eggs and gammon?" Sheffield moved around for a look.

"It involves last night's murder." The earl stared through the lens, willing himself to see something—anything—that might serve as a clue.

"Hmmm. That's odd," murmured his friend.

He turned in his chair. "Kit, I'm in no mood for your bacon-brained jesting—"

"It's just that I recognize the writing."

Wrexford went very still. "You're sure of that?"

"Quite sure," replied Sheffield. "Just look at the curlicues. I've seen enough of the fellow's vowels to be very familiar with them. He's the only man who loses at the gaming tables more regularly than I do."

"Do you, perchance, know his name?" asked Wrexford slowly.

"Yes, of course. The Honorable Robert Gannett." His friend raised a brow. "Why?"

'Because you may well have given us the identity of Elihu Ashton's killer," he replied. "Forgive all my earlier slurs on your intellect. You're brilliant."

Sheffield grinned. "No, just lucky." A pause. "*Now* will you offer me some breakfast?"

"In a moment. Any idea where we might find Mr. Gannett?"

"That will cost you one of your excellent Indian cheroots," quipped Sheffield. Catching the earl's scowl, he ceased his bantering. "We can start by making the rounds of the gaming hells in Southwark. He's been avoiding the more exalted environs of Mayfair because he owes people there too much money."

"Excellent. *Now* you may go help yourself to breakfast." Wrexford leaned back and gave a grim smile. "Then come back again around midnight, and I'll make sure Cook has a lovely rare beefsteak ready for you enjoy before we head off to capture a killer." He allowed a small pause. "Then again, perhaps it's better to keep an empty stomach, in case we have to put a bullet in the bloody dastard."

● ● ●

Charlotte penned a quick missive to the earl, explaining what she had learned the previous night. As to her suspicion concerning Ashton's mutilation . . .

As soon as the boys peltered off to deliver the note, she gathered her cloak and set off to pay a visit to a friend.

"Come to bid me a last farewell, Mrs. Sloane?" Looking up from the worktable of his mortuary shed, Basil Henning ran a hand over his jaw, leaving a dark oily streak on the stubbled whiskers.

Charlotte didn't dare try to identify the substance. The surgeon had a deep interest in the workings of the human body, and often did autopsies for the authorities, along with the care he offered to London's living poor.

"I'm moving to a different neighborhood, Mr. Henning, not the backside of the moon," she replied with a smile. "I still intend to continue my fortnightly class for women who wish to learn to read. So I daresay we won't become total strangers."

His face, which resembled a slab of Highland granite that had been shaped with a dull chisel, softened ever so slightly. "Auch, I'm glad to hear it, lassie. However it's not Tuesday night, and seeing as our paths tend to cross when dead bodies start turning up, I have mixed feelings about seeing you on my threshold this morning." A chuckle rumbled deep in his throat. "Nonetheless, your presence always brightens my day. Would you care for a cup of tea?"

She quickly averted her gaze from the pan on the table, thankful that the flickering lamplight left it wreathed in shadow "Tea would be lovely. Shall I put a kettle on the stove in your office, while you tidy up here?"

His laugh became more pronounced as he picked up a grimy rag and wiped his hands. "You don't fancy boiled kidneys?"

"You have an even more peculiar sense of humor than Wrexford," she chided. "As for dead bodies . . ."

Henning stopped laughing.

"You're right about why I'm here."

Despite his disheveled clothing and less than fastidious personal habits, the surgeon was sharp as one of his scalpels. Frowning, he fixed her with a searching stare. "Your latest print implied Elihu Ashton's death was the result of an unfortunate encounter with footpads."

"That is what Bow Street believes," she said carefully.

"But you have reason to think otherwise?"

Charlotte considered her promise to Wrexford, but quickly set it aside. Henning had become a trusted confidant during the investigation into Holworthy's murder. If the earl wished to ring a peal over her head for sharing the secret, so be it.

"Wrexford does," she answered. "It was he and Mr. Sheffield who stumbled upon the body." Charlotte told him about the slashed clothing and the fact that the killer had carved a crude symbol on the inventor's belly.

Then, after drawing a measured breath, she added, "I'm hoping you can tell me something about the pamphlet I saw here last week when I came to give my lesson."

Henning's expression turned even grimmer. A shiver of silence flitted between them before he turned abruptly. "Follow me." He blew out the lamp's flame and led the way across a muddy yard to his office. Once they were inside, he bolted the door and looked at the stove in the corner of the room.

"I'll stir the coal and put on a kettle. It may take a few minutes for the water to boil.

"We needn't go through the motions of social conventions," said Charlotte softly. "In any case, I daresay you'd prefer a dram of Scottish malt."

Henning's eyes lingered for a moment on the bottle of amber-dark whisky sitting atop one of the bookshelves. "Aye. But I'd better keep a clear head." Chuffing an irascible sigh, he dropped heavily into his desk chair. "You're putting me in a devilishly difficult position, Mrs. Sloane. You know my sentiments on the privileged classes and how they exploit those who work their fingers to the bone for wages that wouldn't feed one of their fancy hounds or horses."

Charlotte nodded. A flinty Scot with radical notions on social equality, the surgeon was outspoken about his contempt for the English aristocracy—though he did make the occasional exception. He and Wrexford recognized each other as kindred souls who shared a healthy skepticism for conventional rules.

"I know that, Mr. Henning, and I wouldn't ask if I didn't feel it was in the best interest of everyone, rich or poor, to make sure that Ashton's murder doesn't turn into the spark that ignites the powder keg of labor unrest in this country."

She drew an unhappy breath. "My natural sympathies are much the same as yours." For more years than she cared to count, she, too, had been among those cobbling together a hand-to-mouth existence. Things were a bit better now, but Charlotte knew how quickly that could change.

"Violence will only beget a more crushing violence," she went on. "The radicals who preach death to those in a position of power will be crushed by the government—and countless innocent poor will suffer even more misery."

Henning grimaced. "Auch, I know that in my head, lassie. But my heart doesn't like it."

"You've told me on numerous occasions that you don't have a heart," she murmured.

A reluctant smile ghosted over his lips. "I was planning on cutting it out. But I've not yet figured out how to use my long-winded diatribes against injustice as an internal steam engine for circulating blood through the body."

"Your secret is safe with me," she murmured.

"Aye, you're very good with secrets." The tension broken, he rummaged around in the welter of books and papers on his blotter—his desktop was as unruly as his appearance—and located a crudely printed pamphlet sewn together with coarse brown thread.

"I take it this is what you're looking for." He slid it across the desk.

Charlotte took it up and studied the cover. MACHINES WILL BE THE DEATH OF US! announced the title. Below it, in boldface type, was an exhortation to join the Workers of Zion. Its symbol was based on the letter Z and featured a distinctive arrangement of lines to create the image.

There was no doubt in her mind—it matched Wrexford's sketch.

"What do you know of the Workers of Zion?" she asked.

"Enough to comprehend that they're preaching some very radical ideas," replied Henning tightly. "They make the followers of Ned Ludd look like cherubic choirboys."

Charlotte's flesh turned cold. According to

legend, Ned Ludd was a weaver who in 1779 had smashed stocking frames in protest over the new technology stealing his livelihood. Whether the story was true or not, his name had become a byword for radicals who over the few years had taken to sabotaging new mills that were using steam power to improve production. The Luddites, as they had come to be called, were currently sparking some serious trouble up north. But the objects of their wrath were confined to machinery.

As for the Workers of Zion . . .

She skimmed over the rest of the contents, growing more unsettled with each turn of the page. "Good God," she whispered. "This isn't just dangerous. It's madness. I, too, sympathize with the plight of the working poor. But smashing machinery and murdering mill owners will only bring down the wrath of the government, not meaningful change. The uprisings will be crushed, the ringleaders hung, the laws tightened—and countless families will suffer the dire consequences. Surely no rational person can see such actions as a solution."

"Desperate people don't think rationally," said the surgeon.

"Which is why you can't allow the group to distribute their pamphlets here in your surgery," reasoned Charlotte. "Your patients are poor, and they're vulnerable and afraid. Allowing the

Workers of Zion to incite them to violence would destroy them and their families."

A war of conflicting emotion played across Henning's grizzled face.

"Your conscience knows I'm right," she pressed. "You must tell me what you know about the group and its leaders, so Wrexford can pass on the information to Bow Street. These men must be stopped from stirring up chaos."

And death.

"Yes, we need change to improve the conditions of workers," she went on. "But it must be done through lawful means."

Henning took a long moment to find his pipe and fill it with tobacco. A plume of pungent smoke rose up as he struck flint to steel, obscuring his expression. "Freedom and change are often bathed in blood." *Puff, puff.* "Look at the revolutions by the French and the Americans."

Charlotte remained silent, trusting that his innate sense of right and wrong would bring him to the right decision.

He exhaled a vaporous sigh. "However, much as I hate to admit it, you're right about the terrible suffering that results from ill-conceived protests." *Puff, puff.* "The fellow who left the pamphlets is tall, dark-haired, and has a mole on his left cheek. He calls himself the Archangel Gabriel." *Puff, puff.* "More than that, I can't tell you."

"You have no idea where he's living?" she asked.

"I don't," replied the surgeon. His mouth puckered around his pipe stem. Charlotte could almost hear the unhappy grinding of his molars. "If he returns, I'll see what more I can learn. He sees me as a kindred soul, so that may loosen his tongue."

"Thank you." Charlotte knew how much the grudging agreement had cost him.

She rose, the pamphlet still in her hand. "May I take this for Wrexford? He needs to convince Griffin that Ashton's murder was not a random attack by footpads."

"Aye," muttered Henning. "God grant that this sordid situation can be resolved without further bloodshed." *Puff, puff.* "But as I'm a hard-bitten cynic, lassie, I doubt that will prove the case."

Chapter 6

Wrexford set aside his book on Priestley's theories, finding it impossible to concentrate on abstract mysteries of science when an all too real conundrum was tugging at his thoughts. A glance at the clock showed it would be hours and hours until Sheffield returned.

"Damnation," he muttered under his breath. Patience was not among his virtues—the list of which would be a very short one.

The thought of lists drew his gaze to his desktop. Mrs. Ashton's sheet of stationery lay next to the note that had drawn her husband to his death. Much as it seemed the lesser of the clues in solving the murder, he decided it would be wrong to make assumptions and ignore it.

Wrexford picked it up and reread it. *Eight names.* The brief notations on how each knew of the inventor's work gave little insight into possible motivation. The widow would of course be able to elaborate . . .

He frowned, recalling her suggestion that Octavia Merton and Benedict Hillhouse—the top two names on the list—would be the ones to consult about any personal conflicts that might have turned violent. She had voiced nothing negative about the pair, but he sensed that beneath all her perfectly proper words there was much left unsaid about the Ashton household.

The inventor, a longtime bachelor, had appeared wedded to naught but his work. The decision to take a bride late in life might have sparked trouble. Scientific observation proved again and again that the introduction of a new ingredient into any mix could often have volatile results.

Taking up the list, Wrexford rose and called for his hat and overcoat.

A short while later, the butler of the widow's borrowed townhouse escorted him into the drawing room and withdrew to inform Mrs. Ashton of his arrival.

It took only minutes for her to appear. "Lord Wrexford!"

He turned from the set of landscape engravings hung above the sideboard.

Isobel stepped into the drawing room and drew the door shut. Her hair was drawn back in a severe bun, its midnight hue combining with the black mourning gown to heighten the paleness of her face. "H-Have you news about Elihu?"

Silently cursing his thoughtlessness, Wrexford shook his head. "Forgive me, Mrs. Ashton. I should have sent word I was coming, rather than shocking you with an unexpected visit. However, I wanted to ask you a few questions about the names on your list."

Isobel touched a hand to her bodice and summoned a smile. "Of course, of course. I didn't mean to suggest that I expect miracles, milord." A tentative wave indicated two facing sofas near the bank of diamond-paned windows. "Please have a seat."

Given Sheffield's surprising revelation about the lethal note, a miracle might be in hand, allowing them to quickly learn the truth about her husband's murder. Wrexford hesitated for a moment, then said, "I may have a lead on the note written to your husband. A friend thinks he recognizes the handwriting. Tonight we are going to make the rounds of the gambling establishments in Southwark, where the fellow is known to play."

Her eyes widened ever so slightly.

"Mind you, I don't wish to raise false hopes. It could very well be a wild goose chase."

"I understand." She took a seat and motioned for him to do so as well. "May I offer you some tea?" A slight pause. "Or brandy?"

Wrexford wondered what she had heard about him. Clearly nothing good about his personal peccadillos.

"Thank you, but I've no need of refreshments." He, too allowed a moment of silence. "But please don't let that stop you from ordering some sustenance."

The widow laughed, its musical lightness at

odds with her somber appearance. "Dear me, I've had so much tea pressed on me lately that I swear, it could float a twenty gun frigate. So I, too, shall forgo the usual social rituals, no matter that tea is considered a panacea for all ailments."

Her sense of humor surprised him. Or perhaps *intrigued* was a better word. He sat up a little straighter.

"Forgive me if that sounds awfully blunt. But I sense that both of us prefer plain speaking," went on Isobel, as if reading his mind.

"Plain speaking is a very polite way of referring to my interaction with people," replied Wrexford. "I'm considered outspoken to the point of rudeness, and am said to have a vile temper."

She arched a brow. "And is it true?"

"For the most part," he replied. "I don't suffer fools gladly."

"Ah." Rather than appear intimidated, Isobel seemed amused. "I shall have to take care not to appear a feather-brained goose." Looking down at her lap, she smoothed at the folds of heavy bombazine fabric, and in an instant all trace of humor was wiped from her face.

"How can I help?" she said softly.

He took out her list and a pencil from his coat pocket. "I'd like to learn a little more about the people on your list . . ."

Wrexford asked a few questions about six of them, jotting a few notes in the margin before circling back to the two names written at the top of the page.

"And now to Octavia Merton." He looked up. "During our first meeting, you suggested that she and your husband's laboratory assistant would know the most about who might wish Mr. Ashton ill."

"Yes," she replied. "They worked very closely with Elihu, so it seems a reasonable assumption."

"So it does," Wrexford hesitated. "You mentioned plain speaking just now, and so I feel beholden to ask you something before we consider any other questions. Do you consider either of them suspects?"

Her expression didn't change, but a certain tension seemed to take hold of her, drawing the flesh taut over the delicate planes of her face. Her cheekbones looked sharp as razors. "If I gave you the impression that I think Octavia or Benedict to be guilty of any nefarious doings, then I am sorry," she replied in a carefully controlled voice. "I did not mean to do so."

"Your sense of noblesse does you credit," he murmured. "But anything less than complete candor will make the very difficult task of finding your husband's killer impossible."

She gave a tiny nod. "I understand, Lord Wrexford."

"Excellent." He watched her for a moment longer, wondering if he had been too harsh.

However she met his gaze with a calm composure.

A woman who doesn't rattle easily. Which was all for the good, reflected Wrexford, seeing as he wasn't very good at tempering his tongue.

"Then let's start with Miss Merton. How did she come to be part of your husband's household?"

"Her parents died in a carriage accident when she was fourteen, leaving her alone in the world. As her father was Elihu's cousin, he offered her a place in his home," answered the widow. "That was nine years ago."

"Would you describe their relationship as cordial?"

"My husband was exceedingly fond of Octavia." She drew in a barely perceptible breath. "And she appeared to feel the same way about him."

"Appeared to?" repeated Wrexford. "You doubt the sincerity of her sentiment?"

Isobel considered the question for a long moment before answering. "I find it hard to discern Octavia's true sentiments about most things. She behaves with perfect propriety, but my sense is, she keeps her inner thoughts very . . . well guarded."

Wrexford considered the answer. But before he could frame another question, she continued, "In fairness, I imagine it wasn't easy for her when Elihu married me. She had run the household and served as his secretary for so long that it's only natural she might feel resentment at the change."

Change was a challenge for most people, reflected Wrexford.

"How would you describe your own relationship with Miss Merton?" he asked.

For an instant, a mirthless smile tugged at the widow's lips. "Coolly correct." Her fingers twined in the silk fringe of her black shawl. "I've tried to kindle a warmer rapport, but with no success."

"And yet you tolerated her presence? I would have thought . . ." He let his words trail away.

"To Elihu she was family," answered Isobel. "It would have been wrong of me to force him to make any painful choices."

Wrexford hesitated. Further personal probing, he decided, would only be jabbing a needle into a raw nerve. The two women were not on friendly terms. How much that colored the widow's assessment of Octavia Merton was hard to know.

"Just one last question for now. Can you think of any reason why Miss Merton would wish harm to come to your husband?"

"No." Isobel hesitated. "But as I've said, I find it difficult to discern Octavia's thoughts." She shifted, setting off a faint rustling of fabric. "Perhaps it would be better if you spoke with her yourself. Shall I ring for her?"

"She's here?" he asked in surprise.

"My husband was always hard at work on his projects, even when traveling. So yes, both Octavia and Benedict accompanied us to London." Wrexford edged forward on the sofa. "Yes, I'd very much like to have a word with her."

Isobel summoned a footman. "Please ask Miss Merton to come to the drawing room." Then leaning back against the cushions, she folded her hands in her lap and turned her gaze to the windows. Her expression was as inscrutable as stone.

He regarded her profile for a long moment and then on impulse asked one more question. "If I asked you to describe Miss Merton in a single word, what would it be?"

Her reply came with no hesitation.

"Secretive." She exhaled a wry sigh. "But then, I suppose we are all guilty of having secrets."

"Another visit te His Nibs?" Raven made a face at Charlotte's request to take a second package to Wrexford's townhouse. "Sending him billy-doos, m'lady?" he murmured, giving a credible pronunciation to the French term for love letters. Though where he had overheard *that* term was an unsettling thought.

She repressed a sigh. He was fast growing out of childhood into adolescence. Given his fierce independence, she had no illusions about the battles that lay ahead. The struggle over name-choosing would likely seem a mere ripple on calm water . . .

"Don't be impertinent," she said tartly.

"Wot's billy-doos?" demanded Hawk.

"A silly jest that doesn't merit a reply." Charlotte finished knotting twine around the package for Wrexford. "Both of you are letting your speech—and your manners—slide into the muck. I know you can do better."

Hawk hung his head in contrition. "I'm sorry, m'lady."

Raven's reaction was harder to gauge. He had always been far better at hiding his feelings than his younger brother. Turning into the shadows, he took a moment to pluck at a loose thread on his sleeve before meeting her gaze.

"Just let us know when your missive is ready, milady," he said in perfect imitation of a proper little Etonian. "It would give us great pleasure to deliver it forthwith to the Earl of Wrexford's townhouse."

Charlotte couldn't hold back a burble of laughter. "Be off with you, Weasels," she said, using the earl's sardonic name for the pair. "And do *not* pester His Lordship's cook for sweets."

A guilty flush colored Hawk's face. "Yes, m'lady."

As they hurried away, she turned and found herself confronted by the still-jumbled assortment of half-packed boxes stacked around the room. Yet another reminder that her whole life was turning topsy-turvy.

Change.

Taking a seat at her desk, Charlotte felt a sudden clench in the pit of her stomach.

Through Wrexford, she had learned the scientific laws of the universe seemed to indicate that everything was in constant flux. *Time. Motion.* Nothing was impervious to change—even a solid slab of granite eroded over the years, worn away by wind and rain.

But somehow such abstract concepts were of cold comfort. She picked up her pen, hoping its familiar feel would help calm her nebulous fears.

Tempora mutantur et nos mutamur in illis—The times are changing, and we change with them. "I, of all people, ought not be intimidated by change," she whispered.

The gravitas of Latin usually served to steady her emotions. And yet, despite the exhortation, a trickle of cold sweat started to slide down her spine.

Closing her eyes, she sought to banish the strange moment of weakness.

After all, her life had been shaped by tumultuous change—and not always for the better. But somehow she had always managed to draw strength from adversity. It was puzzling that a seemingly simple move from one physical space to another was setting off such a sense of trepidation.

Dipping her pen into the inkwell, Charlotte began sketching a series of random swirls on a blank piece of paper. Drawing always helped focus her thoughts, sharpen her insights.

It was, however, a good deal easier to see the faults in others. Still, she made an effort to look at her own situation with the same detached scrutiny she brought to the subjects of her social commentary.

For the past year, since secretly taking up A. J. Quill's pen upon the death of her husband, she had worked in quiet solitude, earning accolades as London's sharpest satirical artist. The peccadilloes of the rich and royal—their scandals over sex and money and politics—provided endless fodder for her drawings. Her popularity with the public had brought a modicum of financial stability . . .

But then had come the murder of the Right Reverend Josiah Holworthy, a rising religious fanatic, whose gruesome killing had captivated all of London. Lord Wrexford had been the prime suspect, and circumstances had brought them together as reluctant allies to uncover the truth about the crime.

Charlotte's pen momentarily stilled as she recalled the dark secrets that had come to light—

both about the reverend and her husband's death.

Secrets which had forced her to face her own hidden past.

Wrexford was right. The truth was, there was no staying still. One made choices every day, both big and small.

Both right and wrong.

It did no good to fret. Whatever the consequences, she would find a way to deal with them.

"I am strong," she reminded herself. As A. J. Quill, she had learned to be tough. Sardonic. Dispassionate.

It was, Charlotte supposed, one of the things that drew her and the earl together. Wrexford shared the same view of the world, though his sarcasm was far sharper than hers. He had no illusions that life was ruled by reason or fairness. And so he could laugh at the fickleness of Fate— even when it came perilously close to putting his own neck in a noose.

She would do well to copy his lead.

Looking down, Charlotte was surprised to see the paper bore a rough sketch of Wrexford's face.

Wrexford. For an instant, an odd little flutter stirred inside her. Just as quickly it was gone. Expelling a sigh, she crumpled the sheet and set it aside.

Enough of maudlin whingings. *Nihil boni sine labore—nothing is achieved without hard work.* Taking a fresh sheet from the stack of watercolor paper, she set to roughing out a sketch for her next satirical print.

"Thank you for coming, Octavia," said Isobel as the door clicked open and a young woman took a tentative step into the drawing room. "This is Lord Wrexford, a friend and colleague of Elihu. He wishes to ask you a few questions pertaining to my husband's work."

Wrexford wondered whether he was just imagining Miss Merton's slight flinch at the word *husband.*

"I hope you will consent to speak with him," went on Isobel. "It may help unravel the mystery of Elihu's murder."

Octavia's eyes widened for an instant, then she quickly dropped her gaze to the carpet. "Y-Yes. Of course."

Isobel rose and inclined a small nod his way. "If you'll excuse me, Lord Wrexford, there are some matters I must discuss with the housekeeper."

It was a tactful way of giving them privacy, but the young woman looked wary as she took a seat on the sofa.

In contrast to the widow's delicate form and dark coloring, Olivia Merton was tall and slender as a stalk of wheat. In the slanting sunlight, her hair reflected tones of honey and russet mixed in the strands of dull gold. She had none of Isobel's fluid grace. Her movements were stiff and ungainly, as if some unseen force was holding her in thrall.

But then, he reminded himself, she had just lost a surrogate father to a vicious crime. The shock and grief of it must be profound.

Unless, of course, it was some other emotion.

"I'm very sorry for your loss," murmured Wrexford. A banal platitude, but nothing else came to mind.

"Thank you," she answered in a toneless whisper.

"I understand you and Mr. Ashton were close," he began, only to see the color drain from her face.

"Who told you that?" asked Octavia quickly.

It seemed an odd response. "Does it matter?" he countered. "That you held each other in high regard is nothing of which to be ashamed."

"No—of course not. It's just that . . ." She drew a shaky breath. "Forgive me, sir. I-I'm finding it hard to absorb the fact that he is gone."

"That's quite understandable, Miss Merton. I shall try to keep my questions short." Wrexford gave her a moment to compose herself, but then pressed on. Perhaps it was cruel, assuming her grief was real. However, if fear and guilt were leaving her vulnerable to making a verbal mistake, he couldn't afford to let the opportunity slip away.

"I've been told that Ashton was on the verge

of completing work on an important invention—one that would change the way many things are manufactured in this country," he said. "Is that true?"

"Yes," said Octavia. "Eli was a genius, and his latest idea promised to be revolutionary." She looked up from her lap and for the first time allowed her eyes to meet his. "You worked with him on a formula for iron, Lord Wrexford. So you know that his intellect was unique. But . . ."

A tiny furrow formed between her brows. " But I don't see what all this has to do with his death."

It appeared that Mrs. Ashton hadn't told Miss Merton about the note that had lured her husband to the stews of St. Giles. Was it because she suspected that her husband's secretary already knew of its existence?

Shaking off such thoughts for the moment, Wrexford replied, "I have reason to believe that someone was hell-bent on snuffing out Ashton's brilliance."

Octavia blinked, the only sign of emotion. "I don't understand. I thought it was a random robbery by footpads."

"On the contrary, all signs point to it having been a premeditated attack. Judging by the state of his clothing, the killer was searching for something. I think it might have been papers." He let the words sink in. "Can you think of anyone who might have committed such a terrible crime?"

Her knuckles whitened as she fisted her hands together. Silence stretched long enough that he thought she might not answer. But when she finally spoke, her voice didn't waver. "No."

"If his invention was as revolutionary as you say, the patent on it would be worth a fortune," pointed out Wrexford.

"Eli wasn't interested in becoming rich," said Octavia in the same measured tone.

The earl couldn't help chuffing a skeptical grunt.

"He wasn't," she insisted. "Any money made on a patent was going to be used—" Her words cut off abruptly.

"For what?" he prompted.

Octavia stiffened her spine against the pillows, her expression remaining stony. "It doesn't matter now. He's dead."

Wrexford thought it mattered a great deal, and made a note to learn more about Ashton's business. Looking at her rigid features, he decided there was little chance in prying more information out of her concerning the inventor's intentions. So he returned to his original line of questioning.

"Ashton may not have been interested in acquiring a personal fortune, but most people are. Greed is a powerful motive. I have a list here of people who knew about Ashton's research." Paper crackled as he raised the list from his lap.

"Do you think any of them capable of violence?"

One by one, he slowly read off six names, each time getting a brusque shake of her head in response.

He looked up from the page. "And lastly, Benedict Hillhouse."

"Benedict!" The shrillness of her voice seemed to amplify as it echoed off the ornate furnishings of the room. She looked torn between fear and fury. "No—never!"

Interesting. The sudden burst of emotion hinted at hidden fire. Miss Octavia Merton was taking great pains to keep a tight control over herself, and yet clearly there were passions bubbling just beneath the surface.

"You seem very sure of that."

"I am."

The answer made him curious to meet Ashton's laboratory assistant. "I should like to speak with Mr. Hillhouse myself. Might you ask him if he will grant me a few minutes of his time?"

"He's out," replied Octavia softly.

"When will he return?" countered the earl.

"I couldn't say."

Couldn't? Or wouldn't?

"Then I shall call tomorrow afternoon. Please ask him to be here at half past three."

She stared at him, unblinking.

Wrexford decided there was no point in continuing the interview. "Thank you for your time,

Miss Merton. For the moment I have no further questions."

Tucking the list into his pocket, he rose and took several steps toward the door, then paused. "If I asked you to describe Mrs. Ashton in one word, what would it be?"

Octavia stared down at the carpet. "I'm not very good with words."

An evasive answer. Which perhaps told him more than she intended.

Lost in thought, Wrexford left the townhouse and began walking the short distance back to Berkeley Square. Amid the many questions swirling inside his head, one in particular was echoing loudly against his skull.

Why the devil had he allowed himself to be drawn into investigating the murder of a man he barely knew?

He wasn't normally plagued by self-doubts over decisions, but this one was bothering him in a way he couldn't quite articulate. Had he been a fool to succumb to Isobel's plea? The case offered naught but devilishly difficult conundrums to unravel. Even Griffin, a man who made his living apprehending criminals, was doubtful about the chances of apprehending the killer.

Was it hubris that had him believe he alone could succeed?

Or some more incomprehensible force?

By the time he reached his townhouse, Wrexford

was in a foul mood from spinning in mental circles.

"Milord," murmured his butler as he stormed through the front entrance and tossed his hat and gloves on the sidetable.

"Not now, Riche," he snapped. "Whatever it is, it can wait."

Undeterred, Riche followed. "Actually, sir, perhaps you had better have a look at the package. The messenger insisted it was of utmost importance."

Something in his tone brought Wrexford to an abrupt halt. "Did it come from Mrs. Ashton's residence?"

"No, milord, it was delivered by a . . . Young Person."

"Describe him."

Riche's face went through a series of odd little contortions. "Actually, considering how he was dressed, I would rather not." He cleared his throat with a cough and held out a small parcel wrapped in brown paper. "He did say his name was Master Thomas Ravenwood Sloane and that on no account was I to hand over these—" Another cough. "—billy-doos to anyone but His Nibs."

Wrexford felt his mouth twitch. "Thank you, Riche." He undid the twine and took a long moment to read over Charlotte's note and the accompanying pamphlet.

Bloody hell. He now felt even more foolish.

While he was floundering around, grasping for clues, it appeared that Charlotte had, with her usual incisive intuition, cut to the heart of the mystery.

With a motive, most crimes became far easier to unravel.

There were still hours to go before Sheffield returned. Looking up, he quickly retrieved his hat and gloves.

"Have Bailin bring round my carriage."

Chapter 7

Charlotte leaned back and assessed her finished drawing. Color had yet to be added, but the black pen strokes—the elemental heart of a print—were strong and sure. Artistically, she was satisfied.

But had she taken the coward's way out?

Yes, the Duke of Cumberland's mistress looked to be involved in another sordid bribery scandal, which threatened to sling yet more mud on the Royal family's reputation. And yes, the public deserved to know. They depended on A. J. Quill to keep the aristocracy's arrogant assumption of privilege in check.

Or so Charlotte rationalized.

But even as she assured herself that she had made the right choice of subjects, a tiny voice in the back of her head disagreed.

Her *Man versus Machine* prints didn't provoke the same gleeful laughter as her satirical skewering of the Royals. Most people wished to chortle at the misery of others. They didn't wish to confront serious questions—especially when there were no easy answers.

Panem et circenses. Bread and circuses. Juvenal, the Roman satirical poet, had possessed a keen understanding of human nature.

Taking up her paintbrush, Charlotte began to

add in the vivid highlights that would bring the black and white drawing to life.

"Tomorrow," she promised to quiet her conscience. "Tomorrow I shall refocus my attention on the plight of the workers displaced by the new steam-powered machinery."

As for Elihu Ashton's murder . . .

Her hand stilled, the pigment-filled brush hovering in mid-air. Gruesome as the act had been, she feared the motives behind the crime were going to prove even uglier. *Hatred, greed, jealousy, betrayal . . .*

A knock on the front door drew her from such dark speculations.

Charlotte reluctantly set aside her work and rose. The visitor was not likely to brighten her mood. She had a feeling she knew who it was.

"You seem to have a sixth sense for crime, Mrs. Sloane," said Wrexford, as he stepped into the entrance foyer and shook a spattering of raindrops from his hat. Pulling the pamphlet from his pocket, he added, "By what unholy magic did you manage to discover this?"

"I'm not a witch or alchemist, as you well know. I simply use my ears and my eyes," she answered.

"And yet you see and hear things that escape mere mortals."

"That's how I make my living." Charlotte gestured for him to enter the main room. "Forgive me, but things are even more cramped than usual," she muttered after pulling a face.

He shifted a wooden paintbox off one of the stools and took a seat. "When do you move to your new residence?"

"The day after the morrow."

His lidded gaze seemed to be searching her face for something. Charlotte turned away.

"You don't sound happy," observed the earl.

"I . . ." How to explain the churning of conflicting emotions? "It's not that simple, milord."

"Few things in life are." He, too, seemed unsettled.

Charlotte cleared off one of the other stools. "Including Elihu Ashton's murder?"

"Indeed." Wrexford drummed his fingertips on the scarred wood tabletop. For a moment, he looked disinclined to leave off his probing into her personal life.

But as she had hoped, his innate sense of pragmatism prevailed.

"Like, you, I've discovered a few more facts since yesterday," he said. "But first, tell me more about the pamphlet, and where you got it. It's given us an exceedingly important clue."

"In studying the sketch you left, I realized that the cuts formed a symbol—one that looked familiar." Charlotte quickly explained about having seen the pamphlet at Henning's clinic, and her visit that morning to question the surgeon about it.

"Radical reformers bent on stopping progress at any cost?" he murmured after she had finished recounting what she had learned about the Workers of Zion. "Well done, Mrs. Sloane. Your discerning eye and instincts have once again proved invaluable."

Charlotte didn't feel quite so heroic.

"Henning wasn't happy about crying rope on the group, and I understand his conflicted feelings. My sympathies lie with the workers as well." She and her late husband had struggled through some very lean times, so she understood the gnawing terror of trying to stay one step ahead of starvation.

"And yet . . ." he added.

Their eyes locked for an instant, and then she quickly looked away. She was still feeling strangely vulnerable and wasn't sure she wanted the earl to see it. He had very sharp eyes to go along with his razor-edged tongue.

"And yet, a radical group here in London is a very dangerous development," went on Wrexford. He expelled a sigh. "I suppose it's no surprise, even though there are fewer factory workers here than in other parts of the country. But it's bad news for the government. The fear of job losses is like a powder keg—it will take naught but a spark to set off an explosion of labor unrest."

"Henning says the Workers of Zion are even more radical than the followers of Ned Ludd," said Charlotte, her throat tightening around the words. "They advocate the killing of factory owners if steam-powered machines can't be stopped by any other means."

"Madness," muttered the earl, echoing her own thoughts on the matter. "The fear is whipped up by leaders who rarely are the ones paying in blood for such demagoguery." The chiseled angles of his face looked even harsher in the subdued light. "You know as well as I who will be the ones to suffer."

Charlotte hugged her arms to her chest. He was right. Social reforms were much needed to protect the working class. But groups like the Workers of Zion would only bring misery upon countless people by urging them to foment chaos and murder. The government would fight violence with violence. And there was no question of who would win.

She shivered.

Wrexford frowned in thought. "But as I mentioned, I, too, have uncovered a telling clue. Thanks to Sheffield, I may be on the trail of the actual murderer, and from what you've just told me, I've reason to believe he'll turn out to be one of the leaders of the Workers of Zion."

He told her about his friend having recognized the handwriting of the note that lured Ashton to his death and the plan to track down Gannett.

It was, Charlotte thought, an extraordinary

stroke of luck. But in her experience, Fortune was rarely so generous . . .

"You really think he will prove to be the culprit?"

Wrexford quirked a sardonic smile. "Tsk-tsk. You're not supposed to be quite as cynical as I am."

"I prefer to call it realistic," she responded.

A gruff laugh. "To answer your question, it's possible. Sheffield is quite sure about the handwriting, so perhaps we will get lucky," he replied. "Luck *does* happen."

"Or perhaps he's merely an accomplice," mused Charlotte. "Most plots involve more than one serpent slithering through the shadows." Her thoughts leapt back to her conversation with the surgeon. "Henning gave me a good description of the man who left the pamphlets at his surgery. I could work with my contacts in the area to track him down."

"If he's the murderer . . ." Wrexford's expression turned grim.

"I know how to be careful, milord."

"Ashton was not a pretty sight," he said softly.

"Nor was Holworthy," countered Charlotte.

The reminder of the reverend's murder did nothing to soften the earl's scowl.

"So unless you have another idea on how to pursue—"

"Actually I have," he interrupted. "Two, in fact." The pamphlet fluttered in front of her nose.

"With this in hand, Griffin will have a damnable difficult time denying that Bow Street should investigate Ashton's murder more thoroughly."

Charlotte mentally conceded the point.

"And secondly," continued Wrexford, "I've already begun looking more closely at the list of names provided by Mrs. Ashton." He gave a terse account of his meeting with the widow and Octavia Merton, along with his intention of meeting with Benedict Hillhouse on the morrow.

"It seems highly unlikely that Ashton's trusted assistants have any connection to the Workers of Zion," she said. "Doesn't it?"

He shrugged. "We both have learned that clues aren't always what they seem at first. Murder has a way of twisting into a serpentine tangle of motives. And I suspect that Miss Merton may know more than she claims."

Much as Charlotte wished to argue, his words held too much truth. Blood spilled by violent death often tainted both the guilty and the innocent.

"Very well. I shall hold off on pursuing the man Henning described." She couldn't, however, resist adding, "For now."

That didn't seem to surprise the earl. In fact, the brusque rumbling in his throat sounded suspiciously like a laugh.

"Then let us cry pax." He paused. "For now."

Peace, however fragile between them, was a welcome offer. Her emotions were in enough conflict. Allowing a small smile, Charlotte rose. "Would you care for some tea?"

Wrexford looked about to refuse the offer, then seemed to have a change of heart. "Yes, thank you." Lowering his voice to a mutter, he added, "Perhaps a hot-as-Hades brew will help wash the bitter taste of this damnable investigation from my mouth."

As Charlotte bustled with filling the kettle, Wrexford made a closer scrutiny of the room and half-packed boxes. The move to a new neighborhood would be simple enough. Her earthly possessions would barely fill a single dray cart.

As for what was weighing on her mind . . .

"Have you settled on schooling for the Weasels?" he asked.

She took her time to measure an exact amount of dried leaves from the tin tea canister. Which in itself was answer enough.

The water came to a boil, sending up a scrim of steam to hide her expression.

"I—I have not yet decided on what to do," Charlotte finally said over the clatter of the cups. "For now, I plan on continuing their lessons with Mr. Keating. It's a long trek, and only for one afternoon a week, but . . ." Her voice trailed off as she carried the tray to the table.

Wrexford noted the shadows flickering beneath her lashes. "But what?"

She let the tea steep for another few moments before pouring. "But I worry about them fitting into a classroom." A sigh slipped from her lips. "It is a more prosperous neighborhood, and I fear their background may make it hard for them to feel at home."

He didn't intrude on her hesitation.

"Raven doesn't trust others easily. And Hawk will copy his brother," she added. "It is . . . daunting, milord." Charlotte sat heavily. "I'm not sure I possess the proper experience to play the mother hen for two wild fledglings."

"Your instincts seem quite exemplary in all else," pointed out Wrexford. "I can't think of any reason why they wouldn't be so in this."

"That's kind of you, sir."

"Actually, it has nothing to do with kindness. I'm basing it on empirical observation, rather than emotion." He took several sips of the steaming brew, then set down his cup. "You know, I may have a solution to your dilemma."

"Yet another one?" she quipped. "If you solve this particular conundrum as well as you did the one concerning names, I may have to start paying *you* for your unique expertise, rather than the other way around."

It was said lightly, but he knew her voice well enough to detect the slight edge.

Ah, so she was still touchy about having accepted his payments for providing information from her sources during the Holworthy murder investigation. He suspected as much, knowing her fierce sense of independence. And it was going to make his suggestion an exceedingly difficult one to present.

"I'm not sure it's worth its weight in gold—or copper, for that matter. But it so happens I know a young man, the son of a tenant farmer on one of my estates, who's recently finished his studies as a scholarship student at Oxford and is looking for work in London. He's a fine fellow, and being from a humble background, he will have a good understanding of the lads, and be able to cater to their needs in learning."

He paused. "It seems to me that a tutor may be a better choice than a formal school."

"The young man sounds exemplary," replied Charlotte. "But at present, I can't afford a tutor."

"You haven't heard his terms," murmured Wrexford.

"As a man of modest means, I doubt he is offering to work for free."

"No . . ." Wrexford wrestled for a moment with how to tactfully phrase his next words. Then with an inward grimace, he abandoned the effort. Be damned with tact—subtlety was not his forte.

"So let us discuss exactly what the cost to you would be."

Her eyes narrowed. "How do you know what the young man intends to charge?"

"I don't." Enough shilly-shallying. "However, it doesn't matter, as I intend to pay his fee."

"The devil you will!" exclaimed Charlotte hotly. "I won't—"

He raised a hand. "Do me the courtesy of hearing me out."

She lapsed into a simmering silence. He could almost see the steam swirling up from her flushed skin.

"Both of the lads showed great courage during the Holworthy investigation, and risked their lives to keep my neck out of the noose. That I wish to express my gratitude in a meaningful way is only natural. Surely you must know that the Weasels . . ."

He paused for a fraction. "But in truth, it's not *my* motives that we ought to be looking at, Mrs. Sloane, it's yours. They're damnably selfish."

A ripple of shock stirred in eyes.

Before she could respond, he continued, "Pride is all very well on a certain level, but when taken to extremes, it's a sin."

"I don't believe my ears," said Charlotte softly. "Are you, of all people, really quoting the Scriptures at me?"

"Perhaps not a sin in your case," he conceded. "But a stubbornly misguided sentiment. Friendship isn't something that ought to be measured in pounds and pence."

She blinked.

"But never mind the fact that it's an insult to my intentions. Refusing my offer is unfair to the lads and robs them of a chance to better their lot in life."

Her flush had now faded to an unnatural white.

"Don't be an arse," he pressed. "Why are you so bloody afraid of letting your friends help you?"

"I . . . I . . ." Charlotte wrapped her hands around her teacup, as if its warmth might bring back some color to her face. "I'm not quite so high in the instep as you think, sir. I *do* accept help."

She gave a brusque wave at the stacked boxes of her possessions. "I could never have managed the ordeal of finding a new residence in a strange neighborhood without the aid of a friend. It was he and his man of affairs who located the house and negotiated the terms of the lease for me."

The announcement took Wrexford completely by surprise. Without thinking, he demanded, "Who?"

"Someone I've known since my childhood." Charlotte turned to stare into the shadows. In the flickering lamplight her profile looked as if it had been sculpted out of alabaster, the hard-edged planes standing out in stark relief against the ink-dark murk.

"His circumstances have changed," she continued. "Back then, he was merely the son of an impoverished gentry family. But by a quirk of fate—and fortune—he inherited a barony from a second cousin."

A friend—a gentleman *friend.* Wrexford knew he had no reason to feel piqued by the unexpected revelation. And yet, he did.

Very much so, in fact.

"You didn't see fit to ever mention this to me?" he said slowly.

Charlotte brushed an errant lock of hair from her cheek, the movement obscuring her expression. "For what reason would I have done so?"

For what reason, indeed?

His innards gave a sudden clench. He realized he didn't wish to give the why it a name.

"You're quite right. Of course it's no concern of mine." Even to his own ears, his reply sounded pompous. Wrexford forced a smile that was likely equally stilted. "My apologies. It is I, not you, who am an arse."

"No, you were right to rail at me about pride," she responded. Darkness seemed to spread over her face, deepening the hollow beneath her cheekbone. "There were times in the past when it felt like it was the only weapon I had against life's vicissitudes. I suppose it's become a habit to keep up my guard."

Wrexford suddenly felt like a toad, not an arse. An uncharacteristic awkwardness seemed to have come over him of late. He had stumbled through the day, making a hash of the interview with Miss Merton, and now was upsetting and embarrassing a woman who had time and again proved her grit and courage in the face of adversity.

"Mrs. Sloane, it was wrong of me—"

"You made a very generous offer, sir," interrupted Charlotte. "It was churlish of me to refuse. If it still stands . . ."

"Of course it does," he muttered.

"Thank you." A conciliatory smile curled at the corners of her mouth. "Once I've settled in the new house, perhaps I might arrange with you to meet the young man."

"I'll see to it." Wrexford rose abruptly, slopping a bit of the tepid tea on the table. He knew it was wrong to leave on such an unsettled note. But she was all too aware of his mercurial moods, his bloody awful temper. "I had best return home in order to be ready for my rendezvous with Sheffield."

Charlotte slanted a glance at the clock and raised a brow. "The midnight hour won't be chiming anytime soon."

"Yes, but I wish to make sure I have ample time in which to clean and prime my pistols," he replied. "With any luck, I'll get a chance to shoot the miscreant."

"You're in a prickly mood," she said slowly. "Is there a reason why?"

"Am I?" In the solitude of his laboratory, his handling of inanimate chemicals was unerringly precise. He understood their qualities and the consequences of combining X with Y. With people, the mixtures all too often blew up in his face.

She didn't reply, but simply fixed him with a searching stare.

"Good day," he murmured.

"Good hunting," she shot back.

Unable to think of a suitable retort, Wrexford picked up his hat and took his leave.

On returning to his townhouse, he quickly sought sanctuary in his workroom. Lighting a spirit lamp, he made himself begin replicating one of Priestley's experiments on the chemical composition of air.

The whisper of the flame, the ritual of precise measurement, the focus demanded for careful observation—Wrexford felt his personal devils give way to curiosity. The mysteries of science were far more interesting than the mysteries of mankind.

Minutes ticked by, their rhythmic cadence slowly drawing him out of his brooding . . .

Then all at once the calm was shattered by a thumping on the door.

"Grab up your coat, Wrex—there's not a moment to lose!" exclaimed Sheffield as he burst into the room. "I've just come from White's where I overheard Davies mention that Gannett is planning to play *vingt et un* at the Demon's Den tonight."

His friend gave an impatient wave at the worktable. "Bloody hell—blow out that lamp and fetch your pistols. If we hurry, we can catch him."

Chapter 8

"Arse," muttered Charlotte. Staring down at the sheet of drawing paper, she added a few more curling lines to her sketch of the donkey.

The question, she thought ruefully, was which face she should put on the beast—hers or that of the earl.

"Who's an arse?" Raven looked up from the book he was reading. He was lying by the stove, a candle pulled close to the pages. "Prinny?" The dancing flame caught the flash of a grin. "If ye ask me, he looks more like a pig."

It was true, she conceded. A handsome man in his youth, the Prince Regent had an appetite for pleasure and had put on an obscene amount of weight. It was well-known that these days he wore a corset to try to contain the damage to his figure.

"Mind your tongue," she chided, knowing full well the hypocrisy of her words. "You mustn't speak so disrespectfully of the man who will be the next king."

"You've called him far worse than that in your prints," pointed out Raven.

"Aye," chirped Hawk, who was playing a game of skittles on the rag rug. "Ye said he was a lecherous old goat, whose pizzle—"

"Enough of barnyard animals," interrupted Charlotte. "Let's keep our minds out of the muck."

Raven made an *oinking* sound, much to the mirth of his brother, but stopped when she shot him a severe look.

"What are you reading?" she asked, softening her expression to a smile.

"Mr. Keating gave me a book on mathematics. Numbers ain't nearly as boring as history. There's all these things called equations, and ye can play games with all the different ways te make 'em add up."

"Is that so?" Charlotte often struggled to make the modest sums of her expense ledger behave as they should, so she was bemused that subject seemed to have captured his fancy. "You find that interesting?"

"It's kinda like putting together the pieces of a puzzle," he answered. "So yeah, I s'pose I do."

"According te Mr. Keating, yer wery good at it," volunteered Hawk.

"Really?" she asked.

Raven shrugged.

It was Hawk who answered. "Aye, he says Raven's got a gift fer it." A pause. "I'd rather have a dog."

As the boys fell to bantering with each other, Charlotte turned back to her drawing. The exchange had only been further proof that

Wrexford had been right to press her about providing a good education for them. Not that she had needed it. In her heart, she had known he was right.

So if anyone had been an arse, it was she. Charlotte sketched in her own likeness for the donkey's face, then added two large equine ears.

Her reaction to their confrontation had been childish. But so had his.

For all his faults, Wrexford was always quick to forgive a quarrel. This time had been different. He had left in a foul temper—for what reason she still couldn't say. If she didn't know better, she would be tempted to think she had wounded his feelings. However, the idea was absurd. By his own admission, Wrexford armored himself in cynicism too thick for any barb to penetrate.

Giving up on trying to figure out what was bedeviling him, Charlotte turned her attention to making a list of all the things that she needed for the coming morning.

Tomorrow would be her last day in this house. Lifting her gaze, she took in in the room, though every nook and cranny was indelibly etched in her mind's eye. Dark and light—the silent flicker of the lamp and candles danced over the tiny details . . . the crack in the window casement that always let in a whistle of wind when it blew from the west . . . the spatter of blue pigment on the far wall where Anthony had once flung his paintbrush in frustration . . . the dent in the stove caused by a mouse who had dislodged the cast iron frying . . .

Memories, memories.

Charlotte sat staring at her own ink-stained hands for a moment longer, then shook off the shadows of the past. It was time to look to the future.

Malum consilium est, quod mutari non potest. Bad is the plan that is unable to change. The words, whether whispered in Latin or English, made it sound so simple. . . .

Pulling a pristine sheet from the stack of blank drawing paper, she set it atop her doodles. Mr. Fores expected a new print by the following evening and as her pen and pigments had not yet mastered the art of creating satire on their own, she set to work.

A potent fugue of distinctly male smells—smoke, sweat and brandy—enveloped Wrexford as he entered the gambling hell. Red-gold flames licked up from the glass-globed wall scones, their oily light casting the jumbled scene of the crowded gaming tables in a Mars-like glow.

War was an apt analogy, he thought sardonically. A cacophony of curses clashing with drunken laughter filled the hazed air. Man's primal urges battling against their better nature.

No question which was the stronger of the two.

"Gannett is most likely in one of the rear salons," murmured Sheffield. "Follow me."

His friend led the way through the press of bodies to a narrow corridor that led deeper into the bowels of the building. The rattle of rolling dice echoed loud as musket fire against the close-set walls. They passed several more dimly-lit rooms before Sheffield came to a halt by a low archway.

"The lowest pit of hell," he quipped. "The stakes tend to be highest in here."

Through the scrim of cigar smoke, Wrexford could make out the vague shapes of men hunched around a half dozen tables.

"Though I'm surprised Gannett is still welcome to play among these devils," added Sheffield. "I've heard he's having trouble paying off his vowels. And those who can't settle their debts aren't looked upon kindly."

Wrexford watched the flash of pasteboard cards as they slapped down upon the green felt. From what Sheffield had told him of their quarry, he found it hard to believe that a wastrel like Gannett had any interest in radical reform. But perhaps the fellow simply found fomenting violence and chaos sent the same thrill bubbling through his blood as gambling did.

Danger was addictive.

"Do you see him?" he asked.

Sheffield shifted a step and squinted into the gloom. "Yes, he's there, in the far corner."

They waited until the hand had been played out, then made their way to the table.

"Gannett," growled Wrexford. "We'd like a word with you."

A man looked up. His face had once been handsome but the sallow skin now sagged from the well-cut bones, giving him the look of a dead cod.

"Can't you bloody well see I'm busy?" His voice was slightly slurred. "Bugger off."

The retort drew a rumble of laughter from his fellow players.

Wrexford fisted a hand in Gannett's collar and yanked him to his feet.

The laughter stopped.

"It wasn't meant as a request," he said.

Gannett tried to squirm free. "What the devil—let me go!" He shot a look at Sheffield. "Hell's teeth, Sheff, I don't owe you—or your ham-handed friend—any blunt. Tell him to release me, or—"

"Or what?" Wrexford gave the man a shake that rattled his teeth. "You'll murder me?"

Gannett went very still. "I-I don't understand . . ."

"You will in a moment." Wrexford turned on his heel, dragging his unresisting captive with him, and bumped his way to the corridor.

"What—" began Gannett, only to have the wind knocked out of his lungs as Wrexford slammed him up against the rough-plastered wall. A look of fear spasmed across his face.

"Tell us about why you murdered Ashton."

"*Murder?*" The word had barely any breath to it. "There's been some ghastly mistake." Gannett wet his trembling lips. "I know nothing of any murder—I swear it!"

"Don't try to deny it," said Sheffield roughly. "I recognized your handwriting on the note luring Ashton to his death."

Gannett's knees buckled and he would have collapsed in a heap if Wrexford hadn't kept a grip on his coat. He tried to speak, but all that the came out was a mewling moan.

Wrexford gave him another shake. "You can either speak to us or have me haul your worthless carcass to Bow Street and let the Runners pry the truth out of you."

"Their methods," growled Sheffield, "will be far less gentlemanly than ours."

The threat seemed to slap away Gannett's initial panic. Drawing a deep breath, he steadied his stance and exhaled a shuddering sigh.

"Y-Yes, I wrote a note. But it was all supposed to be part of an elaborate jest! A stranger's handwriting was needed—or so I was told— in order that the person on whom it was being played wouldn't recognize it. Hell's bells, it sounded like harmless good fun . . . and I was offered money to do it."

Gannett was babbling now. "Come, Sheff, you know what it's like to be sinking in the River Tick. I desperately needed the blunt."

"Why shouldn't we believe that you needed it desperately enough to murder a man you knew was plump in the pocket?" demanded Wrexford, though in truth he didn't think the gamester possessed the nerve to have committed such a cold-blooded crime.

"Because I don't know whoever this Ashton fellow is from Adam!" exclaimed Gannett. "How could I plan to murder a man I've never heard of?"

"You've not read of Ashton's name in the newspapers?" asked Sheffield. "He's one of the leading men of science in England."

The question drew a grimace. "The only printed sheets of paper I read are the racing forms at Newmarket."

Wrexford was inclined to believe him. The gamester struck him as a bacon-brained reprobate. Which meant . . .

"If what you say is true and you didn't have anything to do with Ashton's murder, then you'd better hope to holy hell you can give us the name of the man who hired you."

"Of course I can!" Hope lit in Gannett's eyes as he sensed an escape. "It was Gabriel Hollis."

A ruse? wondered Wrexford. He doubted the gamester was that clever. "Why would he ask you? Is he a friend?"

"No! That, is, we knew each other at Cambridge, but I hadn't seen him since then until our

141

paths recently crossed at a tavern near Covent Garden. We fell into conversation and . . ." Gannett made a face. "After several tankards of ale, he asked me to write that god-benighted note."

Ah—perhaps they were getting closer to the real culprit. "Did he say where he was living?"

"No, but . . ." He gulped in a shallow breath. "But he seemed on very friendly terms with the tavernkeeper. Ask at the Crown and Scepter on Cross Lane off Cattle Street. The man may have the information you seek."

"I know the place," confirmed Sheffield. "It appeals to ruffians and reprobates."

The trail seemed to be growing clearer, the scent stronger. But as for the miscreant's motive, Wrexford wanted to confirm they weren't barking up the wrong tree.

"A last question—has Hollis ever shown himself to hold radical political ideas?"

Gannett blinked away the beads of sweat clinging to his lashes. Or perhaps they were tears of relief. "Good God—yes! He was always ranting about the ills of society, and how the monarchy and the Church stood in the way of creating a true utopia."

His gaze shifted and suddenly he pointed into the gloom. "Just ask Kirkland!"

Wrexford spun around and spotted the dark-on-dark silhouette of a figure standing deep in the shadows. And yet he'd been sure the corridor was deserted just a few minutes ago when he'd slammed Gannett up against the wall.

The man stepped forward, bringing with him a flutter of chill air as he fumbled with the fall of his trousers.

That explained it, thought the earl. The back alleyway would serve as a pisspot for the patrons.

"Come, Kirkland, you knew Hollis during our undergraduate days! Tell them how he was expelled as a troublemaker," pleaded Gannett. "Remember how he was always rattling on about the rights of the common man and the oppression wrought by church and state?"

"No," replied Kirkland. He turned to the earl, and the weak light of the sconce caught the haughty curl of his well-shaped mouth. "I remember no such thing."

"But you must!" exclaimed the gamester, terrified that his alibi was slipping away.

Kirkland expelled a martyred sigh. His face was handsome, with chiseled features—and the look of arrogant boredom that Wrexford so loathed in his peers. He appeared to consider the plea for a long moment before drawling, "I suppose the name rings a faint bell."

With a careless tug, he pulled on a pair of soft leather gloves that matched the burgundy color of his coat. "And yes, as you say, the fellow was a thoroughly dirty dish."

"You see!" said Gannett quickly. Grasping to keep hold of the chance to throw the blame on someone else, he added. "Now that I think of it, Carruthers knew Hollis too. He's throwing dice in the next room—let's go ask him if he knows the bloody bastard's address."

"There seems little to lose," observed Sheffield.

"If you gentlemen will excuse me . . ." With a brusque nod, Kirkland brushed past them. "I must be going."

Wrexford watched him walk away. The man looked vaguely familiar . . . but then, he had likely met every donkey's arse who moved within the beau monde's privileged circle.

"A conceited coxcomb," muttered Sheffield, sensing the earl's interest. "He gambles often and deeply, though usually in fancier places than this one. Not that he has much success, but his purse always seems full." A grimace. "A generous father, I suppose. Which is bloody unfair."

"Aye, *bloody* unfair," agreed Gannett. "Fortune ought to favor—"

"We're wasting time," cut in Wrexford. "Let's see if Carruthers knows where Hollis resides. If not, we'll head on to the Crown and Scepter."

As he expected, the visit to the dice table brought no luck. Against the squawking of Gannett, Wrexford took the precaution of paying the owner of the gambling hell to lock the gamester in a storage closet for the

144

night. However unlikely a villain the man now appeared, the earl wasn't willing to risk making a lethal mistake.

The tavern was, as Sheffield had said, a dingy, dirty hole in the wall that catered to a rough crowd. The owner pretended to know nothing of Hollis, but a fistful of guineas soon loosened his tongue, and they were given an address.

"It's not far away," said his friend as they exited through the back of the building. "Follow me."

Wrexford felt his pulse quicken, their loping footfalls over the uneven cobbles echoing the rush of blood through his veins.

After a quick traverse through a twisting alley-way, Sheffield stopped at the head of a narrow lane and motioned at a brick building on their right.

Pulling the two pistols from his coat pockets, the earl hurriedly checked the priming and handed one over. "I'll lead the way from here," he whispered.

Clouds scudded over the moon, hiding their approach to the rickety entranceway. He slid a thin knife from his boot, prepared to pick the lock. But a touch to the iron keyhole showed it was broken.

The door swung open with a tiny groan.

Up the stairs he went, swiftly and silently taking the treads two at a time. It was dark as

145

Hades, and on reaching the top floor, Wrexford was forced to feel his way along the wall to find the latch to their quarry's lair.

It, too, yielded to the pressure of his palm . . .

Which stirred a sudden prickling at the nape of his neck.

Taking hold of Sheffield's arm, he quickly positioned him on one side of the door. Then, after drawing back the hammer of his weapon, he kicked in the door, and ducked low.

Nothing. No shot exploded from inside. Indeed, the room was dark and unnaturally still. Wrexford waited for another moment before cautiously edging over the threshold. After several steps, his boot hit up against a smashed chair. He reached down and felt broken glass on the floor. The odor of lamp oil swirled up from the planks.

"Damnation." He found a fallen candle and struck a flint to the wick. The spark of light revealed a scene of chaos. A table and three other straight-back chairs had been knocked to flinders. The small desk lay overturned, the contents of the drawers strewn helter-pelter through the puddles of oil. Feathers from the slashed bed pillows had fallen atop the debris, the downy curls looking absurdly delicate against the splintered wood.

The flickering flame also showed a number of pamphlets strewn over the floor. Though the ink was already turning illegible on the paper,

Wrexford easily recognized the symbol and headline.

The Workers of Zion. They had come to the right place.

Sheffield found another candle and lit it. Just as he was about to speak, Wrexford held up a warning hand and went very still.

The sounds were barely discernable—a ghostly creaking from the unseen rafters, a faint *whoosh* of air through the crack in the window . . .

A whispery groan, rhythmic in its rise and fall.

Muttering another oath, the earl moved into the alcove off the main room. A man lay spread-eagle on the floor, his breath going in and out with a labored gurgle.

Crouching down beside him, Wrexford held the candle closer to the sound and saw why. A deep slash cut across the man's throat, leaving the windpipe half-severed. Blood had turned his shirtpoints scarlet.

As the light touched his face, the man's eyes fluttered up, resignation pooled in the dark and dilated pupils.

Perhaps he could see the specter of death moving inexorably closer and closer.

"Hollis?" asked Wrexford.

A tiny nod.

"Who—" he started to ask, but seeing Hollis was trying to speak, he quickly stopped and leaned closer.

The man's lips were moving—a zephyrous stirring of air tickled against the earl's cheek. But no words came forth. Just a deathly wheezing, low and horrible to hear, from the ruined windpipe.

Wrexford untied his cravat and carefully wound it around Hollis's throat, hoping to keep the Grim Reaper at bay for a little longer.

"A-Ashton." Hollis finally managed a sound. "Didn't . . . k-kill . . . Ashton."

"Do you know who did?" he demanded.

Hollis moved his head ever so slightly, setting off a sputtering cough.

The devil take it—the man is choking on his own blood.

"I . . . I know . . ." Another cough. "Find . . ."

"Here, let me make you more comfortable." Pulling off his coat, the earl pillowed the dying man's head to help him breathe.

Hollis grimaced. "Find . . . find . . ."

"Find *who?*" pressed Wrexford, trying to keep a rein on his frustration. Placing a hand on Hollis's shoulder, he gave a squeeze, willing him to hold on.

Exhausted by his efforts, the man let his eyelids fall shut. Pain twisted his features. The Reaper's scythe was cutting ever closer. Wrexford could hear the last gasps of breath dying in Hollis's lungs.

Think, think! Grasping at straws, he mentally

ran down the list the widow had given him.

"One of Ashton's investors? His assistants," he suggested.

A flash of emotion in Hollis's eyes seemed to say *no*. "F-Find N-Nevins . . ." Lifting a hand, he fluttered a wave at the main room. "Numbers . . . Numbers will reveal everything."

"Who's Nevins? And *what* numbers?" coaxed Wrexford.

No response.

"Damnation—don't die yet," he muttered, sliding his hands beneath the man's head and trying to win him a few more precious seconds.

Hollis opened his eyes. His lips formed the faint whisper of an 'H', but in the next heartbeat it was gone.

"Bloody hell. The earl leaned back from the corpse and stared at his gore-covered fingers. If only the carriage had rattled over the cobblestones just a little faster, if only the tavernkeeper hadn't played coy in his haggling . . .

If only he had never walked through the stinking, scum-smeared alleyways of Half Moon Gate.

Sheffield touched his shoulder, bringing him out of his brooding. "I wouldn't second-guess yourself, Wrex. Guilty men are wont to proclaim their innocence right down to their dying breath."

"On the contrary." Wrexford slid his coat free from beneath the dead man's head, grimacing at the blood saturating the soft melton wool. Tyler would likely faint over the task of trying to clean it.

"During the Peninsular War, I saw far more hardened criminals than Hollis shuffle off their mortal coil," he went on. "When faced with meeting their Maker, most men want to make a clean breast of it."

"So you believe him that he didn't do it?" asked Sheffield.

"Yes." A gut reaction. But according to Charlotte, he should learn to trust his instincts.

"But if Hollis didn't kill Ashton . . . who did?"

Wrexford's mouth thinned to a grim line.

"I haven't got a clue." He looked around at the ransacked room and swore again. "And we'd need the Devil's own luck to find anything useful here."

He rose, and out of frustration kicked at one of the overturned desk drawers. The savage *crack* of it exploding into shards was so satisfying that he swung another kick at the second one.

Crack. The base panel split apart, revealing a small hidden compartment in the false bottom. The guttering candles showed a pale glimmer of paper caught in the splinters.

Crouching down, Sheffield quickly eased it free. "Satan be praised," he murmured as he took a quick glance. "Have a look."

Numbers.

Wrexford studied a page full of what looked to be a random jumble of numerals. "Rooms like these are rented furnished," he pointed out. "We've no idea how long this has been in the drawer."

A list of debts, an inventory of some sort—bloody hell, it could be anything!

"True," replied Sheffield. "But perhaps we've gotten very lucky."

"It wouldn't be luck, Kit. It would be a miracle," retorted the earl. Nevertheless he carefully folded the paper and put it into his pocket.

Chapter 9

"Goodbye," murmured Charlotte.

Like the rest of the tiny house, the main room was now bare of belongings. Somehow, it looked smaller, not larger. The emptiness seemed to amplify how little of the place was lodged in her heart.

Memories.

Precious few of them were ones she wished to take with her. She thought hard, trying to recall moments of happiness. Most, however, were less easy to define. They were shaded in subtle hues of regret rather than any brilliant bursts of pure sunshine.

Anthony. Her late husband had been unwell here, both physically and mentally. His ghost still shadowed the place. She turned in a slow circle, watching somber shades of grey dip and dart over the dingy walls. All color had long ago been leached from the space. Even the light had a dullness to it.

Now that she was quitting the house, perhaps he, too, could move on to a better place.

As if in response to her musings, a chill draft—a farewell kiss?—blew in through the damnable crack in the molding that had defied her every effort to fix it. Charlotte gave a wry smile and pulled her shawl a little tighter around her shoulders.

I am leaving an old life to start a new one.

She felt as if she should perform some momentous ritual to mark the occasion. Light a red-tongued bonfire . . . offer a libation to the gods . . . sacrifice a virgin . . .

"M'lady, the carter says the wagon is packed, and he can crack the whip soon as yer ready te be off." Raven moved to her side, and to her surprise, the boy twined his fingers with hers. He usually held himself aloof from physical contact, far more so than his younger brother.

Perhaps that was why the unexpected warmth of his touch felt so comforting.

They stood silently in the shifting shadows for another few heartbeats before he added, "We've saved a spot on the driver's perch fer ye. Hawk and I will ride atop the boxes."

She squeezed his hand. "Yes, I'm ready."

Raven hurried off. Her own steps were slower, but closing the door for the last time didn't feel as daunting as she had feared.

Respice finem. One should only look back at the end.

Keeping careful hold of the satchel carrying her paints and brushes, Charlotte climbed up to her place on the wagon. A flick of the whip set the dray horses in motion. Mud squelched as the wheels lumbered over the rutted lane. In a few short minutes, the house was well behind her.

She didn't twist around for a last glance.

The mud turned to cobblestones as they progressed from the fringes of the stews to a more prosperous neighborhood. Behind her, she heard the boys chattering like magpies. Charlotte wished she knew what they truly felt about their new nest.

But in all fairness, her own emotions were not yet sorted out. It would take time. She must be patient, both with them and herself.

Patience. A self-mocking smile touched her lips. It was not one of her virtues. In that she was like the earl.

Thoughts of Wrexford drew her back to their argument over Ashton's murder. His high-handed order to stay out of the fray had touched a raw nerve. Granted, his arguments had made sense. But that didn't make them any easier to swallow. Her independence had been won at great cost. It was hard to surrender any of it.

Stubbornness, she conceded, was yet another of her many faults.

With her musings straying in such an uncomfortable direction, Charlotte was happy to hear the driver announce that the next turn would bring them to her new street.

She looked up to see a handsome carriage standing by the curb in front of her new abode, its forest green door bearing a discreet crest painted in dark tones of taupe.

Dear Jeremy. Despite all the upheavals in their lives since the days of filching apples together from the local squire's orchard, he had never wavered in his loyalty. They had been the best of friends since childhood. Without his support during her darkest days . . .

"Halloo!" Jeremy—Baron Sterling—stepped into the street and gave a welcoming wave. As usual, he was dressed faultlessly, today's attire being biscuit-colored breeches, polished Hessians, and a coat fashioned from a subtle shade of azure blue merino wool.

If anyone deserved to be a titled aristocrat, it was Jeremy, thought Charlotte with an inward smile. He had always had exquisite taste and an eye for quality. And now he had the blunt to afford to indulge in his passion for the arts and fashion.

He gave an additional hand signal, sending a liveried footman darting forward as the dray rolled to a halt.

"Good heavens," murmured Charlotte, reluctantly accepting the servant's offer of a hand down. "You needn't fuss as if I'm royalty."

Jeremy enveloped her in a quick hug. "You will always be a princess to me," he replied gallantly, just loudly enough for her ears.

She let out a wry laugh. "I seem to have misplaced my enchanted tiara on the journey here. So I'll have to settle on remaining my humble self for now."

"One never knows what the future holds."

"It's only in fairie stories that a common wench is magically transformed into royalty."

He stepped back, his brow crinkling in concern.

Pretending not to notice, she turned to the carter. "Mr. Holson, if you carry everything into the corridor, I shall then direct you as to where it all goes."

Not that it would take much thought.

"My footman will help," called Jeremy. Turning back to Charlotte, he said, "But first, come inside. You look tired." His pause was barely perceptible, as was the tightening around the corner of his mouth. "Let us have some tea."

His jovial tone sounded a little forced. Charlotte knew her friend well enough to sense he had left something unspoken.

"I'm sorry but my kettle is packed somewhere among the boxes," she replied. "So I'm afraid we'll have to forego refreshments."

"As to that. . . ." Jeremy cleared his throat with a cough. "I took the liberty of bringing my housekeeper to fix some sustenance. The boys will be hungry, and I didn't wish for them to starve." A smile. "There are apple tarts from Gunther's. And a custard-filled meringue."

"A low blow," she muttered. He knew how

adamant she was about refusing any monetary aid, no matter how trifling. But in this case it was hard to be angry with him.

Raven and Hawk tumbled down from the pile of baggage, an expectant look on their grimy faces. They occasionally delivered notes to his house, where she suspected the servants plied them with sweets.

"They were spotless when we left," said Charlotte with a harried sigh. "How it is that boys are a magnet for dirt?"

Jeremy answered with a chuckle. "It is one of those immutable truths of the universe. I imagine Sir Isaac Newton has written something about it in his laws of motion."

"Quite likely." She would have to ask Wrexford.

"Oiy!" Raven looked offended. He held up his hands, which for him were relatively respectable. "Look, they be clean as a whistle."

"They *are,*" she corrected, even though she knew the mistake was deliberate. "Now, make your bows to Lord Sterling, and then, if your fingers pass muster when we get inside, you may have some apple tart."

"Huzzah!" They scampered away, pulling their shirttails loose in order to scrub their hands.

"They're good lads," murmured Jeremy.

"They're heathens," she said wryly, hoping her underlying fears did not edge her voice.

"Being clever and curious makes them different. However, that's not a bad thing."

Charlotte hoped that was true. But given her own checkered experience, she wasn't convinced of it. There was something to be said for a staidly conventional life.

Her expression must have betrayed her thoughts, for her friend added, "Living within the tight strictures of society may be safe, but it is challenges that bring out the best in us."

"An admirable philosophy," replied Charlotte. Assuming one was strong enough to survive.

Jeremy offered his arm. "Shall we go inside?"

She looked up. It was naught but a modest century-old stucco and wood building standing in an orderly row of similar structures that stretched the full length of the block. *Two floors. A tiny attic tucked under the pitched slate roof.* But compared to her previous residence it looked like a mansion.

A tiny sigh escaped as she thought of the bare rooms, and her meager furnishings. The stark emptiness of the rooms would not be an edifying sight, but she couldn't very well take the coward's way out and retreat. There was no other place to go.

Numquam rediit retrorsum et deinceps semper. Always go forward and never turn back.

Strangely, it was Jeremy who hesitated. "I must give you fair warning, Charley. . . ."

She stiffened, which made his expression turn more baleful.

"I brought something a bit more substantial than tarts," he went on.

Damn him. Charlotte let her hand slip away from his sleeve. "I take it you aren't referring to a joint of roast beef?"

"No." Her sarcasm brought a slight flush to his cheeks, and yet rather than flinch, he took firm hold of her wrist. "A house needs more than food in the larder. Please do me the courtesy of observing what I've done and hearing my explanation before ringing a peal over my head."

God knows he deserves that much. And so much more.

It didn't mean she had to like it.

"Very well," said Charlotte, swallowing the bitter taste of bile that had risen to the back of her throat. "Lead on."

Set on the far left side of the house, the front door opened into a shallow entrance foyer holding a simple boot box and a Turkey carpet in muted tones of indigo and burgundy red. From there, a corridor, half-filled with a set of narrow stairs leading to the second floor, ran back to the rear of the house. The first door on the right opened to a main parlor with a wide-planked wood floor and well-proportioned mullioned windows.

Charlotte gingerly stepped inside.

A large fireplace occupied one end of the space,

and in front of it a sofa covered in navy and taupe stripes faced two leather armchairs. Between them sat a brass-cornered tea table made of oiled teak.

Sucking in her breath, she shifted her gaze. A large bookcase—already half filled with various leatherbound volumes—was at the other end of the room. A game table inlaid with dark and light checkered tiles, several straight-back chairs and sideboard completed the grouping.

Without a word, Charlotte gave a curt nod, indicating she was ready for Jeremy to continue with the tour.

The kitchen and tiny pantry were at the rear— the boys were noisily eating their pastries under the indulgent eye of Jeremy's housekeeper—then it was up the stairs to the upper floor. Her friend led her past the first door, which was closed.

"We'll come back down here in a moment," he murmured. "First let me show you the attic."

Charlotte dutifully followed, unsure what to expect.

Jeremy had to duck slightly to get through the door at the top of the stairs. A small but snug little room occupied the space. Front and back dormer windows let in a surprising amount of gold-flecked light. Outside, the trilling song of a linnet rose up from the tiny back garden to echo softly against the glass.

Turning slightly, she saw two narrow beds had

been placed side by side against one wall, each with a wooden storage trunk at its foot. Two desks, with a bookshelf set between them, fit comfortably on the opposite wall. A cheery rag rug covered the planked floor.

"I thought the lads would enjoy having their own aerie," murmured her friend.

Charlotte felt a lump form in her throat. She couldn't yet muster any words and merely gave another curt nod.

"Come, we're almost done." Taking no umbrage at her silence, he headed back down to the second floor.

At the foot of the stairs, he threw open the door to the rear room. "Here is the main bedchamber."

It, too, was simply but tastefully furnished.

"You'll find it quieter than the room facing the street, and there's a view over the back garden." He smiled. "Granted, it's no bigger than a farthing, but there's a small swath of grass and a rowan tree."

Oh, Lud. How to respond?

All the furnishings were clearly used but of good quality. A quick mental calculation of their cost showed they would beggar her hard-won savings. She had scrimped and sacrificed in order to build a buffer against any change in her present circumstances. Life, as she well knew, could change in the blink of an eye.

But now. . . .

Charlotte bit her lip. She would never have chosen to squander her blunt on bedsteads and draperies, no matter how pretty. But now, she had been given no choice.

Fury collided with gratitude, leaving her shaken.

Jeremy was already out in the corridor and opening the next door. "Here is another small room. I've told my footman to bring the furnishings from your old house up here and for now to arrange it as a spare bedchamber for now. However, it could easily serve as an informal sitting room if you so choose."

Choices, choices. And yet it felt as the decisions concerning her life were being wrested from her grasp.

"There's just one more room to see," he murmured.

She had seen quite enough. It was only the bonds of longtime friendship that kept her by his side as he moved to the last unopened door.

"One of the reasons I pressed you to take the house was because it had the space . . ." The portal opened ". . . to allow you a proper studio."

A large desk was positioned to take advantage of the sunshine streaming in through the tall windows.

North light. *Artist's light.*

Jeremy had thought of everything.

Tears suddenly pearled on her lashes, the sting

of salt piecing straight through her soul. "H-How can I ever repay you?" she mumbled, holding back the hysterical urge to laugh.

Of course she knew how, and it would ruin her savings.

"I must, of course, do so," she continued. "Though—"

He pressed a fingertip to her lips. "You agreed to hear me out before saying anything."

Charlotte blinked, and suddenly the tears were streaming down her cheeks.

Damnation—I never weep.

"I know how you feel about charity, Charley. Your fierce sense of independence is one of the things I've always admired about you," he continued softly. "But pride can be taken to a fault."

Her insides gave a lurch, his words more painful to hear for how sharply they echoed the earl's sentiments.

"Everything here is from the attics of the late baron's country manor," continued Jeremy. "Rather than let it sit moldering in the shadows, please allow me to share my unearned largess with you. Fate takes strange twists. Why should I deserve a title and a fortune more than the next fellow?"

He lifted his shoulders in a wry shrug. "But there it is, so why spit in Fortune's face? I say we should enjoy it."

All her arguments seemed to dissolve in the

space of a heartbeat. He was right—life's vagaries were absurdly unfair. All the more reason for friendship to triumph over pride.

Friendship.

"Thank you," she said simply, knowing the true depth of her emotions was beyond words.

Sunlight gilded Jeremy's smile. "You're welcome."

It was only then that she realized she was still gripping the satchel containing her brushes and watercolor pigments. To break the emotional tension, she set it down on her new desk and began to unpack the supplies.

"This will be a very pleasant place in which to work," she said. "A good thing, as I am in danger of missing the deadline for my next drawing."

Following her lead, Jeremy turned the talk away from personal feelings. "Speaking of drawings, have you learned anything more about Mr. Ashton's death?" Her recent print had garnered a great deal of attention.

"The authorities still seem convinced it was a random robbery," replied Charlotte carefully. The evidence suggesting otherwise was not her secret to share.

"What a senseless tragedy." He shook his head and let out a mournful sigh. "I shall miss him greatly."

The box of pigments slipped from her fingers and fell to the floor.

"Y-You *knew* Elihu Ashton?"

"Why, yes, we were good friends." Leaning down, Jeremy picked up the paints and set them on the desk. "In fact, I'm one of the investors in his project for a new, highly advanced mill."

Charlotte stared at him in mute shock.

"Apparently, he was working on an innovation," added her friend. "One that he believed would leave current technology in the dust."

Chapter 10

Setting aside the morning newspaper, Wrexford took a quick gulp of his still-steaming coffee and let the brew burn a trail of fire down his throat. Would that it could scald away the coppery taste lingering in his throat. Death had a sweet-sour stickiness that clung to live flesh like a limpet. Something about blood spilled in violence refused to be washed away.

War ought to have inured him to it. But the Ashton affair had stirred feelings he thought had been long ago buried in the past.

Or were they vulnerabilities?

Swallowing the unsettling thought along with another mouthful of coffee, Wrexford turned his attention to last night's murder. There was, of course, no account of it in the newsprint. Death was an all too common occurrence in the teeming stews of the city. Only the well-born or well-heeled merited a mention.

However, he had sent word to Griffin about Hollis's demise, along with a warning about the presence of a radical group in London. Given how fearful the government was about worker unrest, surely Bow Street would have to devote more scrutiny to the puzzle of Ashton's grisly death.

As for Charlotte, he owed her a report on

what had happened. *Quid pro quo*. He couldn't very well expect her to be forthcoming with information if he didn't reciprocate.

"Nothing," announced Tyler loudly as he entered the breakfast room. "You may rest easy on that account, milord. Fores's printshop has nothing new from A. J. Quill."

The news wasn't surprising. Charlotte had strict scruples about keeping her word. However, it did no harm to check, in case she had learned of Hollis's demise from her own sources. At times, her awareness of every shadowy secret in London seemed to surpass that of Lucifer.

"Mrs. Sloane has been preoccupied," answered Wrexford. "She's moving to her new residence today."

"Ah." His valet, who was aware of Charlotte's secret identity, gave a knowing nod. "It's not easy to uproot from one place to another, even when one has decided the auld sod has become barren ground."

The earl regarded him with a quizzical stare. Tyler was a sarcastic Scot, who rarely gave a hint of having any personal feelings beneath his flinty skin.

His valet returned the look, his expression giving nothing away.

In no mood for verbal sparring, he let the matter drop.

"I had better pay her a visit and inform her of

what happened last night." He'd made a copy of the hidden paper found in Hollis's room, though he didn't have high hopes for her deciphering its meaning. Art was her bailiwick. Numbers were numbers. Their message required a different perspective.

The thought sparked a sudden idea. "By the by, perhaps we should send a copy of the list of numbers found in Hollis's room to Isaac Milner."

"The fellow who teaches at Trinity College?" Tyler raised his brows. "Are you conceding that Cambridge has greater expertise than Oxford in the subject?"

"In this particular case, yes," answered the earl. "Milner is the Lucasian Professor of Mathematics. It's a very prestigious appointment—Sir Isaac Newton is a past holder of the chair—and it'd well known that he's a genius with numbers. If anyone can see a hidden message in the dratted paper, it's him."

"I'll make another copy," said Tyler.

"I'll pen a letter to him when I return. We know each other from the Royal Institution. He can be counted on to be discreet."

"I'm no expert with numbers but I'll take a closer look at them, too," added the valet. "I did a little study on the subject of cryptography, and we've some books in the library on the subject. Perhaps some idea will come to mind."

Wrexford nodded absently, then returned his

attention to Charlotte. "Have you got the package for Mrs. Sloane ready?"

"Yes, milord. Though it was *not* easy to get it wrapped." A hint of amusement shaded Tyler's voice.

The earl ignored it. He had no idea what her reaction would be to the items he was bringing. They were, admittedly, a rather bizarre gift to celebrate the move to her new residence. But then, Charlotte was a very unconventional woman. He imagined that she might be amused.

Or perhaps she would be tempted to murder him on the spot.

His mouth twitched. *That* would certainly sell a lot of prints. The public, bloodthirsty as they were, would take great glee in seeing the dark-as-the-Devil Earl of Wrexford hoisted on his own petard.

He rose and consulted his pocketwatch. There was no time to waste if he was to pay her a visit and then make it to his appointment with Benedict Hillhouse at the appointed hour. "Have the coachman bring the carriage around."

"Friends," repeated Charlotte. Given the difference in their ages and interests, the connection between Elihu Ashton and Jeremy took her by surprise. "How did that come about?"

"During the last two years, I've had to spend a great deal of my time at the Sterling ancestral estate." Her friend made a wry face. "I still have trouble calling it *my* home."

Charlotte realized she had never given any thought to his life outside of London. But of course he would have responsibilities to learn, lands to oversee.

"It's located in Hunslet," he explained. "And it was only natural that I became acquainted with Ashton through the soirees and dinners given by local society. I liked him very much. He was a man of great intellectual curiosity and we enjoyed talking about philosophy, as well as art and literature."

"I see," she murmured.

"Indeed, I was so impressed with his knowledge and his progressive ideas on social reform that I decided to join the group of investors who were funding his new venture."

Good God.

"Not only that," went on Jeremy. "His laboratory assistant, Benedict Hillhouse, was a very good friend of mine at Cambridge. And so that was yet another reason for me to think well of him."

Though her mind was whirring over the unexpected revelations, Charlotte forced herself to slow down and think logically. Gather all the pieces to the puzzle—they could be put together later.

"Old friendships are important," she murmured.

"Benedict and I had lost touch over the years,"

mused Jeremy. "I was very happy to rekindle the acquaintance."

"Understandably so." She knew little of Jeremy's life during his university years. She and her late husband had been in Italy . . .

"He works closely with Ashton's personal secretary," continued her friend, "and Miss Merton's company has proved very pleasant as well." His expression turned troubled. "They will both be devastated by his death."

Merton. Hillhouse. The two names at the very top of Wrexford's list of possible suspects.

"I'm so sorry," said Charlotte. Murder was like a stone thrown into a calm lake—the impact sent waves rippling out far from the point of impact.

"As am I." A flicker of unreadable emotion tightened Jeremy's features, but it was gone in an instant. "I hope to provide some comfort while they are here in London. The atmosphere inside a house of mourning can be oppressive."

Especially as, according to Wrexford, there was no love lost between Ashton's widow and her late husband's assistants.

"A walk in the park may be a balm for the spirits," he finished.

"Perhaps Miss Merton would welcome the company of another woman," said Charlotte slowly.

His face wreathed in a smile. "That's exceedingly kind—"

Honesty compelled her to interrupt him. "I'm

not merely being altruistic, Jem. You know I've been working on a series of prints entitled *Man versus Machine*. So for professional reasons, I should very much like to hear her viewpoint on the subject—and that of Mr. Hillhouse."

It wasn't a lie, simply a partial truth, in which she left her part in the murder investigation unsaid.

"If they are friends of yours," she went on, "I'm sure they will be both thoughtful and articulate."

Jeremy hesitated. "They are. And I think you would all like each other very much. However . . ."

"However scandal is my bread and butter," said Charlotte softly. "And you fear I may make a meal of them." She watched a dappling of the north light skate across her desk top. How ironic that it was known for its piercing clarity. With each passing moment she felt herself being drawn deeper and deeper into the tangled murk of secrets within secrets.

"I understand the demands of what you do," replied Jeremy. "And ought not make you decide between friendship and earning a living."

"I would have thought you know me well enough to know which will always come first," she said slowly.

He reached out and slowly uncurled her fisted fingers. "I'd trust you with my life, Charley." His faced paled. "In fact, I have. We both know that."

"Just as I've entrusted you with my deepest secrets." Charlotte hardly dared ask the next question. "I've never regretted it for an instant. Have you?"

A ripple of emotion darkened his eyes. "No. Never."

Her insides unclenched. "I may use my pen as a barb to puncture the pompousness of those who think themselves above the rules. But in cases such as Ashton's death, I hope I am always a voice for truth and justice."

"I don't doubt that." Jeremy pressed his palms to his temples. "But the truth can be twisted by others."

What is he so afraid of? Charlotte thought it a strangely pessimistic comment for someone who had mastered the art of graceful good cheer. But for the moment she forced the question from her mind.

"All the more reason to introduce me," she pressed. "I can, you know, be a powerful force in shaping public opinion—for good as well as for bad."

An involuntary laugh slipped from his lips. "I daresay the Prince Regent himself quakes in his boots at the thought of becoming a subject of your drawings."

"Prinny quakes—and quivers—because he consumes far too many rich pastries and bottles of claret," she responded, hoping to ease the tension in the air.

Jeremy laughed again. He rarely stayed blue-deviled for any length of time, though he had, she well knew, his own personal demons to wrestle with.

Don't we all?

"True," he said in answer to her quip. "But I happen to know that he took to his bed for several days after seeing your parody of his shopping for corsets."

Charlotte carefully shifted the boxes of her pigments. "I have never turned my pen on innocent people. Your friends have nothing to fear from me."

Unless, of course, they were guilty of murdering the inventor. In that case, she believed that Jeremy would also agree that truth must triumph, no matter the personal cost.

And yet. . . .

Their gazes met and held for a long moment. It was he who looked away first, and while it might have only been a quirk of light, a flicker of shadow seemed to cloud his eyes.

"I know that." After perching a hip on the desk, Jeremy smoothed a wrinkle from his trousers. "Forgive my hesitation. I'm happy to arrange for you to meet them. Though I assume it will not be as A. J. Quill."

"No," she agreed. "Just as a longtime friend of yours. Given the connection all three of you have with Mr. Ashton, and the public reaction to the series of prints on *Man versus Machine*, I don't think it will strike an odd note if I'm curious about their views on the subject."

He nodded. "As it happens we've made a plan to meet for a walk in Green Park tomorrow afternoon. Would you care to join us?"

"Yes," replied Charlotte quickly, even as a chorus of voices inside her head began to chant a warning.

Beware of the dangers that lie along that path.

She'd been very careful to stay outside the circle of Polite Society. The Greek myth of Persephone showed the perils of moving back and forth between the land of the living and the land of the dead.

"Then it's settled." Jeremy brushed an imaginary speck of dust from his breeches and then quickly rose again, though without any of his usual grace. "And now, I'd best toddle off and allow you to settle in to your new abode."

"Thank you again for everything, Jem," murmured Charlotte. "I'm . . . I'm truly grateful."

Her friend snapped a jaunty salute and turned with a whisper of well-tailored wool.

As Charlotte watched him walk away, a frown slowly furrowed her brow. They had been kindred spirits since childhood and with her artist's eye for faces, she had always been good at reading the subtle nuances of his expression.

It wasn't that Jeremy had been lying . . .

But for all his show of sunny candor, she was sure he was hiding something from her.

Chapter 11

Wrexford took a moment to survey the surroundings before announcing himself at Charlotte's new residence with a rap of the knocker. Though modest, the neighborhood was far more pleasant than her previous one. The street wasn't a hellhole of muddy ruts, the air didn't ooze with the unwashed scents of the city, and the house showed no threat of imminent collapse.

Her friend—the baron, he reminded himself—had chosen well.

Another mystery regarding Charlotte's past. But like the others, one she fiercely guarded.

The earl was about to bang the weighty brass ring again when the door flung open.

"Wot's that ye got?" demanded Hawk, regarding the canvas-bundle with bright-eyed interest.

"Curiosity killed the cat," he responded.

A grin split the boy's face. " 'S'alright—I'm a weasel!"

"Close enough. They are both small, furry beasties."

"Oiy, but a weasel is much cleverer than a kitty."

"Not if the little beastie thinks it's amusing to annoy a large and irascible predator whose arms are growing tired," warned Wrexford.

The retort provoked a laugh.

Alas, how low the mighty have fallen. His august title no longer intimidated anyone in this household. He shifted his hold on the bundle. "Might I come in?"

Hawk quickly stepped aside. "M'lady, m'lady! His Nibs is here!"

A clatter of steps sounded on the stairs, and a moment later, a breathless Charlotte came hurrying down the corridor.

"Lord Wrexford!" She halted and lifted a hand to catch an errant lock of hair that had fallen across her cheek, twisting it slowly around a finger before tucking it awkwardly behind an ear. "I didn't expect . . . any visitors."

"Forgive me if I'm intruding at an inconvenient moment."

"No—that is, I didn't mean. . . ."

He had never seen Charlotte so flustered.

"It's just that I was arranging some of the furniture upstairs," she finished lamely.

"I imagine there is much to do," he answered. "I won't keep you from your tasks. However there are several things I thought you ought to know. It won't take long."

Charlotte hesitated, and then reluctantly gestured for him to step into the corridor. Her agitation struck him as odd. He was familiar with her old abode and its spartan furnishings—though judging by the entrance foyer, the new house had come with some basic amenities.

"I . . ." Charlotte moved stiffly to a half-open door, her face pinching in embarrassment. "I suppose we can have a word in here."

Wrexford expected the room to be empty. "Mrs. Sloane, there is no need to be . . ." His voice cut off as he crossed the threshold.

"M-My friend—" she began.

"Your friend has excellent taste," he interjected, as he gazed around at the well-chosen arrangements of furniture.

"I-I had no idea of his plans," she stammered. "I didn't . . . I couldn't . . ."

Wrexford almost smiled at seeing her so tongue-tied. But the depth of her distress was no laughing matter.

"It's a very pleasant parlor,' " he said. "Clearly your friend knows you well. You'll be very comfortable here."

Her face turned pale for an instant, then flooded with color. "This was a complete surprise!"

"Good heavens, you need not feel you owe me any explanation," replied Wrexford with a careless shrug. "The sofa looks quite comfortable. Might we sit down? My arms are growing quite tired."

"Do *not* tease me, sir!"

The earl was glad to see her usual fire finally flare to life.

"In fact, this is . . . this is . . ." Charlotte huffed in frustration, then allowed a wry grimace. "In fact, this is all *your* fault!"

He raised his brows. "*My* fault?"

"Yes." Her mouth quirked, hovering between a frown and a smile. "Your lecture on accepting help from friends impelled me to let down my guard."

"Which is all for the good," murmured Wrexford.

"Is it?" Uncertainty shadowed her features. Looking away, Charlotte drew a steadying breath. And then another.

Wrexford remained silent. Whatever battle she was fighting, he sensed he was not the enemy.

When she finally spoke, it was barely above a whisper. "It feels as if my life is at sixes and sevens."

Humor, he decided, was the best way to defuse the situation. "Speaking of numbers, that happens to be the reason I'm here. There's something I want you to see."

Charlotte chuffed a laugh.

A good sign

"Impossible man," she said. "Do you not take anything seriously?"

"On very rare occasions. But this is not one of them." He looked around again, and then added, "In my humble opinion, you are making a tempest in a teapot about this. Your lordly friend has gifted you with some furnishings—which I daresay came from acres of attics crammed with the flotsam and jetsam of past generations. It is a gesture of friendship, not pity. To argle and bargle over it is an insult to his intentions."

She lowered her lashes, hiding her eyes.

"But then," he added dryly, "you're well aware of my sardonic outlook on human nature."

Charlotte shifted her stance, and suddenly her grim expression surrendered to a smile. "If you were looking to singe my hubris, consider it done. I doubt the Devil himself could have raked me over any hotter coals."

"I think you know my intention was not to cause pain." Wrexford quelled the urge to reach out and touch a reassuring hand to her cheek. "You've often told me that looking at a problem from a different perspective can help one see the solution."

"How very lowering to have my own words thrown back in my face,' she murmured.

"Especially when they are right?" He smiled. "If it's any consolation, the reason I'm here is because I, too am at sixes and sevens. Ashton's murder has taken another serpentine twist and I would greatly value your view on it."

"You've discovered another clue?" she asked quickly.

"Yes," Wrexford set down his awkward burden. "But first—"

A quicksilver flutter in the corridor caught his eye. "You may step out of the woodwork, Weasels. This concerns you."

The two boys darted into the room.

"See, I told ye," whispered Hawk to his brother. "It's a corking big bundle."

Charlotte fixed them with a basilisk stare. "Spying on one's elders is ungentlemanly."

Raven returned the look without a flinch. "We weren't spying. We were simply making sure you didn't need our protection."

"Gentlemen are s'posed te be knights in shining armor," piped up Hawk. "Isn't that right, m'lord?"

"In a manner of speaking," Wrexford replied dryly. To Charlotte, he added, "You may have new reason to be furious with me, but the lads mentioned there was a small swath of garden here. And so I took the liberty of bringing . . ."

He gestured at the canvas-wrapped bundle. "May they go ahead and open it?"

Charlotte took a seat on the sofa before answering. The day was unraveling into a series of surprises. She wasn't quite sure she wanted another. However, Wrexford's expression was somewhat reassuring. Despite his show of sardonic humor, he looked a little uncomfortable.

What in the names of Hades was beneath the canvas wrapping? Had it been wriggling, she might have guessed a snake.

Oh, surely he wouldn't . . .

"M'lady?" Hawk's wistful voice roused her from her reverie. "May we?"

Wrexford, she noted, had perched a hip on the arm of the facing chair and folded his arms across his chest. His face gave nothing away.

"Yes," she answered, and steeled herself for . . . only God knew what.

The boys flew to the bundle and made quick work of unknotting the cording. With a grunt, Raven lifted it upright while his brother stripped away the cloth.

Metal clinked against metal as a glint of light flashed off polished steel.

Mother of God.

The earl must have read her thoughts. "Before you're tempted to cut out my liver, allow me to say that the points have been ground off and the blades have been dulled."

"Swords!" Two gleeful shouts rose in tandem.

Charlotte couldn't contain herself. She started laughing.

Clang! Clang!

"Are you *mad?*" she sputtered, as the two weapons hit together.

"Stop!" called earl.

The boys instantly obeyed.

"There are rules," he intoned. "And a code of honor. Break either and the weapons will be revoked. Understood?"

Raven and Hawk nodded solemnly.

"The list is short. Swordplay is only permitted in the garden. No thrusting, and you may only hit with the flat of the blade. And never, ever lash out in a moment of anger, as you may cause serious injury."

Well done, conceded Charlotte.

"Lastly, I leave it to Mrs. Sloane to decide whether any blood or bruises merit the weapons being taken away," continued Wrexford. "Have I your promise to abide by what I've spelled out?"

"Aye, sir," answered both boys.

"Then off you go, Weasels. And mind you, lopping off any tree limbs is also strictly forbidden."

"Huzzah!" In a pelter of playful pushing and shoving, Raven and Hawk shouldered the weapons and staggered off.

Charlotte took some consolation in the fact that the swords were heavy enough that the boys were unlikely to wield them well enough to inflict lasting damage.

Wrexford eyed her warily, waiting for her to speak first.

Any anger she might have felt for his high-handed gift dissolved upon recalling how the boys had told her about a conversation they had had with the earl many months ago, one involving ancestral swords and his long-ago duels with a younger brother.

Raven and Hawk had been wide-eyed in wonder at such swashbuckling adventure.

That Wrexford had sensed their awe was all to

his credit. More than that, it revealed a soft spot in his armor—one he took great pains to hide.

"I suppose," she said slowly, "I should take heart from the fact that you somehow managed to survive such brother-on-brother battles."

"There may be a black eye or two, but that does a lad no harm," he replied. "Broken bones or bruises are badges of honor."

"So I gather." Charlotte sighed. "You seem to think such youthful testing of each other's mettle forges a special bond of brotherhood."

His expression turned unreadable. A Sphinx-like mask of impenetrable stone.

Was he thinking of his dead brother, slain on some bloody Peninsular battlefield? She could imagine the sense of loss must seep into the very marrow of one's bones.

"Do you miss Thomas?" she asked abruptly.

He turned, the play of afternoon light and shadow skittering over the austere angles of his face. Perhaps it was merely a fluttering reflection in the windowpanes, but for an instant the chiseled arrogance seemed to give way to a ghosting of pain.

"Every day," replied Wrexford. "He was a good man. A far better one than I."

She had expected his usual sarcasm, not such naked honesty. "I'm so sorry."

A careless shrug, and the moment was gone. "As Raven so wisely pointed out a while back, the Grim Reaper cares naught as to whether you are a lowly pauper or a highborn toff when he swings his scythe."

Clang, clang—the ring of swords floated in from the garden, punctuated by peals of boyish laughter.

"They will sleep well in their new house," he remarked.

A deliberate deflecting of tender sentiment. His cool smile seemed to challenge any further probing on the subject. Speaking of emotion wasn't something either of them did well.

"If physical exhaustion helps to counter the excitement of having beds and room of their own, I shall be profoundly grateful," answered Charlotte, following his lead. "Though I fear they . . ."

The *clang-clang* of steel against steel echoed her own jumpy nerves.

"I fear they won't be as happy as I wish for them to be," she finished.

"Trust your instincts, Mrs. Sloane," murmured the earl. "I do." Without further ado, he pulled a piece of paper from his pocket. "You've much on your mind. If you'll allow me to explain the real reason for my visit, I shall then leave you in peace."

"A new clue?" The flutter of paper chased all other thoughts from her head. "Did you find Gannett?"

"Yes, and you were right to suspect that he

wasn't working alone." Wrexford came to sit down beside her on the sofa. "He pointed us to a man named Hollis, who, judging by all the pamphlets we found in his room, looks to have been a leader of the Workers of Zion."

The earl's use of the past tense stirred a prickling at the nape of her neck. "And what did Mr. Hollis have to say for himself," she asked. "Assuming you found him?"

"Precious little," replied Wrexford grimly. "His throat had been slashed."

Charlotte flinched.

"He did manage to say he didn't kill Ashton . . ." He blew out a harried breath. "But the rest of his words were naught but a cursed riddle."

"W-What did he say?" she demanded.

"When I asked if he knew the real killer, he said 'Find Nevins'—and before you ask, I haven't a clue as to who he is. Then he added the phrase *Numbers—numbers will explain it all.*"

She stared at the folded piece of paper in his hands. "Have you any idea what that means?"

He slapped it down on the tea table and smoothed it open. "I was hoping you might see something that I'm missing."

Black on white—a string of seemingly random numbers jumped off the crinkled page. Charlotte stared at them blankly and then looked up. "Were it art or symbols I might be of some help. But I've no expertise in mathematics, sir."

"I thought perhaps that might work in our favor," he muttered.

"I take it you were hoping I might spot an unexpected pattern." She made herself take another long look. "Sorry, it looks like Greek to me."

"Damnation." Wrexford grimaced and then muttered, "Would that it were Latin."

Hic sunt dracones—Here there be dragons, thought Charlotte. Early on, she had betrayed her knowledge of the classical language, and the earl had never ceased using it to probe for information about her background.

Ignoring the comment, she said, "You're a man of science. Surely there must be some logic to the numbers and how they add up."

"Not that I've seen. However, I've sent it to a professor at Cambridge who's far more skilled in mathematics than I am. With a modicum of luck, he'll have some ideas."

Of late, Luck had not been looking on them favorably, thought Charlotte.

"I'll leave this copy with you," he added. "Just in case inspiration strikes."

"Tell me more about Hollis and his connection to Workers of Zion," she said after taking the paper. "Perhaps there's some clue we can find there."

The earl recounted all that had happened the previous evening. "I'm convinced Gannett is merely an unwitting pawn. And as for Hollis, I need to meet with Griffin this evening. I sent word to him about the body and the connection to the radical agitators, so no doubt Bow Street will be frothing at the mouth to track down the rest of the group. But I want to convince him to delve deeper into this whole sordid mess. The radicals may be involved, but my sense is Hollis wasn't lying about not having killed Ashton."

"He might have had a falling out with one of the other leaders," mused Charlotte. "Perhaps he meant Nevins is the killer."

"I suppose it's possible, though it didn't seem as if that was what he meant." Wrexford made a face. "I'm not convinced we should abandon the idea that someone close to Ashton is involved."

Charlotte thought for a moment. "I wonder . . ." Looking up, she asked, "What did Hollis look like?"

"A big fellow, dark hair, a mole on his cheek."

"That's the man Henning described as having left the pamphlets!" A sharp exhale squeezed from her lungs. "He said he knows nothing about Hollis, and I believe him, but maybe one of his patients knows something about Nevins and can help point to his whereabouts."

"A good point," said the earl. "I'll pay a visit to his surgery. Hollis did seem to be trying to say a word that began with *H* when he gave up the ghost. It's possible it was Henning's name, and that has to mean something." Wrexford paused. "But first, I'm paying a visit to Ashton's two assistants."

Octavia Merton and Benedict Hillhouse. Charlotte felt her insides clench. She must make a decision, and quickly.

"I've a talk scheduled with Mr. Hillhouse," continued the earl. "I'm curious to see if his behavior seems as furtive as that of Miss Merton."

On one hand, Charlotte wished to pursue her preliminary investigation of the two assistants independently. Working closely with Wrexford stirred its own complexities. At times, she feared it clouded her judgment. Even now she could feel his molten green gaze burning against her flesh as he waited for her reaction.

On the other hand, she needed his help.

"Given your encounter with Miss Merton," she said, "Mr. Hillhouse may be inclined to see you as the enemy."

"That can't be helped," he replied tersely.

"Perhaps it can, milord."

His scrutiny sharpened. "How so?"

The recent scathing lectures on pride versus friendship were still ringing in her ears. And yet, that didn't make swallowing her trepidations any easier.

"Mrs. Sloane?" he urged.

Ah, well. In for a penny, in for a pound.

"It so happens that my friend is acquainted

with Mr. Hillhouse." She went on to recount her recent conversation with Jeremy.

Wrexford listened without interruption, and when she finished, he still said nothing.

Charlotte waited. The silence was a little unnerving. The earl was rarely at a loss for words. However, she had no choice but to go on.

"I've arranged to meet all three of them tomorrow," she explained. "But to do so, I'll need to impose on your friendship—which, I might remind you, is something I was quite forcefully urged to do."

That finally roused a response.

"How so?"

"There's no way for me to mingle among beau monde without adhering to the strictures of Society. It's one thing for me to dress modestly and move through the streets of Mayfair on my own. People see me as naught but a working class woman clinging to the fringes of respectability."

She watched his face, trying to gauge his thoughts. *Ha—the hieroglyphics carved on the Rosetta Stone would be easier to decipher.*

"But if I am to join Lord Sterling and his friends in a social outing, I must appear to adhere to the rules of propriety," continued Charlotte. "And that means I must be accompanied by a female servant."

Wrexford crossed his long legs and drew out the moment by smoothing a crease from his trousers. "I trust you're not suggesting I don skirt and bonnet to masquerade as your maid."

A scowl pinched at her mouth. "You can't have it both ways, milord. You can't take me to task for refusing to trust you, and then turn around and mock me for doing so."

"An ill-chosen jest," conceded the earl.

And yet he wasn't smiling.

"Forgive me," he added.

It was her turn to freeze him with a silent stare.

If Wrexford noticed, he gave no sign of it. "So, what you're asking is that someone from my household serve as your companion?"

"I would imagine," she said through clenched teeth, "that a tweenie or kitchen maid could be spared for a few hours without your mansion falling into rack and ruin."

"I daresay the roof slates wouldn't crumble into dust," he drawled.

"If you insist on being insufferable, I will ask Jeremy," she shot back. "Though I would prefer not to do so. These people are his friends, and I already feel guilty that I've been less than forthright with him about my reasons for wanting to meet them."

"If they're innocent, they've nothing to fear."

Charlotte let out an exasperated huff. "We both know it's not that simple, milord. Everyone has secrets they would prefer to keep buried. Suspicion wields an eager spade. It cares not where it digs, as long as it's turning up dirt."

"A very insightful assessment, Mrs. Sloane," said Wrexford slowly. "Since you so clearly see the complexities—and the dark side—of Truth, I assume you won't object if I add an observation."

Mercurial. His mood seemed to be changing with quicksilver spurts, and she had no idea as to why.

The earl didn't wait for a reply. "Your dear friend—Lord Sterling—is both an investor in Ashton's new steam engine and a comrade of two of the leading murder suspects. Surely it hasn't escaped you that he, too, must now be viewed from a different perspective."

Jeremy guilty of a sordid crime?

A gasp tore free from her throat. "Never," whispered Charlotte, once she managed to find her voice. "I-I know him. He's not capable of such evil."

"You knew your late husband—even more intimately, I presume. And yet you didn't see the real darkness into which he allowed himself to be dragged."

At that instant, she wanted to hate him. "How dare you . . ."

"Because," he replied with infuriating calm, "it's the truth and you are smart enough to know it."

She longed to argue—nay, she longed to spit into his glittering emerald-sharp eyes!

But she couldn't. Her profession had given her

a look at too many gut-wrenching deceptions and betrayals. Evil lurked everywhere, even in hearts where one least expected it.

Slumping back against the cushions, Charlotte fought to bring her emotions under control.

Wrexford tactfully averted his gaze. The clash of steel on steel had stopped, leaving the room shrouded in silence. The boys must have grown weary of fighting.

"Very well," she said, relieved her voice didn't crack. "As you say, Lord Sterling must be considered a suspect." A pause. "But not for long. I intend to prove his innocence."

"I would be happy for you to do so," he replied. "The fewer specters we are chasing, the better."

"Then we had both better get to work." Charlotte rose, too unsettled to remain seated. "Have you made up your mind about allowing me a companion for tomorrow?"

"I'll send someone, along with a carriage, to fetch you."

Charlotte shook her head. "Good God, sir—I can't be seen in one of your carriages! My reputation would be ruined as soon as the wheels rolled into Mayfair."

"Give me some credit, Mrs. Sloane. I'm quite familiar with what a proper lady can—and cannot—do. On occasion, I wish to travel without drawing notice, so I have several vehicles which are unmarked and unrecognizable."

For what reason? she wondered, then quickly pushed the thought away.

"Having a carriage drop you at the park entrance only further enhances your image as a widow of strict propriety," he pointed out.

"That makes some sense," allowed Charlotte, hoping she didn't sound too peevish. "Is there anything else we need to discuss?"

"No." Following her lead, Wrexford got to his feet. "I'll not impose on you any longer."

Charlotte watched him move toward the doorway. The curl of his mouth indicated that his usual dry humor had returned. And yet, a black cloud seemed to surround him.

Specters, indeed. She wasn't thinking straight.

"Lord Wrexford."

He halted and slowly looked around.

"I—I haven't thanked you properly for your gift to the lads."

"You may want to reserve judgment on that." It was said lightly, but like much of their conversation, his words resonated with multiple meanings.

"Let us not part on a discordant note, sir," replied Charlotte. "I . . . ." She wanted to say more, but couldn't seem to find the right words, so merely expelled a harried sigh. "My tongue, as you well know, has a sharp edge. There are times when I ought to keep it sheathed."

"I've a thick skin, Mrs. Sloane. You've drawn no blood."

The mention of blood made her shiver.

"I'm relieved to hear that. Too much of it has already been spilled in this gruesome affair."

"Indeed." He held her gaze for a moment longer. "All the more reason for us to unravel the mystery surrounding Ashton's murder and find the real killer—before he strikes again."

Chapter 12

"Lord Wrexford."

To the earl's surprise, it was Isobel, rather than Ashton's laboratory assistant who opened the drawing room door.

"Forgive me, but I heard you had arrived to speak with Benedict, and I couldn't help wondering . . ." She glanced back into the corridor and then shut the door behind her. "Did you have any success in finding the man who penned the note to Elihu?"

"Be assured I had no intention of leaving without telling you about the evening," he replied.

"I didn't mean to imply . . ."

"My apologies," he quickly added. "I should have sought you out first." It *was* true that he had planned to put it off until after the interview with Hillhouse. Disappointing news was never easy to deliver.

"I take it things did not go well," she said softly.

"No," admitted Wrexford. "We did find the man who wrote the note, but he was merely an unwitting player in what he thought was a harmless jest."

Her expression remained stoic. "I see."

"However, we learned the name and address of

the real culprit," he went on reluctantly. Having to recount the events made him acutely aware of all the little mistakes he had made. "Unfortunately someone else reached him first."

Her breath seemed to catch in her lungs.

"Alas, he'd been stabbed just minutes before we arrived."

"Dear God." For an instant he feared she might swoon, but she steadied herself and with a wry smile waved off his outstretched hand. "I'm not quite so fragile as I look. It's just that I thought . . . I hoped . . ."

"I'm sorry. He was still alive, but the injuries were far too severe for him to survive"

"H-He wasn't able to tell you anything?"

Wrexford shook his head. "I'm afraid not." A lie seemed kinder than offering yet another false hope. The list of numbers could hardly be considered a viable clue.

"I see." Isobel turned in a rustling of heavy black bombazine fabric and gazed out the window. "So that leaves us with nothing to go on."

"Not precisely," he answered. "The man who used the note to lure your husband to his death appears to be part of a radical group called the Workers of Zion. It's possible they are behind your husband's murder. I'm going to press Bow Street to investigate them."

"Radicals?" Her body tensed, and suddenly she reached for the bell on the side table and rang for a servant. "Before you meet with Mr. Hillhouse, there is someone else with whom I'd like you to speak."

When the butler arrived, Isobel murmured instructions, and within minutes he returned with a tall, well-muscled man who was dressed in plain-cut, dark-hued clothing.

"Lord Wrexford, allow me to introduce Mr. Geoffrey Blodgett, who arrived here from Leeds early this morning," said Isobel.

Blodgett darted a quick look around, appearing a little uncomfortable at being in such opulent surroundings.

"He's the supervisor of the mill," she explained, "and has known Elihu since he was a boy."

"A terrible tragedy, milord," murmured Blodgett after exchanging perfunctory greetings with the earl. "Such a loss, both for his family and for our country. Mr. Ashton's innovations touched so many lives."

Wrexford imagined the man hadn't been brought in simply to spout platitudes. "Yes, yes, a brilliant fellow," he agreed, then angled an inquiring look at the widow.

Isobel met it with a knowing nod. "Much as Mr. Blodgett's sentiments are appreciated, he's come here not merely to express his sympathies. There are a number of important matters to deal with in order to keep the mill running without interruption." She gave a sad smile. "I'm fortunate that he's worked with my husband for years and understands all the technicalities of the operation."

Blodgett bobbed his head in acknowledgement of her words.

"More than that, I'm fortunate that he understands how my late husband wished for things to be done. It's a great comfort to me that everything will continue to work at optimum efficiency. It is what Elihu would have wanted."

The earl was finding it hard to hide his impatience.

"However, that's not why I asked Mr. Blodgett to speak with you now. He recounted some things this morning that, in light of what you just told me, may have relevance to Elihu's murder." She turned to the supervisor. "Please repeat to His Lordship what you said when I asked if you had observed any suspicious activity in recent weeks."

"Aye, ma'am." Blodgett cleared his throat. "The mill is a good place to work and pays excellent wages, so our workers have shown little interest in kicking up a dust. But that doesn't stop radicals from hanging around and trying to stir up trouble. A group of them have moved into the area, on account of all the manufacturing we have there."

He swallowed hard and shot a nervous glance at Mrs. Ashton.

"Go on, Mr. Blodgett," she said gently. "You've naught to fear for telling the truth."

The supervisor gathered himself and squared

his shoulders. "The thing is, I spend a lot of time checking the different sections of the machinery and all the outer storage buildings where we keep our raw materials—it's part of my job, you see. So I couldn't help noticing several weeks ago that Mr. Hillhouse was starting to meet with some of the troublemakers—and in out-of-the-way places, as if he didn't want to be seen."

"Did Mr. Hillhouse's duties include negotiating with your workers?" asked Wrexford.

"No, milord. He worked with Mr. Ashton in the laboratory and had no hand in the actual running of the mill. He's very, very clever with mechanical things." The superintendent hesitated. "I mean no disrespect, but in all honesty, I can't say the same about his skill with people."

"The workers don't like him?" asked Wrexford.

"It would be unfair of me to say that, sir. It's more that they find him aloof." A pause. "All of us do."

The earl thought for a moment about what he had heard, trying to remain objective. "Could there have been a reason Ashton asked Mr. Hillhouse to speak with the workers?"

"Yes, I suppose so," replied Blodgett. "If there had been a mechanical problem with a component, it's possible Mr. Ashton would have asked Mr. Hillhouse to speak with the men who ran the machinery. However, it's hard to imagine I wouldn't have known about it."

That made sense, reflected Wrexford. Striving to remain fair-minded, he tried to think of any other question that might cast Ashton's assistant in a brighter light. But nothing came to mind.

"Is there any other information I should know before I meet with Mr. Hillhouse?"

Blodgett dropped his gaze to the carpet, and then slowly raised it again. "Just . . . Just that he seemed on edge and even more withdrawn than usual over the last few months." The supervisor swallowed hard. "But then again, he and I aren't on the best of terms. I've always felt he looked down on me because I never attended university."

"Anything else?" pressed Wrexford.

The supervisor shook his head.

"Thank you, Mr. Blodgett," said Isobel after a long moment. "If you'll wait for me in the side parlor, I'll be along shortly so we can finish going over the production schedule and supply orders for the coming month."

How fortunate that she seemed to have a keen interest in business, thought the earl. Most ladies would need a strong whiff of vinaigrette if asked to make sense of a bill of lading.

"I'll ring for Mr. Hillhouse," said Isobel after Blodgett had left the room. But before she reached for the bell, a discreet knock sounded on the door.

"Forgive me, madam." The butler entered and inclined an apologetic bow. "I've just received word from Mr. Hillhouse that there's been a problem with the toolmakers and he's been unavoidably detained at the shop."

"How unfortunate." If the news annoyed her, she hid it well. "Please accept my apologies for the inconvenience, Lord Wrexford. It seems we will have to arrange another time for you to meet with him."

He waited for the butler to withdraw and then shrugged. "Business must, of course, come first. Is he working on a piece of machinery? Perhaps an element of the new invention?"

"I couldn't say." A pause, which spoke louder than the three short words. "My husband gave Mr. Hillhouse free rein to experiment with the prototypes on which they were working. However, he hasn't as yet seen fit to share the details of his tinkering with me."

That, imagined the earl, was going to change, and quickly. Assuming the fellow wasn't given the sack by suppertime.

"It is, however, unlikely that he will do so," continued Isobel. "You see, my husband's drawings appear to be missing. Whether Elihu had them on his person at the time of his murder, or whether he put them in a place of safekeeping is, as of yet, an unsolved mystery."

Along with too many other unanswered conundrums, thought Wrexford.

He acknowledged her remark with a nod before

shifting a step closer to the door. "I'll take my leave. I'm sure you have much on your mind." There was nothing more to gain by lingering, and she appeared anxious to return to her meeting with the mill supervisor.

Isobel looked grateful and led the way out to the corridor.

"This way, sir," she murmured, indicating a turn to the right. "I'll show you—" Her words cut off abruptly as a gentleman rounded the corner, looking very much at home in the place.

"Ah—forgive me, Mrs. Ashton. Jenkins didn't mention that you had company," he drawled. "I should have sent word that was I coming. Given the tragic circumstances, it's most unfeeling of me to intrude on your grief."

Light from the wall sconce caught the spark of surprise in her eyes as she fell back a pace. If Wrexford hadn't moved to avoid her flaring skirts, he might have missed seeing it change to a flicker of fear before quickly dying out.

"Good Heavens, you need not stand on ceremony, sir. This is your home. Had I known you were planning a visit to Town, I would have insisted on finding other lodgings," replied Isobel tightly. Her lashes fluttered for an instant, and then went still.

A veiled warning? *But of what?*

Before Wrexford could consider the question, she turned abruptly to him and said, "Allow me to introduce Viscount Kirkland, eldest son of the Marquess of Blackstone, the friend of my husband who so kindly offered us his townhouse for our visit to London."

Blackstone. Why was the name ringing a bell?

She shifted again in what might have been a flutter of nerves. "Lord Kirkland, this is Lord Wrexford."

"We met last night," replied the earl.

Kirkland regarded him blankly for a moment. "Ah, yes. So we did." A disinterested smile. "Any luck in finding the fellow you were seeking?"

"Yes," replied Wrexford. The fellow's pretentious arrogance would have been laughable, save for the effect his presence was having on the widow. Her face now had an arctic pallor, as if the blood in her veins had turned to ice.

"Unfortunately he wasn't able to help us," he added slowly, curious to see the other man's reaction.

"A pity." Kirkland's gaze had already returned to Isobel. "I won't hear of you moving, Mrs. Ashton, especially now in this time of great sadness." The viscount lowered his voice to a mock whisper. "Truth be told, I prefer the comforts of my club to staying here. The chef there does a far tastier joint of beef than Cook, but don't tell her I said so."

"What of your father?" she asked slowly. "Perhaps he—"

"Oh, Pater left for Wales last week to visit with some family friends, and from there he is going to one of our Irish estates. Something to do with horseflesh, I believe. He'll be gone for at least a month, so you need not concern yourself." The viscount gave a negligent shrug. "Indeed, I'm not sure he knows yet of Mr. Ashton's unfortunate demise. I've sent the news to Ireland, but God only knows when he'll receive it."

"He may not wish for his house to be involved in such notoriety," pressed Isobel.

The protests seemed more than polite formalities, thought Wrexford. Yet another *why* to ponder.

A low laugh sounded from Kirkland. "Good Heavens, Pater considers himself far above tawdry scandal or gossip. In his world, such things simply don't exist."

If you are sure . . ." said Isobel.

"Quite. So it's settled." insisted the viscount. "I simply stopped by to fetch a selection of Pater's Indian cheroots." He inclined a polite bow. "I'll head on to his study and then take my leave."

Isobel stood frozen in place as the echo of Kirkland's footsteps receded into the shadows.

"Mrs. Ashton," said the earl softly.

She looked around with a start.

"I, too, will see myself out."

"Forgive me," she apologized. "I'm not

thinking straight. I—I fear Mr. Blodgett's news has unsettled me."

"Understandably so," replied Wrexford. Seeing the uncertainty etched on her face, he couldn't help adding, "Whatever the truth is about your husband's murder, we will find it."

Isobel shifted, the heavy rustling of black bombazine stirring a sudden swirl of shadows. For an instant her face was veiled in darkness. "Do you really believe so?"

Truth or lies?

"As a man of science," he answered, "I hold to the principle that every problem has a solution. One just has to find it."

A forced smile. "I shall take heart from your optimism."

"Inquiry takes patience. Answers are reached by taking one small step at a time."

"Yes, of course." But her voice held no conviction.

"Good day, madam." Lost in thought, Wrexford exited the townhouse and began walking back to his own residence.

Yet more threads added to the conundrum. Which was now tangling into a damnable Gordian knot.

It wasn't until he crossed the cobblestones and turned down Grosvenor Street that he remembered why the name Blackstone had sounded familiar. As the principal investor in Ashton's company, the marquess was on the widow's list of people who knew that a revolutionary new invention was in the works.

As Wrexford mulled over the fact, another thought suddenly occurred to him. Surely father would confide in son. Which meant the list was missing a name.

That of Viscount Kirkland . . .

Wrexford slowed to a halt, realizing another one had also been omitted.

That of Isobel Ashton.

Chapter 13

Charlotte awoke the next day feeling tired and out of sorts. She had slept fitfully, her peace plagued by dreams of unseen threats, pressing closer and closer, choking off all air and light.

The morning had passed in a blur—a simple breakfast and the boys made presentable for their first lessons with the new tutor. True to his word, the earl had sent the young man around for an interview the previous evening, and she had found him to be a solid, sensible choice. More than that, he had a sense of humor, which she hoped boded well for his taming the Weasels. As he lived nearby, it had been agreed that Raven and Hawk would go to his rooms this morning to begin the experiment.

She prayed that it would work out. The boys were bright and the chance to expand their horizons would open up new worlds to them. But for the moment it was out of her hands.

A good thing, as she had been unaccountably clumsy in preparing the meal, scorching her fingers on the kettle and dropping a plate of fresh-sliced bread.

After making a few desultory sketches at her desk, all of which were consigned to the wastebin, it was time to dress for her rendezvous with Jeremy and his friends.

Staring into the looking glass, Charlotte sighed on seeing the dark shadows under her eyes. Hardly an auspicious sign for her first official foray into Polite Society.

Imposter. Perhaps she should simply letter a sign to pin on her bodice announcing the fact.

"I don't have to do this," she muttered. And yet, even as she said it, she knew she did.

The why of it seemed to elude words. When she had first assumed her late husband's persona of A. J. Quill, it had simply been a matter of survival. But penning the barbs and satire on frivolous scandals had sharpened her awareness of deeper injustices, and Charlotte had found that truth and fairness mattered far more to her than merely a means for putting bread on the table.

That she could help puncture lies and expose evil with her art had somehow taken hold in her heart.

Semper anticus. Always forward. There was no going back.

Charlotte rose and opened the doors of her armoire. At least she had decent armor in which to march into the fray, she thought wryly. The necessity of having to accompany Jeremy to review the final choices for her new residence had required a respectable gown that wasn't hopelessly outdated. Luckily her network of informants included an Italian modiste who catered to the beau monde. The woman—who was savvy enough about business to pretend she was French—had readily agreed to create a suitable design.

She fingered the whisper-soft merino wool, feeling a little guilty at the pleasure she took in such fripperies. The subtle grey-blue color— the exact shade of twilight in September—was dark enough to convey somber sensibility. And yet there was a hint of mystery. Of elemental feminine allure. As for the cut, by some sort of needle-and-thread magic it seemed to transform her tall and slender shape into something . . . less ordinary.

Her bare bones life had so few enchantments. Perhaps it wasn't wrong to secretly—secretly!— savor the thought of drawing a man's eye. Jeremy had naturally offered flowery compliments. But she had also caught the admiring glances from other men.

Repressing a shiver—and the sudden, unbidden thought of how Wrexford would react to seeing her dressed as a real lady—Charlotte smoothed a finger over the delicate tucking around the bodice and then shucked off her wrapper.

Contrary to folk wisdom, it *was* possible to make a silk purse out of a sow's ear, she thought wryly as she slipped the gown over her head and did up the fastenings.

A twirl in front of the full-length cheval glass confirmed that Madame Franchot—nee Franzenelli—truly possessed bewitching powers.

Trying not to feel like a charlatan, she took a seat at her dressing table, and reached for her brush and pins.

"Let us hope the spell works on Wrexford's servant," she whispered, once she had finished arranging her hair. Taking up the pert little chip-straw bonnet that the modiste had made to accompany the dress, Charlotte carefully looped the ribbons into a neat bow.

The silk suddenly felt a little clammy, as if the breath from a ghost had sent a sigh tickling over her fingers. Charlotte steeled her spine.

No, the past was the past. It would not come back to haunt her.

Grabbing up her gloves and shawl, she hurried downstairs to wait for Wrexford's carriage. Despite her resolve to remain calm, the quickening thump of her heart echoed each passing minute.

Finally, the clatter of iron-rimmed wheels on the cobblestones roused her from brooding.

She rose, a spurt of panic shooting through her veins as the horses halted.

Steady, steady.

As Wrexford had promised, it was a nondescript vehicle, with no fancy footman or tiger clinging to the outside perch.

Nihil sibi metuunt. There is nothing to fear but fear itself. Drawing a deep breath, Charlotte took hold of the door latch and stepped outside.

"You're a hard man to find, Griffin." Having had no luck in tracking down the Runner the previous evening, Wrexford finally caught up with him at an out-of-the-way tavern in St. Giles. "It wasn't so long ago when I couldn't take a step without tripping over your boots."

"That was when I wanted your head on a platter. Now, thanks to you and your penchant for finding dead bodies, I have another murder to solve." Griffin polished off the last morsel of his cheese and pickle, then pushed away the empty plate. "Have you got something for me—other than a wedge of apple pie and another tankard of ale?"

"One would think you'd starve if you didn't know me." After calling the order to a barmaid, the earl took a seat at the small table. 'The answer is yes—I have something meaty for you."

Griffin waited until his pie and ale arrived before murmuring, "I'm listening."

"I think Hollis and the radicals may not be solely responsible for Ashton's murder," began Wrexford. The Runner was not yet aware of Hollis's dying words or jumbled numbers found in the desk, a fact he quickly rectified. He did, however, hold back the mention of Nevins. He had not yet managed to track down Henning, and until he spoke with the surgeon, he wasn't going to send the authorities sniffing around his clinic.

Griffin fixed him with a baleful look. "You didn't think I should have known that right away?"

Wrexford shrugged. While he and the Runner had an unspoken truce, it was a wary one. "As I said, you're a hard man to find."

"Hmmph."

"There are too many possible—and powerful—motives that haven't been fully explored," pressed the earl. "Think about it, Griffin. Why would the radicals leave their symbol on the body? Given the government's fears of labor unrest, they would know it would be inviting the military to hunt them down like vermin."

"You're assuming they think rationally," pointed out the Runner.

"It feels too simple," insisted Wrexford. "I think we need to keep looking at whether one of Ashton's investors was involved in the murder. Or perhaps a member of his household." A pause. "Ashton's assistant continues to avoid meeting with me to discuss the case."

Forking up a bite of pie, Griffin chewed thoughtfully before replying. Ignoring the earl's suggestion, he focused on the facts. "Any luck in deciphering the numbers? That's assuming the paper isn't a child's mindless scribbles from years ago. As you pointed out, there's no proof it was left by Hollis."

"No, I've not yet made any sense of it. But as I said, intuition tells me that along with tracking down radicals you should look more closely at the people around Ashton. The motive of the patent is too powerful to ignore. After all, money is usually at the root of all evil."

"Have you any—*any*—proof of that?"

Damnation. The fellow was like a bulldog, who needed a bone between his teeth before he could chew. "For God's sake, use your imagination."

"My superiors don't pay me to commune with the realm of fantasy, milord." Griffin set his fork down. "The government is extremely concerned about the prospect of workers rioting and mayhem breaking out across the country. There's not a snowball's chance in hell they will allow me to break off my hunt for the radical leaders on a mere hunch. Even from you."

Wrexford swore under his breath.

"Find me some actual evidence of your theory," went on the Runner. "Otherwise you're on your own." He took a long draught of ale. "But do have a care. I should miss the pleasure of your company, milord."

Wrexford rose with a grunt. "And that of my purse."

"Good day, madam." The coachman hopped down from his perch and opened the carriage door.

Charlotte climbed inside, thankful that the small

glass-paned windows let in little light. Shadows would help hide her masquerade.

After settling herself in a swoosh of skirts, she dared to look up at the facing seat.

"His Lordship sends his regards, Mrs. Sloane, and trusts that my company will prove satisfactory."

The throaty voice, edged with a sharp Scottish burr, took her by surprise. She had expected a young tweenie and kitchen maid, not . . .

"I've been told you prefer plain speaking," said the woman who sat facing her. "So allow me to assure you that I'm not easily rattled, nor do I have a tongue that's prone to wagging." A pause. "I'm good at keeping secrets."

"Plain speaking, indeed," murmured Charlotte. She took a moment to assess her companion. A thin, angular face, beaky nose, and bony body—the woman, well past the first bloom of youth, would never be called a beauty, but the glint of lively intelligence in her eyes cut through the gloom.

The tightness in Charlotte's chest slowly released in a silent exhale.

A faint smile played on the other women's lips. "Aye, I ain't much to look at, but His Lordship says you need someone trustworthy, and he knows I can be counted on to keep my mummer shut."

"I'm rather afraid to ask what he's told you

about me," replied Charlotte dryly. "I'm not intending to commit murder or steal the Duchess of Devonshire's jewels."

The smile stretched a little wider. "What a pity. Life has been a little flat lately. An adventure would be welcome." The woman shifted against the squabs. "I'm McClellan."

Charlotte reminded herself that a lady's maid was always called by her last name. "I'm grateful for your assistance, McClellan." On impulse, she held out her hand. "I'll try not to cause you too much trouble."

McClellan responded with a firm shake. "A wee bit of trouble keeps life interesting, Mrs. Sloane."

They rode on for a few minutes in silence as Charlotte sought to sort out her thoughts. Wrexford had a knack of keeping her off-balance . . .

The why of which was a conundrum in and of itself.

A frown pinched her brow. It was maddening to have to keep swallowing her pride. But honesty compelled her to admit that in this case, his unpredictability was most welcome.

McClellan, noted Charlotte, seemed unperturbed by the silence. Another mark in the woman's favor. A chattering fibberwidget would have driven her to distraction.

Her reflections were cut short as the carriage turned down Piccadilly Street. The driver drew to a halt at the entrance to Green Park, and Charlotte soon found herself strolling along the graveled walkway, the very picture of a prim and proper lady, with her maid trailing behind at a discreet distance.

Oh, how looks can be deceiving.

The irony was rather amusing. It was, after all, at the heart of how she made her living.

"Mrs. Sloane." Jeremy was waiting at the appointed spot. "You are looking quite lovely," he said gallantly.

"Save your Spanish coin, Jem. Its glitter doesn't fool me," she murmured.

He chuckled. "You wound me to suggest my compliments are false gold."

"You'll survive."

Seeing his quizzical glance at McClellan, who was standing at the requisite distance required of a servant, Charlotte explained, "I *do* know the rules of Polite Society. However idiotic they are, I must comply if I wish to mingle with the beau monde. McClellan has agreed to play the role of lady's maid for the afternoon."

"How—" began Jeremy.

"I asked a favor," she answered curtly.

He looked about to press the point, then seemed to think better of it. Instead, he merely tipped his hat politely at McClellan before offering Charlotte his arm. "Come, let us observe the maids milking the cows." The park was well-known for the rustic sight of dairy cattle grazing on the lawns. "Miss Merton and Mr. Hillhouse will meet us there by the serving shed."

Charlotte was curious to meet the pair. She wondered whether Wrexford's interview with Ashton's assistant had fared any better than the one with his secretary. Given her own experience with his interrogation techniques, she rather doubted it.

"You say you've known Mr. Hillhouse for some time?" she asked, turning her attention to Jeremy.

"Yes. We were both scholarship students at Oxford. It was a bond of sorts—unlike the fancy swells, we had little blunt for carousing," he answered. "But it turned out we both enjoyed each other's company." A wry grimace tugged at his lips. "His interest in mathematics and science was beyond me, however we shared similar tastes in reading, and spent many an hour discussing art and philosophy."

Radical philosophy? wondered Charlotte. It wouldn't be surprising, given they were intelligent young men without a groat in their pockets. She left the question unsaid. She knew the depths of Jeremy's loyalty. He would curl up tight as a wary hedgehog if he thought she was digging for dirt on his friend.

"Mr. Hillhouse sounds like a very interesting fellow."

The question is whether he is also a very dangerous one.

"That he is," replied Jeremy as he cut around a pair of laughing boys playing catch with a cricket ball.

A breeze ruffled through the air, stirring the sun-warmed scent of grass. Charlotte inhaled deeply, savoring its sweetness. She must think about bringing the boys here, and treating them to a glass of fresh milk. Hawk, who had a love for animals, would be in alt—

"Lord Sterling!" The sudden hail from behind them sounded a bit breathless.

Charlotte glanced around to see a young woman hurrying in their direction. She looked to be alone.

"Miss Merton," began Jeremy. But his welcoming smile quickly faded on seeing her expression. "Is something amiss?"

"No . . . Yes!" Octavia Merton came to an awkward halt.

Whether her face was red from rushing or from embarrassment at making such a dramatic entrance was impossible for Charlotte to tell.

"W-What I mean is," added Octavia in a rush, "I fear something has gone dreadfully wrong."

Jeremy stiffened. "Take a moment to catch your breath, and then tell me why."

Octavia gulped in a lungful of air and let it out in a low *whoosh*. "Benedict has gone missing."

Chapter 14

"Gone *missing?*" repeated Jeremy, his voice pinching to a sharp edge.

Aware that they were beginning to draw curious stares, Charlotte gave him a small nudge. "Let us walk," she whispered.

"Right." Mastering his emotions, he forced a smile and quickly offered Octavia his other arm. "Come, this way."

To her credit, Ashton's secretary obeyed without argument.

Setting a deliberately leisurely pace, Jeremy guided them down a path that led to a copse of trees. A breeze ruffled through the leaves overhead, casting a flutter of shadows over their faces. His steps turned even slower as the path curved deeper into the greenery, and after a careful glance around, he finally spoke.

"Now, please explain yourself, Miss Merton."

"Benedict never returned from the toolmaker's shop yesterday," replied Octavia. Her earlier agitation was gone, replaced by a taut control. "He was supposed to meet with Lord Wrexford, so at first I assumed he didn't want—" She cut off abruptly and shot a wary glance at Charlotte.

Jeremy drew in a measured breath. "Mrs. Sloane is an old and trusted friend. You may speak freely."

But the tiny hint of hesitation made Charlotte wonder whether he truly believed that. He had always supported her decision to take up A. J. Quill's pen, but she knew a part of him didn't understand it.

Gravel crunched beneath their feet as they kept walking.

"At first I assumed he didn't wish to meet with the earl," explained Octavia. "But now I fear something has happened to him."

Jeremy frowned in thought. "Perhaps he simply stopped by a tavern and . . . well, it would be understandable if he sought some solace from the shock of Ashton's death."

Octavia made a rude sound. "Benedict would *never* have left me in the lurch. Not with all the suspicions of—"

She shot another glance at Charlotte, but Jeremy seemed too preoccupied to notice.

"God in heavens, what do you mean?" he demanded.

"I know the newspapers have called Eli's death the tragic result of a random attack by footpads." Octavia lowered her voice to a whisper. "But in truth, there's compelling evidence that it *wasn't* random. And I imagine you can guess why."

"Say no more," said Jeremy, darting a look around. "I think we should return to your town-house, where we can discuss this in complete privacy."

The shadows couldn't hide the flare of anger that lit Octavia's eyes. "Privacy—ha! There always seems to be one of Mrs. Ashton's servants lurking in the corridors, spying on us. And Benedict is quite certain our study has been searched."

"For what?" asked Jeremy with a tightness Charlotte had never heard before in his voice.

Octavia didn't answer.

Ye god. Charlotte wondered what Wrexford would make of the accusation. Assuming, of course, that Octavia wasn't lying. The woman was, after all, a suspect . . .

And then, all at once, Wrexford's ugly suggestion, reared up in her head. So, he had said, was Jeremy.

No. She thrust the idea away. It was unthinkable. She knew her friend too well.

"You think Mrs. Ashton is looking—" began Jeremy, but Charlotte quickly interrupted him.

"Lord Sterling was right to suggest a return to your townhouse, Miss Merton. It's dangerous to discuss such private matters in public." Like Jeremy, she glanced around. McClellan, who had dutifully trailed along behind them, seemed to have sensed the tension in the air. She, too, was surveying the surroundings.

"Words have a way of being overheard," finished Charlotte. Though they seemed safe enough, she knew that dangers were often unseen.

"We'll find a hackney on Piccadilly Street," said Jeremy. And yet he seemed loath to make a move.

"No need. My carriage is waiting there," replied Charlotte. Ignoring his look of surprise, she tugged at his arm. "Come, let us not linger."

The ride back to the Grosvenor Square passed in uneasy silence. Perhaps regretful of her earlier outburst, Octavia had withdrawn into herself. Her face gave no hint of her inner emotions. And while eyes were said to be the windows to the soul, hers were veiled by the thick fringe of her lashes.

Charlotte considered herself a good judge of people, but Ashton's secretary was proving devilishly difficult to decipher. Octavia seemed a strange mix of fire and ice. Her earlier agitation had seemed genuine. But as Wrexford had pointed out, the two recent murders appeared to have been planned with meticulous cunning. Whoever possessed such cold-blooded ruthlessness was likely very good at deception.

Lies and distraction. Smoke and sleight of hand.

As they entered the townhouse, the butler appeared in the main hallway and cleared his throat. "Miss Merton, Mrs. Ashton left word that you were to join her in the drawing room as soon as you returned."

"I shall do so," replied Octavia. "As soon as

I escort my guests to my study and order them some tea."

The man looked unhappy at the answer, but grudgingly stepped aside to let them pass.

"Might my maid wait for me in the kitchen?" asked Charlotte, knowing it was a perfectly proper request to make. Servants tended to gossip about the goings-on in a house, and McClellan struck her as someone who would keep her eyes and ears open.

"But of course, madam." He gestured to her maid. "Follow me."

Octavia checked up and down the corridor before shutting the study door and turning to face them. "Please don't think me a flighty peagoose. I assure you, I've never been accused of having an overactive imagination." She made a face. "Quite the opposite, in fact."

"Benedict has nothing but the highest praise for your intellect and steady good sense," responded Jeremy.

Nonetheless, Charlotte could see something was troubling him. She, too, was finding the sudden turn of events difficult to swallow. Murder, cryptic clues, and now the disappearance of a possible suspect—it was sounding more and more like one of Mrs. Radcliffe's horrid novels.

Octavia didn't miss the shade of doubt in his voice. "Lord Sterling, I don't blame you for wondering whether I'm spinning a Banbury tale. But I can explain." She let out a harried sigh. "I know Benedict considers you a man who can be trusted with any secret . . ."

Jeremy paled.

"So I feel I can—nay, I *must*—trust you. There's evil at play here, and I suspect . . ." She hesitated. "Might I ask you to accompany me to the back parlor, where we may talk in private, sir?"

Charlotte watched as Octavia's gaze shifted to her. "Forgive my rudeness, Mrs.—" A grimace. "I'm sorry. I don't even recall your name."

"Sloane," she said softly. "And it's entirely understandable that you don't wish to confide such life-and-death matters to a total stranger." She allowed a thin smile. "I wouldn't either."

"Thank you." Octavia turned to Jeremy. "Sir?"

Grim-faced, he nodded, but as he moved by her, Charlotte saw it was not just worry that pinched his features.

It was fear.

The door shut with a doleful thump, leaving the room quiet as a crypt.

You were right not to trust me, Miss Merton, thought Charlotte as she quickly moved to the desk and skimmed over the papers lying atop the blotter. Seeing nothing of interest, she made a check of the drawers. It was too risky to start poking through the contents now, but if anything

225

looked promising, she could make a clandestine visit during the night.

However, as she suspected from Octavia's comment about the room having been searched, nothing caught her eye. It had, however, been worth a try.

No matter how clever we think we are, we all make mistakes.

Once again, Wrexford's unsettling words about secrets within secrets stirred like a serpent, sending a shiver slithering down her spine.

Charlotte shook off the sensation. Looking up, she spotted a large Majolica figurine on the far side table, half-hidden between two stacks of books. A specialty of the Tuscan region of Italy, the colorful piece of rustic pottery stirred a sudden sharp pang of nostalgia. It was silly—the gaily-painted rooster had an almost comic naiveté to it. And yet, her breath seemed to stick in her lungs.

How absurd. She should be feeling the urge to laugh, not cry.

Against her better judgment, Charlotte crossed the carpet and with great care picked it up. The weighty heft, the smooth glaze, the pure hues—everything was achingly familiar, right down to the last detail of the beaky smile.

Her late husband had bought a similar figurine on a trip they had made to Florence during the first year of their time in Rome. It had been far too expensive for their paltry purse, but he had insisted on getting it in celebration of her birthday A talisman to the good times and good fortune ahead, he had said. It had sat on their kitchen table, a spot of brightness as the shadows of poverty had slowly squeezed the optimism from Anthony's spirit.

Though she had packed it carefully, the rooster had somehow been smashed to flinders on the journey back to England.

A talisman, indeed.

"Miss Merton." The door clicked open after a perfunctory knock. "Might I have a word with you."

Jarred from her reveries, Charlotte nearly dropped the piece as she spun around.

"*Now,* if you please," added the slender woman who stood framed in the doorway.

"I'm sorry but Miss Merton and Lord Sterling stepped out for a moment." The woman started as Charlotte moved into the ring of light cast by the table lamp. "I apologize for the shock of finding an utter stranger in your house." Charlotte went on, having no doubt that she was speaking to Elihu Ashton's widow. "It was terribly impolite to intrude upon you without a formal introduction. I'm Mrs. Sloane, a friend of Lord Sterling. We met Miss Merton in Green Park, and came back here for . . . tea."

Mourning did not flatter most women, but

somehow the unremitting black only accentuated the woman's delicate beauty. Silhouetted against the dimly lit corridor, her pale, porcelain-perfect face drew the eye, much like a moth to a flame.

"It is I who should be apologizing, Mrs. Sloane. I had not realized Miss Merton had guests," replied Isobel. The dark silk rustled, stirring shadows on shadows. "Please, let us not stand on formalities. I am Mrs. Ashton."

A graceful speech, quickly followed by a smile. And yet, there was no warmth to it.

Realizing the rooster was still in her hands, Charlotte flushed, feeling like a guilty schoolgirl. "I know it's horribly rag-mannered of me to be poking around in another person's possessions, but this reminded me of a piece my late husband and I acquired in Italy." It was manipulative, perhaps, to hint at her own widowhood. But maybe she could turn this initial awkwardness to her advantage.

The chill melted ever so slightly from Isobel's lips. "It brings back fond memories?"

"Yes. But alas, ours was destroyed during the voyage back to England." Charlotte set it back on the table. "Again, I apologize for my bad manners."

A throaty laugh. "I, too, am a guest in this house, so be assured you've caused no offense. Most of the possessions you see don't belong to me either."

The widow had a unique vitality that most

people would find appealing, thought Charlotte, seeing a spark come to life in the other woman's eyes. Most especially men. Strange that Wrexford hadn't made mention of it. He was usually perceptive about such things and quick to comment on them.

"But as it so happens, that rooster did travel here with us," continued Isobel. "It was given to my husband as a jest by some friends. Like an owl, he tended to work in the dark of night, so he was not an early riser."

Charlotte smiled politely.

"He found it highly amusing, though I'm surprised he brought it along on this trip." The widow regarded it for a long moment. "I can't say that I see its charms."

"It has no intrinsic artistic value," agreed Charlotte. "One would have to feel a sentimental attachment to see any worth in it."

"I don't claim to have an eye for art of any kind. I prefer music to paintings." As the sound of approaching footsteps echoed in the corridor, Isobel shifted and then suddenly moved to the table and took up the figurine. "Please, I'd like for you to have it."

"Oh, no, I couldn't," protested Charlotte, taken aback by the unexpected offer.

"You would actually be doing me a great favor," responded the widow. "It would save the trouble of transporting it back to Leeds."

Before Charlotte could reply, Octavia hurried into the room, followed closely by Jeremy.

"Oh, you need not have troubled yourself to come to me, Mrs. Ashton," Octavia exclaimed. The words belied the daggers in her eyes. "I was just seeing to having tea served to Lord Sterling and Mrs. Sloane before responding to your summons."

Isobel eyed Jeremy, her expression inscrutable. "How kind of you to stop by, Lord Sterling."

Charlotte realized that of course they must know each other.

"I'm so glad to have the chance to express my condolences in person, Mrs. Ashton," he answered smoothly, as if he hadn't heard the hint of friction in her voice. "It is a great loss for you, and for all of us who considered your husband a friend."

"Thank you." A pause as her gaze took on a speculative gleam.

Jeremy often drew such looks from women, thought Charlotte. But this one seemed strangely impersonal.

"Elihu enjoyed your company, and your intellectual curiosity," went on Isobel. "Most of his investors are not particularly interested in his ideas, merely what they produce."

Was that an edge of bitterness, wondered Charlotte. Or some other emotion?

Jeremy acknowledged her words with a small nod. "That's very kind of you to say."

The Majolica rooster suddenly felt heavy as lead in Charlotte's hands. The air of perfect politeness wasn't fooling anyone. Beneath it crackled a current of tension.

Octavia's eye was drawn to the flutter of color. "Ah, I see you've found Eli's pet."

The widow stiffened at the use of her husband's name.

"He was very fond of that silly bird," added Octavia.

"It seems Mrs. Sloane had a sentimental attachment to a similar one from her past," replied Isobel. A pause, made with an actress's instinct for effect. "So I've made it a gift to her. I know Elihu would be delighted that it will bring pleasure to someone who'll appreciate it, now that he's gone."

The color drained from Octavia's face. "But . . ."

"But what?" asked Isobel softly. *Steel within silk*. Her looks might deceive a great many people, but Charlotte wasn't fooled. Beneath the widow's fragile femininity, she sensed there was a will that would break before it would ever bend.

Octavia bit her bloodless lip.

"If Miss Merton would take comfort in having it as a token—" began Charlotte.

"She has a great many mementos of my husband, if indeed such things have any sentimental meaning to her," said Isobel firmly. "However, I doubt that is the case. Miss Merton has said on numerous occasions that she prides herself on being ruled by reason and practicality, not emotion." A glance at Octavia. "Isn't that so?"

"Yes." The whisper had no breath behind it.

"So you see, Mrs. Sloane, the matter is settled. It gives me great pleasure to know the piece of pottery will have an appreciative home."

Charlotte had no choice. To refuse the gift would appear unforgivably churlish. "That's exceedingly generous of you."

"Not at all," replied the widow frankly. "True generosity is when you part from something that has value to you."

Charlotte sensed her mettle was being tested. "Then call it charitable. An act of kindness to a stranger."

Amusement touched Isobel's lips. "I would have suggested pragmatic. As I said, it saves me the worry of transporting a fragile object— and the guilt of breaking something which Elihu enjoyed."

"Pragmatism," murmured Charlotte, "is, to my mind, a worthy trait." Especially for a woman.

"Indeed." The windows rattled as a rising gust slapped against the diamond-shaped pane. A spattering of raindrops ricocheted against the glass. Octavia started, but the widow didn't flinch.

Isobel Ashton, decided Charlotte, would be a formidable enemy.

The shadows deepened and darkened within the room. A rattling suddenly sounded in the corridor as well, along with tentative footsteps. Looking uncertain, the young maid carrying the heavily-laden tea tray hesitated upon entering the room.

"Do come in," said Isobel. "And please light the other lamps for our guests."

"I think it might be better if we put off tea to another time," suggested Jeremy. "I sense we've come at an inconvenient time."

"No," exclaimed Octavia. Her chin rose in challenge. "That is, there's no need for you to go. If Mrs. Ashton has something she wishes to discuss with me, I'm perfectly happy to do so now."

Isobel coolly ignored the protest. "Thank you, Lord Sterling. I appreciate your understanding. Another time would be best." To Octavia, she said, "I wish to speak with you about Mr. Hillhouse and his whereabouts. I was obliged for the second time to inform Lord Wrexford that he was not here."

"There's no need for you to see us out," murmured Jeremy. "The maid will do so."

Charlotte shifted her gift and accepted his arm. As they turned to go, she couldn't help but notice that Octavia had slumped back against the bookshelves. Although her hands were fisted in her skirts, they seemed to be shaking. And her face looked like death warmed over.

Chapter 15

As soon as they reached the street, McClellan trailing behind them with the majolica rooster cradled in her arms, Charlotte tightened her grip on Jeremy's arm and turned away from the waiting carriage. "Let us take a walk around the square, before the driver takes me home."

He looked unhappy about the request, but surrendered with a sigh.

"I've really nothing more to report from my private time with Miss Merton," he murmured, once they had crossed to the central garden and passed through the wrought iron gates. "Benedict didn't return home last night, and aside from expressing anxiety, she had no specific reason as to why."

"But it does seem ominous, doesn't it?" pressed Charlotte.

Jeremy lifted his shoulders in sudden exasperation. "The devil take it, Charley—I don't know! Grief grabs people in different ways. Perhaps he's drunk himself into a blind stupor, or perhaps he's sought solace in the bed of some willing wench."

He quickened his pace, sending a spray of pebbles skittering into the grass. "I'm not sure there's any need to panic."

"But Miss Merton seems awfully alarmed,"

pressed Charlotte. "And she knows him very well."

"Not," replied Jeremy through clenched teeth, "as well as I do."

Charlotte stole a sidelong glance at his profile and felt a frisson of alarm. After darting an involuntary look behind her, she demanded, "What is it you're not telling me?"

"Bloody hell—don't badger me!"

She stumbled and nearly lost her footing. Never in all their years of friendship had Jeremy sworn at her.

He caught her arm and steadied her steps. "Dear God, forgive me." Remorse tightened his voice to a hoarse whisper. "It's just that some secrets should stay hidden."

Dread clenched in her belly, turning her insides to ice.

Sensing her reaction, he blew out a harried breath. "It's nothing to do with me, or my sordid secret, if that is what's worrying you."

How can I not be worried—nay, how can I not be terrified?

They walked on in uneasy silence. She dared not press him. Their friendship—now hanging by a fragile thread, she feared—was worth more than the information.

Let Wrexford wield the spade if he wished to dig for the truth.

"I'm not angry with you," Jeremy finally murmured, forcing a ghost of a smile. "I'm angry at the twist of Fate that will unfairly resurrect the past and perhaps send Benedict to the gallows."

Charlotte kept her gaze locked straight ahead. It was up to him to decide how much to confide.

"I know as well as you do that long-buried secrets have a way of coming back to life," he explained. "Given the publicity around Ashton's death, it's inevitable that someone will speak up." He swallowed hard. "Benedict made a terrible mistake in his youth . . ."

Crunch, crunch. The sound of their steps on the gravel seemed to echo the ragged thumping of her heart.

"Like me, he hadn't a feather to fly with at university. It's difficult to be poor, scrabbling for the bare necessities while your peers have bagfuls of blunt for the pursuit of idle pleasures."

Still she remained silent.

Jeremy released a sigh, which was quickly swallowed in the soft swishing of the leaves stirring in the breeze.

"He desperately needed textbooks for his chemistry studies. Expensive ones. So late one night, when he saw one of our wealthy friends in the throes of drink stop in one of the narrow lanes and remove his overcoat in order to take a piss . . ."

Charlotte could well imagine the scene. *Drunken laughter. Hide-and-seek moonlight. A moment of temptation.*

236

"Benedict wasn't thinking straight. He'd just come from the room of a fellow student, who had plied him with ale," went on Jeremy. "On impulse, he rushed in to riffle the pockets and found the man's purse. It took only a moment, but unfortunately he was recognized by two other students as he turned and fled with the money. They gave chase and caught him."

The path forced them to circle back toward the gate.

"Luckily, I heard about the incident right away, and as I had several influential friends willing to help me, I was able to convince the victim not to press charges," said Jeremy, rushing his words. "I also arranged a small loan for Benedict, enough to purchase the books. He finished his studies and left Cambridge several months after the incident."

Oh, Jeremy. A loyal and stalwart friend, no matter how ugly things appeared.

"I know how remorseful Benedict was about his mistake," added Jeremy. "He was desperate to get his education and do some good in the world with his scientific gifts." A pause. "He would never—*never*—have betrayed Ashton's trust in him."

Her friend had the gift of seeing the best in people. As he had with her. Charlotte only hoped that in this case he hadn't let the wool be pulled over his eyes.

"Did Mr. Ashton know of this incident?" asked

Charlotte. Recalling Octavia's frightened face, she added, "And does Miss Merton?"

"I *know* Benedict, and I can't imagine that he didn't tell them. Despite what I just told you, he is honest to a fault." His eyes closed, but not quite quickly enough to hide a ripple of doubt. "But I don't know for sure."

Good Lord, what a coil.

"I think it wise for you to find out," counseled Charlotte.

He nodded bleakly.

She didn't have the heart to add that it would also be wise for him to consider that his friend might well be guilty. For all his worldly wisdom, Jeremy's heart was achingly vulnerable. While she had long ago made peace with life's disillusionments.

Or have I? Charlotte dared not look at him.

"By the by," he said a moment later. "Miss Merton was quite upset about her rudeness to you. She intends to send an apology."

"Her discretion was laudable," murmured Charlotte. "One can't be too careful."

The remark didn't lighten his mood.

They waited at the gate for McClellan to catch up with them, and as soon as she did, Jeremy wasted no time in escorting Charlotte to the waiting carriage.

"I shall walk back to my residence," he murmured, handing her up the steps."

"I will help in any way I can," she replied softly.

The angle of his hat hid his face. "I'm not sure what any of us can do."

She hated hearing him sound so defeated. "Come, it's not like you to sound so Friday-faced," she chided. "If Mr. Hillhouse is innocent, we will prove him so."

That drew a grudging smile. "Or God help the devil who stands in your way."

"Yes, well, I've made it my mission in life to cut devils down to size." She squeezed his hand. "*Semper fortis.*" *Always brave.*

"*Semper fortis,*" he repeated. "Would that I had your innate courage."

As soon as she took her seat facing McClellan, Jeremy closed the door and called for the driver to be off. The whip cracked and the carriage lurched forward, joining the cacophony of wheels and iron-shod hooves clattering along the busy street.

Charlotte sank back against the squabs, and pressed her fingertips to her temples, trying to compose her thoughts. Worry for her friend set her blood to throbbing. She could feel the slow, rhythmic pulse of heat begin to burn through the thin kidskin gloves. The facts so far certainly seemed to cast a grim shadow of suspicion over Benedict Hillhouse. His disappearance, coming on the heels of another murder, roused all sorts of questions. Including ones about the motive of her dear friend.

She couldn't help recalling Octavia's first outburst—*I fear something has gone dreadfully wrong.* It seemed a strange phrasing, one that could imply a plan had been in place.

Wrexford, she was sure, would pounce on that.

The taste of bile rose up in her throat.

A jolt of the wheels caused her foot bump against McClellan's sturdy half boot. Reminded that she wasn't alone, Charlotte hastily looked up. The maid was staring out the windowpanes with an aura of unruffled calm that helped soothe her own inner turmoil.

"Thank you, McClellan," she murmured.

The maid turned, and once again Charlotte was struck by the bright intelligence in her mouse-brown eyes.

"For adding the duties of farmhand to your original assignment," she quickly added, indicating the majolica rooster nested firmly in McClellan's lap.

"Just as long as I'm not expected to pluck any feathers or prepare it for roasting. I'm all thumbs when it comes to kitchen work."

Somehow Charlotte doubted that. "I'm also grateful for you not peppering me with questions," she added truthfully.

A flicker of sunlight caught the twitch of the maid's lips. "It's not my job to do so, Mrs. Sloane."

Ah." She decided to test McClellan's sang froid. "But likely it's your job to answer them, if your employer decides to ask."

"I doubt that His Lordship would," replied the maid.

An astute answer. "But if he did?"

"Then I should recount what I have seen. Which has been mostly the backsides of three well-dressed gentry morts out for an afternoon stroll."

Charlotte couldn't hold back a laugh. "I trust Lord Sterling's posterior helped keep boredom at bay."

"He's a very fine-looking man," agreed McClellan with a straight face. "Well-fitting boots. They look to have been fashioned by Hoby."

"No doubt," said Charlotte dryly. Jeremy *did* have long, shapely legs. "He has exquisite taste in clothes. So I imagine he would choose only the best."

They shared a quick smile.

"As for what you've heard . . ." Charlotte smoothed at her skirts. "Might I ask what sort of talk was going on in the kitchen?"

McClellan took her time in answering. "The recent murder of their houseguest has things in a humble-jumble downstairs. The servants are all aware that there's bad blood between Mr. Ashton's widow and his two assistants. And

241

it seems that one of them—a Mr. Hillhouse—stayed out all night, and has not yet been seen."

"Did they speculate as to why?" asked Charlotte.

"The maids think him a very handsome fellow, and wouldn't be surprised if he was tempted to take advantage of the pleasures London has to offer," replied the maid. "Though one of the tweenies was of the opinion that he and Miss Merton are thick as thieves."

Charlotte straightened. "Indeed?" That was interesting to know.

"Aye. There was also a lot of grumbling about how the master of the house, though rich as Croesus, is a nipcheese when it comes to food and wages."

"I suppose that is how the wealthy stay wealthy," she murmured.

Amusement danced in McClellan's eyes. "I wish I knew."

Charlotte saw that they were turning into her street. "Thank you for your help," she said as she slid forward on her seat. "And your company."

"I should be thanking you, madam. I escaped an afternoon of helping the housekeeper polish the silver."

"A waste of your talents," murmured Charlotte.

"From your lips to God's ear." The maid held out the rooster. "Here, you'll not want to be forgetting this."

In truth, she had mixed feelings about living with a memory resurrected from the past. But too late for that now, conceded Charlotte as her palms cradled the figurine's smooth weight.

Unless it happened to slip through her fingers and smash on the pavement.

A foul thought. The bird deserved a better fate.

The coachman hopped down from his perch and opened the carriage door.

Grasping her gift tightly, she carefully descended the iron steps. "Please tell His Lordship that I'll be sending him a note about the afternoon shortly."

"Very good, Mrs. Sloane."

Once inside her house, Charlotte cocked an ear for any sign that Raven and Hawk had returned. For a long moment, she feared she was alone, which was not a good omen on how the lessons had gone. However, a reassuring clatter from above—Hawk took great delight in polishing the swords to a looking-glass brightness—told her they were up in their aerie.

But first things first. The dratted rooster was too fragile for boyish exuberance. Expelling a sigh, she turned into the parlor. For now, its loud colors would add a touch of whimsy to the quiet respectability of the furnishings.

"Like me, you are a square peg trying to fit in a round hole," she murmured, placing it on the side table near the windows. Sunlight shimmered through the glass panes as the clouds shifted, warming the reds and cobalts to an even brighter blaze.

"Quite right—to the Devil with trying to conform to the dictates of good taste." Charlotte tugged off her gloves and touched a finger to the beaky smile before turning and heading for the stairs.

The aerie door was open and a glance inside showed Raven was curled on his bed, engrossed in reading a book. Hawk had propped the swords up against the wall between the windows and was busy arranging a regiment of lead soldiers that Jeremy had left in the wooden storage trunks.

She knocked softly on the casement to catch their attention. "How did the lessons go?"

"Oiy!" Hawk scrambled to his feet, knocking his troops to flinders. "Mr. Linsley is a great gun! We're going te study lots of wery interesting things, and we practiced our penmanship." He hurried to his desk and fetched a piece of ruled foolscap for her to see. "Look!"

"Very handsome, indeed!"

"I'll soon be able te help ye letter in yer drawings."

"I daresay you'll soon be creating your own satires," she replied with a smile. Hawk had a lovely imagination, and she had already noted his skill with a pencil. "Art is a very gentlemanly pursuit."

Raven made a rude sound.

"A talent for sketching is much admired," she assured his brother before shifting her gaze back to Raven. His nose was still buried in the book, which she hoped was a good sign.

"And how did you find Mr. Linsley?" she asked him.

"He likes mathematics," came the reply. "And says numbers can be used to understand all sorts of interesting things—like how far a cannonball can fly and how ships can navigate by calculating the angle of the sun."

"He gave Raven a book about numbers," said Hawk.

"And you are enjoying it?" she asked.

"Yeah." Raven finally looked up. "I am."

Charlotte smiled, just enough to look pleased, but not interfering.

"Well, then, I won't disturb your reading any longer." She moved to the door. "But after supper might I ask you to run an errand for me? I need to send Lord Wrexford a note and it's important he receives it this evening."

"O' course." Raven's eyes sharpened. "Book learning ain't gonna turn us soft."

"Isn't," she corrected. "You may stay tough as hobnails, and still speak like a proper gentleman."

"Please tell me you've made some progress with the murders." Sheffield entered the earl's work room and slouched into one of the armchairs with a disgruntled huff. "I'm bored. And as my pockets are to let, I've no way of entertaining myself."

"Take up a hobby." Wrexford looked up from trying to make any sense of the jumbled numbers he had found at Hollis's quarters. Frustration had his temper on edge. He had still not managed to track down Henning, which along with Hillhouse's absence, had him feeling that he was simply spinning in circles.

"Reading, perhaps?" he added sarcastically. "The laws of probability would make an excellent subject to study."

"Oh, please." Sheffield gave a theatrical wince. "I'm trying to relieve the ache in my head, not slam a spike through my skull." After crossing his legs and staring moodily at the tips of his boots, he added, "Is there really nothing?"

Wrexford set aside his pen. "Nothing overly useful. The assistant, Hillhouse, contrived to be absent from our arranged interview, so I've yet to have a word with him. However, Mrs. Sloane was engaged to meet with both him and Miss Merton earlier this afternoon. So perhaps she will have learned something meaningful." Though in truth, he was beginning to fear that the case was tangled in so many knots that it might never be unraveled.

Sheffield straightened. "I swear, there are times

when her powers to conjure information out of thin air is rather frightening. How the devil did she bring about that connection?"

"In this case, the answer is far more mundane than magic. They have a mutual friend, who has arranged the meeting."

"*Who?*"

"A friend from her youth, who apparently attended university with Hillhouse."

"What sort of friend?" pressed Sheffield.

The question only exacerbated Wrexford's simmering frustration. "If you are so bloody curious, ask her yourself," he snapped. "Perhaps, for once, you'll get lucky."

As soon as the words were out of his mouth, he regretted them. "My apologies, Kit. That was a rotten thing to say."

"Aye, it was." Sheffield, however, didn't look offended. "But no less deserved. I make a mull of many things." He gave a wry grimace. "Though you have to admit, I do seem to have some skill in helping you ferret out dastardly villains."

"That you do." Wrexford was grateful for the show of good-humored camaraderie. For all his faults, Sheffield was a loyal friend. And he knew that his own mercurial moods were not easy to tolerate.

"I shall take that as permission to pour myself a glass of your excellent brandy," murmured Sheffield.

As he watched his friend saunter to the side-board, an idea occurred to him. A way not only to make amends, but also to pursue an idea that had slowly, unwillingly been taking shape in his head. "You know, now that you mention villains, perhaps there *is* something you can do to help."

Sheffield paused, decanter in hand.

"You recall the donkey's arse we encountered at the gaming hell—Kirkland?"

A nod.

"I thought nothing of it—a mere chance encounter—until I met him again at Mrs. Ashton's temporary residence here in London. It turns out he's the son of her late husband's primary investor." Wrexford went on to explain about the viscount's unexpected appearance, and the widow's reaction to his presence.

"It wouldn't surprise me if Kirkland is involved in something havey-cavey," said Sheffield, once the earl had finished. He set the brandy back on the tray. "Word is, he's become badly dipped lately and is desperate to find the funds to pay off his debts—not only his gambling vowels but also his loans from the cent-per-cent men."

"He's had dealings with moneylenders?" Wrexford frowned. A desperate sign, indeed. They charged exorbitant interest, up to one hundred percent on a loan, and failure to come up with the blunt at the appointed time had very unpleasant consequences. Unlike their clients, the cent-per-centers made no pretense of being gentlemen.

"And yet," he mused, "the viscount's father is extremely wealthy."

"Kirkland is extremely profligate with his money," answered Sheffield dryly. "I assumed he was being given unlimited funds for his carousing. But perhaps his pater has tired of refilling the coffers."

"One has to assume Kirkland knew about Ashton, and the success of his previous inventions," said the earl. "And if he was aware of the new project, he would likely know the value of a patent."

"The viscount isn't stupid, merely reckless," observed his friend. "And his father has become a very wealthy man through making savvy investments in business ventures. I seem to recall he's part-owner in a number of highly profitable coal mines in Wales."

"So, Kirkland, of all people, understands the potential of metal and steam to generate money," interjected Wrexford.

"Yes," said Sheffield, warming to the subject. "But even assuming he was clever enough to come up with a plot to steal Ashton's invention, it seems to me he would need to partner with someone who possessed technical expertise. Wouldn't it stir suspicions if he were to claim such an innovation on his own?"

A good point. But like a spider spinning and spinning, the conversation was starting to weave a tantalizing web of connections.

"It would," agreed Wrexford. "However, as Kirkland has grown up amidst talk of business dealings, he'd be aware of that." Steepling his fingers, he paused to think back on what he knew about some of the earlier steam engine patents. "Let's take a moment to follow this thread. Ashton's idea for financing his work wasn't new. There's a precedent for an inventor forming a partnership with investors in order to fund the actual manufacture of the machinery. The genius of James Watt and his innovation in steam power might never have seen the light of day had not he forged an alliance with Boulton, who had the money to make the concept a profitable reality. Watt and Boulton steam engines have dominated the mining and textile manufacturing industries for nearly half a century. A radically different model which offers a whole new level of performance would revolutionize production."

"And who could afford not to buy one?" said Sheffield, finishing the earl's thought.

"As we've said, the key to the plan is having someone who's knowledgeable in the technology, not only to be a credible applicant but also to build a working model that proves the idea is not just hot air." Wrexford paused. "And what more perfect person than Hillhouse?"

"Science is a popular topic of conversation these days," he went on. "The talk has sparked an awareness of how scientific discoveries will shape the future. If Kirkland could convince some rich acquaintances that he had a friend who had created a revolutionary new engine, it's reasonable to think he and Hillhouse could form a powerful, well-funded consortium. That in turn would allow him to cut more favorable terms with the cent-per-centers."

"All this assumes he wouldn't hesitate to cut his father out," said Sheffield.

Wrexford smiled grimly. "Rivalry between fathers and sons is as old as history."

"It all does seem to fit together rather nicely." Sheffield appeared equally willing to follow the thread of thought. "There might be people who smell a rat, but inventors tend to be secretive, and as Ashton never made his sketches public, it would be hard to accuse Hillhouse of having stolen the idea."

Wrexford rose and began to pace, mulling over the sudden shifting and reshaping of the puzzle's pieces. Was it true perception or was the lens distorted by wishful thinking?

"Speculation is all very well," he muttered. "But as a man of science, I know it's imperative to base conclusions on facts and empirical knowledge, not mere conjectures."

"Then I had better get to work and see what

facts I can learn about Kirkland," responded Sheffield.

His friend, noted the earl, hadn't touched a drop of brandy. As he had long suspected, Sheffield, if given a choice, seemed to find a cerebral challenge more intoxicating than idle dissipation.

"I'm grateful, Kit. Keep in mind that any information you can dig up on his relationship with the lovely widow would also be most helpful," he said. "And the sooner, the better, before we trip over any more dead bodies." As Shakespeare had so aptly observed, family tragedies had a penchant for being written in blood.

"*Cherchez la femme?*" quizzed his friend. "Mrs. Sloane might take umbrage on our assuming that there is always a woman lurking behind the evil of men."

"Mrs. Sloane reads the classical literature. I've seen the books on her desk—including the *Iliad*."

"It's your hubris she'll skewer, not mine, Wrex," replied Sheffield. "Thank God."

"She's welcome to prove me wrong. I'm quite willing to sacrifice my pride, as long as it's on the altar of Truth."

His friend raised an empty glass in a mock toast. "To *Veritas*."

Yes, to Truth, thought the earl. Whatever it might be.

Chapter 16

The note duly written and dispatched to the earl, Charlotte made herself enter her work room and take a seat at her desk. Of late, she had been woefully neglectful of her art. Ink and pigment had been shoved aside by the overwhelming demands of reality. The move, the murders, the worries about the boys adjusting to a new life.

Her own feelings were, she admitted, still a little topsy-turvy. Hidden away in the shadows of slums, she had a certain degree of simplicity to her life, allowing her to focus all her passions and ideas through her pen. Art and commentary were her voice.

Now things were infinitely more complicated. Anonymity had been a protective cloak. With each inch that she pushed back its concealing hood, she was making herself vulnerable.

Change entailed risk.

Charlotte shifted her gaze to her open sketchbook. She had only to look at the preliminary sketches for her *Man versus Machine* series of prints to see that.

Taking up her penknife, she set about preparing a fresh quill. Mr. Fores had actually proved to be surprisingly supportive of the serious subject. Though the prints didn't sell quite as well as the ones ridiculing the Royal family, he took satisfaction in the fact that nearly every government department and all the leading politicians were sending messengers to purchase copies of them. That his shop was seen as shaping public opinion was, to his canny mind, a worthwhile investment.

More than that, Charlotte was of the opinion that, at heart, Mr. Fores was a secret supporter of social reform.

The pen was now ready. There was nothing new she could—or would—say about Ashton's death. However, there were still myriad questions to explore about the revolution sweeping through manufacturing in England. What place did people have in a world where machines made their efforts obsolete? What lay ahead for those who toiled with their hands?

These were important issues. And ones fundamental to what sort of society the country envisioned for its future.

The smoothness of the shaft, the softness of the feathery filaments grazing her knuckles—Charlotte realized how much she had missed creating the images and words that challenged people to think and react.

Science and technology were important. But so was art and abstract ideas.

A quick dip loaded the point with ink. Turning

to a fresh page in her sketchbook, she began to rough out a preliminary idea.

"Milord, you have a visitor who is demanding an immediate audience."

Wrexford didn't look up from his laboratory notes. Having abandoned his efforts with the numbers, he was using his earlier experiment to keep his mind occupied. "What can you be thinking, Riche? You know the rules about interrupting my work."

"My thoughts, sir," replied the butler with a sniff, "are that I would prefer to face your ire than risk having the Young Person cut out my liver with the nasty-looking knife he has clutched in his grubby fist."

"Ah." The earl snapped the pages shut. "I take it Master Sloane is at the door."

Tyler, who was busy cleaning the scientific instruments on one of the work counters, let out a snicker.

"Yes, milord. May I show him in?"

"I suppose you had better do so. It would be a cursed inconvenience to have to hire a new butler."

"Indeed it would," quipped Tyler. "Finding someone willing to tolerate your moods would be no easy task."

Riche padded off without comment.

"M'lady said this was urgent," announced

Raven without preamble as he hurried into the room and slapped a folded sheet of paper down on the earl's desktop.

"Thank you." Wrexford picked it up. "Where's your shadow?"

"We came in through the alleyway by the mews. One of the grooms was currying a big black stallion and he said Hawk could stay and watch." Raven looked around. "Wot's that?" he added abruptly, his gaze fixing on the large brass apparatus Tyler was polishing.

"A microscope." He cracked the wax seal. "Its lenses magnify things to many times their real size."

The boy continued staring.

The note was longer than Charlotte's usual terse missives. "Tyler, show the lad how it works while I have a look at this."

The sound of their voices faded to an indistinct hum as Wrexford read the news of Hillhouse's disappearance. Had they finally stumbled on to the scent of the villains? His blood quickened at the thought that the hunt was on in earnest. But he made himself hold his excitement in check.

A difficult a task, as Charlotte's very next sentences spelled out the details of Hillhouse's youthful moral lapse. Granted, a single mistake didn't damn a man for eternity. However, if money had proved an irresistible temptation once, it might well again.

Evidence. At least he was beginning to gather evidence, rather than just sit and spin theories. After re-reading the note, he took his time to consider the facts and what they might mean. Hillhouse, Kirkland . . . and Isobel Ashton? Lost in concentration, he wasn't sure how many minutes had ticked by when a muted exclamation pulled him from his thoughts.

"Oiy!" Raven lifted his head from the microscope's eyepiece, a look of wonder warring with wariness. "Yer bamming me, ain't ye?" he said to Tyler. "It's a trick—that ain't really the eye of a gnat?"

The valet grinned. "It is, lad." He slid out two thin glass plates and showed the boy the tiny insect pressed between them.

"How does it work?" demanded Raven, touching a curious—and none-too-clean—finger to the gleaming metal.

Tyler winced but bit back any chiding, choosing instead to launch into an explanation of the convex and concave lenses.

The boy, noted Wrexford, asked very intelligent questions.

"Come, let me show a drop of water," said the valet, warming up to the subject. "You'll be amazed at what the naked eye can't see."

As Wrexford rose, he saw Raven's face fall. "Ye got a note ready fer me te take back?" he asked, reluctantly sliding down from his stool

The earl had not yet decided how to respond in writing. Charlotte's message seemed to confirm that he and Sheffield were pursuing a promising path, but there were many questions he wished to discuss with her. It was all still conjecture, and with a sudden start, he realized how much he had come to value her judgment.

The boy darted a longing look back at the microscope.

Clenching his teeth in frustration, Wrexford realized that a visit was not possible at this hour. Now that she had settled in to a more respectable neighborhood, the rules had changed. He could no longer come and go without stirring malicious gossip.

"No need for you to rush off quite yet. I need to think for a bit," he said to Raven. He turned for the door, and then added, "Tyler does have a tendency to rattle on like a loose screw, so if you're finding him a posy bore, you are welcome to wait in the kitchens."

"Naw, s'alright, I don't mind," replied Raven, exaggerating an indifferent shrug.

Once in the corridor, Wrexford headed for his study, the thump of his steps stirring the emptiness to life. Shadows uncoiled from shadows, dark, taunting shapes twisting and turning through the flickers of lamplight.

Questions, questions. And precious few solid answers.

He felt strangely uncertain.

The fading light of late afternoon had left his study shrouded in half-darkness. Leaving the lamps untouched, Wrexford poured himself a brandy and took a seat by the unlit hearth. A cold-fingered chill seemed to creep out from the black coals and wrap itself around his boots.

His was not a tender heart—not since the days of his callow youth, when the razor-sharp cut of feminine wiles had left it irreparably scarred. These days, women rarely upset his peace of mind. And yet, Isobel Ashton seemed to have gotten under his skin.

The brandy filled his mouth with a sudden heat, and burned a trail down the back of his throat.

Though he didn't want to, he found her attractive. Alluring. Intriguing. In the beau monde world, it was de rigueur for females to be colorless pasteboard cut-outs. Mere silhouettes swathed in silks and satins. No wonder the widow's aura of self-assured individuality stood out like a blaze of fire.

Wrexford spun the glass between his palms, feeling the prickle of cold cut crystal facets. He had never met anyone quite like her. Beautiful, but with an unusual strength and intelligence giving far deeper meaning to the superficial surface.

There was Charlotte, of course. But she was different.

He frowned as he tried to find words to describe how.

Irritating? No, that was unfair. She provoked him, she challenged him.

And what man liked that?

More than that, she forced him, by the sheer strength of her own unwavering passions, to care more deeply than he wished to about such notions as right and wrong.

Another swallow of brandy. Cynicism was much more comfortable.

Forcing his thoughts away from Charlotte, the earl made himself confront the specter of Isobel Ashton—and the fact that she might be involved in her husband's murder.

No question in his mind that she was clever enough. She had fire, but it was tempered by ice.

And that, he slowly realized, was the elemental difference between her and Charlotte. The widow, he sensed, would be capable of murder. While Charlotte's elemental warmth would never—*never*—allow for such a cold-hearted act.

That he might have misjudged Isobel's character so badly stung. After the painful lesson of his youthful folly, he thought his brain had become a less primitive organ than other parts of his anatomy. But perhaps he was mistaken.

Brooding, however, was the coward's way out. Whatever the spell that had drawn him to Isobel, it was broken by the fact that he could think her capable of cold-blooded murder.

Wrexford rose and went to his desk. A spark of flint and steel lit a single candle, and after quickly penning a note, he sealed it with a circle of molten wax.

"Weasel," he called, as he returned to his workroom.

Tyler held up a warning finger. "A moment, milord. Let us finish."

"Finish what?" Curious, Wrexford approached the counter where Raven was sitting, shoulders hunched, head bent low. The sound of pencils scratching over paper rose above the faint hiss of the oil-fueled Argand lamp.

The valet gestured to an open ledger book sitting amidst a bunch of other books. "The bantling saw the open ledger when I was showing him our work. He thinks he's spotted an error in my addition of the monthly expenditures. We are both in the process of rechecking the final tally."

"By all means, carry on." Another minute or two of delay would make no difference.

Scratch, scratch.

And then Tyler let out a low whistle through his teeth. "Bloody hell. My apologies, lad. You're right."

Raven made a last calculation before setting down his pencil with an owlish blink. "Yeah, looks that way."

Wrexford moved closer and surveyed the page. "You first found the error by adding this all up in your head?"

The boy nodded. "Are ye angry at me fer pointing it out?"

"Not in the least," replied the earl. "You appear to have a knack for numbers. It's an excellent skill to have."

"Ye think so?" Raven slowly met his gaze, a hint of a question lurking in his eyes. "Dunno what's so special about it. But Mr. Linsley says a great many interesting things can be explained by numbers."

"He's quite right, it's a fascinating subject, lad." Yet another surprise in a day filled with surprises. "And I look forward to talking with you at greater length about the wonders of mathematics." Wrexford held up the sealed note. "At the moment, however, m'lady is waiting for my reply."

Punctuating the papery crackle with a low oath, Charlotte crumpled the earl's missive and dropped it into her desk drawer.

"We have much to talk about," she muttered, repeating the first of the two sentences he had deigned to write. The second one merely stated, 'The carriage will call for you tomorrow at noon.'

His high-handedness caused a clench of resentment in her chest, even though she knew he was right to respect the strictures of society. It was the brusqueness of his message that felt a little like a slap in the face. Charlotte had thought their friendship, though fraught with complexities, was a bond that had grown into something deeper than mere pragmatism. Perhaps she was wrong.

Which brought into question her judgment on a great many things concerning the earl. Including her own feeling for him . . .

The clench suddenly tightened with a fierceness that forced the air from her lungs, and for an instant she feared her ribs might crack.

No, I am stronger than such weak-willed longings, she told herself, forcing away thoughts of the earl. *Survival depends on being pragmatic.*

Willing the iron-fisted grip to relax, Charlotte found she could breathe again.

Picking up her pen, she returned her gaze to the unfinished drawing on her desk. There was nothing like the need to put bread on the table to focus a clear-minded clarity on the moment at hand. She had promised it to Mr. Fores by tomorrow and had never failed to keep her word to him. With that in mind, she set to work.

It was close to midnight before Charlotte scraped back her chair and flexed the stiffness from her shoulders. The composition had demanded a dramatic balance of black and white, one that required a laborious series of cross-hatched shadings. But as she cast a critical eye over the details, she decided she was satisfied with the result.

Painting in the colored highlights could wait until morning. Fatigue was hazing her head and hanging heavy on her lashes. Charlotte found she could barely keep her eyes open as she rose and made her way into the night-dark corridor leading to her bedchamber. Still, she paused by the narrow set of stairs leading up to the attic aerie and cocked an ear to catch the soft stirrings of the boys asleep in their beds.

Rustling wool, a snuffled breath—the sounds were reassuring. Of late, their nocturnal ramblings had grown less frequent. A sign, she hoped, that they were adapting to a more settled life.

For the moment all was well, and yet Charlotte lingered, thinking about the hopes and fears that came with love.

Love.

The heart was safer in solitude. Was that what was keeping Raven at arm's length? The boy had seen enough of life's cruelties to sense the dangers of caring too much.

As for her own emotions . . .

Charlotte looked up, though the slumbering gloom revealed no answers. She was curious as to what had happened at the earl's townhouse. Hawk had come home looking blissfully happy—the pungent smell of horse that clung to his clothing explained why. Raven, too, had seemed pleased about something, though her gentle probing had failed to elicit more than a cryptic smile.

She wished . . .

"Ah, but if wishes were winged unicorns, I could fly a chariot to the moon and back by dawn." A yawn punctuated her murmur. Time for sleep, before her thoughts spun any further quicksilver silliness.

A discreet knock on the workroom door roused Wrexford from his brooding.

"Milord, Mr. Henning wishes to speak with you. He says it's rather urgent."

Thank God for small favors, thought the earl. He hadn't been in any mood to go out searching through the stews again. "Show him in, Riche."

As the surgeon shuffled into the room, looking even more disheveled than usual, Wrexford added, "Where the devil have you been? Gabriel Hollis has been murdered."

"An outbreak of influenza had hold of the rookies near the Foundling Hospital. I've been there for several days." Henning came closer, and as he ran a hand over his unshaven jaw, the lamplight caught the circles of fatigue bagged beneath his eyes. "As for Hollis, I heard." He withdrew a small packet from his pocket and dropped it on the desk. "That's why I thought you had better see this without delay."

As Wrexford snatched it up, Henning let out a

sigh and looked around. "Might I pour myself a wee dram of that lovely malt?"

"You may have the whole damn bottle," muttered the earl as he stared down at the words written on the outer wrapping.

From Gabriel Hollis. To be given to William Nevins in the event of my death.

"I found it shoved under my door when I returned home this evening," said Henning as he shuffled to the sideboard. "Hollis was a prescient fellow, it seems."

"Yes," muttered Wrexford. "Sheffield and I found him wheezing his final breath night before last. Like Ashton, his throat was sliced open." Taking up his letter opener, he cut a slit in the wrapper. "Any idea who Nevins is?"

"I've just learned he's one of the leaders of the Workers of Zion."

Inside was a duplicate of the sheet of numbers he had found in Hollis's rooms. That answered one conundrum—it was indeed written by the radical leader. And it seemed Nevins was the key to deciphering it. "I need to speak with him right away."

Henning's expression, never terribly encouraging to begin with, turned even grimmer. "I'm afraid that won't be possible, laddie. One of my patients told me his body was discovered in one of the side alleys near Seven Dials this morning. With his throat cut."

The bloody villain, fumed Wrexford, was staying one teasing, taunting step ahead of him.

After taking a loud slurp of the whisky, Henning leaned in for a closer look at the paper. "Any idea what that means?"

"No. And now, without Nevins, our chances of guessing which sort of code he's using is virtually nil."

"For what it's worth, I've been listening to talk in the stews, and word is Hollis and Nevins were shocked at Ashton's murder and claimed they had nothing to do with it."

"I'm inclined to believe them," replied Wrexford. "But proving it has just become a great deal more difficult."

"Aye. But then again, you seem to like dancing along a razor's edge." Henning drained his drink. "Just take care not to lose your balance."

A breeze ruffled through the night mist, stirring a sudden swirl of ghostly tendrils that kissed up against the window glass. The thick twines of ivy growing up the stucco and timber wall sighed, the breathy whisper just loud enough to cover the quick-footed steps moving over the damp grass. Clouds drifted over the moon, cloaking the garden in darkness.

Crouched low, the black-clad figure melded into the leafy shadows of the shrubbery as it moved slowly, stealthily to the back of the house.

Darkness hid the flick of a knife blade sliding between the window frames, seeking the latch.

Charlotte came awake, unsure what had dragged her from the depths of slumber. Her heart was jumpy, her muscles tensed.

"A bad dream," she whispered, trying to chase away the sharp sense of unease.

She slowly sat up and looked around. The armoire . . . the dressing table . . . the washstand with its cream-colored pitcher glowing softly in the dappling of moonlight. Nothing was amiss.

Exhaling a self-mocking sigh, Charlotte made herself relax. All the little flitterings and creaks of her new residence were still unfamiliar. Like the *tit-tit* of the yew bushes against the back of the house as the breeze set them to swaying.

The sounds ceased, making her feel even more the fool. At least she was not yet imagining the clank of chains or the moan of a spectral ghost.

And then the scrape came again, this time louder and sounding more metallic.

Charlotte threw off the bedclothes and snatched up her wrapper. Sending up a silent prayer that the floorboards wouldn't give her away, she moved swiftly to the stairs and crept down just far enough that she could steal a peek at the main corridor.

Footsteps sounded, moving from the pantry to the kitchen.

Only then did she realize she hadn't thought to grab up a weapon of some sort.

Too late for that now. Someone was coming.

Shifting her weight to the balls of her feet, Charlotte clenched a fist. Her late husband had taught her to throw a decent punch. And besides, the thought of an intruder harming the boys made her angry enough to commit murder with her bare hands.

However, the shadowed figure hurried past the stairs and ducked into the small drawing room.

Charlotte waited for several moments, then tiptoed down the remaining treads and took up a position to one side of the doorway. From her vantage point, she could make out the dark-on-dark silhouette making a slow circuit of the room. She eased in a breath and tried to quiet her pounding heart.

Thankfully the intruder appeared unaware of her presence. Steeling her spine, she made herself study her enemy, looking for any weakness. His face was hidden by the upturned hood of a cloak, whose heavy folds fell to mid-calf of the snug-fitting leather boots. He was of ordinary height and looked to be slim and wiry—an in-and-out man rather than a bludgeoning brute.

His steps halted, his head swiveled from side to side . . . Looking for valuables, no doubt.

An experienced thief would have known better than to expect silver candlesticks or precious baubles in this neighborhood. But perhaps word had gotten around that a fancy carriage had been spotted during the hustle and bustle of moving day.

The man had made a grave mistake in choosing his victim, thought Charlotte, fear giving way to primal fury as she watched her home being violated. Her blood was up. Even if the miscreant tried to scamper away empty-handed, she didn't intend to let him escape.

He turned his back and headed to the side table.

Charlotte seized the chance to slip inside the room and took cover behind one of the armchairs. Several moments passed and then she heard a faint scrabbling, followed by the swoosh of wool. Venturing a quick look, she saw the intruder turn from the table and in one herky-jerky motion slip the majolica rooster inside his cloak and set off for the door.

Another step or two would bring him abreast of her hiding place—

The silence was suddenly shattered by a pelter of thumps and clanging steel as Raven charged in from the corridor brandishing one of Wrexford's swords. Hawk was just behind him, trying manfully to keep his weapon from bumping along the floor.

"Oiy!" cried Raven, taking a swing as the intruder tried to dodge past him. The flat of the blade smacked the fellow's leg, knocking him to the ground.

"No!" screamed Charlotte, springing to her feet and rushing to put herself between the boys and danger.

Agile as an eel, the intruder wriggled back just as Raven slapped out another strike. It struck only a glancing hit as, with a grunt, the man managed to dart around the sofa.

Hawk dropped his sword and, fists flailing, flew toward the other end of the sofa to cut him off.

"*No!*" cried Charlotte again. The boy was no match for a cornered man. She lunged to stop him, just as his older brother did the same. They collided and Raven's sword clattered to the floor as they fell in a welter of tangled limbs.

Twisting free, she saw the intruder knock Hawk aside with a flying elbow and bolt for the door, the stolen bird still cradled in his cloak.

No, no, no!

The man was quick—but Raven was quicker. Slithering forward, he grabbed the sword and flung it like a spear, aiming low at the man's feet and flapping cloak. The missile caught in the cloth and fell between his legs, once again sending him sprawling.

Raven was on him in a flash, fists punching at the hooded head. Not to be outdone, his brother flung himself on the man's kicking legs and held on like a limpet.

Pushing the hair out of her eyes, Charlotte snatched up Hawk's sword. "That's enough!" she shouted, stepping up and placing the point just inches above the intruder's throat. His head was turned to the side, the folds of fabric still hiding his face. "Get off him now and back away."

The two boys reluctantly obeyed.

"Ye ought te let us chop him into mincemeat," muttered Raven, rubbing at his knuckles.

"Oiy," agreed his brother, who couldn't resist giving a last little kick to the prisoner's shins.

A muffled sound rumbled from within the wool.

"Gentlemen don't strike an enemy once he's surrendered." Charlotte looked away to wag a chiding finger. "It's not honorable."

Taking advantage of the distraction, the intruder made one last grasp for escape. Rolling sideways, he popped to his feet. Freedom was just a scant few strides away.

She had no choice. Steel flashed as the weighty sword sliced through air and smacked a hard blow between his shoulder blades. The force of it staggered him. Charlotte struck again—a palpable hit that spun him spun around.

Half-crazed by a surge of battlelust, she dropped her weapon and seized him by the cloak. "Bloody bastard!" she cried, swinging him around and slamming him up against the wall.

The rooster slipped free and fell to the floor.

The *crack* snapped Charlotte out of her daze.

Shaking her head to clear away the last vestiges of madness, she looked down in dismay, just as Raven rushed in to help.

"Holy hell," hissed the boy, staring at the shards. He crouched down and plucked a shaft of tightly bound papers from the broken pottery.

"Holy hell," echoed Charlotte as her gaze flew from the papers back to her captive.

The hood had slipped during the struggle, revealing a pale face—now sporting a fast-purpling bruise on the tip of the chin—and a mass of tumbled wheaten curls.

"*Merde*," said Octavia Merton, her shoulders slumping in resignation.

Chapter 17

Her mind flooded with a myriad of questions—but Charlotte forced them aside. First things first.

"Hawk, find some rope," she ordered, keeping a firm grip on her captive. "Raven, have you got your pocket knife?"

"Aye, m'lady." The blade opened with an ominous snap.

"I'm no threat to you," said Octavia softly.

"Two people have been murdered, their throats sliced open with gruesome precision, so I prefer to err on the side of caution." Charlotte darted a look at Raven. "Hand it over."

To her relief, he did so without arguing. Unlike her, he wasn't tall enough to keep the point pressed against Octavia's neck. "Now search her for any weapons. And if you so much as twitch, Miss Merton, I won't hesitate to add a third corpse to the count."

"There's a knife in the right pocket of my cloak—only because I needed something to pry open the window latch," said Octavia calmly. "Other than that I'm unarmed."

Raven fished it out. "She's telling the truth," he muttered a few moments later. "Now what?"

Charlotte saw Hawk emerge from the pantry, a coil of rope slung over his shoulder. "Take your brother and fetch a chair from the kitchen," she answered.

The two of them were back in a trice.

"Place it there," said Charlotte, indicating a spot by the sofa.

"Your sons?" asked Octavia, watching them jump to the task.

"My wards," answered Charlotte, giving her captive a small shove forward. "But no less dear to my heart. You made a grave mistake in threatening those I love."

"They were never in any danger."

"Forgive me if I don't take your word for it. You've been lying through your teeth about a great many things."

"I have," conceded Octavia, allowing herself to be seated on the hard slats of the straight-back chair. "But not about what you think."

Charlotte gave a noncommittal grunt. "Raven, tie her to the chair—snugly enough that she can't wriggle free."

"Let yer arms hang down by yer side, miss," he ordered before looping the rope around her middle. Moving swiftly and methodically, he had the job done within moments.

The knots, observed Charlotte as she lit a single candle, would have done a naval midshipman proud.

"Excellent. Now go fetch your coats and boots. I need for you to deliver two messages."

Wrexford must know about this. And so, she decided, must Jeremy. The earl wouldn't like it, but her friend deserved her trust . . . until he proved unworthy of it.

"They seem very brave and resourceful lads," murmured Octavia as they raced off. "Most children would have been paralyzed by fright."

"They are," replied Charlotte curtly, "unlike most children."

Octavia nodded thoughtfully, then turned her head to stare out the window facing the street. Charlotte wasn't sure why. The mist had thickened to an impenetrable veil of ghostly greys and the opaque glass showed naught but the blurred reflection of their silhouettes limned in the weak candlelight.

What thoughts were swirling in Octavia's head? wondered Charlotte as silence settled over them. The young woman's face was expressionless.

She felt a chill tickled at the nape of her neck. A ruthless killer would need just such a cold-blooded detachment. And unlike most people, Charlotte had no illusions about whether a woman was capable of murder.

The boys soon reappeared, dressed and ready to brave the night.

"Raven, you go rouse Wrexford."

Octavia started at the earl's name, her first real sign of emotion.

"Tell him to come immediately," went on Charlotte. "Hawk, you must head to Lord Sterling's residence and give him the same message."

Raven gave a solemn nod. "We'll fly like the wind, m'lady." A low whistle to his brother, and they were gone.

"Wrexford," repeated Octavia. "So, you were spying for him."

Charlotte didn't answer. She was slowly unrolling the sheaf of papers that had been hidden inside the rooster.

"Who are you—his mistress?"

Ignoring the insult, Charlotte took a seat on the sofa and smoothed open the top sheet. And then another and another.

Dear God. Curled in the roll were page after page of technical drawings, rendered in meticulous detail. *Ashton's missing sketches?*

"It is *I* who should be hurling nasty accusations, Miss Merton."

The low light caught the flush of color rising to the other woman's cheeks. "I-I can explain . . . But you won't believe me." Her mouth twisted. "Isobel Ashton seduces most every man who crosses her path. Clearly the earl is under her spell. And you . . ."

"And I had never met the widow before this afternoon," pointed out Charlotte. "She has, I agree, a certain magnetism. Whether that makes her guilty of any crime is not something I feel ready to judge. Your behavior, however, has been highly suspicious." She paused. "There is an old adage—*if it waddles like a duck and quacks like a duck, then it likely is a duck.*"

"You're hunting the wrong bird," replied Octavia bitterly. "Look to the swan. A beauty now, but since you wish to throw out adages, keep in mind that a swan is notoriously ugly in her youth. And does one ever really change one's feathers?"

The young woman's passion was palpable. Octavia was either a consummate actress. Or she believed what she was saying.

Charlotte looked down at the papers, feeling a twinge of doubt. She was beginning to question her judgment of people. And the realization left her a little shaken. "An elemental question, I agree. But let us wait for the gentlemen to arrive before we pursue it. They'll have questions, and I doubt you wish to go through an interrogation twice."

Octavia shifted slightly, setting off a harsh whispering of tightly wound hemp.

"I'm sorry if you're uncomfortable. But I imagine you understand why, Miss Merton."

"Of course I do." Octavia drew in a ragged breath. "I'm a woman who's dared to defy the conventional path for those of our sex. In my experience, prim and proper ladies of the ton are appalled by that—and their reaction is even more vitriolic than that of gentlemen. I threaten all you hold dear, so of course you're willing to think me guilty of any horrid crime—even murder."

"I am," murmured Charlotte, "more open-minded than you might think. If you are innocent, I'm perfectly willing to be convinced." The candle flickered, sending skitters of light across the shadowed sketches. "But it will require more than mere histrionics."

She held up the top drawing, depicting an intricate meshing of gears and levers. "The late Mr. Ashton knew it was imperative to show clearly why something was true. Like him, you'll need to build a solid argument for why we should believe you."

"Benedict and I have carefully assembled an explanation for what has happened, and can draw you a perfect diagram," shot back Octavia. "Our suspicions have been confirmed by several sources. As for proof . . ."

Charlotte waited as a spasm of pain pinched the other woman's lips to a taut line.

"Oh, what does it matter?" went on Octavia in a bleak whisper. "Without Benedict, all hope is gone." Her face had gone ashen, accentuating the bruises from the struggle. "Go ahead, throw me in Newgate Prison. But it will mean that Mrs. Ashton will, quite literally, be getting away with murder."

"That's a very serious allegation, Miss Merton."

"Yes, it is," came the unhesitating reply. "Which is why I wouldn't say it unless I was certain it was true."

Wrexford looked up sharply from the book he was reading. The sound came again—the *ping,*

ping of pebbles hitting up against the diamond-shaped panes of glass.

He rose and twitched back the half-closed draperies of the workroom's windows. The back garden was a netherworld of dark, leafy shapes rising up from a quicksilver sea of mist. The low ornamental trees swayed in the fitful breeze, their black-fingers branches twining with the tendrils of fog.

Squinting into night, the earl tried to spot any furtive movement within the plantings. The stones hadn't launched themselves. He waited another moment, then unlatched the casement and cracked it open.

"Hell's teeth," he muttered as a gust of night-damp air slapped against his cheeks.

"Yer not supposed to swear in front of children." A hand appeared from the gloom below and grabbed hold of the ledge. Wrexford heard the rustling of ivy an instant before Raven swung a leg up and hauled himself to a perch on the narrow jut of stone.

"You're not a child. You're an *afreet* who's been released from some devil-cursed bottle in order to plague mankind."

"What's an *afreet*?"

"A demon." He offered a hand. "Come inside. It looks like a squall is blowing in."

"Can't," replied Raven. "M'lady says ye're to come quick-like."

Wrexford felt a frisson of alarm. "What's happened?"

"An intruder broke into the house—"

"Was she hurt?" he interrupted sharply.

"Naw, we pummeled the miscreant into submission," answered the boy. "And then tied 'em to a chair right and tight. M'lady's standing guard, but she wants ye to see what happened."

"What the devil is that supposed to mean?" called the earl as he hurriedly fetched a pistol from its case.

"You'll see fer yerself," said Raven darkly. "Shake a tail feather, sir. We need te hurry."

Bloody Hell. All sorts of dire possibilities flashed through his head. *Why was she always so infernally afire to charge straight into the maw of danger?*

An idiotic question. Wrexford blew out a breath, exasperation warring with admiration. Because she was the Warrior Queen, possessing more passion and principle than was good for her.

"Meet me on the far side of the square," he called. "It will be quicker to take a hackney part of the way than to go the entire distance on foot."

The flash of gold urged the driver to fly through the deserted streets like a bat escaping from the bowels of hell. They careened to a halt a few streets from Charlotte's residence, and Raven led the way through a series of alleys to the back garden.

"Through here," said the boy, loosening several hidden pegs and shifting a loose board to make a narrow gap in the fence.

The house was completely dark, which stirred yet another pinch of worry as Wrexford waited for Raven to refasten the secret entrance.

"Hurry," he snapped. "The cursed fellow may have gotten free."

"Not from my knots," replied Raven as he signaled for the earl to follow him. "And even if the prisoner did get free, m'lady would knock her arse over teakettle again."

Her? The rustling leaves must have distorted the words.

"Let me go first," whispered Wrexford, holding Raven back once the boy's key released the kitchen door's lock. Drawing his pistol, he eased through the opening and entered the darkened corridor.

The faint sound of voices was coming from up ahead. He slowly eased back the hammer and started forward.

Then came a loud clink—metal hitting against metal. Wrexford broke into a run.

The drawing room door was half closed, the weak aureole of light making it hard to see what was going on. Charlotte had her back to him. She was leaning over . . . a sudden silvery flicker flashed behind her—

"Don't anyone move!" he ordered, kicking

open the door and raising the snout of his pistol.

Charlotte slowly turned. "Thank you for coming, Wrexford. My apologies for rousing you at such an ungodly hour." A ghost of a smile touched her lips. "Would you care for some tea?" she added, gesturing at the steam-swirled pot sitting on the pewter tray.

"Ye untied her," said Raven with a scowl as he joined Wrexford in the doorway.

"Yes, she convinced me she was no threat," replied Charlotte.

Wrexford stepped into the room and slowly looked from Charlotte to Octavia, who was seated on a straight-back chair and chafing her wrists amid a tangle of rope. "Is this your idea of jest?" he demanded. "If so, it's not remotely funny."

"I assure you, sir, I would never stoop to such puerile pranks," replied Charlotte. "Though there are times when your high and mighty attitude richly deserves it."

The earl bit back a retort as he took in Octavia's disheveled clothing and the bruises on her face. It was only then that he realized Charlotte was wearing naught but her nightrail and a wool wrapper. Her feet were bare.

His gaze then found the shards of shattered pottery on the floor and the two swords propped against the wall. "Might I ask—with all due humility, of course—what's going on here?"

"Sit down, milord." She indicated one of the

armchairs, which along with the sofa had been knocked askew. "It's going to be a lengthy conversation. However we must wait for one other person to arrive before we begin."

If he were in need of a libation, decided Wrexford, it would be brandy, not tea.

"Hawk will be bringing—" She cocked an ear. "Ah, I believe they are here now."

The earl turned to see the boy's familiar face—though covered with more than its usual streaks of grime—appear in the doorway. Behind him, still mostly in shadow, was a tall, slender stranger, whose well-tailored garments announced he was a gentleman despite looking as if they had been thrown on in a hurry.

"Charley, are you sure you're not injured?" exclaimed the fellow to Charlotte. "And Miss Merton . . ." He paused to take in the disarray of the room. "Good Lord."

"I'm quite fine, Jem," replied Charlotte. To Wrexford she said, "Allow me to introduce Lord Sterling."

Her dear friend and benefactor. The reminder did nothing to improve his mood.

"This may be a tea party, but let's dispense with the bloody formalities, shall we?" growled the earl. "I'm Wrexford," he said brusquely to Jeremy. "Now, can we cut to the chase? I assume that we're both anxious to hear why we've been summoned here by Mrs. Sloane."

Jeremy raised his brows at Charlotte, a silent seconding of the earl's statement.

She wordlessly picked up the sheaf of papers from the tea table and held them up.

Jeremy made a choking sound in the back of his throat. "Are those Ashton's missing drawings?"

"That," replied Charlotte, "is something I'm hoping Miss Merton will explain to us." A pause. "Along with a great many other things. She's made some serious allegations to me, which she claims can be proven. "

Plumes of pale vapor wafted up from the teacup Octavia had cradled in her hands, blurring her face. It struck Wrexford as an apt illusion. Everything about the inventor's murder seemed to dance in and out of focus, taunting every sense of perception.

"Let me begin with an explanation of what happened here earlier, before I let Miss Merton speak for herself," went on Charlotte. "I awoke to hear an intruder entering my house and went downstairs to investigate."

"Did it not occur to you how dangerous that was?" said Wrexford.

She ignored the question. "I saw a cloaked figure slip into the drawing room—Miss Merton, as I later discovered—and steal the majolica rooster which Mrs. Ashton had given to me. Intent on stopping the theft, I confronted her, and with the help of the boys—and the earl's swords—we managed to subdue her."

"Good God." Wrexford shook his head. "You risked your life for a piece of pottery?"

Her chin rose to a pose he had come to think of as Stubborness Personified. "It was a matter of principle."

Principle. A word that brought out the best and the worst in her.

"And besides, it turned out to be a *very* valuable bird. During the struggle, it fell and shattered—revealing the technical drawings hidden inside." Charlotte hesitated and took a moment to pour herself some tea. She suddenly looked exhausted, but several swallows seemed to revive her. "Those are all the facts I possess. For further explanations, we must turn to Miss Merton."

Silence filled the room. Even the boys stopped fidgeting. Octavia looked away. She seemed to shrink into herself with each slow undulation of the candle flame.

"Enough shilly-shallying, Miss Merton," said Wrexford impatiently, deciding it was time to play the iron fist to Charlotte's velvet glove. "Would you rather we summon Bow Street?"

"Octavia," appealed Jeremy. "Please. If we are to have any hope of helping you and Benedict, you must tell us the truth."

The young woman slumped forward and took her head in her hands. "I confess—Benedict and I did it."

Chapter 18

The tea turned cold on Charlotte's tongue. Octavia's passionate avowals of innocence while waiting for the gentlemen had struck a deep-seated chord within her—and so she had trusted her instincts.

A mistake, apparently.

Charlotte set down the cup and closed her eyes, feeling like an utter fool.

"Did what, exactly?" asked the earl dryly, breaking the taut silence. "There are a number of heinous crimes for which you and Mr. Hillhouse are the prime suspects."

Octavia's head snapped up. "Good God, I didn't mean . . . that is . . . Forgive me, I'm not making any sense." She gave a self-mocking sigh. "Truly, I'm not usually a featherheaded peagoose. I—I had better start from the beginning."

"Take your time," encouraged Jeremy, assuming a seat on the sofa and crossing his legs.

Wrexford, noted Charlotte, perched a hip on the arm of the upholstered side chair. In the harsh shadows, the sharp planes of his face looked even more forbidding than usual as his eyes narrowed and he fixed the poor woman with an intimidating scowl.

"Sterling might be willing to dally here until

dawn," he snapped. "But I'd prefer to get on with it, Miss Merton."

She bobbed a small nod. "Several months ago, Benedict and I began to notice small irregularities in Eli's study and in his workshop. Tiny things, but to our eyes, items were out of place, as if someone had been riffling through papers and examining prototypes. When we mentioned it to Eli, he shrugged it off, but we noticed that he became more careful about locking up drawings and the parts to his new engine. We did as well."

Octavia brushed an errant curl from her face. "It was then that we also noticed Lord Kirkland had come for a stay at his father's estate and was making frequent visits to the Ashton residence. Benedict noted that he started loitering around the textile mill as well."

"That was unusual?" asked Jeremy.

"Very," answered Octavia. "Kirkland very rarely paid a visit to Blackstone Abbey. And when he did, word was he only came to rusticate from creditors and wheedle more money out of the marquess. He certainly never showed any interest in Eli's mill—other than to see how many guineas he could squeeze from his father's profits."

"His father was a primary investor in Ashton's business," mused the earl. "Did Kirkland not own an interest in the company, too?"

"No. In fact, Benedict often heard Lord

Blackstone speak disparagingly about his son's intelligence and his inability to understand the fine points of finance," answered Octavia.

Charlotte considered the information. "You implied to me earlier that you and Mr. Hillhouse suspected that Kirkland's growing interest in Ashton's affairs was personal."

"We did." Octavia's expression turned grim. "Eli was spending more and more time with Benedict in the workshop, which is located in an outbuilding on the grounds. As my work was in the study, I was more aware of the comings and goings within the main house. Kirkland began appearing almost daily to take tea with Mrs. Ashton." Her expression turned sardonic. "That is, tea was delivered to the parlor. What took place behind the closed doors I cannot say."

"But you can venture a guess?" asked Wrexford.

"It's *not* that I have a sordid mind, sir," replied Octavia somewhat defensively. "But Eli was like a father to me, and knowing how much he loved his wife, I worried that he might be crushed by a betrayal." She drew in an unsteady breath. "So Benedict and I began making some inquiries. And the secret we discovered chilled us to the very marrow."

Charlotte slanted a glance at Wrexford. His expression remained unchanged. Jeremy, on the other hand, was looking increasingly uncomfortable.

Secrets. No matter how deeply buried, they had a way of slithering their way back up to the light of day.

"In her youth," continued Octavia, "Mrs. Ashton faced a time when she was in dire financial straits. Her father had lost his business, and on his death she was faced with being thrown into the streets. However, despite her lack of money, she did have two very valuable assets—her striking looks and her ability to bewitch men. She used them both to attract a wealthy protector."

"Lord Kirkland?" guessed Charlotte.

"Lord Kirkland," confirmed Octavia.

"You have proof of this?" demanded Wrexford.

"I'll get to that in a moment, milord," answered Octavia. "We also discovered that Kirkland had taken to playing cards with Neville McKinlock at a gaming hell in London that caters to deep play."

Wrexford's expression turned grim. "The owner of Locke and Wharton?"

"Precisely, sir."

"Locke and Wharton is Ashton's main competitor," explained the earl to the others. "Their steam engines are very good, but if Ashton had come up with a way to make his models more powerful, then McKinlock's company would be left in the dust."

"Exactly," said Octavia, her voice rising in

urgency. "So when we learned that Kirkland owed McKinlock a veritable fortune in gaming debts, we began to see how it all began to fit together."

"Conjecture," murmured Wrexford.

"We realized that, sir," countered Octavia. "We knew we had to assemble proof to convince Eli that he was being doubly betrayed."

"What you're saying is that his wife and Kirkland were conspiring to steal Ashton's invention," intoned Jeremy.

"Yes! Giving it to McKinlock would allow him, not Eli, to file for the patent. Locke and Wharton is skilled in steam power. It would have been nigh on impossible to contest their filing." She lifted her shoulders. "The legal precedent is, the victor is always the one who files first—and to him go the spoils."

"A riveting tale," drawled the earl. "But again, have you proof of this?"

A spasm of emotion flitted across Octavia's face, but it passed too quickly for Charlotte to tell what it was.

"We put together the story through conversations with trustworthy people, but we're not naïve, Lord Wrexford," responded Octavia. "We began gathering actual evidence to corroborate what we had heard. However . . ." Her voice faltered for a moment. "However, Eli was murdered—"

"And then Hollis," interjected Wrexford.

"That only added urgency to the task," said

Octavia. "To put a fine point to it, Benedict was worried that we might be in danger if Kirkland or the widow got wind of what we were doing."

Charlotte couldn't help but wonder about one thing. "What about Ashton's drawings? How did you know they were in the rooster?"

"We put them there for safekeeping." A wry grimace. "We were aware that our things were being searched, and knowing Mrs. Ashton disliked the bird, we thought it a clever place in which to conceal the papers."

"Too clever," murmured Charlotte.

"Yes, you can imagine my chagrin when she made a gift of it to you." Octavia sighed. "I'm not sure whether it was high drama or high farce."

"Perhaps," she mused, "it turned out for the best."

"Let us return to Benedict and his disappearance," urged Jeremy. "Or was that merely an act to throw us off the scent?"

Octavia looked stricken. "No!" she exclaimed. "I swear it! Benedict was making a visit to the toolmaker's shop but after that, he was going to meet with a former maidservant at Mrs. Ashton's love nest, who said she had some letters written by Lord Kirkland to his paramour. However . . ." She swallowed hard, struggling to keep her voice from cracking. "However, he never returned."

Her gaze turned to Jeremy, who looked as if he might be ill. "As I told you, I fear something terrible has happened. Benedict would *never* simply slink off and leave me."

"You seem very sure of that," said Charlotte softly. But knowing what she did about the young man's past, a very ugly thought leaped to mind.

"I am." Octavia hesitated. "You see, we've made no announcement of it yet on account of the troubles, but we're engaged to be married."

"Love." Wrexford chuffed an exasperated snort. "As if we haven't enough youthful follies to plague our patience."

Charlotte shot him a warning frown.

Glowering, he fell silent.

No one seemed anxious to speak. Jeremy rose and moved to the window. The draperies tremored as he leaned in and pressed his forehead to the fog-misted glass.

Her heart ached for him. It looked as though bile was churning, hot and acid, in his belly. She guessed that he, too, was thinking the same thing she was.

Octavia watched him, her gaze turning troubled. "Lord Sterling? Is something wrong?"

For a long moment, it seemed Jeremy hadn't heard her. He held himself so still that his form slowly faded into the surrounding shadows.

If only it were that easy to escape from fears that threaten all we hold dear.

Jeremy finally tore himself away from his own inner demons and turned to face them. "Miss

Merton, much as it pains me to do so, I must ask you how much Benedict has told you about his past."

A tiny muscle jumped at the base of Octavia's throat as she swallowed hard. "You are, I presume, referring to a misunderstanding he had at Oxford concerning a friend's missing purse."

A look of anguish flooded Jeremy's eyes.

Octavia saw it and stiffened in alarm. "It was a *mistake,*" she said. "Benedict had picked up his friend's coat, thinking the man had left it in the lane, and was accused of—"

"It was no mistake," interrupted Jeremy. "Benedict was driven by a desperate need of blunt for his books, and made a bad choice. It was I who helped extricate him from the affair and see to it that he was not charged with the crime."

"No," she whispered. "I don't believe it. Benedict doesn't have an evil bone in his body."

"Nonetheless it is true," replied Jeremy tersely. "He is a dear friend—do you imagine I take any pleasure in digging up old scandal?" He pressed his fingertips to his temples. "I don't think one mistake damns a man forever. I've always believed in Benedict's integrity. But I have to accept that I may be wrong. We can't turn a blind eye to the fact that money once lured him to set aside his scruples."

"And if he has done it once," intoned Wrexford, "the odds are, he would do it again."

"I don't believe it," repeated Octavia, keeping her chin up even though she looked white as a corpse.

Charlotte found herself liking the young woman for not throwing Benedict to the wolves. And yet . . .

"We must consider the possibility that Mr. Hillhouse has succumbed to the temptation of money and is in some way connected to Mr. Ashton's murder," she said. "But we must be equally open to the fact that he may have poked a stick into a nest of vipers."

"In which case," said Octavia with tightly-wound calm, "Benedict is likely dead."

"Not necessarily," countered Charlotte. "He may have been forced into hiding, or he may be a prisoner."

"Held deep in a dungeon by supernatural forces?" muttered Wrexford sarcastically. "Come, if we all chime in, I'm sure we can write a horrid novel that will outsell *The Mysteries of Udolpho*."

"As you are so fond of pointing out, sir, we would be wrong to assume the man's guilt without any tangible proof," replied Charlotte. "I'm simply saying we must keep an open mind to all scenarios."

Wrexford gave a grudging nod. He began to pace in slow, measured steps around the perimeter of the room, past the boys, who had moved to a spot behind the sofa in hopes of going unnoticed, past the bookshelves, and past the slivers of pottery scattered on the dark-grained floor.

"An open mind," he murmured. As he spoke, he stopped abruptly and hefted one of the swords. A winking of light danced along the length of its blade. "Instead of flinging wild conjectures willy-nilly, let us employ the scientific method and start using reason and logic to guide us as to what next steps to make."

The boys shifted, watching as the earl stared meditatively at the blunt tip of the weapon and waggled it up and down. He held its weight easily, observed Charlotte, exuding an aura of command. She found herself mesmerized by the flickering sparks reflecting off the smooth steel.

"What good will mere thinking do?" asked Jeremy. "Mrs. Ashton is insisting to Bow Street that her husband's death was not the result of a random robbery. She wants a culprit caught—and we now can imagine why." His hands clenched at his sides. "Once Benedict's secret comes to life, Bow Street will be frothing at the mouth to see him swing for murder."

"Oh, ye of little faith," murmured Wrexford. "If what Miss Merton says is true, there will be a way to prove it."

"And you are willing to help us do so?" challenged Octavia.

"I am willing to see that justice is done," corrected the earl. "Whether that is the same thing remains to be seen."

A very Wrexford response, thought Charlotte, a faint smile momentarily touching her lips. His mercurial moods could be maddening, but when it came to intellectual conundrums, he was able to detach his emotions and become a stickler for precision. She hoped that would work to their advantage.

The sword cut back and forth, setting off more quicksilver flashes of light. And with a start, Charlotte realized how much she wanted to prove Benedict Hillhouse innocent of any crime. Her first impression of Octavia hadn't been a positive one. The young woman had struck her as evasive and untrustworthy—understandably so, based on what she now knew. But the young woman's daredevil disregard for her own safety and tigerish defense of the man she loved had won a grudging respect.

"What can we do te help?" piped up Raven from his spot in the shadows.

"Nothing at the moment," replied Charlotte quickly, suddenly conscious of the fact that they had overheard more than she would have liked. "You and Hawk should return to your beds."

"Not quite yet," said Wrexford, earning two grateful grins. "They might as well stay and hear us out. I may have a task for them."

Charlotte wasn't quite sure she liked the sound

of that. The last time the earl had enlisted the boys in one of his investigations, they would have been transported to the penal colonies half a world away had they been caught.

"That might not be possible," she replied tersely. "Their lessons with Mr. Linsley demand a great deal of time and study."

Raven uttered a word that Charlotte pretended not to hear.

The sword angled to point at a spot on the sofa. "Do me the favor of hearing me out before you decide to cut out my liver with your pen knife."

Reading each other's thoughts was a skill that cut both ways, acknowledged Charlotte to herself as she took a seat. "Very well, sir."

"It seems to me we have three avenues to pursue," said the earl without further preamble. "Firstly, there are our two main suspects." He resumed his pacing. "We need to learn more about Lord Kirkland and Mrs. Ashton—their past history and if they are indeed conspiring together. And of course, we'll need to consider McKinlock, too."

"How—" began Jeremy, but was cut off by a *swoosh* of steel.

"As it happens, I've already asked my good friend Kit Sheffield to dig around for information on Kirkland," replied the earl. "The gaming hells should be fertile ground for whatever dirt there is."

"Is Sheffield trustworthy?" demanded Octavia.

"Absolutely," answered Charlotte.

The answer seemed to satisfy the young woman. She sat back without further protest.

"It's also imperative to gather proof of any perfidy," continued Wrexford. "To whit, it would be helpful to get our hands on the love letters that Mr. Hillhouse was seeking. And knowing the pair's daily movements—who they are meeting, where they are going, especially if it involves McKinlock—could be a key in confirming our suspicions."

Wrexford had circled around to Charlotte. "Mrs. Sloane, I'll leave the love letters to you and your network."

Octavia once again edged forward on her seat. "How—"

"Never mind," murmured Jeremy. "But be assured they can run rings around any Bow Street Runner."

"Weasels, you play a part in this too," went on the earl. "Can you recruit your reliable raggle-taggles for surveillance duty?" The boys had a trusted circle of smart, savvy street urchins who had proved extremely helpful in solving the Holworthy murder case.

"O' course," replied Raven. "Skinny, One-Eyed Harry, Alice the Eel Girl, Pudge—"

"I leave it to you to assemble the group," interjected Wrexford. "I'll inform you of the assignments by the end of tomorrow."

Octavia was looking more and more mystified but she kept any further queries to herself.

"Then there is the question of finding Mr. Hillhouse." Wrexford shifted his stance to face Jeremy. "You know him well. As, it appears, does Miss Merton. The two of you are tasked with thinking of where he might have gone to ground if he were in trouble."

"He would have come back to the house," insisted Octavia.

The earl looked down his long nose at her. "And lead whatever danger was pursuing him straight to you?"

"Oh," she said in a small voice.

"I've some ideas," said Jeremy. "I'm sure Miss Merton will too, once she's thought about it.

"Do any inquiries discreetly, Sterling," cautioned the earl. *Swoosh, swoosh.* He was moving again. "Given your background, I assume you can manage that."

"If you're asking whether I can manage not to trip over my aristocratic feet, yes I think I can manage that," came the cool reply.

"I can search Mrs. Ashton's parlor and private quarters when she is occupied elsewhere," suggested Octavia.

"No," said Charlotte firmly. "You must promise to do nothing. As you've discovered, clandestine activities are not quite so easy as you might think. Alerting the widow that she's under suspicion could be disastrous. The element of surprise is key if we are to catch them red-handed."

Octavia looked unhappy, but as Charlotte had hoped, her innate good sense prevailed. "I understand."

The list was already daunting, but the earl had mentioned three avenues of pursuit. "And what, sir," asked Charlotte, "is the last thing?"

Chapter 19

Wrexford's peregrination around the room had brought him back to the doorway, where the other sword stood propped up against the wall. "We can't ignore the possibility that the real villain is someone else entirely. Our suspects aren't the only ones who would reap enormous profits if they possessed Ashton's invention. And as a man of science, I've learned one must consider all factors when one is conducting an experiment."

He slowly set his weapon next to its mate. "Else you risk having it blow up in your face."

"Yes, but . . . where do we begin?" mused Charlotte. "With Mr. Hillhouse in God knows what difficulty, time is of the essence."

"The answer is actually very simple. We—or rather, I—start at the Royal Institution, where all the latest gossip concerning the world of science echoes through its august corridors before it ever reaches the public." Wrexford allowed a cynical smile. "Men tend to be even more loose-lipped than the drawing room tabbies. If McKinlock's company has any new projects in the works, one of the Institution's members will have heard rumors about it."

Charlotte nodded slowly. "An excellent idea, milord. It makes sense that whoever is looking to make a fortune from the invention would want to partner with someone who already manufactures steam engines."

"It would, indeed." Wrexford cast his gaze on Ashton's technical drawings, which Charlotte had placed on the table by the sofa. "Miss Merton, I know you've gone to great trouble to retrieve these, but I'd like to keep them for now. Not only will they be safe in my townhouse, but it will also give me and my laboratory assistant the chance to understand on what sort of revolutionary innovation Ashton was working."

"Valves," whispered Octavia. "It's all about valves."

Steam power, he knew, had to do with heat, condensation and creating a vacuum. The quicker and more efficiently an engine could cycle through the process, the more pressure—and power—it could create.

"I've not the technical expertise to give you more than a rudimentary explanation of how the design works. It involves *four* valves in each cylinder. The linkages for open and shutting them are independently controlled, which keeps the temperature at a constant. The result is far more power. In addition, Eli and Benedict calculated that the new engine will be far more efficient, and run on thirty percent less fuel."

"Revolutionary, indeed," murmured Wrexford.

"As for keeping the drawings, I'm hardly in a

position to argue," added Octavia with a cynical shrug. "Besides, I agree that they are probably most secure in your hands."

As the earl leaned down to pick them up, Charlotte cleared her throat. "A thought just occurred to me. Without these as reference, would someone have the knowledge or expertise to build the new engine?"

A good question. Wrexford was already taking a closer look at the schematics.

"The toolmakers who've been fashioning parts for our experiments have an inkling of what Eli was doing," answered Octavia. "And some of the investors might have a general idea that a new concept of valves is involved. But the devil is in the details. The exact design is exceedingly complicated, and I doubt there is anyone capable of imagining his creative thinking." The tiny tic of hesitation seemed amplified by the stillness of the room.

"Except, of course, for Benedict," she added softly, "who knows the plans by heart."

"Then I daresay we need to find Mr. Hillhouse," said Wrexford, "as it appears he is a key to unlocking this mystery." Paper crackled as he tried to focus on the tiny mathematical equations scrawled on the margins. His mind suddenly felt muzzy with lack of sleep.

"However, there's nothing more to be accomplished at the moment. We all need clearer heads before attacking our appointed tasks." He touched a hand to his jaw and felt the faint prickle of whiskers rasp against his flesh. It stirred the uncomfortable sensation that he was missing something.

And yet he couldn't put a put a finger on what it might be.

The demands of the here and now pushed the thought aside. "Sterling, you must see Miss Merton safely back to Mayfair. And I suggest you do it now, before the city begins to stir to life."

Jeremy nodded. Octavia rose and gathered her cloak.

"One of the lads will lead you out to where a hackney can be flagged down without attracting unwanted attention."

Raven nudged his younger brother. "Ye heard His Nibs. Take them out te High Street, and be quick about it."

Charlotte waited until the sound of hurried footsteps had faded into the night before asking, "So, what do you make of this latest twist, sir?"

Wrexford couldn't help but quirk a smile. "You're the one who's attuned to interpreting intuition, Mrs. Sloane. My limited intellect must depend on facts and logic. Both of which are proving damnably elusive in this case." He took a moment to twist the drawings into a tight roll. "Fetch me some twine, Weasel."

Raven looked loath to leave, but hurried toward the kitchen.

"My sense is that Miss Merton is telling the truth," said Charlotte.

"The truth as she understands it," muttered the earl.

The candle sputtered as wax dripped down the pewter stick. It was burning low.

"There's that," conceded Charlotte. After a lengthy pause, she continued, her voice betraying a troubled note. "There are tantalizing leads, but precious few facts. So much seems to depend on Mr. Hillhouse, and whether he's a force of good or evil."

"Kind o' like a complicated mathematical equation." Raven materialized from out the gloom and held out a length of twine. "Ye know, where ye have te figure out the value fer x or y before ye can work out the correct answer."

"Precisely, lad," replied Wrexford. He started to secure the roll but was only half-aware of his fingers working the knots. *Out of the mouth of babes* . . . the boy's words had stirred an even sharper sense that he was forgetting something.

Charlotte looked up with a start "Mathematics!" she exclaimed. "Why, we've made no mention of the page of numbers you found in Hollis's rooms. And yet his dying words said the answer to Ashton's death was in the numbers."

Damnation. Wrexford felt like an idiot.

"I take it you haven't heard anything from the professor at Cambridge?" she asked.

The earl shook his head. "I shall write to him again. But Henning came earlier this evening with proof they were written by Hollis." He quickly explained about the note left for Nevins and how they still had no clue how to interpret the strange jumble. It was a reminder of how his usual clarity had been strangely clouded during this investigation. The reason why was not something he cared to contemplate.

And yet he must.

"Wrexford . . ."

Charlotte's sharpness roused him from his momentary brooding.

"I must ask you an uncomfortable question."

"Go on," he drawled. "I daresay you'd do so with or without my permission."

She didn't smile. Not a good sign, he decided, though he wasn't sure what misdeed of his had brought such a serious expression to her face.

But first Charlotte turned to Raven. "It's time to return to your aerie. You must get some sleep if you are to be sharp enough to keep watch on our suspects." Seeing he was about to argue, she raised her voice a notch, something she rarely did with the boys. "Go." Her lashes flicked, darkening the shadows around her eyes. "I need to have a word with His Lordship in private."

Raven looked unhappy, but reluctantly obeyed. Charlotte waited until she heard the creak of the stair treads before clearing her throat.

Another bad sign, thought Wrexford. She never shied away from crossing verbal swords with him. It was one of the things he respected about her.

This strange hesitation put his nerves on edge.

"It seems to me that your usual dispassionate detachment has been missing from the very beginning of this case," she began. "Is there a reason?"

"If you're implying that I ought to be able to solve any crime, no matter how complex or—"

"That's not at all what I mean," she interrupted brusquely. "I think you've let your emotions become involved—and as you once warned me, that's asking for trouble."

Wrexford couldn't summon any clever quip. He wouldn't insult her by pretending he didn't know to what she was referring. Charlotte, with her unholy gift of intuition, appeared to have sensed the truth even before he had.

Not that he thanked her for it.

Charlotte took his silence as confirmation of her surmise. "I've met Mrs. Ashton. The widow has . . ." A tic of hesitation as she chose her words carefully. ". . . a powerful presence. She's attractive. Alluring. And—"

"And you think her womanly wiles have seduced me?"

"I think they have clouded your judgment," replied Charlotte flatly. The candle guttered and with a dying hiss went out. Uttering a low oath, she fetched an oil lamp from the side table. It took her several strikes of the steel and flint to light the wick.

"Whether she's warming your bed is none of my business," continued Charlotte. "What does concern me is your emotional state. If you can't view the investigation with a dispassionate eye, it puts us all in an untenable position. Not only will it make it nigh on impossible to uncover the truth, but it may also place people who are dear to me in peril."

In other words, thought the earl, she worried that he was being ruled not by his brain, but some other portion of his anatomy.

"I *must* be able to trust you, Wrexford."

For a moment, he kept his gaze on the carpet, watching the flitting of dark, nighttime shapes dart through the weak aureole of lamplight.

Then he looked up and met her searching stare. "Mrs. Ashton is, without question, a beauty who exudes an innate sensuality."

Charlotte's expression didn't change. Like stone—impervious to the elements swirling around it.

"That's not uncommon among the beau monde. Women have little else but their allure to use as bargaining chips when negotiating with men," he went on slowly. "However, the widow also possesses a sharp intellect, which is far rarer.

Granted, I found that intriguing. So, yes, . . ."

Was it merely a quirk of light, or did Charlotte's eyes betray a flicker of pain? It was gone so fast he decided he was mistaken.

"So yes, perhaps that was a distraction."

She released a pent-up breath, softly, so that it barely stirred the surrounding air. "One that might prove deadly."

"It might," agreed Wrexford. "Assuming, as you so delicately implied, that my response to her remained primal rather than cerebral."

Despite the gloom, there was no mistaking the rise of color to her cheekbones.

"There's a steely secrecy to Mrs. Ashton—"

"And God forbid that women have secrets," whispered Charlotte. "But at times, they are our only defense. As you so sagely said, we have precious few ways to counter the power that men hold over us in this supposedly civilized society."

Their eyes met, and on seeing the momentary flicker of naked vulnerability, it was all he could do to keep from drawing her into the protective shelter of his arms. Once again, he wished he knew what lay in her past.

"I don't disagree with you on that, but kindly allow me to finish," he said, somehow keeping his voice level. "There's a secrecy to the widow, and though there's a passion burning somewhere in her depths, it's impossible to discern what it is. My sense is, it's very private. And it's tempered by ice. She's not likely to ever really open her heart."

"You underestimate your own powers, Wrexford. Most women, I imagine find you . . ."

He raised his brows, waiting for her to go on.

Her flush deepened. "But I need not flatter your vanity. My point is, Mrs. Ashton's passions are—"

"Personal," he said flatly. "Unlike yours, which are roused by your compassion and commitment to ideals that are larger than yourself. I can't imagine her risking her neck, as you do, for abstract concepts like truth and justice."

A look of astonishment crept over Charlotte's face. "Y-You find my passions infuriating."

He allowed a small smile. "Yes, but that doesn't mean I don't admire them. Indeed, it's in comparing her to you that I've clarified my thinking."

Charlotte rendered speechless was a rare sight to behold. He took a moment to enjoy it.

"However suspect my judgment is about women, and God knows I've been fooled in the past, I've come to the same conclusion as you about the widow," he explained. "Whether she's ultimately proven to be guilty or innocent, I suspect idealism isn't part of her nature. Whatever attraction I might have felt—and by the by, she was never warming my bed—it is gone. You have my word on it."

"Then the matter is settled," said Charlotte, still appearing a little flustered.

"Not quite," he responded as she turned to the tea table. "Attraction cuts both ways, Mrs. Sloane. Lord Sterling is up to his teeth in this mystery. For you to be blind to that because of the obvious bonds between the two of you could also be dangerous to us all."

"Jeremy and I are friends, nothing more."

"*Dear* friends," stressed Wrexford, repeating her earlier words. "Perhaps it is *you* who under-estimate yourself. He looks at you—"

"He looks at me like someone he's known since childhood!" interrupted Charlotte.

She appeared unnaturally upset by the sugges-tion of a romantic entanglement, though the earl wasn't sure why. Was she oblivious to her own undeniable allure?

"The bonds you sense are those of two kindred souls who didn't fit into the conventional strictures of their worlds," she went on haltingly, clearly fumbling for words. "We've helped each other through . . . difficult times in the past. That builds . . . an elemental trust that is hard to explain."

"And that doesn't make you apt to give him the benefit of the doubt?"

The pulse point on her throat jumped as Charlotte looked away to consider the ques-tion. Her hair had loosened from her night braid, the dark, curling strands obscuring her profile.

She looked achingly beautiful in the softly shifting shadows. He felt a sudden spurt of raw jealousy for Sterling and the closeness he had with her.

"I'm no stranger to facing terrible truths, Wrexford. My bond with Jeremy, however strong, will not override my sense of right and wrong."

"I can't help but wonder what deep, dark secrets you share?" Though he said it lightly, he was deadly serious.

"They have nothing to do with this case." Charlotte's breathing turned ragged. "I assure you, there's naught but friendship between us."

Wrexford didn't think she was lying, but something wasn't quite adding up right. "I'm not sure Sterling feels the same," he pressed.

"He does," she insisted.

"How can you be so sure?"

The uncertain light couldn't hide her reaction. All the color suddenly drained from her face, leaving her looking pale as death. "I—I accepted your word without challenge because I feel that we, too, have developed a certain degree of trust. I ask that you do the same for me."

Perplexed, the earl held himself silent, a furrow forming between his brows. Charlotte was always so plainspoken. Why the devil was she talking in circles? It made no sense.

His frown deepened. Unless . . .

The realization dawned on him as he watched a

fearful war of emotions tighten her features. She wasn't afraid for herself.

"Ah," he said softly. "I think I finally comprehend what you are saying. Sterling's feelings for you are . . . platonic."

"Yes," she whispered, locking her gaze with his. "I have just made myself vulnerable to you. And him as well. But it's important that there be no misunderstandings between us, sir. We must be able to trust each other without reservation."

"Agreed. Trust is a matter of honor—it's sacrosanct between friends." He read the silent appeal in her eyes and added, "You have often said that no secret is ever safe, but rest assured that despite my many faults, I'll never betray your confidence."

"Thank you." Relief resonated in the faint stirring of air between them. "I—I hope that you, who have a healthy skepticism for convention, will not judge Jeremy too harshly."

"Mrs. Sloane, I am far too concerned with the precarious state of my own salvation to give a fig about the so-called sins of others."

Paper crackled as he took a step back and shifted the roll of drawings from hand to hand, intent on giving her a moment of privacy. Charlotte, too, moved away, the soft clinking of the tea things helping to break the tension.

"Thank you," she repeated. "For being . . . such a good friend."

Friend. The word had been barely a whisper, and yet its echo seemed to fill the room with a thrumming that reverberated right down to the marrow of his bones.

Wrexford shifted, trying to shake off the sensation. And yet, after several slow, thudding heartbeats, honesty compelled him to admit that his feelings for Charlotte had somehow become far more than mere friendship.

"Wrexford . . ."

He looked up.

"You . . . don't seem yourself."

I'm not—and perhaps I'll never be quite the same.

She edged around the table, closing the space between them, and to his surprise reached up to place her palm against his cheek. The warmth of her skin sent sparks shooting from his scalp to his toes.

Without thinking, he covered her hand with his. They stood for a long moment, still and silent, before he reluctantly released her and drew back a step.

"I'm simply fatigued, that's all," he murmured.

Charlotte nodded and quietly returned to the task of straightening up the table. "So, is there anything else we need to discuss?" she asked after carefully arranging the cups and pot on the tray. "Otherwise, I suggest you return home and get some sleep."

"I think not," replied the earl. "Our strategies

are in place." He made a small farewell gesture and started for the door. "We shall see how they play out."

Shaken by her confrontation with Wrexford, Charlotte found herself too on edge to sleep. At the top of the stairs, she turned sharply, heading into her work room instead of her bedchamber. It had certainly been a night of revelations, though how they would all intertwine was impossible to predict.

Truth and lies, with no way to discern one from the other.

As for the personal conundrums . . . Charlotte pressed her palms together, aware of the raspy warmth lingering from Wrexford's bristled jaw. How could he be so hard and yet so soft?

Questions, questions—her emotions were too tangled to try to sort out right now.

Instead, she took refuge in the murder investigation. There *must* be a way to put her intellect to work. After pacing back and forth, she took a seat at her work desk. Exhaling a breath, she opened one of the drawers and took out the copy of the numbers Wrexford had found in Hollis's rooms.

Simple symbols, wrought clearly in black on white. Charlotte squinted. Surely she should be able to see some sort of clue, some sort of pattern. Picking up a pencil, she made a stab at converting the numbers to letters.

Gibberish.

Defeated, she slumped back in her chair.

"M'lady?"

Raven's cat-footed stealth was always a little unnerving, but his sudden appearance just an arm's length away nearly caused her to jump out of her skin.

"Sorry," he apologized, stepping back so quickly that tea sloshed over the rim of the steaming mug cradled in his hands. "I—I just thought ye might want something hot te drink."

"How thoughtful! Indeed I do." Charlotte patted the desktop. "Come, put it down, before you burn your fingers."

As soon as he did so, she drew him into her arms, no matter that he usually shied away from hugs. She suddenly needed to feel the softness of his cheek and the reassuring thud of his heart through his shirt. How quickly he was growing out of childhood. He'd been all skin and bones when they first met. Now his scrawny body was filling out with frightening speed and he was shooting up like a weed.

In another year . . .

"Oiy." Raven shifted uncomfortably. His cheeks were tinged with red, but a flicker of a smile softened his grunt.

Charlotte reluctantly loosened her hold.

"Are ye snuffling?" he asked in sudden alarm.

"A bit of dirt from your shirt must have gotten

317

in my eyes," she answered, blinking back tears. *Ye god, Wrexford has really knocked my emotions out of kilter.* "And here it was just laundered yesterday. What do you do—turn cartwheels through every mud puddle between here and Hades?"

He grinned. "Got te practice being agile if I'm te stay one step ahead of the Devil."

She ruffled his hair. "You've done enough twisting and turning for one night. Go to bed."

"Yeah, well, ye should do the same."

"I will." Steam swirled up from the mug. "As soon as I drink my tea."

Raven, too, had shifted his gaze, not to the silvery plume rising up from the mug, but to the piece of paper sitting on the blotter.

"Is that the clue His Lordship mentioned?"

How would Wrexford answer? No sooner had the question formed in her head then Charlotte found herself forced to swallow a laugh. *With brutal honesty*, she conceded, recalling his long-ago conversation with the boys concerning death and the vagaries of the Grim Reaper. With him there was no spooning of sugar-coated platitudes. He didn't treat them like children.

"Yes," she replied. "It is."

Raven craned his neck for a better look.

She pushed the paper closer to him, the shift uncovering her own silly scribbling of letters.

Propping his elbows on the dark-grained oak, he leaned in to study the numbers. Although a curling tangle of uncombed hair shaded his face, she saw his eyes narrow in concentration.

Shamed by how easily she had given up, Charlotte felt compelled to look again. Seconds turned to minutes, and still her mind remained depressingly blank.

"You seem to have a knack for numbers. Have you any ideas on what these might mean?" she finally asked.

A frown pulled at the corners of his mouth but he merely lifted his shoulders in a vague shrug. Whatever thoughts were taking shape in his head, he was, in a very Raven-like way, keeping them to himself.

"But the cove wrote them all down in this order," mused the boy, "so they must mean something."

Charlotte stared balefully at the paper, willing it to whisper its secrets.

And pigs might learn to sing an aria from one of Mozart's operas.

"Yes, they must. Wrexford said . . ." She thought hard, making her recall the exact words he had said when first handing her the copy. "Wrexford said the murdered man's last words were, *Numbers. Numbers will reveal everything.*"

"They ain't saying anything," quipped Raven after several long moments of silence.

"No, they aren't." Swearing a silent oath, she refolded it and set it aside on her blotter. Her hand lingered on the dark leather. The dark-fingered night chills had long since squeezed the heat from the house. A gust rattled in the chimney and she felt a shiver spiral straight down through her marrow.

Grasping the mug, Charlotte took a long swallow, grateful for the ripple of warmth now pooling in her belly. This case had unnerved her—she couldn't seem to find her bearings. Perhaps it had been hubris to think she could pick up and move from one life to another without leaving something of herself behind.

"The tea's turning cold." The lamplight caught the spark of concern in Raven's dark eyes. "I can fetch ye a fresh brew."

"Go to bed, Weasel." Charlotte deliberately used the earl's sardonic nickname.

That made him smile.

"I'll do the same as soon as I finish what I have."

That seemed to satisfy the boy. He nodded and padded off toward the door. Whether he would head to his nest in the attic aerie, or find the allure of the night too strong to resist wasn't a question she dared confront at the present moment.

In diem vive. Live one day at a time, she reminded herself.

A hard-won lesson she'd learned in life was that to have any hope of vanquishing an opponent, one had to find a way to use one's strengths.

"And God knows, I haven't done that in this case," she muttered into her tepid brew. Her best weapon was her pen, and it had been strangely silent in this affair. Poking, prodding with her art and commentary to find an enemy's weak spot and trigger an errant move had proved highly effective in the past. She had somehow lost sight of what she did best.

Plucking a quill from its holder, Charlotte opened her inkwell and placed a blank sheet of sketching paper on her blotter. Numbers might be a mystery to her, but words and images were kindred souls. She began to sketch, letting her thoughts flow freely, without censure. Imagination could be edited.

The details of Ashton's death and the dark suspicions concerning the radical workers couldn't be revealed to the public. But there was always another angle to take in flushing evil from the shadows. She just had to see it.

The nib looped and looped through a series of elaborate curlicues. And then suddenly Charlotte smiled as finally an idea took shape.

Hell's bells, it was so obvious—how had she not thought of it before?

Money was always a subject that titillated the public's interest. Which would make patents a provocative topic for her series. One that might serve to stir a few serpents from their dark hole.

She quickly grabbed a pristine piece of watercolor paper and set to work.

Chapter 20

Wrexford shrugged out of his overcoat and let it drop to the floor as he turned for the sideboard, intent on pouring a much-needed glass of brandy. Or perhaps a Scottish malt. He needed a good jolt of—

"Bloody hell." Two oaths, equally indignant, collided in the darkness.

"I think you might have broken one of my bones," added Sheffield in a querulous mutter as he rubbed his bruised shin.

The earl winced, having tripped over his friend's outstretched legs and hit up against the sharp corner of one of the worktables. "Why are you sleeping in my armchair rather than your own bed?"

"Your selection of beverages is better than mine," quipped Sheffield.

In no mood for banter, Wrexford limped over to the tray holding the crystal decanters. The near-tumble had definitely tipped the odds in favor of the whisky. He poured himself a glass.

"As it happens, I've been waiting here since before midnight, a perfectly respectable time," added his friend. "Which begs the question of what activities you've been up to in the witching time of early morn."

Wrexford took a moment to strike a flint to the wick of the sideboard's oil lamp and turn up the flame. "There's been another unexpected twist in the case."

The yawing yellow-gold light caught the sharpening of Sheffield's features as he straightened from his slouch, suddenly looking wide awake. "Not another murder?"

"No," he answered. "Though a rather colorful rooster did meet an untimely demise."

"A rooster?" Sheffield raised his brows. "If I were you, I'd set aside the whisky. Your wits are befuddled enough without demon drink."

"Not at all," said Wrexford after savoring a long sip. "In fact, my night's foray demanded clear-headed thinking in order to untangle all the threads. Suffice it to say, my efforts have resulted in a momentous discovery."

"As have mine," responded Sheffield. "And if you'll stop being an arse and pour me a wee dram of that lovely malt, I'll tell you about what I've found."

A more than fair trade, conceded the earl. Having tasked Sheffield with mucking through the smoky, sweaty gaming hells for any rumors about Kirkland, his friend likely deserved a key to the entire wine cellar.

"*Slainte mhath*," he murmured, handing Sheffield a generous helping of the whisky. Their two glasses came together in a crystalline clink, setting off a wildly winking pattern of amber light on the side wall.

"I shall cede the honor of going first to you," Wrexford added. "My explanation will likely be the longer of the two."

Sheffield dropped all pretense of ennui. Setting aside his drink, he edged forward in his chair. "I decided to try my luck at one of the less-frequented gaming hells in Seven Dials, as I recalled that Herrington, a fellow who's said to run in Kirkland's circle, tends to play faro there. And sure enough, I struck gold."

To his credit, his friend didn't overplay his hand.

"It cost two bottles of damn expensive brandy—for which I expect reimbursement—but Herrington's tongue then began to wag," recounted Sheffield. "Apparently, the current Mrs. Ashton was, some years ago, Kirkland's paramour. He paid the rent on a charming little townhouse in the village of Morley, near Leeds, and supported her in style."

Wrexford nodded. "Well done, Kit. That confirms what I've just heard."

Sheffield's face fell. "You already knew?"

"Only by a scant hour or two. I'll explain in a moment, but first finish your account."

"Harrington wasn't sure what broke up the previous arrangement. However, he said that Kirkland has recently been telling his cronies that he's rekindled the relationship and expects to be a very rich man once the mourning period is over and the widow can remarry without scandal."

"That is gold, indeed." Wrexford cocked a toast.

Sheffield looked pleased. "Now, tell me of your night's activities."

"One might better call them adventures," said the earl dryly. "It all began with one of the Weasels coming to alert me that an intruder had broken into Mrs. Sloane's house."

"What!" exclaimed his friend in alarm. "Was she injured in any way?"

Wrexford chuffed a quick laugh. "You need ask? Given the two little demons and her own hellfire resolve, the Devil himself wouldn't stand a chance of gaining the upper hand."

Sheffield sank back in his chair. "Who—"

"Miss Merton, one of our suspects. You see, she was after a ceramic rooster . . ." As promised, it required a rather lengthy explanation to apprise his friend of all the evening's surprises.

"Bloody hell." His friend let out a low whistle through his teeth when the story was done. "What next?"

"Sterling will try to trace Hillhouse's where-abouts and the Weasels will organize their urchin friends to keep a close eye on Kirkland's movements—and those of the widow," answered the earl. After a long, meditative swallow of whisky, he added, "I'm considering confronting Mrs. Ashton, now that you've corroborated the scandal in her past."

"Have you told Griffin of these developments?

It seems to me you've all but solved the case for him." Sheffield pulled a sardonic face. "Greed, lust, and betrayal—it's a primordial triangle that has played out countless times throughout human history."

"So it appears, but until I'm certain, I've decided to stay mum. Bow Street is caught on the horns of a difficult dilemma." Wrexford pursed his lips and stared into the amber spirits. "The government is anxious to apprehend the radical leaders quietly while letting the public continue to believe Ashton's death was simply the result of a random robbery gone wrong. Unless there's indisputable evidence, Griffin would be risking his own position to press them to start sniffing around a high-born aristocrat like Kirkland, especially as his father is such an influential man."

"And you are thinking you can wrest a confession from the widow?" Sheffield sounded skeptical. "It seems to me she has ice in her veins. She won't be easily intimidated."

"She may have ice in her veins, but she also has a clear-eyed pragmatism whirring inside her clever brain." The earl gave a grim smile. "Ratting on one's partner to save one's own neck is also a common theme throughout human history."

"How cynical you are."

Wrexford finished his drink. "But that doesn't make my words any less true."

That earned a sardonic laugh. Then Sheffield,

seeing a hint of dawn beginning to tinge the night sky, gave a lazy stretch and recrossed his legs. "When will breakfast be served?"

"As soon as I've had a few hours of sleep." The earl rose. "If the ivories continue to roll in our favor, the day will demand that our wits stay sharp."

His friend gave a gusty yawn. "Wake me when coffee is brewed."

Charlotte set down her paintbrush and rubbed at her bleary eyes. She could barely see straight, but a last inspection of the finished artwork left her feeling satisfied. Exhausted, but satisfied.

A good night's work. Though in truth, it was well after dawn. The pale, pearlescent light was softening the shadows on the street and the houses opposite her own. Somewhere in her back garden, a wood pigeon was cooing a welcome to the new day. She slowly rose, feeling weariness penetrate to the very marrow of her bones, and rolled the drawing in a protective sheet of oilskin.

Upstairs the boys were stirring. No doubt they would welcome an early morning run to Mr. Fores's print shop, especially if she added a shilling for a treat of hot sultana muffins from the bakery near Covent Garden.

Charlotte waited for the patter of their steps on the aerie stairs before stepping into the corridor.

Raven stopped short, fixing her with a basilisk

327

stare. "Ye told me a bouncer, m'lady. Ye said ye were going to go shut yer peepers, if I did the same."

"I fully intended to, but I had a sudden idea." She held up the roll containing her drawing. "And as I've been lax about meeting my deadlines for Mr. Fores, honor compelled me to finish it without delay. He deserves no less."

"I s'pose," conceded Raven. He took the package. "After we deliver this, we'll go find Pudge and have him help us alert the others that His Nibs has work fer us."

Charlotte passed him several coins. "You must be sure to stop and buy some muffins for your breakfast."

"Muffins!" Hawk eyed the silver hungrily. "Huzzah!"

She reached out and ruffled the younger boy's hair. "Be off with you now." She hesitated, then couldn't help adding, "And be careful. You heard more than I might have wished for last night, but let it serve as a reminder that we are dealing with very dangerous adversaries, who'll stop at nothing to get what they want."

"Milord." Riche entered the earl's workroom after giving a knock on the door.

"Ah, is it time for tea?" asked Sheffield, looking up from the novel he was reading.

"Good God, we just finished breakfast. Given

how much food you consume, it's a wonder you don't weigh more than an ox," observed Wrexford, which earned a snicker from Tyler, who was busy polishing the scientific instruments on the far side of the room.

Setting aside Ashton's technical drawings, he checked the clock on the sideboard, then raised an inquiring brow at his butler. He had only a half hour before he must leave for his appointment at the Royal Institution. "Yes, Riche?"

"Master Thomas Ravenwood Sloane wishes to speak with you."

"Show him in."

Sheffield looked surprised. "Has Mrs. Sloane a younger brother?"

"It was decided that the Weasels needed proper English names to fit into their new neighborhood. Be assured the civilizing effect is only skin deep . . ." As Raven entered the room, covered in more than his usual filth, the earl quickly added, "If that much."

"We've alerted our friends," said Raven without preamble. "They'll meet me in the alleyway behind St. Stephen's church in an hour te receive their instructions."

"Excellent," replied the earl. "Sheffield has ascertained that Lord Kirkland is playing cards at White's and will be there for the rest of the afternoon. McKinlock is attending a lecture at the Royal Institution, and my footman has confirmed with Miss Merton that Mrs. Ashton hasn't left her townhouse. So we may put the surveillance into place."

The boy nodded alertly, but to Wrexford's eye, his expression looked a little clouded.

"Is something amiss, lad?"

Raven hesitated before answering, "Skinny hasn't been seen since the day before yesterday, and it isn't like him te be gone from his spot sweeping the muck on Silver Street."

"Perhaps he's feeling poorly."

"Naw, that wouldn't keep him from work," replied Raven. "Ye can't afford te be ill."

Friends were friends, reflected Wrexford, no matter what age or social standing. "Let's give it another day, then we'll see what we can do." Though there was precious little, he feared. The perils for an urchin living alone in the stews were too numerous to count.

Raven knew that as well as he did, and merely shrugged. "Not much anyone can do if the Reaper decides it's yer time."

True, but it was sobering to hear such a hardened sentiment from a boy so young. Still, he'd not insult him with sentimental claptrap. Instead, Wrexford changed the subject.

"Where's your brother?"

"In the stables, looking at yer horses." The boy shot him a wary look. "Do ye mind?"

"Not at all." The earl picked up his notebook

and perched a hip on his desk. "Let us set the surveillance assignments, shall we?"

The next few minutes were spent going over logistics. The plan was for a pair of urchins to shadow Kirkland, McKinlock and the widow—one to race back to inform them if the two suspects met, while the other remained in place. As Wrexford had learned from Charlotte, the master at gathering information, few people paid any attention to children, which made them the perfect spies.

Raven was sharp-witted and though he noted the details in his head rather than on paper, Wrexford was confident that all would run like clockwork.

"Just one last thing. Remind your friends that their quarries must be considered highly dangerous. They are to shadow them from a distance, that's all. Understood?"

"Oiy." The boy shuffled his feet, seeming loath to leave, even though their business was now done. "Can I ask ye a question? It's about numbers."

The earl noticed that Tyler stopped his polishing and cocked an ear. "Of course, lad."

"M'lady and ye were talking about the page of numbers ye found with the second murdered cove. Ye sent it te some expert in mathematics, and I was just wondering whether ye really think numbers can be made to hide a message?"

"Yes, there's a long history of numbers being used to construct codes, lad. The trouble is, there are infinite possibilities, so the chances of our figuring out which system is being used are not good."

"Even for an expert," added Tyler. "I've been taking a long look at the possibilities myself, and from what I can tell, it may be a variation of a Vigenère Square that uses both numbers and letters. But if so, we're hopelessly out of luck, for one needs to know the key word. So we had better pray it's one of the others."

"No word yet from Milner?" interrupted the earl.

"Not yet, milord. He could be away giving a lecture somewhere." Turning back to Raven, the valet tapped a finger to a thick book on the counter. "Come, lad. If you like, I'll show you a diagram of the Square, as well as some of the other well-known codes from the past. "

The boy shot an eager glance at Tyler, then slowly fixed Wrexford with a questioning look.

"You would be doing me a great favor to provide him with an audience," he said dryly. "Otherwise I might have to subject myself to a lecture on Caesar shifts, and I'm already in danger of being late for a meeting."

Raven hurried across the room and took a stool next to the valet.

"I shall leave the pair of you to it," murmured

the earl as he rose. To Sheffield he asked, "What are your plans?"

"I shall toddle back to White's and keep an eye and ear on Kirkland," replied his friend. "Unless you have another task for me."

"Not at the moment. For now, we'll wait for the next move of our adversaries."

The shaft of sunlight roused Charlotte from a bone-deep slumber. Though fatigue still weighed heavily on her, she found her thoughts were too agitated to think of further sleep. After dressing and fixing a pot of tea, she felt more awake, and yet that only exacerbated the question of what to do next.

Granted, she was to put in motion her informant network to see if they could find the love letters. But that felt maddeningly removed from the action. All that was required were a few cryptic notes to key people, and those would be delivered by the boys.

They were in the thick of things. As was Wrexford.

It chafed to feel so passive.

After penning the requests in readiness for Raven and Hawk, Charlotte took a fresh sheet of paper and began to doodle. Drawing always seemed to stimulate her imagination. There *must* be some creative way to help—she just had to see it.

Scratch, scratch. Several sheets were soon

covered in bold, black scrawls. It wasn't until the fourth one that an idea suddenly took shape. It would, she acknowledged, take a little improvising.

And Wrexford wouldn't like it.

Charlotte thought for a moment, uncertain how to deal with that thought. Something had changed between them last night. She had felt the thrum of it in the momentary joining of their hands— and she was sure he had felt it, too. But as she couldn't yet define what it was, she made up her mind to put it aside for now, and simply trust her own judgment.

Yes, the plan was a risk, but one which she felt confident in taking.

She quickly returned to her bedchamber and changed into more fashionable clothing. Casting a critical eye at the cheval glass, she did a slow spin to ensure all was in order. She must appear a perfect pattern-card of propriety. *Or rather, a wolf in sheep's clothing.*

How very apt, as Mrs. Ashton was wearing the same disguise.

Satisfied that she looked the part, Charlotte gathered up her cloak and reticule. Once on the street, she flagged down a hackney and made the journey to Mayfair, where she descended several streets away from the widow's borrowed residence. A short stroll brought her to the front entrance.

"Please ask Miss Merton if she's free to receive Mrs. Sloane," she said to the butler who opened the portal.

"Yes, madam." He gestured for her to enter "If you'll wait here in the parlor, I shall inquire."

Octavia appeared in a matter of minutes. "Mrs. Sloane. How lovely to see you," she said politely, though a questioning look was evident in her eyes.

"Forgive me for arriving unannounced," replied Charlotte a little louder than necessary. "But my modiste is not quite finished with a pelisse I ordered, and as the delay promised to be a bit lengthy, I left my maid to wait for the item while I came to see you." A pause. "I hope you don't mind."

"Not at all. Come to my study and I'll order us some tea."

"Tea would be most welcome," she agreed.

The charade of good manners continued until they were settled in the room and the maid had delivered the refreshments. Octavia waited until the door shut, then quickly rose and pressed her ear to the paneled wood for several long moments.

"We're alone, at least for now," she said in a conspiratorial whisper as she returned to her chair and nervously smoothed at her skirts. "Is there any word on Benedict?"

"It's far too early for that," replied Charlotte.

"Then why are you—"

"I've an idea. But it requires your help."

Chapter 21

After giving a brusque wave in answer to the porter's greeting, Wrexford hurried through the grand colonnaded entrance of the Royal Institution and took the stairs up to the laboratory area two at a time. Horatio Johnson, an irascible fellow to begin with, tended to become insufferably grumpy if kept waiting.

"Hmmph. About time." A tall, reed-thin man with a thick shock of ginger hair and prominent side whiskers, looked up from an assortment of machine parts on his workbench and shot an irritated glace at the ship's chronometer mounted above his bookshelf.

The hands, noted the earl, read precisely 2:53.

"Anything less than a minute does not qualify as late," he said, regarding the jumble of pistons and rods with interest.

"Precision, Wrexford. Precision," chided Johnson. "You're a decent natural philosopher—as shown by your chemistry in creating different tensile strength in iron—when you pay attention to the minute details."

"I've not your talent for patience." Men of science, who, for the most part, toiled and tinkered in solitude, were prone to a little flattery, so Wrexford added. "Nor your genius for precision."

"Hmmph." The grunt was a good deal less huffy than the first one.

"I was wondering whether I might ask your opinion on a concept concerning steam and the power it can generate." Johnson's passion was the internal combustion engine, and he'd been working for over four years on refining the hydrogen-and-oxygen-powered design patented by the Swiss inventor, Francois Isaac de Rivaz. But his background in steam power made him an authority in that field as well.

Johnson sat back and tugged at the points of his waistcoat. "I daresay I can be of some assistance to you," he replied with exaggerated modesty, "having a small degree of experience in that field."

Wrexford unfolded the notes he had made after analyzing Ashton's plans. "Say one could engineer a way to put four valves in a cylinder and create a controlling valve gear for steam admission and exhaust which did away with the wide swings in temperature during the cycle," he explained. "That would generate a whole new level of power, wouldn't it?"

"*Four* valves?" Johnson frowned in concentration. "A radical notion . . ." After a search of his pockets, the inventor found a small notebook and the stub of a pencil. Opening to a page, he began to scribble a quick diagram. "You'd need to transfer motion from a single eccentric to the four valves. . . trip valves . . . some sort of wrist plate . . ."

He pursed his lips. "Yes, it's theoretically possible—and yes, it would be a revolutionary advance in power. But it would take a technical wizard to design a workable model." A few more scribbles and *harrumphs*. "No, too deucedly difficult. I doubt that even Hephaestus, the Greek god of metallurgy could create such an innovation."

"Difficult, but not impossible," mused the earl.

"And then, of course, there would be the question of the iron. The added pressure of such valves would require a very strong metal, as you well know."

"I imagine that could be done," replied the earl. "Again, difficult, but not impossible."

"Don't tell me you are thinking of taking up engineering? I wouldn't advise it. It takes great patience, which I've heard isn't your strength." Johnson pulled a face. "But perhaps you've got a prototype of your valves ready to unveil to the public." The idea seemed to amuse him. "Ha, ha, ha."

"Ha, ha, ha," echoed Wrexford. "Alas, no. A friend and I were discussing the matter and disagreed over the concept. You've been very helpful in settling the argument." He refolded his papers and tucked them back into his pocket. "Thank you. I'll not take up any more of your valuable time."

"Quite all right," said the inventor, his eyes straying back to his notebook. "Hmmph, you'd need a ratchet gear . . . a dashpot . . ."

Wrexford left Johnson muttering to himself, and after stopping to speak with a few other fellow members took his leave from the Institution. No one had heard any word about McKinlock having new plans on the drawing board.

From there he made a stop at a toolmaking workshop renowned for its precision work. The proprietor, Joseph Clement, was a gruff, rough-spoken man, but his technical skill was unquestioned throughout the scientific community. Anyone looking to build complicated mechanical devices sought him out. A short conversation— and that only because he had greased Clement's palm with a few guineas—confirmed Johnson's assessment that Ashton's valves could work with the right engineering and materials.

The plans found in the ceramic rooster were indeed worth a fortune, thought the earl as he began walking back to Berkeley Square. Assuming someone had the expertise to finish the last little details not shown on the drawings.

And as he further mulled over the matter, the only name that came to mind was that of Benedict Hillhouse.

"It will demand a steady nerve if we are to be successful," Charlotte went on to explain. "If my hunch is right, we may find the evidence we need to prove Mrs. Ashton's perfidy. However, we must be very careful. If we make a mistake, it will have grave consequences."

Octavia didn't bat an eye. "Tell me what you need me to do."

"I need to get upstairs and have access to Mrs. Ashton's bedchamber. I'm assuming, given the layout of the house, that your quarters are close to hers?"

"Yes, but how—"

"I'm going to have a sudden attack of megrims and will need to lie down for a bit. You'll escort me up to your chamber with a great show of solicitous concern, of course."

Octavia's eyes lit up in understanding. "You're thinking of any notes between her and Lord Kirkland? Very clever. But you told me clandestine activities aren't quite as easy as they may seem."

"I'm experienced in such things," replied Charlotte firmly.

To her credit, Octavia didn't question how, but merely nodded for her to continue.

"And yes, there's a good chance she has incriminating letters. After all, Kirkland is here in London, and they are likely communicating. If I were her, I wouldn't dispose of them, as a servant might find them. I've an idea of where to look," explained Charlotte. "But it's key we have the floor to ourselves. Think hard, Miss Merton—are there usually any maids working there at this time of day?"

"No," replied Octavia. "Their tasks are always completed in the morning hours."

"Excellent. Now, once you escort me upstairs, your task will be to stand guard at the top of the stairs. If you hear Mrs. Ashton or a maid about to come up, you must find a way to delay them long enough for me to quit her chamber—raise holy hell about me needing absolute silence, or some such thing. Can you do that?"

"Yes," came the resolute reply. "As it happens, we're in luck. Mrs. Ashton is currently meeting with Mr. Blodgett, the mill supervisor, as he's leaving later today to return to Leeds."

Fortuitous, indeed. Would that their luck would hold. "Then come, let us not waste any more time."

Charlotte slapped her cheeks to bring a rush of color to her face, then pulled loose some strands of hair and undid the top fastening of her high-collared gown. "Give me your arm," she said, rising from her chair, "and help me into the corridor."

Leaning heavily on Octavia, she followed her friend's lead with unsteady steps, hoping her instincts were right and that the other woman would keep her nerve.

Octavia immediately proved her mettle, putting on a very convincing show of fussing in concern as a tweenie carrying an empty coal scuttle passed them.

So far, so good.

"Well done," Charlotte murmured once they were half way up the stairs.

"You play the role of invalid to perfection," whispered Octavia admiringly. "Why, you have *me* believing you are on the verge of a deathly swoon."

"Necessity is an excellent teacher of play-acting," Charlotte replied dryly. Then, as they reached the top landing, she dropped all pretense of languor and came to full alert. "Describe the layout," she demanded.

"My quarters are the first door on the left, the next is the suite used by Mr. Ashton," pointed out Octavia. "Mrs. Ashton's rooms are accessed through the last door."

"And on the right?

"Just two linen closets. The door opposite mine leads to Benedict's quarters."

Charlotte took a moment to survey her surroundings, gauging the distances between the rooms. Satisfied, she said, "Wait here. You know your role. If you must play it, be sure that I hear you."

"I understand." Octavia looked pale but determined.

Feeling her pulse quicken, Charlotte swiftly traversed the passageway and entered the widow's quarters. Slipping into her second skin—the woman who had learned all the tricks necessary to survive in the stews—felt far more comfortable than the fancy clothes she was wearing. It took only a moment to assess the small sitting room. The escritoire might be a possible hiding place, but she thought it unlikely. Even the most cunning and clever people, Charlotte had learned, allowed primal urges to overrule reason when it came to precious possessions. One kept them close.

A jewel case, a travel desk for private correspondence, a box of lace fichus. Her feeling was that any incriminating letters would be kept in an intimate, portable place. As time was of the essence, a thorough search wasn't possible. She would have to trust her instincts.

Without hesitation, Charlotte continued on to the bedchamber.

No feminine frills were in evidence—it was decorated in the same dark, masculine colors that dominated the rest of the house. The furniture was mahogany, heavy with ornate carvings. There was no warmth to the room, and yet she sensed that the widow felt at home there.

Charlotte immediately moved the dressing table, where a set of silver-backed brushes and an array of crystal cosmetic pots were aligned on either side of a large looking glass framed in a brass pedestal.

Mrs. Ashton's iron-willed self-control extended to her toilette.

To the right of the brushes sat a small rosewood chest, its lid inlaid with an intricate rosette made of ivory. Dropping her gaze, she saw a large brass keyhole.

A quick tug confirmed it was locked.

Charlotte pulled a steel hairpin from her top-knot and with a few precise jiggles and twists was rewarded with a satisfying *snick*.

The top velvet-lined tray contained several pairs of earrings and matching bracelets. Garnets and peridots—nothing flashy. Beneath it was a larger divided compartment, with a double strand of lustrous pearls coiled on one side and a filigree gold necklace on the other. She lifted the jewelry out of the chest and carefully inspected the velvet lining, poking and prodding with her pin see if there was any sign of a false bottom.

Nothing. And a quick check with the span of her fingers confirmed that there was no hidden space. After replacing everything exactly as it had been, she closed and relocked the lid.

Charlotte was allowing herself a quarter hour for the search. She gauged that she had maybe eleven minutes left.

The chest of drawers contained nothing but

gloves, shawls, and small clothes. Moving around the four-poster bed, she saw the night table held only a glass-globed oil lamp and a book. Within its pages was a bookmark, but no other papers.

Behind her, the clock on the mantel was ticking off the seconds.

Hearing no disturbance in the corridor, she ducked into the dressing room. A large painted armoire held a number of gowns, while next to it sat two trunks with several smaller traveling cases stacked next to them. Faced with a choice, Charlotte made her decision quickly and headed for the luggage. If the letters were hidden within the silks and satins, they would remain safe from her prying eyes.

Unlatching the small brass-banded box that sat atop the others revealed a collection of pens, bottled inks, and sealing wax. No papers, and the thin layer of felt was glued tightly to the interior wood, allowing no hiding place.

The sense of urgency was growing. Drawing a breath to settle her spiking nerves, Charlotte quickly shut it and moved on to the next one.

Damn. It held only ribbon-trimmed ballroom slippers.

The dark, smooth ebony of the bottom case was cold to the touch—or maybe it was just that the blood pulsing through her fumbling fingers was heating to a hellfire pitch. It took several tries to open it before she realized it was locked. Once again, she plucked the pin from her hair and worked the catch free.

Charlotte felt a spurt of surprise on seeing the contents were all items belonging to a gentleman. She picked up the handsome pocketwatch and turned it over. *EJA* were the ornate entwined initials engraved in the gold case. *Her husband's personal effects?* That made perfect sense. Mrs. Ashton would naturally wish to ensure they were kept safe.

Logic said there was nothing to be gained by a further search. But a hunch was prickling at the tips of her fingers so Charlotte delved deeper. Several briarwood pipes . . . a pouch of watch fobs, a battered leather sketchbook . . .

Was that a noise coming from the corridor?

She pulled it free and began thumbing through the pages. *Faster, faster.*

More sounds—she couldn't linger any longer.

As the cover snapped shut, a small folded sheet of stationery fluttered free. A rushed look showed it was addressed to Isobel. That was enough to make up her mind. Charlotte jammed it down her bodice and hurriedly put everything back in order.

A quick dash brought her to the doorway, where she halted to cock an ear.

Octavia's voice rose from the foot of the stairs. ". . . suffering a *beastly* headache. I fear the smallest sound will be *agony* to her."

Charlotte rushed to Octavia's door and after fluffing her skirt, assumed a slow, shuffling step as she headed for the landing.

"I apologize for upsetting the household," she said weakly.

Both Mrs. Ashton and Octavia looked up. A man was standing several paces behind the widow. He, too, darted a glance at Charlotte, then quickly averted his eyes. Head bowed, he began toying with the brim of his hat.

"There is no need to apologize, Mrs. Sloane," said Octavia. "Illness is nothing to trifle with. You must rest for as long as need be." She turned to Mrs. Ashton. "I'm sure you agree."

"Of course," answered the widow slowly. "I simply need a moment to fetch some papers from my desk for Mr. Blodgett before he leaves, then we'll leave you in peace and quiet until you're feeling better, Mrs. Sloane."

"That's very kind of you, but it's truly not necessary. The worst has passed." Charlotte started down, leaning heavily on the bannister. "Indeed, I think it best if I return to my residence, where I have powders to help prevent a further attack. My maid is still delayed at the modiste shop . . . but Miss Merton, if I might trouble you to accompany me in a hackney . . ."

"I would be happy to do so." With a rustling of skirts, Octavia joined her on the stairs. "Please allow me to assist you."

"Thank you," murmured Charlotte, accepting her friend's arm.

Mrs. Ashton stepped aside to let them pass. "I do hope you'll recover quickly."

"Thankfully the attacks come infrequently, but alas, they give no warning." She gave a small wince. "And tend to be severe while they last."

"Then please don't let me keep you," replied Mrs. Ashton.

Blodgett shuffled back deeper into the shadows to make room for them to move through the archway leading to the entrance hall. He was a handsome man, noted Charlotte in passing. His gaze kept darting to the widow—the woman seemed to attract men like flies to honey—but as he shifted, his eyes met with Charlotte's for an instant.

Passion. For all his show of proper subservience, Charlotte caught the hot spark of some fierce emotion before he looked away.

Was Blodgett another of Isobel's conquests? Or was it infatuation from afar? He was the mill's supervisor . . . Good God, could he, too, be involved in taking control of Ashton's business?

She forced herself to push such thoughts away until later. Her nerves were on edge—perhaps she was merely seeing specters.

Playing her role well, Octavia guided Charlotte down the front steps. Neither of them spoke until they were in a hackney and navigating through the crush of carriages on Piccadilly Street.

"Well?" Octavia was whispering despite the noise of the traffic. "Did you find anything?"

"Perhaps." Charlotte withdrew the paper from her bodice—now slightly crumpled—and smoothed it out in her lap. "You're familiar with Ashton's writing." She held up the top note. "Is this his hand?"

The reply came without hesitation. "No."

"Take a closer look. I need for you to be absolutely certain."

"I've handled Eli's correspondence since I was fifteen," replied Octavia. "The slant and the roundness of the letterforms are all wrong. He did *not* pen that note."

Charlotte accepted her word for it. "Then yes, I think we've found something interesting. You see, it begins *My Dear Isobel*, and since you're sure it wasn't written by Ashton, it certainly stirs suspicions." She went on to explain where she had found the note and why she had taken it.

Octavia edged forward on her seat. "What does the rest of it say?"

A slow smile tugged at the corner of her mouth as Charlotte skimmed the short message.

"*My Dear Isobel*," she read, "*There's no need to worry that anyone will learn of our sordid little secret. Just remain calm and do as I tell you, and we'll both get what we want.*"

Charlotte looked up. "It's simply signed with the letter *D*."

"Lord Kirkland's Christian name is Dermott," said Octavia.

"I'm aware of that." Her smile widened. "Granted, it's still circumstantial. But we may be slowly tightening the noose around the necks of the villains responsible for Elihu Ashton's death."

The wheels lurched as the hackney rolled onto the narrower streets and rougher paving stones of her new neighborhood. A reminder that Mayfair, with all its glitter and glamor, was still a world apart from hers.

I must never forget that.

"Mrs. Sloane . . ."

Charlotte was roused from her own musings by the tentative words.

"Might I ask you a question?"

Shadows flitted between them, sharp and jumpy, like the rattling of the vehicle and clattering of hooves. She nodded an assent, careful to make no promise to answer it.

"I can't help but be curious on how you seem so skilled at clandestine activities."

"There is an old adage about curiosity killing the cat," murmured Charlotte.

Octavia didn't smile. "Which is to say you aren't going to give me an answer?"

"Correct."

The sigh was swallowed in the street noise. "My guess is you're a government spy." Octavia plucked at a fold in her skirts and gave a wry grimace. "But I don't suppose you would admit to it if that were true."

"You have a very creative imagination, Miss Merton. However, allowing it to run wild can lead to trouble. Let's just say that life's challenges have taught me certain pragmatic tricks for survival."

Octavia remained silent, a pensive look shading her face.

Charlotte turned her attention to the note still in her hand. She read it again, then refolded it and tucked it back into her bodice. Wrexford must, of course, see it without delay. Sheffield would likely recognize Kirkland's handwriting from seeing the viscount's gaming vowels. Bow Street couldn't ignore the web of intrigue woven by the short message . . .

The hackney slowed to a halt.

"What do we do next?" asked Octavia as Charlotte took hold of the door latch. "Benedict—"

"Patience, Miss Merton," she cut in. "For now, discretion is the better part of valor. You must concentrate on giving nothing away to Mrs. Ashton. Lord Wrexford and I must have a council of war. Our enemy is clever . . ."

From outside came the sounds of the horse snorting and stomping.

"But so are we."

Chapter 22

"Pressure, volume, temperature," muttered Wrexford to himself as he entered his town house and headed straight for his workroom. "If the temperature remains unchanged within a closed system . . ." He flung open the door, and marched to the bookshelf above the spirit lamp. "Then the absolute pressure and volume of a specific mass of enclosed gas is inversely proportional."

"Boyle's Law," said Tyler, without looking up from the eyepiece of the microscope.

"Yes, Boyle." The earl quirked a grimace. "Do you, perchance, recall if he experimented with steam?"

"With a name like that, one would hope so," quipped Tyler.

"Stubble the attempts at humor, if you please. As the patron saint of modern chemistry, the fellow deserves the utmost respect from the likes of you."

"I do know the august history of science in our realm, sir."

Ignoring the comment, the earl selected several volumes on chemistry and carried them to his desk. "But enough on the past. Let us focus on the present. I've just come from speaking with Horatio Johnson and Joseph Clement, and their answers to my questions have convinced me that Ashton's new design for a steam engine is technically feasible and will work."

"I'm not surprised," said the valet. "He was one of those rare geniuses who was not only a brilliant theorist, but actually possessed the engineering skills to fabricate what he envisioned."

"Yes," agreed Wrexford. "But there's just one problem." He began thumbing through the pages of the top book.

"Which is?" prompted Tyler.

"The chemical composition of the iron used in the boiler. Ashton's increase in power is based on his revolutionary valve design, which creates much higher levels of steam pressure than in previous engines. To ensure new machines won't explode, the iron has to be strong enough."

Tyler frowned. "Surely he must have been aware of that."

"Yes, but he wasn't a chemist. And to my knowledge, neither is Hillhouse."

Wrexford took a long moment to ponder the problem. "My guess is the formulation of the iron was the last element to address before he could build a full-size working model."

The drumming of his fingers beat a soft tattoo on the open pages.

"Are you thinking it's possible—"

"Possible that he was murdered by a chemist who decided to steal the invention for himself?" interrupted the earl. "The thought has occurred to me." The drumming grew louder. "Though it wreaks havoc with our assumption about the widow, Kirkland, and McKinlock."

Tyler pushed his chair back from the worktable. "Well, as you are so fond of pointing out, one mustn't make assumptions about the outcome of an experiment. One must base the answer on empirical data."

"Thank you for throwing my words back in my face," grumbled Wrexford. He made a face. "However, you're right." Silence, save for the tap, tap, tapping. "So we must consider two more things. Firstly, I need to learn more about gases and pressure."

"Avogadro." Tyler shot up from his seat and hurried to the bookshelf at the far end of the room. "He's the leader in that field. And we just received the latest book on his work."

"Excellent. I'll begin reading while you head to the Institution and make some inquiries on who might be working with the composition of metals."

"Very good, sir." The valet brought over the volume. "And when I'm done there, I think I should visit several of the taverns where the iron-workers and toolmakers congregate. They may have heard some useful gossip."

As he turned to take his leave, Wrexford muttered, "Would that your questions will help us untangle this damnable coil."

• • •

Charlotte shot yet another impatient glance out the window and muttered an oath under her breath. The sun, shining with an unholy brightness, seemed glued to its spot in the sky rather than following its natural course to drop below the horizon. Even the clouds seemed to be taking perverse pleasure in prolonging the day. They were nowhere to be seen, allowing the light to sparkle with a brilliance that drew an additional unladylike word from her lips.

Darkness—that concealing cloak which allowed her freedom of movement—couldn't come soon enough.

With the boys absent because of their surveillance duties, she had no one to carry a message to Wrexford, leaving her no choice but to do it herself. He wouldn't be happy about the choice, but so be it.

In for a halfpenny, in for a guinea.

The odds were good that he was already furious with her because of today's print.

Forcing herself to sit down at her work desk, Charlotte picked up her pen and slid a blank piece of sketching paper onto her blotter. Mr. Fores would expect a new drawing as soon as possible. The topic was provocative—and he would expect to profit from it.

The ink-rich nib moved in a series of skirling circles as an idea began to take shape. It was, she decided, time to press a little harder on the subject of just how much money a patent could be worth.

"Kirkland has finally moved on from White's," announced Sheffield as he sauntered into the earl's workroom. "Having lost a goodly sum, I might add."

Roused from a deep study, Wrexford needed a moment to react. Pinching at the bridge of his nose, he realized day had turned into evening. The room was wreathed in shadows, the last muted purple and gold hues of twilight fast fading into shades of charcoal.

"What time is it?" he asked.

"Well past the supper hour," responded his friend. "I asked Riche to bring in a collation of meat and cheese, along with a bottle of claret, to keep starvation at bay."

"Do you think of nothing but your stomach?"

"Occasionally I contemplate my cravats. Do you think my valet uses too much starch?"

"Remind me again of why I allow you to run tame in my house," snapped Wrexford. His eyes were aching. Avogadro's book had proved less helpful than he had hoped . . . and his stomach was growling, which only exacerbated his fast-darkening mood.

"Because there are times I prove useful," replied Sheffield. "To my point, you turn snappish when your breadbox is empty, and thus don't think as clearly. So you ought to be thanking me for ordering the food."

The earl gave a grunt.

"But even more importantly . . ." Sheffield held up the roll of paper he was carrying. "I brought you A. J. Quill's latest print."

Wrexford felt a stab of unease. Charlotte had been silent of late, honoring his request that she refrain from stirring up public interest in Ashton's murder. But all that pent-up passion for justice was a powder keg just waiting to explode.

"And?" he said.

"And you had better have a look for yourself."

He accepted the print without comment and, after shoving his books aside, slowly unrolled it.

Sheffield clasped his hands behind his back and began to whistle softly through his teeth.

Mozart's Requiem in D Minor, decided the earl. Music for a funeral. His friend's sense of humor was nearly as sardonic as his own.

"You're digging your own grave," he warned. "Another note and my pantries and wine cellar will close up tighter than a crypt."

The sounds immediately stopped.

Focusing his attention on the art, Wrexford made a thorough study of the image and words, willing himself not to react until he'd considered all the ramifications.

It was, he conceded, very cleverly done.

Diabolically clever, in fact. The question of who profited from patents fit into her overall theme of *Man vs. Machine,* so in some ways could be seen as an innocent question. But there were just enough allusions to Ashton's mill and his earlier improvements in steam power to stoke the fires of speculation on whether his unfortunate demise had a darker meaning. After all, in every circle of London society, A. J. Quill's hints of intrigue were known to have substance.

"That ought to poke a stick into the nest of vipers, whoever they may be," observed Sheffield.

"It is," said Wrexford in a carefully controlled voice, "a very good thing the infernally infuriating A. J. Quill is not present. Else I might to tempted to—"

A leathery *thump* cut off his words. The room suddenly turned colder as a sharp gust of air, redolent with the damp smokiness of night, swirled through the open window.

"If you wish to vent your spleen, milord, do so at me." Charlotte straightened from her jump down off the sill and stomped a clump of mud off her boots. "Not the poor messenger of my misdeeds."

"Good evening, Mrs. Sloane." Sheffield inclined a polite nod. "As always, you look very fetching in breeches."

Wrexford signaled him to silence. "Impossible

woman—are you looking to get your throat cut?" he demanded without preamble.

Charlotte didn't flinch. "I take it that is a rhetorical question?"

"Actually, it's not," he retorted. "A.J. Quill's identity may be well-guarded, but as you are so fond of telling me, no secret is ever really safe."

"Yes, well, we're all gamblers in one way or another." Charlotte paused to tuck a loose curl under her floppy wool cap. "And as *you* are so fond of telling *me,* a careful weighing of chance and probability before playing a hand turns the odds in one's favor."

"Theoretically," he shot back. "When a gambler loses, it's usually one's purse, not one's life."

She shrugged.

"And it's not just you who will pay the price. You've two young boys who depend on you."

Her mouth quivered for an instant. "That's a low blow, sir."

"Yes, it is. But no less true."

Their gazes locked and Wrexford could almost hear the steely clang of rapier against rapier.

Charlotte held his eyes a moment longer, then looked away. "The stakes are higher," she conceded. "But before you continue ringing a peal over my head, please hear me out."

He, too, backed off. "I'm willing to listen."

Charlotte was about to begin when a knock on the door sounded. She looked to the window, but

Wrexford stopped her with an exasperated chuff.

"Never mind. My butler is growing used to the eccentricities of my acquaintances."

"Thank God," quipped Sheffield. "Supper is about to be served."

"Excellent. I'm famished." She smiled on seeing the earl's scowl. "Come now, sir, you're always more cheerful when your stomach is full."

"It's a moot point, seeing as what you're about to say will likely rob me of any appetite."

"Stop brangling," commanded Sheffield as he stepped aside to allow the earl's butler to place a large tray on the tea table and then quietly withdraw. "It's bad luck to break bread in anger."

Wrexford drew in a sharp breath, but held back a retort.

"Do go on, Mrs. Sloane," said the earl's friend after helping himself to several slices of beefsteak and a wedge of buttery cheddar.

She took a seat on one of the work chairs, suddenly looking smaller and more vulnerable than she had a moment before. He looked away quickly, uncomfortably aware that the thought triggered feelings that he wished to keep at bay.

Damn her for somehow prying open a chink in his defenses. It was far simpler to snap and snarl at the world from within a suit of armor. Caring about another person . . . was dangerous.

"You may think my actions rash, milord, but in truth I thought very carefully about my drawing and its timing," began Charlotte after removing her heavy moleskin jacket. "We have our main suspects under surveillance, and touching a raw nerve, so to speak, may cause them to react without thinking and make a mistake."

Shaking off his musings, Wrexford made himself focus on the problem at hand. "The trouble is, after paying a visit to a fellow man of science at the Royal Institution and a skilled toolmaker this afternoon, I have reason to believe we may be looking at the wrong people," he replied. "There's a good chance the real culprit is a chemist."

Her reply was quick and decisive. "I think you're wrong."

"Why?" he challenged.

She took a piece of paper out of a hidden pocket in her shirt. "Because of this."

Her thoughts, Charlotte knew, ought to be strictly focused on the evidence and convincing the earl that she was right in her reasoning. Still, as she watched him unfold the note, she couldn't help thinking what graceful hands he had. Strong. Sure. And yet capable of great gentleness, as she'd witnessed when the boys were in trouble. One wouldn't have guessed it from his outward show of snappish sarcasm.

A man of contradictions and complexities.

Which, she supposed, was rather like the pot calling the kettle black.

"What am I looking at?" he demanded.

"I found it hidden in a locked case in Mrs. Ashton's dressing room. As you see, it's written to her and signed with a *D*. As Kirkland's Christian name is Dermott, I presume it was written by him." She looked at the earl's friend. "I'm hoping Mr. Sheffield can confirm that."

Wrexford passed it over without comment.

"Yes, I'm quite certain this is Kirkland's handwriting," said Sheffield after subjecting it to a careful scrutiny. "Mind you, gambling vowels tend to have mostly numbers but while I don't remember cards overly well, I've a good eye for letters."

The earl took it back. "Might I be so bold as to inquire how, precisely, you came to be in Mrs. Ashton's dressing room?"

She expelled a resigned sigh. "I see we are about to have another round of pyrotechnics. But after the sparks die down, might we call a short truce in which to enjoy refreshments?"

He didn't smile, but she thought she detected a tiny flicker of grudging humor in his eyes. To his credit, the earl was one of those rare men who was able to laugh at himself.

"It wasn't nearly as risky as you might think." An overstatement, perhaps, however Charlotte sensed his temper was on edge and a further clash would do neither of them any good. "Miss Merton was instrumental . . ." She gave a quick explanation of the ruse, and how it had gone exactly as planned.

"That was devilishly dangerous, Mrs. Sloane," said Wrexford after a long moment of silence. "If the widow is involved in her husband's murder, she wouldn't have had any qualms about sticking a knife between your ribs."

"It was no more dangerous than chasing into the stews after the man you thought responsible for the hideous slashing of Ashton's throat."

His eyes narrowed. "That's different."

"Because I am a woman?"

Sensing that he was being maneuvered into a verbal corner, Wrexford quickly sidestepped the question by countering with one of his own.

"If Mrs. Ashton and the viscount are alerted to our suspicions, it may give them time to cover their tracks. How can you be sure she won't notice that her rooms have been searched?"

Charlotte fixed him with a level gaze. "Because I'm very good at what I do, Wrexford. I wouldn't stay in business if I wasn't."

"The beef is excellent," murmured Sheffield. "As is the cheddar. May I fix you a plate, Mrs. Sloane?"

"Thank you. That would be most welcome."

"Wrex?" asked his friend.

The earl's answer was to pour himself a glass of claret.

"Come, let us set aside our differences and

have a constructive conversation on what to do next," said Charlotte after savoring a few bites of the food. "By the by, Mr. Sheffield is correct—the beef is delicious."

The earl finally surrendered his scowl. "It had better be," he replied, fixing himself a generous helping from the platter. "I pay my chef an obscene amount of money."

"I imagine he earns it," she said.

Wrexford surrendered a low laugh. "You know, most people show a modicum of respect for my exalted position."

"I am not like most people," pointed out Charlotte. "And besides, an occasional pinprick keeps your vanity from ballooning to exalted heights."

"No chance of that with you two around," said Wrexford, once he had swallowed a mouthful of beef and bread.

Sheffield smiled. "You loathe toadeaters."

The banter—and the refreshments—appeared to have improved the earl's mood. Setting aside her empty plate, Charlotte decided it was time to get down to business.

"So, assuming you agree with the assessment that Kirkland and Mrs. Ashton are the most likely suspects, we must decide what to do next."

Wrexford took a long sip of his wine. "Given your discovery, I agree that it makes the most sense to pursue the pair. So the question is, do we wait for them to rendezvous and then confront them together? Or do we choose one of them and see if we can force a confession?"

"Both have merits," mused Charlotte. "For the moment we hold a certain advantage in knowing of their illicit past. However, it seems to me, Benedict Hillhouse is the unknown factor in all this. We don't know how close he is to completing a working model of the engine, or how that might factor into the timing of applying for a patent. We may not have much time."

"I take it you are suggesting bold action." At her confirming nod, Wrexford tapped his fingertips together. "So, who do we confront—the viscount or the widow?"

"The widow," responded Sheffield without hesitation.

Charlotte expected no less. Men liked to delude themselves with the notion that women were, by their nature, prone to betrayal. But in her experience, the opposite was true.

"Mrs. Sloane?" murmured Wrexford. "You are unnaturally silent on the subject."

Sheffield, she noted, put down his plate and went very still. Perhaps he was expecting further fireworks.

"I disagree," she answered. "Especially as, for pragmatic reasons, I wouldn't be permitted to take part in the interrogation."

The earl's gaze turned hooded. "Would you care to elaborate on your objection?"

"Women are not always the weak vessel you men assume them to be. A strong and clever female knows how to turn such prejudices to her advantage," replied Charlotte. "In short, I think gentlemanly scruples will prevent you from being too rough on her. While I, on the other hand, would keep my hands around her throat and squeeze harder if I sensed it would draw out a confession."

Sheffield's expression altered slightly—whether in admiration or revulsion she couldn't quite discern.

Wrexford's face remained a cipher.

She waited, trusting his innate good judgment to conquer any lingering vestiges of ill humor.

"An interesting conjecture," he finally commented. A hint of a smile touched his lips. "The idea of being at your mercy in any interrogation is terrifying."

"Nonsense, milord. Nothing terrifies you, least of all me."

The dark fringe of his lashes stirred ever so slightly. But whatever he was going to reply was cut short by a sudden loud rustling in the ivy vines outside the window, followed by the hurried scrabbling of leather on stone.

Quick as a cat, Wrexford shot up and moved to the rosewood case containing his pistols. Steel flashed in the wildly flickering candlelight as the hammer cocked with a sharp *snick*.

Charlotte came to her feet as well, just as a hand grasped the fluted granite ledge.

"Oiy!" Raven hauled himself up to the sill, red-faced and struggling to catch his breath.

In two quick strides, the earl was at the window. Grabbing hold of the boy's collar, he pulled him into the room.

"Ye got te come fast! Kirkland—" exclaimed Raven, his words tangling in a gusty wheeze.

Wrexford thumped him several times between the shoulder blades to jar the air back into his lungs. "Steady, lad."

"Kirkland—" gasped Raven.

"What about him?" urged Charlotte.

"He's been murdered!"

Chapter 23

"At least, it looks that way," amended Raven quickly. "I can't be sure, seeing as ye ordered us not te follow him into any building, and we kept our word."

"Thank God," rasped Charlotte, falling to her knees and enfolding him in a hard hug.

Much to the boy's chagrin, noted Wrexford, as he uncocked the pistol's hammer.

"Good God, this is *blood!*" she suddenly exclaimed, fingering a dark patch on the front of his coat.

"Don't get all argy-bargy. It ain't—it isn't—mine," protested Raven. "I'm trying te explain—"

"If the lad isn't hurt, let him tell us what's happened," ordered Wrexford. To Raven he added, "As quickly as you can, but try not to leave out any important details."

The boy squirmed free of Charlotte's hold. "Me 'n Pudge were the ones keeping watch on White's. Lord Kirkland left right after eight."

Sheffield nodded in confirmation

"He didn't hail a hackney but headed north on foot, by way of Dover Street. At the corner of Hay Hill, another man came around the corner from Berkeley Street and hailed him. They spoke fer a few moments—friendly-like as far as we could tell. We didn't want te get too close and give ourselves away."

"Wise thinking," said Wrexford. "Go on."

"They fell in step together and walked fer a bit before cutting through the passageway on the east side of Bruton Lane, which brought them to a cul de sac running along the back of two buildings on Hay's Mews."

The earl knew the place. Even Mayfair, with its elegant streets and thoroughfares, had a maze of twisting passageways threading through the neighborhood, which allowed for the coal mongers and nightsoil men to do their business without offending highborn sensibilities.

"Lord Kirkland and the other man entered the one on the right," continued Raven. "I found a place te hide behind some broken crates, while Pudge scarpered around te the front of the place te make sure they didn't leave that way. We weren't there more than five minutes when the other man came out the back entrance, moving quick-like, but taking care te keep te the shadows. He passed close te where I was crouched and tossed something into the jumble of crates, then disappeared around the corner."

"Did you see what he threw away?" asked Sheffield.

"O'course I did," answered Raven as he drew a knife from inside his coat, dried blood still clinging to the blade.

Charlotte paled.

Thinking, no doubt, of how the boy had been within a hairsbreadth of the man who had wielded it, gauged Wrexford. But there wasn't a moment to spare for sympathy. Time was of the essence.

"Where's Pudge?" he demanded.

"I set him te watching the rear of the building while I came te fetch ye."

Grabbing up the other pistol from its case, the earl looked to Sheffield. "Stay here. When Tyler returns tell—"

"Be damned with that!" cut in his friend, holding out his hand for one of the weapons. "I'm coming with you."

"As am I," said Charlotte.

Deciding argument would only waste precious seconds, Wrexford passed over a pistol. "I'll allow you to lead us to the spot, Weasel, but after that you're to come back here and wait for Tyler."

"I ain't!" responded the boy.

The earl caught him by the scruff of his coat. "Yes, you *are*. I'll have your word on it, or in you go to the storage closet." He swung Raven around. "As you see, it has a bloody big lock."

Raven's next words weren't a promise.

"Very well, lad." He took a step toward the heavy oak portal.

"Oiy, oiy! I swear to it."

"Then let us fly."

Following Raven's lead, they scrambled out

through the window and trooped swiftly and silently through the winding byways. On approaching the entrance to the cul de sac, the boy slowed and gave a low whistle.

An answering one cut through the gloom.

"That's Pudge," confirmed the boy. "This way."

The urchin popped up from within the spiky silhouettes of broken slats. "Nuffink—nobuddy's come or gone," he reported.

Wrexford fished out a guinea from his pocket. "My thanks, lad."

Pudge gave an awestruck grin. "Anytime, Yer Nibs." The coin disappeared into his pocket, and in the next instant the wraith-like urchin was gone, too.

"There's the entrance." Raven pointed to a shadowed doorway.

"Wait here, lad." The earl didn't bother giving orders to Charlotte and Sheffield. He knew they would do whatever they damn well pleased.

He hurried across the uneven ground, unsurprised to hear the light-footed tread of steps behind him. On reaching the portal, he found it slightly ajar.

Drawing his pistol, he waited for the others to join him. "I'll go first," he whispered. "Mrs. Sloane, stay right behind me. Kit, cock your weapon and bring up the rear."

The hinges creaked as the door swung open. The dank scent of decay immediately assaulted his nostrils. Wrexford stepped inside, crumbled mortar from the bricks crunching under his boots. An air of abandonment pervaded the place. The windows were tightly shuttered, allowing no light to dribble in, and the utter silence as he halted amplified the impression of emptiness.

Empty, save for a lingering aura of evil. The sensation was palpable, sharp as a knifepoint prickling against the back of his neck. He felt the tension in Charlotte as her shoulder brushed up against his.

Whatever reason had brought Kirkland to this spot, its malevolence still swirled, blacker than the shroud of shadows. Shifting his stance, Wrexford hit up against a hard object on the planked floor. A lantern, by the feel of glass and metal.

"Have you a match?" he whispered to Sheffield. Stealth seemed pointless.

A flare of phosphorous pierced darkness. His friend quickly lit the wick, and with an oily sputter, a flame came to life, casting a weak aureole of light.

Nothing.

Wrexford ventured another step deeper into the murk and lifted the lantern higher.

Charlotte let out a shivering gasp.

Kirkland lay face up, his sightless eyes gleaming with a pale pearlescence in the fluttery light. His once-white cravat was now stained a rusty red, and dark-fingered rivulets were snaking out from the pool of viscous liquid forming beneath his ravaged neck.

"Ye god," uttered Sheffield. "Another slashed throat."

"Yes," said the earl, "Our villain, whoever it may be, appears to have an unholy skill with a blade."

Charlotte crouched down for a closer look. "Given his height and bulk, I don't think it could have been Mrs. Ashton. She couldn't have managed the reach and angle—not to speak of the fact that this sort of damage would require a goodly amount of strength."

"You're likely right. But perhaps it's time we take the offensive and find out for sure." Wrexford felt a sudden surge of fear as he glanced at the pooling blood. Charlotte was in mortal danger until the murderer was apprehended.

She looked up and met his gaze through the hazy light. "You're suggesting we pay a call to her townhouse *now?*"

"Surprise is a weapon unto itself," he replied. "If we can knock Mrs. Ashton off balance, she may make a fatal slip."

Her expression turned troubled.

"It doesn't matter who wielded the knife," he explained. "If the widow is conspiring with the murderer, then her own neck is in danger from the hangman's noose. By striking hard and fast, we may be able to frighten her into betraying her cohort by offering her a choice between life and a very unpleasant death."

"Choices, choices," responded Charlotte in a tight voice. "Why is it that women are, more often than not, the ones caught between a rock and a stone? We seem to be damned if we do and damned if we don't."

Sheffield cleared his throat with an uncomfortable cough.

"With the rules of society weighted so heavily against us, it's no wonder we are forced to rely on cunning and guile," she added softly.

Wrexford eyed her intently, but said nothing.

"What about him?" ventured Sheffield after the silence stretched out for a moment longer. Kirkland's gaping wound looked ghoulish in the sickly yellow light cast by the cheap lamp oil.

"Leave it to me," said the earl curtly. He turned away and snuffed out the rancid-smelling flame. "Let's be off."

Charlotte wiped her palms on her rough wool breeches as she rose, and yet the residue of murder was not like blood or muck. It didn't come off with a casual scrub. Rather, it seemed to seep beneath the skin.

In absentia luci, tenebrae vincunt. In the absence of light darkness prevails.

Was violent death an insidious poison, she

wondered, which over time would pollute the soul?

Perhaps that was a question whose complexities were best left to philosophers. For now, she simply wished to see justice done. If that was morally suspect, then so be it.

"Weasel," summoned Wrexford in a low but commanding voice.

Raven darted out from the shadows.

"It's time for you to return to my townhouse. Wait for Tyler and tell him he's to send one of the footmen to Bow Street at first light with a note for Griffin—and only Griffin, understand?"

The boy gave a solemn nod.

"He should inform the Runner of Kirkland's murder and give him the precise location of the body. More importantly, he needs to tell Griffin I have an idea of how this all ties together and ask him to be patient. I shall endeavor to meet with him as soon as possible." The earl paused. "Can you remember that, lad?"

"Yes, sir," replied Raven.

"One last thing," added Wrexford. "Griffin should have the corpse taken to Henning's surgery. There may be some clue Henning can see."

A weak scudding of moonlight caught the silent movement of the boy's lips. Committing the words to memory, realized Charlotte. For all his fierce sense of independence, Raven always held himself a little straighter in the earl's presence.

"Yes, sir," repeated the boy.

"Then away with you."

The shadows skirled, as if caught in a momentary gust of air, and then settled back into stillness.

The earl was already striding to the alleyway.

Charlotte shook off her musings and hurried to catch up with him.

"How do you intend to gain entrance into the widow's residence?" she asked. "The doors are likely barred, so picking a lock won't work. And besides, it's not a wise idea—the footmen may have orders to shoot any intruder."

He didn't look around but merely quickened his pace. "There are times when having a high and mighty title proves useful."

Charlotte fell in step behind him. Whatever force of nature had him in thrall, it wasn't going to yield to anything she said.

One turn, then another, and suddenly the silvery silhouette of Grosvenor Square's fancy mansions, all elegant angles and decorative pediments, rose out of the gloom ahead. Moving in single file, the three of them circled around the central garden, hugging close to the leafy shadows overhanging the fence. The residences lining the far side of the square were swathed in silky silence, the pale limestone and stately marble porticos sleeping peacefully in the hide-and-seek shadows cast by the wrought iron street lights.

Lord Blackstone's townhouse was set near the

far corner. Wrexford took the treads of the marble entrance stairs two at a time and grabbed hold of the heavy brass knocker.

Bang, bang! Several staccato raps shattered the quiet tranquility.

"If you are intent on rousing the dead, we could simply summon a regiment of the Royal Hussars to gallop through the streets," quipped Sheffield.

The earl paid him no heed and pounded out another tattoo.

Charlotte glanced around. No light flared to life in the nearby windows, but as she turned back, she thought she detected the glimmer of candle deep within the residence.

Sure enough, a wary voice, muzzy with sleep, sounded on the other side of the paneled oak door.

"Who's there?"

"The Earl of Wrexford."

She'd never heard him sound so imperious.

"Open up immediately and wake Mrs. Ashton," he added. "It's a matter of life and death."

"B-B-But the h-hour . . ." stammered whoever had the misfortune to be keeping the midnight watch.

"Open up *now!*" commanded the earl. "Or I promise you, there will be hell to pay!"

The rasp of wood scraping through an iron bracket announced the man's surrender. The bolt drew back, the latch lifted, and the massive slab of oak slowly swung open.

Wrexford shouldered his way past the nervous servant and started for the stairs.

"Milord! You can't—"

"Oh, but I can."

Keeping her head down, Charlotte hurried after him. The earl had not yet thought to protest her presence, and she didn't intend to give him a chance to do so. Her disguise was good, but experience had taught her that the best cloak of concealment was the fact that people saw what they expected to see.

An urchin was an urchin. Mrs. Ashton would have no cause to think otherwise.

Wrexford paused on the upper landing. A single wall sconce was lit, its flame turned low, the flickers quickly disappearing in the darkness.

"Which is Miss Merton's bedchamber?" he asked as Charlotte joined him.

She pointed it out.

"Wake her. Her presence may be useful."

"I doubt she's still asleep." A hurried rustling behind the door confirmed the surmise. Lowering her voice, Charlotte added, "Remember, sir, I'm merely one of your informants. Let it not be you who makes the dangerous slip."

"Be assured, I don't intend to make any mistakes."

There was an edge to his voice she had never heard before. But there was no time now to puzzle it out.

378

The door latch of Octavia's room rattled. Charlotte heard Sheffield start up the stairs.

Drawing a deep breath, she edged back into the recessed alcove of the linen storage closet.

Wrexford turned and was ready when Octavia stepped into the corridor, a wrapper thrown haphazardly over her nightrail, her hair sticking out in disarray from a loose braid.

"Lord Wrexford!" Her breath caught for an instant in her throat. "Is it Benedict? Oh, God— is he dead?"

"I've no news on Hillhouse," he replied. "I'm here on another matter. One that I hope will put an end to the bloody trail of lies and deceit."

Octavia slumped against the molding, whether in relief or a sense of impending doom was impossible to tell. Charlotte felt a stab of sympathy. She feared that things were not going to end well for her friend.

"Go wake Mrs. Ashton," commanded Wrexford to Octavia.

"There's no need." From the far end of the corridor came a tiny explosion of light as a candle suddenly sparked to life. Its dancing glow illuminated the widow's face. Framed by her midnight-dark hair and the surrounding gloom, it held a spectral beauty, her pale, wraith-like features appearing to float disembodied above the undulating flame.

Fire and ice, thought Charlotte.

379

"I am here," said Isobel. Her bloodless lips curled upward. "I take it this is not a social call?"

"No," replied the earl. "I think you know why I'm here."

The widow started forward, her slow, steady steps silent save for the soft swoosh of fabric around her legs. As she came closer, Charlotte noted that her nightclothes were pure white.

A reminder that the difference between devil and angel was so easily shaded by perception.

"I can hazard a guess," replied Isobel with chilling calmness. "It seems my past sins have caught up with me."

Chapter 24

Wrexford stared at her, feeling a momentary flicker of pity. Her intelligence and humor deserved more than to have been corrupted by lust and greed.

But passion, he knew, rarely followed reason.

"Indeed, they have." His voice seemed to deepen and darken as it echoed off the walls. "I'm glad to see we share a pragmatism, madam, if nothing else, and may avoid the unseemly spectacle of false tears and protestations."

Isobel shrugged. "I'll not insult either of us with such histrionics. You're a clever man, Lord Wrexford. I assume you've uncovered proof." The candle shifted, throwing her eyes into shadow. "Though I had hoped your scrutiny would stay on Eli's murder, rather than stray to my peccadilloes."

"A rather benign term for your betrayal," he replied. "And how could you have hoped I wouldn't connect the two when they are, in fact one in the same sin?"

A look of puzzlement flitted across her face.

"I trust you'll give me a full confession, and tell us who wielded the blade—especially now that your other conspirator lies dead."

"Dead?" Isobel stared at him blankly. "Who?"

"Your paramour, Lord Kirkland," piped up Sheffield. "We found him a scant twenty minutes ago with his throat foully slashed. Just like the others."

"Murderous bitch!" exclaimed Octavia, her face twisted in fury. "What have you done with Benedict?"

Keeping his eyes on Mrs. Ashton, Wrexford waved them to silence. If he didn't know better, he would have found her show of shock convincing. Her knees buckled slightly, and her hand flew to her breast as she fought to steady her stance.

"Kirkland is *dead?*" She shook her head in disbelief. "My only confession is that I can feel no sorrow at the news. He was a thoroughly dirty dish, devoid of all honor."

"You have the gall to use the word honor?" jeered Octavia. "For shame—"

"Silence, please, Miss Merton," Wrexford cut in. "Allow me to do the questioning." To Isobel, he said, "Are you claiming that you and the viscount weren't responsible for your husband's murder?"

"I may be guilty of some sins, but not that. *Never* that." Her chin rose. "I respected and admired my husband. And while we didn't flame with love's passion, we were very fond of each other."

"You're lying," said Octavia.

Isobel ignored the accusation. "You can't claim to have proof of my involvement in Elihu's death, Lord Wrexford, because none exists."

"A note was found in your dressing room," he countered. "One in which Kirkland warns you not to panic and you'll both get what you want. How do you explain that?"

"Ah. Miss Merton and Mrs. Sloane . . ." Isobel glanced at Octavia with a grim smile. "I should have suspected something havey-cavey was afoot."

"Rather the pot calling the kettle black," murmured Sheffield.

Isobel's brow furrowed in a pensive frown. "I recognized Mrs. Sloane from the past . . ."

Out of the corner of his eye, Wrexford saw Charlotte start within the shadows.

"But decided it was her own business if she wished to keep her true identity to herself."

Secrets tangled within secrets. What skeletons, wondered Wrexford, were about to come rattling out of the closet to join the fresh-killed corpses?

"Just who do you think she is?" asked the earl in a carefully measured voice.

"I, of all people, sympathize with the desire to conceal past mistakes, especially when one is a woman," replied Isobel. "It's not always for nefarious reasons, so I shall leave it to her to decide what to tell you."

Wrexford fought to keep his questions about Charlotte from overpowering all the others. Time enough for that confrontation later, he told himself. Murder and mayhem must take precedence.

Whatever secret she was hiding, he didn't believe it involved a trail of dead bodies.

"Very well," he responded. "Then let us return to the note. How do you explain it?"

"In very stark and simple terms," said Isobel coolly, "Lord Kirkland was blackmailing me to keep the fact that I'd been his paramour in my youth from becoming a public scandal. Elihu knew about it—I had told him, of course, before I accepted his proposal of marriage—but I couldn't bear to have my past tarnish him and his work, just when he was on the cusp of a revolutionary new invention. So I acceded to the viscount's demands." She made a face. "A mistake, as once a blackmailer gets his claws into you, he never lets go."

"I-I don't believe you," said Octavia, but there was less force behind her outrage than before.

"Miss Merton, you have always chosen to think the worst of me." Isobel finally chose to meet her nemesis's accusing gaze. "Change is upsetting, and often frightening, to people. Your cozy, comfortable world was suddenly not the same with me in it."

Octavia's mouth quivered, but she couldn't seem to muster a retort.

"I don't suppose you have proof of your claim," asked Wrexford.

"In fact, I do," said Isobel, a note of challenge shading her words. "If you'll come down to my study, I'll show you some of Kirkland's other notes, along with a few other documents that may cast me in a different light."

Yet another dizzying twist, thought the earl. For all their racing around had they merely been spinning in circles?

"By all means," he replied. "I welcome the opportunity to have empirical evidence resolve the question of your guilt or innocence once and for all."

"I trust scientific reasoning will triumph over prejudice and preconception," murmured Isobel. "I simply ask that you keep an open mind."

The comment brought a flush to Octavia's cheeks.

"I am as anxious as you are to see that justice is done for Elihu." Isobel started walking for the stairs, and then stopped abruptly as she noticed the still-as-a-statue shape sheltered within the recessed doorway. "I take it this is one of your companions, and not some errant intruder, Lord Wrexford?"

"The lad runs a network of urchins," he replied without hesitation. "They are my eyes and ears on the streets—an invaluable and effective resource in conducting my investigations. It's he who informed me of Kirkland's murder."

"Clever," commented Isobel. Her gaze lingered

on Charlotte for a fraction longer, then she continued on to the landing.

"I'll join you very shortly," said Wrexford, nodding a subtle signal at Sheffield to accompany the women downstairs. "I need a private word with Phoenix."

"Phoenix," repeated Charlotte softly, once the others were out of earshot. "I would have thought you might choose *Crow*." A pause. "Or perhaps *Vulture*."

"Phoenix seems far more appropriate," replied Wrexford.

Though she deliberately avoided meeting his gaze, she could feel the heat of it on her skin.

"A bird that bursts into fire and burns to a crisp," he continued, "only to rise from the ashes and reform itself anew."

"Yes, I've changed my plumage. But not as you might think." This was hardly the time for personal revelations, but somehow it mattered to her that he not think her favors could be bought so casually. "I have an inkling of where Mrs. Ashton might have seen me. But be assured it was *not* serving as some gentleman's lightskirt."

His expression was unreadable. "You've made it quite clear that your past is none of my concern."

"Wrexford . . ." Charlotte hesitated. *What to say?* "I . . ."

The earl was quick to cut her off. "We've

no time for personal matters right now. Mrs. Ashton's confession must take precedence over all else."

Including mine, thought Charlotte.

"You're right, of course." Reaching up, she took a moment to adjust the angle of her hat in order to compose her thoughts. "So, we need to consider logistics. I ought not come down to the study. The widow may question why an urchin needs to be present. Not to speak of the fact that the lighting will be brighter, and she's proved herself to be a careful observer."

The wall sconce sputtered weakly, sending up a thin plume of smoke. The oil was burning low.

"A damnable shame," she added. "I'd very much like to hear and see what proof she offers of her innocence."

"Your assessment is important," replied Wrexford. "Let me think . . ."

Charlotte watched his face carefully, and was relieved to see only his usual calm concentration.

"I can say that you've been involved in the investigation from the beginning, and given your knowledge of London's underbelly, it's imperative for you to hear the evidence."

"That might fadge," agreed Charlotte.

"When we enter, I'll order you to stand by the door and listen. It won't seem amiss if an urchin isn't invited to join the inner circle."

She nodded. "That should suffice."

"Then let's go." He turned without waiting for a reply.

Charlotte followed along behind him, the hurried thumping of their boots the only sounds passing between them.

Wrexford entered the study several strides ahead of her. "Guard the door, Phoenix, and make sure we're not disturbed," he barked as she reached the threshold. "And keep your ears cocked as to what goes on in here. If you've any ideas on who the villains might be and where they've gone to ground I'll want to hear them."

Charlotte slid into a niche by the bookcase, some distance away from the others. Sheffield, she noted, had settled the women on the sofa near the hearth, and had taken a seat in one of the facing armchairs. A lamp was lit on the side table, another on the large pearwood desk. Her own spot was untouched by the soft circles of light.

Wasting no time, the earl immediately confronted the widow. "Is there a reason we're waiting for the papers, madam?"

Isobel appeared unintimidated by his scowl. "I assumed you would wish to watch me fetch them, in order to assure yourself that I performed no witchcraft or sleight of hand."

He gave an impatient wave. "There's been enough drama as it is, Mrs. Ashton. We need not play any scenes from Shakespeare. Get your proof."

Charlotte was well placed to see everyone's face. Repressing a quirk of amusement, the widow rose and went to her desk. Reaching inside her nightrail, she found the gold chain looped around her neck and unclasped it. A key hung from its links, and with a quick twist she unlocked one of the drawers.

Octavia bit her lip as Isobel lifted a slender Moroccan leather portfolio from beneath several ledgers and carried it back to the sofa.

She took several folded sheets of stationery from atop the pile and offered them to Wrexford. "I assume you are familiar with Kirkland's handwriting."

The earl wordlessly handed them to Sheffield, who after looking them over carefully, nodded in confirmation. "They look genuine."

"Might I have the courtesy of knowing who sits on my jury?" asked Isobel.

A fair request, thought Charlotte. She was growing surer and surer that the widow was telling the truth.

"The Honorable Christopher Sheffield," said Wrexford curtly. He took the notes back from his friend and began reading them.

Isobel settled back against the pillows, but Charlotte saw the tension in her body. She was not quite as cool as she wished to appear. Next to her, Octavia couldn't sit still, her fingers plucking and pulling at the folds of her wrapper.

"Hmm." Paper crackled as the earl reread the notes a second time. The seconds seemed to stretch out to eternity. He finally looked up, his gaze spearing straight to Isobel.

"I suppose this seems clear enough." Without further ado, he began to read aloud, *". . . It seems a small pittance to pay for my silence, dear Isobel. After all, you have a great deal of money because of my discretion to this point, and I do not, as my Father has tightened the purse strings. Share your favors—I recall how very good you are at doing so—and there will be no scandal. We'll all get what we want."*

Isobel's expression remained stoic.

"The others have similar threats and wheedling," said Wrexford.

"You're sure they aren't forgeries?" asked Octavia in a small voice.

It was Sheffield who answered. "Yes. There's a faint but distinctive watermark in the paper—a small pitchfork—which is made specially for a gambling club called Lucifer's Lair. I doubt any woman would have access to blank sheets."

"Perhaps if I give a few more details of my sordid past, it will help further allay suspicions," offered Isobel. "My father was a prosperous merchant in Newmarket, but when a friend of his convinced him to invest his savings in a stock offering, he ended up losing everything."

She paused to draw a tight breath. *"Everything.*

Including his life. He couldn't bear the shame and shot himself one night. I was eighteen and destitute. My only relative, my father's cousin, wouldn't hear of taking in a disgraced family member. So I had to find a way to survive."

Octavia's face pinched.

"I'm not proud of it, but when Lord Kirkland, who had been sniffing around my skirts while in town for the racing season, offered to set me up as his mistress, I made the decision to accept." Isobel kept her voice devoid of emotion. "Until I could figure out another, more acceptable, way to support myself. Thankfully that came maybe six months later when a fortuitous meeting with an elderly acquaintance of my father led to me being offered the position of a lady's companion."

Charlotte saw a look of affection flicker over Isobel's features.

"The dowager Baroness Weston was considered an eccentric bluestocking for her intellectual interests, but that suited me quite well. I've always been keen on learning. It was at her weekly evening gathering for like-minded men and women that I met Elihu."

Isobel took a long moment before going on. "We enjoyed each other's company." She looked at Wrexford, a glint of humor in her eyes. "You might say there was a certain chemistry between us. And, well, he asked me to be his wife. I accepted, but only after revealing my history. He said it didn't matter."

"I-I assumed . . ." stammered Octavia. "You were so very beautiful . . . b-but so very cool and distant."

"It wasn't easy for me. I felt I must present a very prim and proper façade. And of course I sensed your dislike. Unsure of what else to do, I decided to make the best of it, so as not to upset Elihu, who loved you dearly."

"I . . . I . . ." Octavia blinked, the candlelight catching the pearling of tears on her lashes. "I-I'm sorry if I misjudged you. But—"

Wrexford cleared his throat with a brusque cough. "Perhaps we could leave recriminations and reconciliations for some other time. We've a murder to solve, and the mystery has just grown more knotted."

"F-Forgive me, but I just have one more question concerning that." Octavia fixed the widow with a searching stare. "Benedict and I are quite certain that our workroom and desks were searched. We assumed you were trying to take the final plans because . . . because Eli had decided that he didn't want to profit from the patent. He was planning to share the profits from his inventions with his workers. We discussed plans for building housing, and a school, and—"

"And a hospital," interrupted Isobel. "Yes, I know all about that. Indeed, Elihu and I came up with the idea together." She drew another document from the case, and placed it on Octavia's lap. "You know his handwriting—and mine. There is his first draft for how to use the money, along with my notes in the margin suggesting some minor changes." She held up a second sheet. "Here's the final version."

Secrets within secrets within secrets. Charlotte gave an inward sigh at the serendipitous twists that Fate could take. A knot here, a knot there, and all of a sudden, the threads have formed a disastrous tangle.

Octavia needed only a moment to check over the paper. "I'm so sorry. It seems I have much for which to apologize," she whispered. "But as Lord Wrexford said, let us leave that for later. What matters now is to figure out who was riffling through our work."

Isobel made a wry face. "My study was searched as well. I confess, I thought you and Hillhouse might be the guilty parties. You would have made a pretty penny by taking the invention for your own."

"We would *never* have done that."

"You may be certain of your own intentions, Miss Merton" interjected Wrexford. "However, the evidence against Hillhouse is rather black."

"Yes, he made a mistake in the past." Octavia glanced a little guiltily at Isobel. "But as we have learned, that shouldn't damn a person for life."

"He let a desperate need for money overcome his scruples," pointed out Sheffield. "We can't overlook that."

Frowning in thought, Wrexford began pacing back and forth before the unlit hearth. Charlotte clenched her teeth in frustration. Would he think of the right questions . . .

To the devil with it. She had already cast caution to the wind.

"Oiy, m'lord," she said, pitching her voice low and rough.

His head jerked up.

Charlotte gestured for him to join her.

"The lad is welcome to join us," said Isobel.

"He'd not be comfortable doing so," replied the earl quickly. Several swift strides brought him into the shadows, where he took up a position with his back to the others, effectively blocking their view of her.

"Numbers," she said hurriedly. "Remember Hollis's last words—he said numbers will reveal everything, so it stands to reason that we should find out who, if anyone, knew of Ashton's plans not to profit from his patent."

A flicker of understanding lit in his eyes. "A good point," he growled.

"And ask Octavia if she knows anything further about what Jeremy is doing to find Hillhouse. He didn't tell me his plans, but he may have confided in her."

The earl nodded. "Anything else?"

"Not at the moment," she answered, though something was nibbling at the edge of her consciousness.

A moment passed and yet he made no move to return to the others. "What think you," he asked slowly, "of the widow's revelation?"

"I think she's telling the truth," replied Charlotte without hesitation.

The answer seemed to settle some of his uncertainties. His shoulders relaxed slightly.

"Furthermore, my sense is she's a formidable ally. She's highly intelligent and thinks with incisive logic. Press her on any scientific connections Kirkland might have had. I find it hard to believe his death is not in some way connected to Ashton's murder."

Wrexford fingered his chin, which was starting to shade with a faint stubbling of whiskers. "Yes, the same thought occurred to me." He stood for a moment longer in contemplation before making his way back to the others.

"Miss Merton, have you heard anything from Sterling?" he asked.

"He has gone to Cambridge," she answered. "On the off chance some of Benedict's friends at the university may know something of his whereabouts."

Doubtful, thought Charlotte. Her sense was things were black or white—Hillhouse was either one of the villains, or he'd turn up as yet another victim of their killing spree.

The earl queried Isobel next. "We think there's a chance Kirkland was involved in a plot to steal your late husband's invention and sell it to a competitor."

She frowned.

"We know the viscount owes gambling debts to McKinlock. But is there anyone else in the scientific world with whom he has a connection?"

"Science?" responded the widow with a grim huff of laughter. "Dermott had absolutely no interest in *anything* intellectual. It was a great bone of contention between him and his father. In fact, his son's indolence and debauchery made Lord Blackstone so livid that he had recently cut off all funds to his son." She made a wry face. "Indeed, I'd be tempted to say Blackstone was angry enough to mur—"

Her words cut off abruptly. "Forgive me. What a ghastly thing to say," she apologized. "Good heavens, I shall have to write to the marquess and inform him of his son's demise. Though God only knows when he'll receive it."

"Anyone else you can think of?" pressed Wrexford after allowing a short interlude of silence.

"No," said Isobel. "But I've had no contact with Kirkland, save for our own sordid personal business."

"M'lord." Trusting that her street voice would serve as adequate disguise, Charlotte couldn't hold back a suggestion. "Be there any udder morts what knows of the invention?"

"A good thought," agreed the earl, and then translated, "The lad asks who else knew Ashton was close to a technological breakthrough?"

"The investors," said Isobel. "Lord Blackstone, Lord Sterling . . ." She named three others, and explained they were elderly intellectuals and longtime friends of her late husband. "I can't imagine any of these men wishing Elihu any harm."

"What makes evil all the more powerful is the fact that it's often well-hidden under the most respectable guises," replied the earl. He resumed his pacing, and then suddenly stopped after several strides. "The fellow who was here the other day—your mill supervisor. Does he know as well?"

"Yes," said Isobel. "Mr. Blodgett is highly skilled in mechanical workings and often assisted Elihu and Mr. Hillhouse in the laboratory."

Charlotte suddenly recalled what was niggling at her thoughts and felt compelled to interrupt again. "Oiy, m'lord. Word is there may have been mingle-mingle between the two of 'em."

Wrexford frowned. "The lad says I need to ask you whether you've been having an intimate relationship with Mr. Blodgett."

397

"Blodgett?" Isobel's brows shot up. "Good God, no."

Given all else she had heard, Charlotte didn't doubt the denial. She nodded at Wrexford.

The earl cleared his throat. "Then getting back to Blodgett's motivations, might he have been bribed to disclose the secret?"

Isobel considered the question. "No, I can't see him doing that. He was paid handsomely, and aside from the question of money, he had worked with Elihu since he was a boy and was quite devoted to him."

"Geoffrey—that is, Mr. Blodgett—could be very high and mighty with the rest of us," offered Octavia. "I have to say, I noticed how he looked at you, and I . . . well, I thought it was envy of Eli. It just seemed Geoffrey always thought he deserved more than he had," She paused. "But in fairness, Benedict and he didn't rub together very well, so I'm not a neutral observer."

"What did they quarrel about?" asked Wrexford.

"Nothing in particular," answered Octavia. "I just had the sense that Geoffrey resented the fact that Benedict had the same modest background, yet had managed to attend university. He was always trying to show that he was smarter."

"It sounds like a natural competition," pointed out Sheffield. "Two young men eager to win the approval of their mentor."

"You're probably right," responded Octavia. "As I said, I'm not the best judge."

So, no real leads as of yet about the numbers, and who stood to gain from Ashton's death, mused Charlotte. And yet, she felt in her bones that would come down to how the money added up. But in the meantime, there was still another important question to address . . .

"M'lord," she rasped. "Ye ain't tried te cobble who searched this house."

"Hell's teeth, there are no end of questions," he muttered. "And damnably few answers."

"Are you sure the lad would not care to come join us and make himself comfortable?" quipped Isobel. "He seems to be looking at things more clearly than the rest of us."

"No need," snapped Wrexford. "He thinks better on his feet."

Sheffield rubbed at his temples. "And I think better when I've had my breakfast. It *is* morning, isn't it?"

"I could wake the cook—" began Isobel, but the earl cut her off.

"Not necessary. We're almost done," said the earl. "The lad asked if you have any idea who might have searched the house?"

"Kirkland and Blodgett were here, so I suppose they both had the opportunity," she answered. "Other than that, no."

"Then it seems to me that there's nothing more

we can accomplish for now. We all ought to get a few hours of sleep—and pray that it sparks some new thoughts on how these murders all tie together."

"A wise suggestion." Sheffield rose and took his leave from the ladies. To Wrexford he said, "I'll call at your townhouse later in the day, in case I may be of use."

Charlotte thought about slipping away while the others were occupied, but the earl had other ideas. "Come with me, Phoenix. We've a few points to discuss before we part ways."

She held her voice until they had crossed the cobbled street and came to a halt in the shadows of the square's central garden. "Wrexford, I know I owe you an explanation . . ."

He turned to face her. Charlotte bit her lip, wishing she could read his eyes through the flitting swirls of darkness.

"I assume," he said softly, "you will share your past with me if and when you decide I can be trusted with your secrets."

Charlotte had expected one of their usual clashes. His reply seemed to wrap around her heart and cause it to skip a beat. "I do trust you." More than anyone else in the world. "And I mean to tell you. I—I just need a little time to order my thoughts."

"That's probably wise," he said dryly. "I daresay we've had enough shocks for one night."

Charlotte mustered a ghost of a smile. "Right. Well then, unless there's anything else to discuss, we . . . we should both think of getting some sleep."

"There's actually one last thing." He drew her deeper into the leafy shadows of the branches overhanging the wrought iron fence. "But it won't take more than a moment since I've no intention of brangling with you over it. I'm going to send McClellan to stay with you until we've found the people responsible for the murders."

"Wrexford—"

"She knows how to load and fire a pistol with pinpoint accuracy. Two extremely useful skills that aren't in your arsenal," he continued. "She'll arrive later today."

"Wrexford—" But Charlotte found herself hissing at thin air. The earl had, with infuriating cat-like quickness, already disappeared into the gloom.

Chapter 25

Charlotte slept fitfully, exhaustion too weak to fight off the dark dreams clawing at her peace of mind. She finally gave up any further attempt at repose and threw off the bedcovers, wincing as a blade of afternoon sunlight cut across her face.

An apt metaphor, she decided, for how her life had been turned upside down. She always rose at the crack of dawn. Only indolent aristocrats had the luxury of lingering in the silky cocoon of sleep, blissfully ignorant of the inevitable everyday triumphs and disasters taking shape.

As she splashed cold water on her cheeks, Charlotte found herself yearning for her old life, her old world, where the hours were, for the most part, filled with ordinary tasks. *Shopping, washing, cooking, drawing.* A hard rhythm, perhaps, but one that had grown comfortable because of its familiarity. This new life was even more complicated than she had expected.

And about to get even more complicated, given her promise to Wrexford.

After dressing, she hurried downstairs, filled with a sudden resolve to fend off her worries, at least for an interlude, with mundane tasks. The larder needed to be restocked, her paints and paper replenished.

The boys had left a note—thank God they had not shirked from heading off to their lessons. She hoped that boded well. Both of them seemed to like their new tutor. Wrexford had chosen well.

Wrexford. Charlotte didn't want to think about him and all the conundrums and confusion entangled in their relationship. Death and disaster were the forces that had brought them together. And now, she must face giving up her most vulnerable secret . . .

No wonder her emotions were out of sorts.

Taking up her cloak and marketing basket, she headed out to the street.

Coffee—thankfully as dark and scalding as boiling pitch. Blowing away a cloud of steam rising from the cup, Wrexford took a quick swallow, hoping its burn might jolt him fully awake. He had slept for a goodly number of hours—a glance out his work room windows showed that dusk was already falling—and yet his brain still felt muzzy. He needed to get his thoughts in order.

And quickly.

Riche had left a note on his blotter informing him that Griffin had stopped by earlier. The Runner couldn't afford to be patient much longer. The government was likely pressing him for answers about the radical group's involvement in Ashton's murder.

Wrexford reread his butler's missive. Griffin would be heading to Henning's surgery later that evening after finishing his official duties, and expected the earl to be there. The 10 o'clock rendezvous time was clearly an order, not a request.

Damnation. He had been hoping to have an idea or two about who might have murdered Kirkland to offer Griffin. But unless any of the others had a suggestion . . . He rubbed at his temples, then took another swallow of coffee.

Still no inspiration.

He decided there was nothing to lose by paying another visit to Mrs. Ashton. Between her husband's business and her own personal problems, she had been in the thick of the plot. Surely she must have some conjecture, now that she had had some time to think on it.

After finishing his coffee, Wrexford shuffled through the documents he had on the investigation, and then jotted down a few more notes. His overcoat and hat were still on the armchair where he had tossed them, and perhaps the short walk in the brisk air would help clear his head.

He exited his house and circled around from the elegant square to the alleyway behind the mews, following the way through several sharp turns before it intersected with an even narrower passageway. Overhead, clouds scudded over the rising crescent moon and scattering of stars, dimming what little glow was left by the fading twilight.

As he ducked through the opening, the earl heard the pelter of footsteps up ahead. They were coming towards him, and at a dead run. On instinct, he closed his hand around the butt of his pistol and moved quickly to take cover within the crevasses of the uneven buildings.

A small black blur came flying out of the gloom.

"Weasel!" called Wrexford as the boy took shape, feeling a spurt of alarm at his obvious agitation. His first thought was of Charlotte and how vulnerable she was.

"M'lord! m'lord!" Raven skidded to a stop and hurriedly grabbed a paper from inside his jacket. "Look! Look!"

The clench in his chest relaxed. A note from her meant there was no reason to panic. The boy would never have left her alone if she were in any danger.

"What is it, lad?" Wrexford asked, the rush of relief sharpening his voice.

"The answer!" The boy waved the paper as he gasped to catch his breath. "The answer!"

A cryptic reply, considering how many lethal mysteries they were facing.

"Slow down," he ordered. "What has Mrs. Sloane discovered?"

"Not m'lady," responded Raven in rush. "Me!"

Wrexford found the paper thrust right under his nose.

"*Look,* sir! Mr. Tyler was right—the numbers are a code! M'lady left the copy ye gave her on her desk, so I borrowed it and began te play to with the patterns he showed me."

The earl grabbed both the paper and the boy, then hurried to a spot in the passageway where a weak dribbling of light from an overhead window afforded a bit of illumination.

"Ye see, Mr. Tyler said he thought it was some sort o' Vigenère Square, so I just decided te make some tries with the diagram he showed me," explained the boy. "Ye use a keyword to encrypt the message, otherwise it will just come out as goobledy-gook. Then ye got to convert the numbers te letters of the alphabet—A equals 1, B equals 2 and so on."

Raven paused to gulp in a breath. "Mr. Tyler had been trying a passel of words, like *Ashton* and *steam.* But m'lady told me the murdered cove who wrote the note said *numbers—the numbers reveal everything.*" Another gulp of air. "So I tried *numbers.*"

Good God—the simple insight of a child. Wrexford heard no more. He was too engrossed in reading what Raven had decoded.

Nevins—I've been duped and set up to appear Ashton's killer. I know who the real culprits are.

The earl swore on reading the names, as all the topsy-turvey pieces of the puzzle finally fell into place.

> And I can guess why—I've learned from a friend that Ashton truly did plan to use the profits from a patent to better the lives of his workers rather than line his own pockets. I think the miscreants intend to take the inventions for themselves. You must unmask them for the blackguards they are, for they've made our group appear guilty of the heinous crime.

He looked up to find Raven watching him expectantly. "Did you show this to Mrs. Sloane?" he demanded.

"She was out when I came home and started work on it. And she hadn't returned by the time I finished. So I decided I'd better come show it to ye."

"You did exactly the right thing, lad." Wrexford pocketed the note, along with his pistol. "Now, let us hurry back to your house and tell her what you've discovered."

A new clench of fear had taken hold of him. One of the villains had seen Charlotte with Miss Merton. No matter that McClellan was a crack shot, he worried that she was now in grave danger. From now on, until all the miscreants were under arrest, he wasn't going to let her out of his sight.

"Then we're all going to head to Henning's surgery," he added, turning away from the light and urging the boy forward. "Griffin will be arriving there later this evening, and we can finally put the wheels of justice in motion."

Her basket brimming with purchases, Charlotte turned the corner to her street. She had been away longer than expected, but a stop at the workshop entrance of her modiste's fancy shop had resulted in the invitation to share tea with Madame Franzenelli. It had been a very pleasant diversion to talk about Tuscany's beauty and the latest fripperies of fashion instead of ghoulish murders and menacing dangers. Indeed, she had lost track of time. It was now past suppertime, and the boys would likely be starving.

A quick rummaging in her reticule located her key. She unlocked her front door—and froze at the sound of voices coming from the parlor.

Setting down her basket, Charlotte groped for the small pocket pistol concealed in her cloak pocket. Thank God she'd been wise enough not to venture out unarmed. She cocked the hammer, careful to make no noise, and started forward, feeling as if her pounding heart had leapt up and lodged in her throat.

A lamp was lit inside the room, its outer ring of light just edging out through the open doorway and into the corridor. Charlotte crept along the wall, and then, weapon held ready, she ventured a peek inside.

A sound—something between a gasp and a laugh—slipped free from her lips.

Hawk turned quickly, the heavy sword nearly twisting from his grip and whacking the captive seated in the wooden chair.

"I captured another intruder!" exclaimed the boy proudly.

"I knocked," said McClellan, a smile tugging at the corners of her mouth. "And on finding the door ajar, I took the liberty of entering, to make sure nothing was amiss."

"My apologies," said Charlotte, lowering the pistol. "Untie her, Hawk. At once, if you please."

His face fell. "She ain't the enemy?"

"She *isn't*," replied Charlotte.

"But I commend you on your vigilance, young man," said McClellan as Hawk fell to unknotting the ropes binding her to the chair. "You were entirely right to be on your guard. Better to be safe than sorry." A pause as she looked back to Charlotte. "Did His Lordship inform you I was coming?"

Charlotte had, in fact, let the fact slip her mind. "Yes, but—"

"But you're not pleased."

"It's not that," she answered. "It's . . ." *How to explain?*

"It's just that you prefer that other people don't make such decisions for you," suggested McClellan.

She gave a wry grimace. "That's one way of putting it."

McClellan chuckled. "I understand. But perhaps I may be of practical use while I'm here." Flexing her freed wrists, the maid thanked Hawk politely and stood up. "I'm a credible cook. Allow me to fix supper while you take a moment to settle in from your errands."

"I don't expect you to toil at household tasks," protested Charlotte.

The reply was brusquely dismissed. "Nonsense. I'm far happier when I'm not sitting in a corner twiddling my thumbs. And besides, my feeling is you have more pressing things to think about."

Charlotte decided not to argue. The suggestion made sense. "Thank you. But first, allow me to show you to your quarters. I must warn you, though, you won't have the same fancy comforts—"

McClelland cut her off. "I'm comfortable anywhere, Mrs. Sloane."

Charlotte turned to Hawk—and suddenly realized that in the unexpected helter-pelter of her return she hadn't registered Raven's absence. "Where's your brother?"

"I dunno. He was here one minute, and then when I looked again, he was gone."

Raven was often running in and out, so there was no reason for alarm. "Well, if he doesn't return soon, he will have to eat his stew cold." She reached out and ruffled Hawk's hair. "That was very brave of you to protect our castle."

"Oiy, well, the earl says a gentleman must always take care of his family and friends."

She held back a skeptical laugh. Wrexford would rather eat nails than ever voice such a maudlin sentiment in her presence. But she found it rather endearing that he had said such a thing to the boys.

"Indeed. However, I think we'll have no further need for swashbuckling adventure tonight. Pick up your sword and carry it back in your room."

Quickening his pace, Wrexford emerged from the passageway and crossed the small square at the head of Adam Street, his boots beating a staccato tattoo on the uneven cobbles. Behind him, still hidden in the murky darkness, Raven broke into a run to catch up.

The *slap-slap* of the hurried steps brought him out of his brooding. He came to a halt and turned, surprised the boy had been dawdling.

"You're usually swift as quicksilver," he said. "What's—"

"There's somebody following us," whispered Raven.

Wrexford came instantly alert. If the boy sensed trouble, the earl was sure it was there.

Sure enough, an instant later, a man burst out from the shadows, a pistol in each hand. At the same time, a second figure clattered into the square from the adjoining alley. He, too, was armed, though only with a stout cudgel.

Wrexford cursed himself for a bloody fool. He had been one precious step ahead of the enemy but had let the advantage slip away. Mind whirring, he sought a way to salvage what he could of the situation.

"Don't move, milord," ordered the man with the pistols, as he slowed to a stop a short distance away. "I would dislike putting a bullet through your brain, but I'll do so if necessary."

"Aren't blades more to your liking than bullets?"

The retort earned a nasty laugh. "I'm equally skilled with either."

"No need to shed any blood," said the earl calmly. "Let me get rid of the beggar boy and then we can conduct our business in a civilized manner." From his pocket he pulled the folded paper and, keeping it hidden in his palm, quickly passed it to Raven.

"Here's a farthing, brat, now be off," he barked, punctuating the order with a sharp shove and praying the boy would understand that flight was a far better choice than senseless heroics.

Raven, to his credit, flew for cover.

The man with the pistols hesitated for a

heartbeat, then seemed to realize his mistake and squeezed off a shot.

Shards of stone exploded just as Raven darted around the corner of a building.

Had the boy been hit? Wrexford couldn't tell.

Swearing, the man took aim with the second pistol, then thought better of it. "Smythe!" he cried. "Go after the guttersnipe and finish him off." To Wrexford, he demanded, "What did you give the filthy brat?"

"Naught but a coin," said the earl calmly "I hope he spends it wisely."

The man's face darkened for an instant, but he quickly released his anger with a laugh. "You've a clever fellow, milord. That bodes well."

For what? But before Wrexford could begin to parse its meaning, the man's accomplice returned.

"There's a trail of blood—quite a bit of it—but it leads into a maze of alleys. Seemed a waste of time to follow," called Smythe as he reappeared from the gloom. "I swear, I saw the bullet hit him. He won't last long."

"Say your prayers. You'll soon be a dead man," said Wrexford softly to his captor.

Another laugh. "No, I'll soon be a very rich man," sneered the man. He flashed a hand signal to his accomplice. The cudgel swung through the air with a sudden whoosh and cracked against the earl's skull with a sickening thud.

• • •

Feeling a tad guilty, Charlotte listened to the faint clatter of dishes being washed and dried in the kitchen before returning her attention to her sketchbook. McClellan had proved to be an excellent cook, and after the meal refused to allow any help with the cleaning. It would have seemed like a luxury, save for the fact that it forced her to confront the taunting, devil-cursed dangers still at large.

Who was the enemy?

Charlotte uttered a frustrated oath. She felt she should have seen the answer by now. Noticing the telling little details was supposed to be her strength. And yet, her mind remained blank as a pristine sheet of paper.

Picking up a pencil, she forced herself to set aside conscious thought and simply start sketching. Why not let intuition have a try, as intellect had failed?

To her surprise, Charlotte found she was drawing Lord Kirkland's face. How strange, she thought, as she had seen it only once and for just a few moments as it lay devoid of life and painted a sallow yellow by the greasy flicker of lamplight. Even so, the viscount's features had possessed a saturnine beauty.

Why do they seem familiar?

She moved the pencil point to a blank part of the page and started again. This time, another face—similar, yet different—took shape. She stared at it, trying to place the slightly hooded eyes and well-shaped mouth.

And then it hit her—a man brushing past her in the closeness of a corridor, his face all the more memorable because of his fire-bright eyes.

Dear God. It took a stretch of the imagination, but all at once she saw how it all could make perfect sense.

Charlotte quickly folded the sketch and hurried to her bedchamber to change into her urchin's garb. After tucking the paper safely into her shirt, she went downstairs and found McClellan busy reorganizing the shelves in the kitchen foyer.

"I'm going out," she announced, feeling McClellan deserved her trust. Besides, she needed her to keep the boys in check. "I have to find Wrexford."

The maid slowly wiped her hands on her apron. "The thing is, His Lordship ordered me to stay with you, Mrs. Sloane, and not allow you to hare off on your own."

"Circumstances demand that we improvise," she shot back. "Time is of the essence, and I'll move faster alone."

McClellan's brow pinched as she considered what to do.

"It's vitally important," added Charlotte. "Lives may depend on it."

"Then I suppose," said the maid slowly, "we

had best act on the old adage that it's better to ask for forgiveness than to ask for permission."

Charlotte nodded her thanks.

"Do you need a weapon?"

"I have one, though apparently I'm not nearly as skilled as you are in its use."

"Like anything, marksmanship takes practice," said the maid. "It is, perhaps, a skill you would find useful to acquire."

"Quite likely." Charlotte tugged at her cap. "I need you to keep Hawk from dashing after me. Can you do that?"

"Yes."

"And when Raven returns, you must see to it that he doesn't leave," she added. "Though that won't be an easy task."

"I've a good deal of experience with fiercely stubborn lads," assured McClellan.

"Thank you." Charlotte reached for the latch of the door leading out to the back garden, only to have it flung open by some unseen hand.

"Raven!" she cried as the boy stumbled in, his face half-covered in blood.

"Never mind that!" he exclaimed, fending off her attempt to enfold him in her arms. "It's just a scratch from flying stones!"

McClellan had been quick to fetch a wet cloth from the kitchen and offered it to him. "She'll calm down if you don't look like death warmed over."

"It ain't *me* who's in any danger of meeting the Reaper! It's His Nibs—He's been coshed on the head and abducted." Raven plucked a paper from his pocket. "By a bloody bastard named Geoffrey Blodgett!"

Chapter 26

It was the throbbing pain—like an iron spike hitting with a clanging rhythm against the back of his skull—that slowly brought Wrexford awake. He squeezed his eyes open and shut several times, feeling dizzy and disoriented as he tried to bring the murky gloom into focus.

He was lying on a stone surface, surrounded by a strange dampness that seemed both hot and cold. The metallic rattling grew louder, punctuated by a steady stream of hissing and whooshing.

Perhaps I'm dead and consigned to the bowels of Purgatory or the belly of a dyspeptic dragon.

No, he decided, tentatively shifting his limbs. If he had given up the ghost, he'd be in Hell and it would be decidedly hotter. Which was small consolation, as it felt like a regiment of devils had run roughshod over his head with their cloven hooves.

"Awake, are you?" asked a voice from somewhere close by in the ink-dark murk.

Wrexford grunted and managed to sit up. "No thanks to you, Blodgett." His fingers gingerly felt at the lump behind his left ear. "I assume you have a reason for abducting me rather than slitting my throat."

A steel struck flint, taking several tries to spark a candle stub to light.

"I've no idea why you've been added to our motley band." The flame illuminated the face of an utter stranger. Behind him, the earl could vaguely make out several boys huddled up against a brick wall. "But I'd guess it has something to do with The Behemoth."

Whoosh-clang, Whoosh-clang. A serpentine swirl of silvery vapor suddenly slithered in from under the heavy planked door. Wrexford winced, realizing the noise and steam were not a figment of his imagination.

"Who the devil are *you?*" he asked warily.

"Benedict Hillhouse," came the answer. "Who the devil are *you?*"

"His Nibs—Lord Wrexford!" answered a reedy voice.

The earl turned and saw it belonged to a painfully thin boy who looked to be half a head shorter than the two others. He looked familiar . . .

"Oiy, remember me—I'm Skinny," volunteered the boy. "A friend o' Raven 'n Hawk."

Skinny. One of the clever little urchins who had proved so useful in during the Holworthy investigation. "I'm glad to see you alive, lad," he said.

"Yeah, well, I don't fink we'll be suckin' wind fer much longer," said Skinny matter-of-factly, which set the other boys to whimpering. "We seen their phizes, so they ain't gonna let us get live, once they've no more use fer us."

"We'll see about that," muttered the earl. "How did they come to snatch a clever fellow like you?"

The boy made a rueful face. "Billy Bones had filtched some ale from the tavern where he sweeps up and shared a tipple wiv me while we wuz rolling dice. So I wuz bosky when a cove arsked me iffen I wanted te make a shilling by helping 'im carry some coal te his wagon. Udderwise I wudda been smart enough te smell a rat. Before I knew it, he whacked me in the brainbox, an' well, here I be."

"Don't fret, lad. The game isn't over yet," said Wrexford, and then turned back to Benedict. "You've led us on a merry chase, Mr. Hillhouse. I take it you're not part of the plot to steal Ashton's invention."

"Bloody hell, no!" exclaimed Benedict. He quickly added, "How is Octavia? Is she—"

"Safe and well," he assured.

"Thank God." Benedict pulled a face. "To think we were so blind! We suspected the widow—and perhaps you—of nefarious doings, only to miss the obvious suspect. We should have immediately thought of Geoffrey Blodgett. He's always felt he's been dealt an unfair hand by Lady Luck. For years, he's simmered with resentment that he didn't have money, privilege, fortune." Another grimace. "And now I know why."

Wrexford frowned. "What do you mean?"

"He's Blackstone's bastard," replied Benedict.

"But for a piece of paper, he would be the marquess's heir. He's a month older than Lord Kirkland, but born on the wrong side of the blanket."

"Kirkland's dead," interjected the earl.

"Oh, yes, Geoffrey has boasted of that. He comes in every day to taunt me with the diabolical details of how clever he and his father have been." Benedict shook his head. "He's always been an arrogant sot, though he hid it well from Eli. It defies all sense of decency that a father would conspire to kill his own son, but apparently Blackstone and Geoffrey are bound by morals as well as blood."

"The marquess knows Blodgett murdered his half brother?"

"Aye, it was at his orders that Kirkland was killed. Apparently he was wheedling the widow for money—I don't know why—and Blackstone was furious that it would interfere in his own plan. Which, by the by, is to patent Eli's innovation as their own—"

"Yes," interrupted the earl. "We figured that out. However, we assumed it was you and the viscount, and that you'd be selling the idea to McKinlock, as he has the money and means to manufacture it."

Benedict flashed a rueful smile. "Lud, I should have thought of that," he said dryly. "But no, it's the marquess and Geoffrey. They will go through the outward signs of mourning Eli, while they secretly build a prototype based on his innovations. Geoffrey is very skilled with mechanical devices, and his expertise with steam will make it plausible to most people that he came up with the idea on his own."

"The key is in filing the patent," mused Wrexford. "The one who claims it first has the great advantage."

"Precisely," agreed Benedict. "They are betting on the fact that Mrs. Ashton will flounder in trying to run the mill. Geoffrey, of course, will use his guile to see to it that things go awry. Eli's investors will be convinced by Blackstone to back a new steam engine company—run by Blackstone, of course—as Ashton's company will be seen as worthless with a woman at the helm."

The earl shifted, trying to dispel the lingering muzziness in his head. "By the by, Mrs. Ashton is not an enemy. She has always been completely loyal to her husband and his work. Miss Merton will explain all the details, but she and the widow have reconciled their misconceptions of each other. They believe the motivation for the heinous murders is the fact that Ashton was planning on using the profits from the patent for improving the lives of his workers rather than lining the pockets of already wealthy men."

"Yes, that's true," confirmed Benedict. "Blackstone lusts for money, though he's already a very rich man. However, from what I've gleaned from the talk here, it's also a lust for power and establishing a legacy for the ages. Geoffrey is smart, ambitious and ruthless—exactly the sort of son Blackstone yearned for. Together, they dream of becoming titans of the British economy. The world is changing, trade is expanding around the globe. They intend to dominate it."

Their own empire within an empire, thought Wrexford.

"Though there does seem to be some friction between them," added Benedict. "I overheard a rather heated argument yesterday. Blackstone was furious that Blodgett killed a second radical agitator. Said he was getting too bloodthirsty, and that too many bodies would wreck all their plans."

The earl rubbed at his still-throbbing skull. A great many pieces of the puzzle were finally fitting together. And yet . . .

"So," he asked slowly, "what is it they need from you?"

And what is it they need from me?

"Ah, yes, why are we enjoying the comforts of their hospitality?" Benedict cracked his knuckles. "If you notice, our hands aren't bound. That's because they need our skill to—"

A rap on the door cut off his words, followed by a gruff order. "Stand back!" Metal scraped against metal as the lock released and the hinges pivoted.

Wrexford squinted as a blade of lanternlight hit him square in the face.

"I see you're awake, Lord Wrexford." Blodgett, still armed with a brace of pistols and accompanied by the brute with the cudgel, motioned for the earl to rise. "Come with me."

Charlotte forced herself to fight off the fear taking hold of her heart. She must think. *Think!*

Her guess had been right, but it had come a heartbeat too late. But at least the enemy was now known, she reasoned, and Raven's rushed explanation of the earl's abduction offered some faint thread of hope.

The boy had managed to hide himself and watch as Blodgett's accomplice had found a hackney and, with jesting comments about their drunken friend, maneuvered the earl into the cab. With a clear description of the vehicle, there was, she assured herself, a good chance that through their network of street urchins and night creepers they would be able to track it to its final destination. After all, there must be a reason they were keeping the earl alive . . .

She looked up and met Raven's grim gaze.

"I'm gonna rouse Hawk, and we'll spread the word on what we're looking fer," he said, a note of defiance edging his voice.

"You're hurt," she replied, though there was little force behind her words.

"Bugger that," he retorted. "We ain't gonna leave him in the lurch."

No, we ain't.

"We'll set up a command post here," said McClellan to Raven. "If anyone has something to report, have them send it here. When you and your brother finish making your rounds, return here—no, on second thought, you must stop and inform Tyler of what has happened, and have him alert Mr. Sheffield. Then return here at once. Mrs. Sloane may need you."

Raven nodded and dashed off for the stairs before any protest could be raised.

"Thank you," said Charlotte simply. The maid's show of calm, quick-witted competence helped steady her own nerves. A plan of her own was now taking shape. "I must head to Mr. Henning's surgery." Raven had told her about the rendezvous with Griffin. Though she dreaded what it might entail, there was really no choice.

She had always known that her recent decision to change her life might threaten her hard-won independence.

"Isn't science beautiful?"

Wrexford stood at the edge of the cavernous room and watched the rhythmic rise and fall of pistons through a silvery scrim of mist.

"It's just a small test model of the new condenser," explained Blodgett. "The actual prototype engine, our beautiful Behemoth—" He gestured at a huge, hulking silhouette at the far end of the room "—awaits a just few more refinements before we fire it up."

"Impressive," answered the earl, his gaze straying to the two sweaty, soot-streaked boys feeding coal into the firebox of the test model. "Save for the fact that it's fueled by blood."

"Oh, come, we've heard you're not a sniveling sentimentalist, Wrexford," scoffed Blodgett. "Progress rarely comes without a price. Though in this case, it was naught but a pittance."

"You hold life so cheap?" he asked.

"Three of the men were worthless," countered his captor. "And Ashton had outlived his usefulness. He would have frittered away his genius, rather than building on it."

Wrexford didn't bother arguing further on ethics. Like Blodgett, he preferred to put his creativity to practical use.

How to stop the dastards? Preferably with a plan that saved the lives of Hillhouse, Skinny and the other captives—as well as his own.

"You take a coldly pragmatic view of the world, I see," he murmured.

"And so, I trust, do you," said Blodgett, "once you've applied your usual steel-sharp logic to the matter."

"I think you ought to go ahead and tell me why I'm here."

Blodgett smiled, perhaps sensing a kindred soul. "We're offering you an opportunity to help forge the future. And reap a handsome profit in the bargain."

Wrexford moved closer to the working model and took a closer look at its mechanics. "Tell me more."

"I knew most of the plans for Ashton's innovation, but he became secretive and a few crucial details about the valves were missing. We've convinced Hillhouse to share them." The smile grew more sardonic. "He has a weakness for Miss Merton."

A fatal weakness, no doubt, for both of us if Blodgett gets his wishes.

"As for your role, we've just forced an alarming fact out of Hillhouse. The boiler for the prototype is made with the wrong type of iron for the amount of pressure that will be generated. We know you worked with Ashton on the composition of iron for his previous boiler. We need your expertise in chemistry to create the right formula for this one. And time is of the essence. We've a very rich man from one of the German principalities coming to see a demonstration of The Behemoth in a week. His investment is the first cog in building our empire."

"I'd need a proper laboratory and furnace," said

the earl. He allowed a small pause. "Assuming I agree to help you."

"It's already been assembled in one of the other rooms in this building. There's also a forge and furnace room, as the building was formerly used for making repairs to naval armaments," replied Blodgett. "I've stocked it with coke and iron ore for the smelting process."

That explained the tidal smells mingling with the odor of burning coal. They must be near the river.

"As for agreeing, we're aware that you're known for being impervious to emotion. You've no close friends, no paramours. You are, in a nutshell, a man without a heart."

The earl shrugged. "A vastly overrated organ when it comes to sentiment, though a rather efficient pump."

"However . . ." His captor's smile turned feral. "My father sent some of his minions to inquire around your country estate. It seems there is an elderly nanny by the name of Miss Beckworth settled in a snug little cottage. Word is, she raised you and your younger brother, and served as a source of solace when your mother fell victim to influenza, especially to the dear, departed Thomas. He was particularly fond of her, wasn't he?"

No secrets are safe. Charlotte's frequent warning echoed inside Wrexford's head. For an instant, he held back any outward reaction, and then thought better of it. Two could play at cat and mouse games. Let Blodgett think he had touched a raw nerve.

Satisfaction sparked in Blodgett's gaze as Wrexford let anger tighten his features. "Your tenants natter away about how kind you are to the old hag, and how she wants for nothing." He let out a mournful sigh. "But then, the elderly are fragile. I doubt it would come as no surprise were you to learn she simply stopped breathing in her sleep one night."

"Your depravity knows no bounds, does it?" he said softly.

"None at all," said his captor with an unrepentant laugh. "So, milord, do we have an agreement?"

"Have someone find me a pot of coffee," growled the earl, quickly thrusting aside all emotion to think of how to turn the situation to his advantage. "Then show me to the laboratory."

A nervous twist of the knob turned the lamp's flame down to a bare flicker, setting the yawing shadows to dancing higher and darker on the far wall. After re-angling her chair, Charlotte sat and pulled her hat down even lower on her brow.

Dare she hope that Henning's idea would work? The chances were . . .

Wrexford would of course be able to calculate

the exact odds if he was here. But he wasn't, and she would likely never hear his infuriating drawl again unless they could engineer a miracle.

Science gave short shrift to the supernatural. In art, however, magic was acknowledged as an integral part of imagination. One had to have faith.

From behind the closed door, she heard the scuff of steps and voices. Her insides gave a lurch. Henning's rough Scottish burr rubbing up against the clipped growl of Griffin, the taciturn Bow Street Runner.

He was, alas, no fool. Which was, in this case, a two-edged sword.

The latch clicked, and Charlotte's nerves jumped again.

"I don't see why we're playing addlepated charades, Henning." Griffin's voice was suddenly clearer. "If you've an informant who knows something, just bloody well bring him front and center and have him spit it out."

"I told you, Wrexford has made a solemn promise to Phoenix that the lad's identity will remain a secret." The door was open but Henning's stocky body was barring entrance to the room. "The earl depends on him for information, so unless you give us your word you'll abide by our terms, Phoenix will disappear out the back exit. He adamantly refuses to have his face or voice known to Bow Street."

Griffin hesitated, then surrendered with a grumbled oath. "Bloody hell—yes, I agree. Don't make me regret it."

"You stay here." Henning indicated a chair by the door and waited until the Runner seated himself before continuing on to Charlotte. "Never fear, lassie. You're naught but a dark shape from back there," he whispered. "I've explained about the deciphered note and the fact that Blackstone and Blodgett are the culprits. Naturally, Griffin has a number of questions, but if you just follow our plan, and let me relay your answers to him instead of speaking up for yourself, we should come through this unscathed."

Charlotte was grateful to Henning for thinking of a way to keep her from being unmasked as a woman. She had been in no state of mind to think of protecting herself.

Wasting no time, Griffin began his questioning. "Tell me about the earl's abduction," he demanded.

Charlotte repeated exactly what Raven had told her, which Henning dutifully relayed. The Runner, she saw, was making notes.

"Describe the hackney—the color, the horses, any detail that might help identify it . . ."

For the next ten minutes, he continued to pepper her with queries. By saying certain things had been told to her by Tyler—as she couldn't very well admit to having first hand knowledge of them herself—Charlotte was able to pass on some vital information. Whether Griffin would take the word of a street urchin was impossible to know. But his instincts were good and he had shown himself to be a man dedicated to bringing criminals to justice.

And the Runner and Wrexford had developed a mutual respect, despite their differences. She trusted he would put all his efforts into helping find the earl.

"I have nothing further to ask," Griffin finally said. "For now."

"Phoenix has spread word throughout the city about the hackney," offered Henning. "If any of the people who inhabit the streets saw it pass, we'll hear of it and send word to you."

Griffin gave a grunt as he rose and snapped his notebook shut. "Let us hope, for His Lordship's sake, that the brat's network of informants is half as good as the one run by the infernal A. J. Quill."

Chapter 27

A long, planked work counter ran the length of the laboratory wall opposite the forge. It looked recently constructed, crude but serviceable, and a quick look showed it stocked with all the necessary equipment. *Crucibles, copper cauldrons, an array of chemicals in glass jars . . .*

"If there is anything else you need, you have only to ask, Wrexford."

The earl turned to see a tall, impeccably attired gentleman had come to stand behind Blodgett. A light dressing of Macassar oil sheened his thick hair, making it gleam bright as polished silver in the lamplight.

"I should like to think of us as partners rather than adversaries," went on the newcomer. "You, of all people, have the vision to look beyond the strictures of convention and see the future."

"A pretty speech in theory, Blackstone," said Wrexford. "But theory is never quite as neat as reality, is it?"

"A bit of blood has been shed," conceded the marquess. "But think of all the lives that will be improved by the revolution in steam power."

And the few select pockets that will be lined by your murderous greed.

"Which makes the toll worth paying?" he asked. "I wonder if Ashton, Hollis and Nevins agree. Not to speak of your son."

Blackstone's face darkened. "My wastrel son was a blight on humanity. A leech. The world is better off without him."

"It's dangerous to usurp the power of the gods," murmured Wrexford. "The Greek tragedies give ample warning of how the deities punish human hubris."

"Ancient history!" scoffed the marquess. "I believe in looking to the future. What about you, Wrexford?"

"As a pragmatist, I'm most concerned with the present."

Blackstone laughed. "A wise philosophy. Do what we ask, and—"

"And you might let me live?" said the earl, a sardonic smile flashing within the flitting shadows.

"That depends." The marquess touched a hand to Blodgett's shoulder. "Come see me when you've finished here, Geoffrey." The well-manicured fingers curled in a quick caress. "You've done very well. I'm proud of you."

Blodgett's face came alight. He waited until the sound of his father's receding steps had been swallowed by the thrum of warehouse noises before expelling a pent-up breath. "Is there anything else you need?"

Wrexford took a long moment to survey the rest

of the workspace. And then repressed a smile. *A ray of light.*

"I need one of the boys to help me with the various potions. The cauldrons need to be arranged in close proximity, so bring me the small, skinny one. He'll work best in tight quarters." The earl allowed a stretch of silence before adding, "You had better bring Hillhouse, too, along with plenty of paper and pencils. He'll need to explain to me the way the new valve system works so I can understand the exact amount of pressure we're dealing with."

"I know the valves," protested Blodgett. "I can tell you what you need to know."

Trusting his instincts, Wrexford took a gamble. "Practical knowledge of the mechanics is one thing. But do you know the mathematical equations for calculating volume and pressure? The scientific formulas for various chemical compounds? This isn't guesswork. It requires highly advanced knowledge."

A spasm of fury twisted at Blodgett's handsome face, which was all the answer he needed.

The bastard son, brilliant but barred from all the privileges of his wastrel half brother. His hunch had been right.

"So you see," said the earl. "I need Hillhouse and his Cambridge education."

Anything else?" came the taut reply.

"Another pot of coffee." Wrexford peeled off his coat. "But first, bring me my helpers."

. . .

A huffing, puffing dragon, snorting fire and scalding clouds of steam, flapped its scaly wings. It was coming closer and closer—her throat was burning, she couldn't breathe—

"Wake up, Mrs. Sloane." McClellan gave another gentle shake to Charlotte's shoulder. "You're having a bad dream."

Blinking, she slowly released her suffocating grip on the pillow pressed against her face and groggily sat up. A baleful glance around showed that she'd fallen asleep fully dressed on the sofa. *Damnation.* Her boots had left streaks of mud on the lovely fabric . . .

"I thought you might like some tea," added the maid.

Charlotte felt a tickle of benign vapor float caress her face. "Thank you. Tea would be divine." She accepted the cup and felt her stomach flip-flop as she took in the shaft of bright sunlight shining through the window-panes. How many hours had trickled by?

"Any word yet?" she demanded.

"A few promising leads," replied McClellan. "Raven and Hawk are out organizing more help to follow up on them."

"We'll find him," announced another voice.

Charlotte swung her gaze around and saw Sheffield was sitting in one of the armchairs, looking rumpled and wan from lack of sleep.

"We're having the lads pass the word that there will be a very large reward for whoever leads us to the hackney's destination." His jaw tightened. "We'll find him," he repeated. "Satan would find Wrex's sarcasm far too annoying to let him stay in Hell."

She smiled, as he had intended, but then, to her horror, realized that tears had pearled on her lashes and several had spilled to her cheeks. Turning away, she made a show of fanning her face. "Lud, the tea is hot as Hades—just the thing to chase the fog from my brain."

McClellan tactfully busied herself with the tray, pretending not to notice the momentary show of emotion.

Charlotte took another scalding sip, welcoming the burn on her tongue. Damn Wrexford for being so . . . so . . .

Principled.

Infuriating man. She wished she could shake him until his teeth rattled. It was *she* who let passions take her to where angels feared to tread. Not him. He wasn't supposed to care. Drawing a shuddering breath, she set aside the cup, aware that her hands were trembling.

Damn, damn, damn. Time was not on their side. Every minute that ticked by made it less likely they would find the earl alive.

Rising, Charlotte began to pace, feeling like one of the caged lions at the Tower menagerie.

Thump, thump. She knew Sheffield and McClellan were watching her in concern. Wondering, no doubt, whether she was going to wear a hole in the floorboards.

The sound of steps suddenly grew louder.

She whipped around as the two boys came racing into the parlor.

"We're now sure the hackney headed down te Limehouse," exclaimed Raven between great gulps of air. "Alice and Pudge are talking with the mudlarks around the river and Harry is checking with the barrowmen around Limekiln Dock te see if we can learn which street."

"I think we should alert Griffin," said Sheffield. "He can muster a force of men and wait for further word in Princes Square, which is close enough to the area to allow them to move in quickly, once we've located the building." He rose. "I'll go. He'll trust me."

Charlotte nodded. "A good plan."

"I need te go back te Bell Wharf and wait fer reports," said Raven. To his brother he ordered, "Ye need te stay here, in case further messages need te be relayed."

"Quite right," she confirmed, then grabbed up her wool cap from the sofa. "However, I'm coming with you."

A series of rasping clicks rumbled from within the heavy iron lock and Wrexford heard the mechanism release, allowing the thick-planked door to swing open.

"A word of warning, Wrexford," came Blodgett's voice from the corridor. "The building is well guarded, and this door will be locked at all times. You or Hillhouse make one wrong move, or don't have the formula ready in time to cast a boiler for the demonstration next week, and first Miss Merton will die, followed by Miss Beckworth." A shuffled step. "Then I'll slice Mrs. Sloane's throat. She and Miss Merton looked thick as thieves, so I assume she's also a friend of yours."

Two burly men shoved Benedict and Skinny into the laboratory, then stepped back as Blodgett moved into the doorway and gave a menacing wave with his pistols.

Weapons make mere mortals feel like gods, reflected the earl. But strip them of steel, he reminded himself, and they were once again just quivering mounds of flesh and blood.

"If she's not," added Blodgett with a wolfish grin, "then it's bad luck for her."

Wrexford reacted with a bland shrug. "You needn't waste your breath with puerile taunts and threats," he said. "Kindly close the door and let me get to work."

As the portal slammed shut with a doleful clang, Benedict marched to the work counter and dropped the sheaf of paper and pencils with a muttered oath. "Bloody hell, you can't mean to meekly sit down and do that dastard's dirty work!"

He gestured at the chemicals. "We need to fight back! We can burn through the door hinges with acid, or . . . or set the planks on fire!" Flinging an arm up, he pointed to the forge. "And we can forge spears from the test scraps of iron! I know how to work metal . . . we can sabotage the Behemoth . . . we can . . ."

Wrexford listened in amusement until the other man had exhausted his ideas. "Bravo, Hillhouse. I commend you for your imagination. I daresay you could write a novel that would outsell those of Mrs. Radcliffe. However, I'm feeling rather lazy after all the rushing around needed to unravel this tangled plot. So I'd rather just be rescued."

"Ha! And pigs may fly!" retorted Benedict.

"No, just a scrawny little lad," replied the earl with a smile.

"What the devil do you mean—"

"I'll explain in a moment." He smoothed out a sheet of paper. "Skinny, they've had you moving coal around, so think carefully and describe as much of the building as you've seen." Taking up a pencil, he drew a rough rectangle. "Show me the entrances and the position of the guards."

The boy, as he knew, was keenly observant and quickly helped him sketch in some key information. It should, he decided, be enough.

"Well done, lad. Now, Raven tells me you've worked as a chimney monkey. Is that right?"

"Oiy!" answered Skinny.

Wrexford grasped the boy's bony shoulders and turned him around. "See that iron grate up there?" He pointed out a small air vent set just below the high ceiling. "If we can get that loose, can you shimmy through it?"

The boy made a rude sound. "I ken wiggle through a wormhole, m'lord. That opening's as big as bloody Piccadilly Street."

"Excellent." He scribbled a quick message on the diagram, before folding it and handing it to the boy. "Once you're out, fly to Raven and Hawk as fast as you can and tell them where we are. You know their new residence?"

"Oiy!" Skinny held out a grubby hand. "It 'ud be a lot quicker if I squibble a hackney. Ye got any blunt?"

The earl dug out several coins from his pocket and handed them over.

Benedict assessed the height of the wall with a critical squint. "Even if I stand your shoulders and the boy stands on mine, we'll be three or four feet short."

"Yes, but . . ." He pointed to the iron anvil mounted on a sturdy block of wood. "I didn't bring you here for your brains, Hillhouse. I figured that between the two of us, we should be able to move the cursed thing."

A smile finally chased away Benedict's frown as he flexed his muscles.

Wrexford drew the thin-bladed knife from the hidden sheath in his boot and handed it to Skinny. Blodgett had made the mistake of assuming that a fancy aristocrat knew nothing about the dirty little tricks of the rookeries. "This should make short work of the screws holding the grate in place."

Flashing a gap-toothed grin, Skinny took the weapon and tested the point on his thumb. "I'll have dem out in two shakes of a bat's arse."

"Drop it back down here when you're done, bantling." Turning back to Benedict, the earl rubbed his palms together. "Don't worry, I do have an alternative plan in mind if this comes to naught. But in my scientific experience, the best solution to a problem is usually the simplest one."

Pewter-dark clouds, heavy with the promise of impending rain, scudded across the grey sky and a chill gust blew in from the choppy river, bringing with it the fetid smells of the ebbing tide. Charlotte huddled deeper within the cluster of pilings at the foot of the wharf and turned up the collar of her coat. The wind-whipped spray clung to her lashes, the drip-drip of its salt stinging her skin. Every bone in her body ached from fatigue. That she could will herself to ignore.

I am stronger than pain.

But fear . . . Like a serpent, fear coiled around her ribcage, squeezing so hard that her heart was thrashing wildly against the bones to keep from being crushed. Fear bubbled through her blood, burning like a bilious acid. It rose up in her gorge, so overpowering that she could taste it.

Raven had darted off to fetch a hot meat pie for them to share. And while the warmth would be welcome, the mere thought of food made her nauseous.

Charlotte closed her eyes for a moment, trying to puzzle out how Wrexford had come to have such a commanding presence in her life. It wasn't physical—they saw each other infrequently. Yet by some cerebral sleight of hand, he had managed to squeeze himself into her head, crowding her thoughts until few of them weren't touched by his shadow. Whether wrestling with a concept for her art or simply dealing with a mundane moment of everyday life, she often found herself asking, *What would he say? What would he think?*

That she might never hear his shouts, his growls, his laugh . . .

That she might never have the chance to tell him . . .

"Here, the barrowman had lamb—yer favorite." Raven sat down beside her and broke off a chunk of the still-steaming pastry. For a moment, the stink of decay gave way to the sweet fragrance of herbs and spices.

"Ye have te eat," he ordered, his dark eyes narrowing, daring her to disobey.

Charlotte choked back a brittle laugh at the irony of having their roles reversed. That her little lamb—well, in truth he had never been a lamb, but more like a lion cub—was willing to fight tooth and claw rather than lose heart and surrender to the darkness made her feel ashamed of her moment of weakness.

She took a small bite and found it helped her swallow the worst of her terror.

"We're going te find him, m'lady," said Raven softly.

She smiled, and in an instant her despair dissolved, transformed by some esoteric alchemy into hope. Wrexford would likely have a scientific theory about the chemistry of it. She must remember to ask him—and watch him huff and snarl about the illusions of sniveling sentiment.

"Of course we're going to find him," answered Charlotte. And when they did, she was going to thrash him within an inch of his arrogant, devil-be-damned life.

The earl winced as Benedict's boot heels dug into his shoulders. Feet planted firmly on the anvil, back braced against the wall, he couldn't see what was happening up above.

He heard a scraping of metal against metal. Benedict grunted and shifted again. "Skinny has pried out the screws. I've got the grate."

A good sign. As was the slithering sound of wool against brick and the iron-grey crumbs of mortar raining into his hair.

Another excruciating few moments passed, then suddenly the knife plummeted past him—a hairsbreadth closer and it would have nicked his ear—to bury its razored point in the planked floor with a quivering *thwack*.

"The lad is out!" exclaimed Benedict in an excited whisper. "By God, your plan worked."

"Yes, well, it's just the first step in the experiment." Wrexford twisted awkwardly, his back pinching in protest as they slowly untangled themselves and dropped down to the floor. "As a man of science, you know it's too early to gauge the final result."

After placing the knife back into his boot, he dusted his trousers and went to examine the chemicals arrayed on the workbench more closely.

Benedict joined him. "Now what?"

"We wait," replied the earl as he lit the spirit lamp and poured a measure of oil of vitriol into one of the copper cauldrons. "Or rather, *you* are going to wait. I'm going to try to stop Blackstone from leaving. Otherwise, we may never be able to bring him to justice."

"But how?" Benedict cast a dubious look up at the tiny opening in the wall. "Even if you could reach that pinhole, you'd never get a leg, much less your shoulders, through it."

"Not to speak of the fact that the effort would likely ruin a very expensive pair of boots," replied Wrexford dryly. Seeing that the acid had come to a boil, he selected several other chemicals and added them one at a time. "Which is why I intend to go out through the door. As I said earlier, simplicity is always the most elegant of solutions."

"But how—"

"There are benefits to employing a valet whose skills go beyond the ability to starch a cravat. Tyler's knowledge of locks and how they open is most impressive." He selected several other chemicals and added them one at a time. "Give me a hand and wipe the empty vials clean with the cloth on the workbench."

Benedict did as he was told, then eyed the bubbling potion. "What are you concocting?"

"*Sturm und drang,*" answered the earl. "Thunder and lightning." The ancient gods were adept at hurling bolts of fire and fury at those who dared to defy the order of the universe. Perhaps Zeus, in his infinite wisdom, would give his blessing to striking down the overweening hubris of Blackstone and son.

Wrexford knew he would likely need a little

divine intervention to pull off what he had in mind.

The soft *pop, pop pop* of the boiling chemicals appeared to be having a mesmerizing effect on Benedict. He sat unmoving, unblinking, his gaze drawn deep into the swirling vortex of crystalline color. Then, with a sudden start, he looked up and read over the labels on the empty vials. "Holy hell, you're mixing an explosive, aren't you?"

"Evil alchemy deserves evil alchemy." The earl crouched down and adjusted the spirit lamp's flame. "The explosive is for defensive distractions." He then turned and gathered several more glass jars from the work counter. "I'm also concocting a mixture of acids with which to sabotage The Behemoth. That will make it impossible for Blackstone to demonstrate that Ashton's invention works in an actual engine."

He uncapped one of the containers. "Alas, I'm going to destroy all your lovely work on the valves. Otherwise they could run the boiler at three-quarter speed and prove it works. But once the dastards are arrested, there's no reason why you and Mrs. Ashton shouldn't take rightful ownership of the prototype. After you've repaired the damage, and I formulate iron for your new boiler, it should function perfectly, allowing you and the widow to file for the patent and carry on your mentor's work."

Benedict's face lit with a beatific glow at the

mention of the invention. "Our new steam engine will change the world, and for the better." But his smile quickly gave way to a sigh. "How unfair that Eli is not here to see it."

"You, of all people, ought to know that life is rarely fair." Wrexford methodically stirred the potion.

"You know about my past?" asked Benedict in a small voice.

"As we parsed through all we knew about your disappearance, Sterling was forced to tell us. He never doubted you for a moment." The earl checked the liquid's color. "Nor did Miss Merton."

"I don't deserve her," came the hollow reply.

Ah, the follies of youth. Though given his own romantic history, Wrexford conceded he wasn't in any position to feel smugly superior. He paused for a moment, watching the bubbling chemicals . . . and was suddenly struck by the realization that he wasn't ready to cock up his toes just yet. For some reason, it bothered him—a great deal, in fact—that he hadn't yet had the chance to tell Charlotte . . . how he felt about her.

Love. Had he just admitted that? Perhaps not, as the earth hadn't erupted in fire and swallowed him into the deepest pit of hell. Still, the word didn't feel half so frightening as he had imagined. Indeed, it seemed to have settled somewhere deep in his chest and was pulsing a very pleasant warmth throughout his whole being.

He looked up. "If you would slink away from the lady you love because you think yourself unworthy, then you likely are."

Benedict blinked.

"For God's sake, let her decide for herself! She seems to have a brain, and knows how to use it."

It seemed to take several heartbeats for his words to penetrate the young man's despair. "W-Why thank you, sir! That is very sage advice—"

"Of course, it's all a moot point if you stick your spoon in the wall here." On that note, Wrexford extinguished the flame. "So help me fill the vials and refasten the lids—and bloody hell, don't spill any of the mixture on yourself. I'll close the door as I leave, so you should be safe in here. I don't expect that anyone will come check on our progress for at least several more hours—and if Skinny reaches the place I sent him, I expect help will be here before then."

Assuming Raven had survived and passed word of what had happened to Charlotte, and that she, in turn, had mustered the full force of their friends. That he refused to believe otherwise was perhaps a sign of his newfound sentimental weakness. Charlotte would likely tease him unmercifully for being such a romantic.

A clash of verbal swords I would gladly welcome.

Wrexford indicated the vials. "I'm leaving the

explosives with you. Stand guard at the door, and if you hear anyone take hold of the latch, let it swing open and wait until they enter the room before smashing the glass at their feet. The oak is thick enough to shield you. Give the flames a moment to subside, then run like the Devil and make your escape."

"Like hell I will." Benedict fixed him with a resolute scowl. "I'm coming with you. You may need help in fighting the guards."

Wrexford heaved a sardonic sigh. "Have you any experience in fighting for your life?"

Benedict's expression betrayed a baleful twitch.

"I didn't think so. And as I'd rather not die because of your bumbling, I'd prefer you stay here."

"I'm good with my fists," began Benedict.

In no mood to waste time with further arguments, Wrexford threw a quick punch that caught the young man square on the jaw.

"So am I," he murmured as Benedict dropped like a sack of stones to the floor. If things went awry with his own plan, it might save the fellow's life to be found bruised and unconscious.

But with a little luck we might both prove wrong the old adage that no good deed goes unpunished.

After rubbing the sting from his knuckles, Wrexford pocketed the acid, drew his knife, and set to work on the lock.

Chapter 28

"Someone's coming." Raven tensed and shifted slightly, trying to peer through the heavy, muffling mist swirling around the wooden pilings. Charlotte heard it, too—the soft slap of steps on the muck-slickened cobbles.

"Don't move," ordered the boy, slipping a hand inside his boot as he tried to slither forward and shield her with his scrawny body.

Charlotte held him back. "Stay where you are," she ordered. He had already taken far too many risks. "I've got a pistol, which is—"

Two short, fluttery whistles cut off the need for any protest.

"It's Hawk," said Raven and gave an answering signal.

A moment later, his younger brother darted out of the fog, shadowed by the wraith-like figure of a second boy, and found their hiding place on the wharf.

"We've found him! We found him!" said Hawk, his words tumbling out in a breathless rush.

Charlotte felt a fizz of heat surge through her veins and suddenly the ice was melted from her blood.

"And look who brought the news—"

"Skinny, ye little bugger," cut in Raven, reaching

out to cuff his friend on the shoulder. "We thought you was dead."

"Oiy, I wudda been feed fer de fishes iffen we hadn't diddled them scurvy bastards wot had us in limbo."

Pulling the urchin into her arms, Charlotte gave him a fierce hug. "Thank God you're safe, Skinny."

The boy's face—what little skin could be seen beneath the coating of filth—turned beet red. "Ain't the Almighty ye gots te thank. It's His Nibs, who be a wery clever cuffin."

"He's unhurt then?" asked Charlotte quickly.

"Oiy," answered Skinny with a gap-toothed grin. "And God help them shamming cads when he tickles their ribs wiv his blade."

She was suddenly cold again. "How many men is he up against?"

"Dunno exactly." Skinny frowned in thought. "There be two leaders, an mebbe three or four brutes guarding the building."

Six against one. And Wrexford had the nerve to accuse *her* of being reckless.

"We need to go help—"

Raven caught hold of her cloak as his brother darted out to the wharf and gave another whistle. "O'course we're going te help him. Hawk says Mr. Sheffield will be here in a tic. He's got Griffin with him, and a half dozen other Runners."

Sure enough, a group of men, moving quickly

452

and quietly, materialized from the mists. Reining in her impatience, Charlotte drew her hat down lower on her brow and took care to stay several steps behind Raven and Skinny as they moved out to join the others.

"More guttersnipes?" Griffin made a face. "Your band of informants appears to be more numerous than the rats that infest these hellhole rookeries, Mr. Sheffield."

"And a good deal more useful," snapped the earl's friend. "So don't bite the paws that feed you, Griffin. Filthy though they may be, they're going to make you smell sweet as roses to your superiors."

The Runner gave a grunt. "Let us hope they're not just blowing stinking smoke up our noses."

"We ain't!" piped up Skinny, every bony angle of his body bristling in indignation. "So shut yer gob and prime yer barking irons." The boy skipped a few steps toward one of the narrow streets leading away from the wharf. "Move yer pegs and follow me."

The lock mechanism quickly yielded to the probing point of Wrexford's blade. Pressing his palm to the age-dark oak, he slowly eased the door open. There was no sign of movement, save for the shadows, their sinuous slithers crowding out the weak aureoles of light cast by the widely spaced wall lanterns. He slipped into the corridor, keeping deep in the darkness, and crept toward the muffled sounds of life to his left.

As he came to a turn, Wrexford peered around the corner and saw two guards up ahead. They were crouched down on the floor, half hidden in the opening of a small side room, their weapons set aside as they took turns rolling dice through the flickering of their own lantern's flame. If he could sneak past them, another turn would bring him to the room with the steam engines.

With luck, their boredom would play in his favor, thought the earl. As would their greed. The pile of coins on the floor was growing. He waited, timing the rhythm of the rattling ivories and the resulting hoots of triumph and disgust.

"Bloody hell—Lady Luck be a she-bitch."

A few quick steps, then Wrexford held himself very still.

The guard added another oath. "Gimme a swig of yer gin."

As light winked off the pewter flask, the earl darted past the doorway.

So far, so good. He waited another moment, but the clatter of the dice showed the game was continuing. Moving quickly, he turned another corner and followed the ghostly wisps of steam to the engine room. His blade made quick work of the lock, and as he ventured a glance inside, the glow of the wall sconces showed the space was deserted.

Whoosh-clang. Whoosh-clang. The small test model of the valves was running at quarter speed, the noise sounding like a sleeping dragon that had swallowed a hammer. Hurrying around the spitting, sweating metal, Wrexford approached the much larger machine, which was sitting in silent slumber at the back of the room. Though the light was dim, he had no trouble locating the condenser. From the nearby tool bench he grabbed up a small wrench and removed several bolts, allowing him access to the interior. One by one, he emptied the half dozen vials of his potent corrosive acid mixture into the casing. The precision valves would quickly be ruined, and as the villains didn't have the drawings, the demonstration couldn't happen—even if he and Hillhouse weren't rescued.

Wrexford replaced the cover and bolts. It was now time to sabotage Blackstone's departure.

Making his way around the workbenches, the earl slipped between two coal bins and was just coming abreast of the hissing prototype when a noise at the door signaled someone was about the enter. He quickly took shelter in a deep alcove near the bins.

The portal bumped open with a bang, and a moment later the earl saw why. Black with coal dust, the two pitifully small boys he had seen imprisoned with Skinny were struggling to push a large wheeled container over to the bins.

"Ye lazy buggers, stop slacking." The brute with the cudgel was behind them. Quickening his steps, he lashed out a vicious blow with his stick that knocked one of the boys to the ground.

Outrage boiled through his blood, but Wrexford kept a grip on his wrath, reminding himself that stopping Blackstone would put an end to such torments. Temper, temper . . .

And then with a nasty laugh, the brute began kicking the boy, his thick hobnailed boots drawing blood. Another few blows and—

Be damned with the consequences. Wrexford shot out of his hiding place and caught the brute by his collar.

"Only craven cowards hit children," he growled as he swung his foe around and smashed a hard blow to his face.

Grunting in pain, the brute staggered back, then regained his balance and swung his cudgel at the earl's head.

Wrexford ducked under the stick and with a swift pivot slammed his knee into his foe's crotch. A gasp—followed by a thump as the brute dropped to the floor, writhing in agony. Still caught in the haze of fury, the earl swung his foot, taking savage satisfaction in the *thud* that knocked the brute unconscious.

The sound seemed to snap him out of his rage. Rubbing at his brow, he paused for a moment as his senses cleared. He wasn't proud of the last kick—but he had never claimed to be a saint.

He hurried to the fallen boy, who had been helped to his feet by his comrade. They both stared at him uncertainly, looking torn between fear and hope.

"Listen carefully, lads," he said softly. "I'll have you out of here in a tic, but you need to do exactly as I say." Taking their hands, he led them to the door. A quick check of the corridor showed the sounds of the struggle hadn't been heard over the noise of the engine. "Go quickly and quietly to the door leading to the coal pile. Once you're outside, run like hell and lose yourselves in the alleys. Understood?"

The boys nodded.

Another check. "Go!" urged Wrexford, and watched them dart off. They were street-tough urchins, used to surviving the cruelty of the rookies. The odds of escape were in their favor. More so than if they had stayed locked up with a violent brute.

Charlotte would likely tease him for having a conscience. A smile played over his lips. Was his cynicism softening?

Interesting though the question was, he had other things to think about. Skinny had indicated that the stairs to the upper level were to the left and at the end of the corridor. Wrexford gave the boys a moment longer to escape, then left the engine room, taking care to draw his knife and re-engage the lock to imprison the brute before continuing on his way. The gloom deepened, the wisps of steam dissolving to dampen the air with an oppressive chill. He had just reached the stairwell and set his foot on the first tread when an icy tickling touched the nape of his neck.

And then the chill suddenly turned coldly metallic.

"You surprise me, Wrexford," said Blodgett over the click of a pistol being cocked. "Word is you're a cold-hearted bastard, but it seems you have a fatal weakness for little boys."

A weakness, to be sure. Whether it would prove fatal remained to be seen.

"I dislike cowards who prey on those too small to fight back," he replied calmly.

"Bad luck for you." Blodgett laughed and jammed the pistol barrel harder against the earl's neck. "Up you go. You've become a thorn in my side, and I think it time to remove the irritation once and for all."

They climbed in single file to the top of the landing. A twitch of the weapon told Wrexford to turn right.

"Open it," ordered Blodgett as they came to a closed door.

Lord Blackstone looked up from the pile of papers on his desk and slowly removed his gold-rimmed spectacles.

"He was in the engine room, and managed to free the urchins," announced Blodgett.

A frown thinned Blackstone's mouth, but his expression quickly relaxed. "Come, Geoffrey, it's nothing to worry about." A curt laugh. "Even if the brats dared to tell anyone, who would believe them?"

"I say we shoot him now. It's clear he's not going to do as we asked."

The marquess's face hardened to a frown. "You're becoming a little too fond of shedding blood," he said sharply. "As I've cautioned you, a smart man solves problems with his brain, not his more primitive instincts. Put down the pistol." A slap of his palm indicated a spot on the desk. "Now."

Blodgett paled but did as he was told. "Y-You thought it an exceedingly clever plan to murder Ashton and frame Hollis for the deed," he muttered, moving back to stand by the side table covered with tools.

"So it was. But Nevins was unnecessary. And now . . ." Blackstone leaned back and tapped his fingertips together in thought.

It was a gamble, thought Wrexford, but perhaps the tension between father and son could be turned to his own advantage. Otherwise, he would soon be a dead man.

And he wasn't quite ready to shake hands with the Devil.

"Since I'm not long for this world, Blackstone, kindly satisfy my curiosity on how you put all of this together. I'm assuming it was Blodgett who killed Ashton and carved the symbol on his belly. But Hollis—"

"Hollis had received a note—one he thought was from Ashton—revising the rendezvous at Half Moon Gate to twenty minutes after the original time," exclaimed Blodgett hotly. "You frightened him off before the night watchman I sent could catch him."

Ah, the noise he had heard by the body, thought Wrexford, as more pieces of the puzzle fit together. But there was still something that wasn't clear. "How was Hollis drawn into the plan?"

"I knew him from his loitering around the mill," answered Blodgett. "It was pitifully easy to have one of our hired men convince him that Ashton was, like himself, an altruist and wanted to discuss sharing the profits of any new inventions with his workers. However, Hollis was warned that he needed to set up a rendezvous during Ashton's visit to London, and that it needed to be done with great secrecy, as Mrs. Ashton was dead set against giving any blunt away."

"Clever," conceded Wrexford. "But—"

Blackstone sighed. "But then I fear Geoffrey overreacted. He felt it necessary to eliminate Hollis so he didn't start putting two and two together and figure out he had been set up to take the blame."

"I tell you," muttered Blodgett, "I had reason to believe he had overheard us in Leeds talking about the patent papers."

"I fear you have an overactive imagination," murmured the marquess.

Wrexford didn't correct him. Instead, deciding to play thorn-in-the-side to the hilt, he thrust the point in a little deeper. "It was, as Blodgett said, an exceedingly well-thought out plan," he said loudly. "Even Hollis's death might have slipped by without the authorities connecting it to Ashton. But . . ." He looked at Blodgett. "Killing Kirkland was the nail in your coffin."

The earl then slowly shifted his gaze to Blackstone. "And yours, too. I doubt the House of Lords will show mercy to a man who kills his own firstborn son."

"*I* was first," rasped Geoffrey. "Just as I was always first in my father's affections. Kirkland was an indolent wastrel, while I had the intellect and ambition of a true Son of Blackstone."

"Yes, yes, no need to get yourself in a pucker, Geoffrey." Blackstone rose, his eyes never leaving Wrexford, and went to stand close to his bastard son.

The earl wondered whether the move was meant to calm Blodgett or to block him from making a rash move for the weapon on the desk.

Either way, his needling seemed to be getting under the skin of both men.

"You have no evidence to link us to anything," continued the marquess. "We were very careful. And now, with Hillhouse's disappearance, it will be believed that he is the guilty party. Once we clear out this warehouse and move the machinery to another location, his body will never be found."

"On the contrary, said Wrexford calmly. "We have a witness who saw Blodgett's face clearly when he was walking with Kirkland. He saw the two of them enter the building, and then, a few minutes later, he also witnessed Blodgett run out and toss away the knife. We have the weapon, still covered in your heir's blood."

"That's a lie," spat Blodgett. "No one was there."

"The fellow was pissing behind the crates where you threw the knife." He shook his head. "It was rather sloppy of you not to notice. Hubris can be a weakness, too, Blodgett. A fatal one."

Blodgett started to take a step but his father held him back. "Is it true, Geoffrey?" he asked. "Did you throw away the knife as he described?"

"Yes, damn him. It's true. But I tell you, it doesn't matter! The authorities aren't going to take the word of some drunken streetsweep over that of a marquess. You can swear I was with you."

"The witness is the son of a duke, whose lineage goes back even further than your father's family," lied Wrexford, sensing Blackstone was listening carefully and coldly calculating all the ramifications. The marquess was known to be a brilliant but ruthless man in business. The flat opaqueness of his lordly eyes reminded the earl of a snake. A sleek, sinuous predator, devoid of emotion.

"Not that *you* have a peerage to protect you, Blodgett," added Wrexford, driving his needle in deeper. "In the eyes of the authorities, you're no better than the streetsweep you just disparaged."

A look of pure hatred twisted on Blodgett's face. "He's lying, Father. Let me shoot him."

Blackstone held his position, blocking the way to the desk. Eyes narrowing in speculation, he looked back to the earl. "The son of a duke? Pray tell, who?"

Wrexford's skill at bluffing was well known in the gaming hells of London. Without batting an eye, he replied with another lie. "Lord James Greville." The man had returned from the West Indies several weeks ago, but from what the earl knew of the fellow, he was not prone to pissing in alleyways.

"Greville?" Blackstone lapsed into a pensive silence.

As his son watched him with growing dismay, Wrexford slowly inched toward the desk and the weapon.

"Greville," repeated the marquess. A mournful sigh followed.

Wrexford could almost hear the aristocratic gears turning in Blackstone's head. A life of well-oiled privilege, of ingrained entitlement, was allowing him to spin the wheels to align with his own self-interest.

"An unimpeachable witness," pressed Wrexford, as he slid a touch closer. He knew the arrogant assumption of God-like privilege held by many of his fellow peers. Blackstone would think himself above the law. All he had to do was give the marquess another little nudge. "But of course, there's no witness to *you* being part of any perfidy."

"Then I suppose . . ." Blackstone sighed again, the only sign of emotion. "I suppose Geoffrey will have to swing for the crime. A pity—he's intelligent, but apparently not quite as clever as he imagined."

"Father!" gasped Blodgett.

Blackstone eyed him coldly. "It's purely business, my boy. When a deal goes bad, you simply have to cut your losses." Turning back to Wrexford, he added, "You're right—there's no evidence to prove I knew about any of this. I've been away in Wales and have people who will swear to that." An evil smile touched his lips. "And who would ever believe that a father would have his heir murdered? "

"But it was *your* idea!" exclaimed Blodgett. "Y-you *promised!*" His voice broke for an instant. "You promised we would build a glorious business empire together! You promised I would be rich! Important! Respected!"

"So I did," said his father calmly. "But the key to success in business is the willingness to improvise."

Blodgett sucked in a shuddering breath, his face turning white with fury. His hands fisted for an instant, then quick as a cobra, he yanked a knife from his boot and before Wrexford could react, lunged and stabbed the marquess in the chest.

Blackstone looked down in disbelief as blood spurted from the wound, turning his snowy shirt-front crimson. He staggered back a step, his fingers feebly touching the hilt.

As his father's body crumpled to the floor Blodgett spun around and snatched up a hammer from the tools lying on the side table. Swinging it high with a keening cry, he rushed at the earl.

A sudden flash of fire flared in the gloom outside the open doorway just as Wrexford pivoted and threw up his arm to parry the attack. *Too late!* The devil-dark hammer was but a hairsbreadth from—

Crack!

Wrexford flinched as a second flash exploded with a deafening bang. Blodgett stumbled and fell, the weapon slipping from his hand as the echo of the gunshot died away.

The thumping bounce of steel on wood sounded unnaturally loud in the sudden silence.

"Ye god, another dead peer I have to explain to my superiors," drawled Griffin. The scrim of smoke floated away, revealing the Runner standing in the corridor. He lowered his pistol. "At least you didn't set half of London on fire this time, Lord Wrexford."

"I am growing more cautious in my old age," replied the earl dryly. "My thanks, by the by, for not letting that madman smash my skull."

"Oh, it isn't me you should be thanking . . ."

It was only then that he noticed Sheffield standing in Griffin's shadow.

"My weapon misfired, but thank God your friend is better at marksmanship than he is at gambling." The Runner flicked a speck of burnt powder from the barrel of his weapon and slid it into his coat pocket. "It seems he's a clever fellow when it counts."

"Clever, indeed." Wrexford locked eyes with Sheffield and held them for a long moment before giving a gruff nod. "I'm most grateful, Kit."

A smile twitched on his friend's lips. "A purely selfish reaction. Who else would be so generous with his port and brandy?"

"Aye. I'm grateful as well," interjected Griffin. "I would sorely miss my excellent suppers."

"I owe you an extra apple tart for rushing to my rescue," replied the earl.

A flash of humor sparked beneath the Runner's heavily lidded eyes. "And a wedge of Stilton."

His gaze then moved back to the bodies of Blodgett and Blackstone.

Wrexford looked down as well, watching the dark rivulets of liquid pooling together on the planked floor. *Tied together by blood, in life and in death.*

"On second thought, milord, you owe me the whole bloody wheel of cheese," murmured Griffin with a martyred sigh. "You've given me an unholy mess to explain to the government."

"Actually it's as simple as the Seven Deadly Sins to explain. Greed, envy—mankind simply can't resist the Devil's temptation," said the earl. "To spare themselves the embarrassment of having to admit that we aristocratic arses are as bad as the rest of humanity, your superiors can blame it all on Blodgett, a bastard son who murdered Blackstone and Kirkland, as well as Ashton, in hopes of stealing the patent for himself."

"That will likely work," mused the Runner. "The only trouble is, given the swarm of your urchin informants flitting around here, it's almost certain word of what really happened here will reach that infernal scribbler, A. J. Quill. He has eyes and ears everywhere."

"The urchins and I have an understanding. Trust me, A. J. Quill will have nothing to say on what transpired here today."

"Hmmph. If you manage that miracle, then it's *I* who owe you dinner."

"Given the fact that you kept me from sticking my spoon in the wall, I'm happy to fork over the blunt for a beefsteak and ale." As Wrexford paused to blink the grit from his eyes, he suddenly realized that Sheffield had come to stand beside the Runner. And behind Sheffield was a slender figure wreathed in shadows . . .

And then suddenly, the figure—moving nearly as quickly as the pistol's bullet—shot past Griffin. The Runner made to follow, but Sheffield grabbed the latch of the open door and swung it shut in both their faces.

Chapter 29

"What the devil—" began Griffin.

"Come, come—don't you think you and your men ought to search and secure the rest of the building before badgering Wrexford with any more tedious questions?" Sheffield released his hold on the latch, and spun around to place a restraining hand on the Runner's chest. "The corpses aren't going anywhere, whereas their villainous minions might be making their escape."

Griffin's gaze narrowed to a suspicious squint.

Sheffield batted at the ghostly puffs of steam that were swirling up from the floor below. "Not to speak of all the devil-cursed racket the machinery is making. Shouldn't you see to having the bloody things shut off so they don't blow us all to Kingdom Come?"

"Why is it I smell a rat, Mr. Sheffield?" growled Griffin, looking to the oaken door and then back at the earl's friend. 'Was that Phoenix—"

A shout from one of his men echoed from the bowels of the building before he could go on.

"We've found another prisoner!" A flurry of muffled bangs and thumps followed. "Says his name is Hillhouse!"

"Ah, Ashton's missing assistant!" Sheffield gave Griffin a little shove. "Let us hurry. Surely he'll know what to do about all the infernal hissing and clanking."

The perversely sweet stink of death clogged her nostrils as Charlotte darted around the slowly spreading pools of blood and flung her arms around the earl. His coat smelled of horse dung, noxious chemicals—and some indescribable male essence that she had come to recognize as uniquely his own.

"Wrexford!" She pulled him into a fierce hug and held him tightly, feeling the strong, steady beat of his heart shudder through every tiny fiber of her body.

Thud, thud. Its pulsing warmth slowly penetrated through the layers of damp wool and softened the clench of dread that had hold of her vitals.

Thud, thud.

Filling her lungs with a ragged inhale, Charlotte pulled back in one swift, herky-jerky motion and smacked her fists against his chest.

Thud, thud.

"Of all the bacon-brained, beef-witted, *foolhardy* things to do!" *Thud, thud.* "God in heaven, you bloody idiotic, infuriating man! What were you thinking to confront a vicious killer and goad him into a fury?"

Wrexford raised a dark brow. "I am," he drawled, "assuming that is a rhetorical question."

How dare he appear amused! One didn't taunt

the gods by cocking a snoot at Death. Not when its snapping, snarling jaws were a mere hairsbreadth away.

"However, as to my state of mind—" He stopped abruptly, his gaze pinching to a wary stare. "Are you crying?"

"No, of course not!" She blinked the tears from her lashes. "Bloody hell, I never cry."

"I didn't think so." He touched a fingertip to her cheek and gently wiped away a bead of moisture. "It must be the steam from Ashton's invention."

Charlotte nodded, unwilling to trust her voice. Now that all her pent-up fears had spent their fire, her mouth felt filled with ashes. She hadn't realized just how terrified she had been at the thought of losing him from her life.

And how terrified she was now at having to face her innermost feelings.

"It works, you know. Ashton was right about the new design," went on Wrexford, seemingly unaware of her inner turmoil.

Thank God—one never had to fear that the earl's ironclad scientific reasoning would ever bow to emotion.

"I suppose we may take a small measure of satisfaction that its power has been saved from falling into evil hands," he mused, "and will, as Ashton intended, be used for good."

"No small thanks to you, Wrexford," pointed

out Charlotte. "You refused to give up on finding the truth."

"As did you." His smile had its usual mocking curl. "You have to admit, we make a formidable team."

"Yes, God help any miscreants who cross our path," she murmured, taking care to match his sardonic humor. "They usually end up dead."

At the offhand mention of death, her brooding concerning the earl quickly gave way to another unsettling thought. "Speaking of which, if Blodgett was the villain, what of Mr. Hillhouse? Poor Miss Merton—"

"There's no need to worry," interjected Wrexford. "Hillhouse is safe in one of the rooms below. It turns out the fellow is entirely innocent. He was abducted and forced to build the valves—the one missing part to the new engine design—because Blodgett threatened to harm Miss Merton. And then Blodgett nabbed me because . . ."

He paused. "Well, it's rather a long story—"

"Then I suggest you wait to tell it," said Charlotte. "As Miss Merton and Jeremy, along with Mr. Sheffield and Mrs. Ashton, have played an integral part in fighting Blackstone and Blodgett's evil plot, they deserve to be present to hear all the gory details at the same time as I do."

Charlotte darted a glance at the massive iron-hinged door. "And besides, I'm not sure how long Mr. Sheffield can hold off Griffin. The Runner didn't see through my disguise last time we met, but it would be foolhardy to press my luck."

At the far end of the room, lit by the oily glow of a single lantern, was a narrow stairwell.

"So I think it best if I slip away." A coward's retreat perhaps. And yet she suddenly wasn't sure how to express her emotions—or whether Wrexford would welcome them. "But first, promise me something."

The floorboards creaked loudly as Wrexford shifted his weight from foot to foot, an oddly uncertain expression rippling to life in the shadow-dark depths of his eyes.

"Promise me that you will be more careful next time you decide to take it upon your lordly self to solve a heinous murder."

A short, cynical laugh rumbled deep in his throat. "I would think my demise would be cause for celebration—you wouldn't have to endure any more of my awful moods and irascible snarls."

It was said lightly, yet the simple statement seemed to quiver in the air, tangling itself in multiple meanings. Or perhaps it was just her own overwrought imagination that was tied in knots.

"If you're implying that I would be happy if you had met your Maker, I do confess my first impulse was to throttle you myself. However . . ." A pause. "However, life might be a trifle dull without your sharp sarcasm and overbearing arrogance to stir scandal and gossip."

Charlotte let her gaze trace the angled ridge of his cheekbone, where the faint stubbling of a bruise was darkening to purple. Strange how all the subtle contours of his face had become so familiar—the shape of his eyes, the aquiline jut of his nose, the tiny creases pulling at the corners of his mouth when he wasn't quite as sure of himself as he wished to appear.

It was that small hint of vulnerability that impelled her to go on. "Do I hope there won't be a next time?" she said. "Yes, of course I do. However, I fear a passion for justice has burned itself into your blood."

"I don't have passions," pointed out Wrexford. "Merely ill-tempered flaws."

"But you have an unyielding sense of honor." She reached up and tucked a tangled lock of his hair behind his ear. "Which may be even worse."

"Me? Honor?" He made a self-mocking face. "Ye god, don't let *that* cat out of the bag."

Their eyes met and Charlotte couldn't hold back a smile. "I—" The rest of her words caught in her throat as he suddenly caught her hand and brushed his lips to her knuckles.

Her heart thumped against her ribs. "Was that a . . ."

A kiss? No, surely not.

"If it was," he murmured, "don't tell anyone. It would ruin my reputation."

"As you know, I'm very good at keeping

secrets," she replied, too confused to think of a clever quip.

"Speaking of secrets . . ." Wrexford suddenly took her arm and drew her toward the stairwell. "To the devil with Griffin. He'll have his hands full cleaning up this sordid mess, so he can wait until tomorrow to question me. Given all the secrets within secrets we've unraveled, you are right to insist that our friends deserve to hear the report without delay."

They were quickly swallowed in shadows, the *clump-clump* of their boots sounding unnaturally loud on the age-worn stone steps.

"I take it the Weasels are close by? And Skinny?" he asked as the stairs made a tight turn and continued downward.

"Yes. McClellan was clever enough to bring Skinny back from my house in your unmarked carriage to where Griffin and Sheffield were waiting. The boys are waiting with them." The darkness was giving her a welcome respite in which to compose her emotions. Though Wrexford had appeared not to notice, she feared her face couldn't help but give away the true state of her feelings.

"Excellent. We'll have the Weasels go spirit Hillhouse away from the Runners, and then we can all head to Mrs. Ashton's townhouse."

"McClellan already dispatched word to Jeremy in Cambridge telling him about your abduction. I assume he's already on his way back to London," said Charlotte. "Her efficiency is very impressive, as is her fortitude. She seems remarkably unrattled by the havey-cavey antics of my household. Most maids would swoon at the sight of her mistress dressed as an urchin and brandishing a pistol."

"McClellan is no ordinary maid," murmured Wrexford, "and no stranger to havey-cavey antics."

"Which begs the question of how she came to be part of your household."

"She's Tyler's cousin," he replied. "Apparently she made some sort of mistake in her past—I know not what, nor do I care. And when he asked me if I might consider hiring her so she could get out of Scotland, I was happy to do so. It's my belief that everyone deserves a second chance."

A second chance. Charlotte flinched, her boot catching in a crack and causing her to stumble. How much had he already guessed about her past?

"Steady." Wrexford caught her arm.

A mirthless laugh nearly slipped from her lips. *Steady?* Of late, it felt as if her life had been wrenched loose from its moorings and was spinning-spinning-spinning in whirling vortex of dangerous crosscurrents.

Suddenly feeling dizzy and disoriented, Charlotte hurried down the last few stairs and flung open the door to the back alleyway.

Rain was spattering the rough-hewn cobbles, forming dark puddles of water over the uneven stone. A sharp gust tugged at her hat, pulling free a tendril of hair that danced in and out of the silvery drops. Hugging her arms around her chest, she lifted her gaze to the sky and drew in great gulps of salty air. The sting helped her shake off the fugue of panic.

I am stronger than fear. As the wild thumping of her heart slowed, Charlotte found her eyes held by the ever-changing play of grey against grey. There was a stark beauty to the infinite range of hues and the way they never stood still. Mixing and moving, the effect was subtle, but all the more intriguing for it. Gulls winged through the breeze-ruffled mist, stormclouds scudded across the pewter-dark patch of horizon peeking up from behind a warehouse. She held herself still, soaking in the sense of calm and feeling the chaos within her begin to subside.

Wrexford let her go, slowing his steps to allow her a moment alone. He sensed the tension thrumming through her body, and the very un-Charlotte-like confusion pinching at her face. In truth, his own emotions weren't on a very even keel. Being within kissing distance of death brought a certain clarity, he supposed.

But what he had seen had left him a little shaken. On reaching the doorway, Wrexford paused to watch the quicksilver wisps of vapor dip and dart through low-hanging roofs of the facing buildings. It was, he reflected, strange how one's own deepest thoughts played the same taunting games within the cracks and crevasses of the mind. *Hide-and-seek.* He didn't often care about chasing them. But during the few fleeting moments of Charlotte's hug, the oddest sensations had taken hold of him.

He had found himself acutely aware of how perfectly they fit together, even though all their individual shapes and contours were so very dissimilar. A conundrum, to be sure. As was the fact that the closeness had felt good in ways he couldn't begin to define. It wasn't sensual in the erotic sense of the word. For that, the words could come easily and glibly to his tongue. It had been something deeper. An elemental connection between them that contradicted logic, given that they lived in such different worlds.

Love. Perhaps that was the simple answer that cut through all the complexities.

The sharp crunch of her boots shifting on the scattering of pebbles brought Wrexford out of his musings. He took a tentative step out into the spitting mizzle just as her voice broke the silence between them.

"You've told me that you men of science think everything in the universe is in constant motion— the sun, the moon, the stars, the tide . . . the hearts that thump inside our chests." she said. "Constant motion, which means constant change—it's an elemental law of Nature."

He saw her profile pinch in a pensive frown.

"So, it seems ironic that change is so terrifying to us."

"The world is full of beautiful contradictions," responded Wrexford. "Perhaps someday we will have rational answers for all its workings. But I rather doubt it. Some things simply defy logic." He allowed a wry smile. "Which to my way of thinking is all for the good, as rules are meant to be broken."

She chuffed a laugh, though it rang a little hollow. "Now you are speaking like an artist."

"I think we've both come to understand that there's never just one way of looking at a conundrum." He took a step closer to her. "What is it that has you so terrified?"

"The past," whispered Charlotte. "The future."

"Fears often lose their terror when they are shared." He waited a long moment and then, after releasing a to-hell-with-the consequences sigh, drew her into his arms. "Perhaps that's because love has the power to keep them at bay."

"L-Love," she stammered. "B-But you don't believe in love!"

He pressed his mouth to her cheek, a throaty chuckle reverberating against her skin. She tasted of salt, and something far more exquisitely sweet.

"My dear Charlotte, it's occurred to me that I may not have gathered enough empirical evidence to come to a definitive conclusion. So I concede that the subject may deserve further scientific study."

"You?" She drew back, surprise widening her eyes. "Are you saying you're willing to be open-minded about emotion?" Her expression quickly turned unreadable. "I find that hard to imagine."

"I beg to—" he began, only to fall silent as her lips feathered against his.

"You're much too arrogant, Agamemnon," she whispered.

"And infuriating," murmured Wrexford after taking his time to savor their closeness. "Not to speak of annoying."

Once again, he was acutely aware of how, against all reason, their every subtle contour and curve fit together like the pieces of a puzzle. Even all his sharp edges seemed to find their perfect niche.

"By the by, I think my name is Aloysius."

"Is it?" A nibble tickled at the corner of his mouth. "I could have sworn it was Alexander."

It was several long moments before either of them spoke again.

"Speaking of names . . ." Wrexford slowly framed her face between his palms. "Don't you think it's time to tell me your real name?"

"Talk about change—that would truly change everything," she replied softly.

"No it wouldn't." he countered. "A name is merely a name. Who you are—your passions, your courage, your kindness, your strength—is already intimately familiar to me."

"I . . ." Her sigh was quickly swallowed by a gust of salty air.

Wrexford waited. Charlotte had taught him patience. Along with a great many other things. The world, both physical and cerebral, looked different through the lens of their friendship. Color, perspective, conceptual ideas—all took on subtle changes he never would have seen on his own. She challenged herself to push past the expected. Which had helped shake him out of his own complacency.

"I . . . I think perhaps you're right," she finally said. "Love does seem to make all of life's challenges a little less frightening."

He smiled. There, they had both said the word 'love.' Granted, in a somewhat oblique way. But it was a start.

One step at a time. Wherever the journey led, it would be . . . interesting.

Charlotte stepped back, needing some space between them in which to give up her secret. "My name *is* Charlotte Sloane," she began. "But I was born Charlotte Sophia Anna Mallory."

"Mallory." His brow furrowed. "That would make you—"

"The daughter of the Earl of Wolcott," she confirmed. "But if you ask my family, I have ceased to exist, all traces of me pruned from the ancestral tree."

"For what heinous crime?" asked Wrexford.

"Eloping to Italy with Anthony Sloane, my drawing teacher." A pause. "I had just turned seventeen."

"Ah." He maintained a solemn expression, but she saw a glint of unholy amusement dancing in his eyes.

"Oh, fie, Wrexford. Here I have just bared my soul to you. Don't you *dare* laugh at me!"

"I'm not." However, his lips twitched. "I'm simply surprised, given your imagination, you didn't do something more spectacularly explosive to make your rebellion."

Charlotte gave a wry grimace. "Give me some credit. I was barely more than a girl. And I promise you, for a young lady that was quite explosive enough." *My life as I knew it was blown to flinders.*

How to explain that mad, devil-be damned decision?

"You see, even at that age, I knew I was different. I couldn't bear the idea of living my life as a perfectly proper young lady—a pasteboard cutout, painted in naught but insipid pastel shades."

She watched a flicker of his emerald eyes flash through his dark lashes. "Not when the very depth of my being craved bright, bold colors."

Wrexford smiled.

"I would have faded to nothing and crumbled to dust being cooped up within the rigid confines of a gilded cage."

He nodded thoughtfully. "Yours is the sort of spirit that needs the freedom to spread its wings and soar." A pause. "Does your family know you are back in England?"

"No. And they wouldn't want to know. I am a stain on their pristine pedigree and—" Charlotte paused on catching the odd little twitch of his lips. "I know, I know, my decisions must strike you as madness. You're far too rational to have ever listened to your heart instead of your head."

"Perhaps some day," drawled Wrexford, "I'll tell you the story of how I made an utter fool of myself over a very pretty but very mercenary young lady."

"You?" She shook her head. "I find that hard to believe."

"Oh, believe it." He gave a sardonic smile. "My brother tried to make me see what was happening . . . Ah, but Love is blind." A pause. "No doubt because so many of us mortals have pulled Cupid's damn arrows out of our arses and flung them back into his eyes."

Wrexford has been hurt by Love? The day was rife with revelations. Which in turn opened up other questions . . .

"What a pair we are," she replied softly. "I can't help but wonder—"

A sharp whistle rose from the head of the alleyway before she could finish. She looked around to see Raven snap an urgent wave before darting back into the shadows.

"Further questions will have to wait. We had better get moving," murmured Wrexford.

Charlotte turned and fell in step beside him. "I'm not ready to share my secret with the others quite yet," she said after several strides. "I need some time to think about how it—" *And whatever it was that just happened between us* "—will change the life I've made for myself."

"We'll find a way to muddle through it all," he answered calmly. "Yes, there are unknowns and uncertainties. But you have friends to help you through them." The squall had blown through, allowing a peek of sunlight to break through the clouds. "And after all, a little mystery is what keeps life interesting."

"Mystery." She slanted a look at the chiseled angles of his profile and hint of humor lurking in the depth of his gaze—and suddenly the future didn't feel quite so daunting. A smile quirked at the corners of her mouth. "Let us hope that in our case, mystery doesn't always keep appearing in the form of a dead body."

Wrexford let out a low laugh. "As to that, m'lady, we shall just have to wait and see."

Author's Note

One of the many reasons I love writing Regency-set mysteries is because the era has so many parallels to our own time. Society was changing—and at such a rapid pace that it was very frightening to many people. The old ways of doing things were being questioned in nearly all aspects of life—the traditional social order was changing, women were beginning to demand equal rights, and workers were flexing their newfound economic muscle. Art, music and literature were changing as well, reflecting a new emphasis on individual expression. And across Europe, the Napoleonic Wars were reshaping borders and countries.

In short, everything was in flux.

As in our own world, technology was a big reason for all the changes. In fact, the Regency era is considered by many to be the birth of the modern world. Scientific innovation was a powerful catalyst for reshaping the way people lived, and it's one of the main themes I enjoy weaving into the plots of my Wrexford & Sloane mystery series.

In *Murder at Half Moon Gate*, steam engines lie at the heart of the mystery. My inventor, Elihu Ashton, is fictitious, but the ramifications of the changes steam engines were creating were very, very real. They were powering the start of the Industrial Revolution—factories were starting to mass produce goods, which in many fields made the old traditions of handmade craftsmanship obsolete. And while mass production generated great profits for the factory owners, machines were putting people out of work. As a result, labor unrest and violence, as mentioned in Charlotte's cartoons, were a serious issue of the time, and the radical Luddites—named after Ned Ludd—did exist. (The name is still used today to describe people who are opposed to new technology. However, my "Workers of Zion" are merely the creation of my own imagination.) Like my fictitious Charlotte, many of the satirical artists of the era dealt with these conflicts, and their visual images capture the fears and bitter differences of opinion concerning "progress."

New innovations in steam power were, as you can imagine, very profitable as they revolutionized productivity. And so, as I describe in my book, a patent on a specific technological invention was incredibly valuable—as it is in our day! Inventors were very secretive, and the competition could be cutthroat to be the first to file for a patent and win the rights to profit from the innovation. (And yes, as in our day, it's no surprise that lawyers were very much involved.)

James Watt, and his partner Matthew Boulton

pioneered the development of steam engines for commercial use. Watt's patent for a condenser made his new engine far more efficient than the old Newcomen engine. My own fictitious inventor also creates a new engine improvement, and while I take liberties with the valve innovation, which didn't actually occur until early Victorian times, I like to think that a brilliant scientist could have come up with the idea years earlier than it did in real life.

For those of you interested in reading more about the Regency, *The Birth of the Modern*, by Paul Johnson, is a wonderful magisterial overview of the world and how it was changing in the early 1800s. And for those of you interested in steam power and patents, *The Most Powerful Idea in the World: A Story of Steam, Industry and Innovation*, by William Rosen is a fascinating resource.

—*Andrea Penrose*

Books are produced in the United States using U.S.-based materials

Books are printed using a revolutionary new process called THINKtech™ that lowers energy usage by 70% and increases overall quality

Books are durable and flexible because of Smyth-sewing

Paper is sourced using environmentally responsible foresting methods and the paper is acid-free

Center Point Large Print

600 Brooks Road / PO Box 1
Thorndike, ME 04986-0001 USA

(207) 568-3717

US & Canada:
1 800 929-9108
www.centerpointlargeprint.com